ONE DECISIVE VICTORY

JEFFERY H. HASKELL

aethonbooks.com

ONE DECISIVE VICTORY
©2022 JEFFERY H. HASKELL

This book is protected under the copyright laws of the United States of America. No part of this publication may be reproduced, stored in a retrieval system, or transmitted, in any form or by any means, without the prior permission in writing of the publisher, nor be otherwise circulated in any form of binding or cover other than that in which it is published and without a similar condition including this condition being imposed on the subsequent purchaser. Any reproduction or unauthorized use of the material or artwork contained herein is prohibited without the express written permission of the authors.

Aethon Books supports the right to free expression and the value of copyright. The purpose of copyright is to encourage writers and artists to produce the creative works that enrich our culture.

The scanning, uploading, and distribution of this book without permission is a theft of the author's intellectual property. If you would like to use material from the book (other than for review purposes), please contact editor@aethonbooks.com. Thank you for your support of the author's rights.

Aethon Books
www.aethonbooks.com

Print and eBook formatting by Steve Beaulieu. Artwork provided by Vivid Covers.

Published by Aethon Books LLC.

Aethon Books is not responsible for websites (or their content) that are not owned by the publisher.

This book is a work of fiction. Names, characters, places, and incidents are the product of the author's imagination or are used fictitiously. Any resemblance to actual events, locales, or persons, living or dead is coincidental.

All rights reserved.

ALSO IN SERIES

AGAINST ALL ODDS
WITH GRIMM RESOLVE
ONE DECISIVE VICTORY

CHAPTER ONE

IRON EMPIRE SPACE - 4MAY2935

Princess Elsa Faust, daughter of the sitting Emperor of the Iron Throne, and second in line for the Empire, balled her fists in impotent rage. Six-hundred souls of the light cruiser Speerspitze we're dead. Murdered by a weapon that shouldn't exist. One moment Speerspitze prepared to board a pirate ship, the next second she exploded like she had run full throttle into an asteroid.

A shudder ran through the passenger ship as the pirates docked their smaller vessel to the emergency airlock on the starboard hull.

Elsa backed away from the port side window and put a hand out to the bulkhead to steady herself. The weapon used was unimaginable. No one had such technology. Not by any stretch of the imagination.

Klaxons wailed as the outer airlock was forced. Her feet were frozen to the deck, and her mind desperately raced through what was about to happen. None of it was good for her.

"I have to move," she said, trying to kick-start herself into action.

They were coming, and she needed to escape. *Among the Stars'* registry showed her as a Terran Republic luxury liner with seven thousand passengers. In reality, she was a Schnell-class liner and had a minimal crew with only one passenger—a princess who also worked for her father's security services. The ship was on a mission to investigate the disappearance of foreign flagged vessels in Iron Empire space.

The head of her security detail, Scharführer Jorgan Wagner, pointed toward the lifeboats.

"Princess, this way." The urgency in his voice startled her brain, and she hustled past him. "Any word from our escort?" he asked.

She shook her head, finding it hard to move the muscles in her neck. "They're gone, Jor. Destroyed."

She sensed him stiffen. His demeanor changed from the friendly man who had protected her since she was a child, to a hard, no-nonsense killer.

"It's no wonder no one has come back to report on what's happening out here," she said as they stormed down the hatchway.

"What do you mean?" Jor asked.

"They destroyed *Speerspitze* with a single shot. Just one. If Father knew about this technology, our fleet would flood the area."

The lift dinged, and the doors slid open as they approached. Jor remained two steps behind her. She turned and realized that he'd drawn his menacing 10mm P3 sidearm.

"If it comes to that"—she glanced down at his pistol—"we're in trouble."

"Princess, you and I both know it *will* come to that. My duty is to get you off this ship." He pressed the lowest button in the lift. The doors slid shut with a whoosh, and her stomach flopped as they descended to the lower decks.

The worst-case scenario her team had anticipated involved three or more pirates emboldened by the disintegrating Terran Republic and carefully targeting foreign-flagged ships in the hopes of avoiding Imperial attention.

The pirates had wrongly assumed her father wouldn't care about foreign-flagged vessels. However, the public image of her father's empire wasn't remotely accurate. He was truly, genuinely committed to what was best for his people, and pirates of any sort were a parasite regardless of who they targeted.

Part of that commitment was making sure his children were capable of ruling when he was gone. Which was why she found herself on an empty liner under boarding action by pirates. Pirates who somehow had a weapon on their ship that shouldn't exist.

The lift opened on a checkered red and yellow sign with an arrow pointing toward the lifeboats. "Jor," she said before leaving the lift, "give me your backup."

He didn't hesitate, spinning his main gun around until the butt faced her. "Take this one, Your Highness." With his other hand, he produced a more compact version of the same pistol.

She grabbed the weapon, and it beeped, acknowledging her authority to use it. She felt her pulse jump as they drew closer to their only escape. Her shock ebbed, replaced by fury.

Whatever happened next, she had to warn her father of what was happening out here. It wouldn't change anything for those who had died, but it would let them rest easier—and keep more from joining them.

"Here it is," Jor said. The lifeboats were on the other side of a four-way intersection. Elsa covered the right as Jor crossed the passageway. He slapped the controls to activate the boat's internal power supply.

"Freeze," a man growled.

Elsa reacted on instinct. Spinning, she brought her pistol up and fired. The P3 discharged a pellet at near-supersonic speeds, blasting through the air, striking the man in a fury of burning plasma. His scream died in his throat as his chest vanished in a thousand-degree inferno.

Her mind caught up with the scene. Elsa had spent her life around professional soldiers. These "pirates" weren't wearing uniforms, but she knew a soldier when she saw one.

Behind her, Jor shouted as more came from the opposite direction. Bolts of plasma burned down the passageway, forcing Elsa away from the lifeboat.

"Elsa," Jor barked, using the shelter of the lifeboat's hatchway to return fire. He frantically waved for her to cross the corridor. Three meters separated her from freedom. Green beams of ionized plasma filled the air between them. Maybe she could make it... but odds were she would be cut to ribbons.

She fired again, forcing the reinforcements to fall back for a second. Then she realized the problem—it would take a solid thirty seconds to launch the boat. In that time, the "pirates" could blast through the hatch and kill them both.

She saw only one option. "Jor, go!" she shouted.

He shook his head. In his eyes, though, she could tell he'd reached the same conclusion.

"You need to do your duty, *Scharführer*. Tell my father," she said.

Duty warred within him. He had sworn an oath to protect her, but a greater oath to protect the Empire. No single life was above that.

"I will come back for you," he said, backing into the boat bay. As the hatch closed, he slid his pistol across the deck to her.

Elsa swiped it up, waiting the half second for it to register her as authorized before she ducked out of the corner and laid down a volley of fire. Two men who were making their way down the hall died, screaming in flame as the plasma pellets disintegrated them.

Next to the lifeboat entrance, a digital readout showed the number of passengers and the countdown to launch. She used the timer to measure her return fire. Every three seconds, she ducked out from the corner and fired. They were waiting for her each time, but she didn't come out at the same place, and their initial shots missed.

With five seconds left to go, the bulkhead she hid behind glowed with enough heat to burn her skin without touching.

"Charge," a man with a gruff voice barked.

Booted feet pounded down the hallway, and the fear and shock she'd felt earlier were washed away by the fire of anger, purified through a singular focus. No matter what, she was going to make them pay for the *Speerspitze*. At the last possible moment, she dove out from behind the melting bulkhead, firing as she went. A dozen men were at point-blank range, and she rained down hell on them.

The first one's head vaporized. Another died clutching his burning throat, and a third screamed as the blazing plasma severed him at the waist. Her weapon ran dry, and they were on her.

A heavy boot stomped on one hand. Another kicked her in the stomach. Someone grabbed her hair, yanking her head back. Pain, unlike anything she'd ever felt, blasted through her as they beat her with hands and feet, reducing her to a whimpering, sobbing thing, cradling herself on the deck.

"Put a collar on her, and let's find the rest of the crew," a man with a thick bushy beard snarled.

Cold steel wrapped around her neck. Jorgan appeared in her mind, and she wished with all her might that he succeeded and her father would come for her. Then blessed unconsciousness took her.

CHAPTER TWO

ONE MONTH LATER

Nadia huddled under her coat, pulling the blue scarf up over her nose to keep out the cold. Omega-Centauri Four certainly won the prize for coldest winter. Even Zuckabar, with its zero-degree average, didn't match the thirty below of the frozen border world.

However, Omega-Centauri Four rested in a neutral zone between the two nations. Its unique position between the Terran Republic and the Iron Empire allowed for a certain amount of intelligence gathering on both sides. Many governments held embassies on the planet, and all agreed they would have no military presence outside the embassies. Over time, hundreds of embassies had popped up and Omega-Centauri Four had turned into something of a political neutral zone.

Snow crunched behind her, and Nadia spun, losing her footing on the ice-covered ground, causing her to slide back. She recovered, hand going to her sheathed plasma knife, the only weapon she could easily purchase on the heavily regulated colony.

"Whoa, sorry. I didn't mean to startle you," Chén said, his hands at waist level in a sign of surrender.

Nadia pressed her lips together as the muscles in her body tightened on high alert.

"You were supposed to approach from the west," she said through clenched teeth. She'd planned every detail of this meeting, and it wasn't starting off the way she would like.

"Yeah, you said that, but you might have noticed how frigging cold it is out here? I didn't want to add five minutes to hike around the Flats in order to come from the west. Are we doing this or not?" he asked.

"The Flats" was the local name for the squat, two-story concrete apartments that dominated this part of town. They were short, to avoid damage from the high winds, and sprinkled haphazardly around the hill the embassies dominated.

Chén stamped his feet in the snow, trying to stay warm. His movements were tight, stiff, not from fear, but expectation.

Nadia's eyes narrowed. She looked past him, seeing nothing, but with the wind and snow, she couldn't see more than twenty meters. Her intuition warned her that something was wrong.

His jumpiness could be the cold... or something more sinister.

"Do you have it?" she asked.

"You're not going to like it," he replied.

Carefully, in full view so the jumpy woman didn't kill him, he reached inside his coat pocket and pulled out a data stick. "RISS picked this up an hour ago. Why does the Alliance care about pirate activity in Imperial space?"

She shook her head. The drive was marked with the official seal of the *Republic Security Services*. Chén didn't move.

Nadia reached for the disk and he jerked his hand up at the last second.

"Not so fast. I want double the money. It's treason if I'm caught."

Nadia had dealt with this before. It was a negotiation, like most of the transactions in her line of work. Everyone had a price—this was Chén's way of letting her know he set a steep price for his conscience. While they had agreed on a price, the true price was never known until the last second. She had come prepared.

The irony of her work wasn't lost on her. In one respect, she couldn't imagine betraying the Alliance for any reason, let alone something as trivial as money. On the other hand, she exploited people who would gladly betray their own governments.

She pulled a stack of crips bills from her front pocket.

"Two hundred thousand... Terran trade currency," she said.

Chén's eyes followed the cash as she idly moved it back and forth.

"Damn, I should have asked for more—"

Chén stepped back, triggering her reflexes. Nadia's adrenaline kicked in. Her perception amped up, and she threw herself forward into a roll. Air swished above her as a plasma sword burned through the spot she'd occupied a second before.

She came up, slamming her own plasma knife into, and through, Chén's stomach. He howled from the pain as the superheated blade sliced his intestines. With her free hand, she palmed the data stick and turned to face her opponent.

A shimmering outline in the snow, barely more than a mirage faced her. He wore a blackout suit, something Nadia herself used on multiple occasions.

Nadia forced the lump down her throat. The kind of tech he wielded was not only illegal, but expensive. She backed away, giving herself some room to move while holding Chén's moaning body as a shield.

"Who did you sell me out to, Chén?" she asked the dying man.

He opened his mouth to respond when the assailant whipped the sword across and severed the traitors head from his body.

She let her training take over, responding with muscle memory of a thousand hours she'd spent in practice. It didn't matter who he worked for—if she died at the end of his blade, then her mission would fail.

She pushed Chén's headless corpse at him to buy herself a second. The body forced him back.

Nadia feinted left, and he followed. When she jerked herself in the opposite direction, the ice-covered ground wouldn't let him completely recover his footing. He lunged as she ran, the sword burning through her arm.

A dull ache warned her of the damage to her cybernetic arm. Relief ran through her that the blow hadn't connected with flesh.

Running through snow on ice-covered ground was twice as hard and half as fast. She grunted from the exertion, jerking her limbs back and forth as she fought to keep her feet.

"Mike-Seven-Echo, India-One-Five. I need immediate evac, LZ is hot. I say again, LZ is hot," she called out over the emergency frequency. Her original plan called for her to insert and extract through civilian channels, but that plan had died with Chén. Military evac risked the Alliance's standing on the planet, but if the information on the disk was what she thought it was, then the risk was more than worth it.

Nadia scrambled for a hold as she slid through the snow, around a corner, and into a closed outside market.

"India-One-Five, copy. ETA three mikes," a distorted voice replied.

India would home in on her transmitter and pick her up on

the move if need be. All she had to do was stay alive for three minutes. If she climbed to higher ground, they would find her that much faster.

An idea struck her. She grabbed the lip of the closest stall and pulled herself up. More footsteps crunched in the snow and she was thankful for the frozen ground and snow. With their blackout suits, Nadia would never have known they were there if not for the sound of crunching snow.

The civilian part of her screamed to fall to the ground and curl up in a little ball. She ignored it. Instincts were well and good, but training trumped them every time. Escape and evasion were her meat and potatoes as a spy.

She would make it.

From the stall, she climbed up to the low-level warehouse where the vendors stored their goods when they weren't open. A hot beam of superheated plasma burned past her. Another vaporized a section of the stall she climbed on, igniting the building on fire.

She clambered up the last story, her boots digging for purchase, fingers aching as she used paper-thin handholds to lift her body.

Biting her lip, she pulled herself over the ledge, fell and sprawled out on the roof.

"No time to rest. Come on," she encouraged herself.

Rolling to the side, she recovered her feet and sprinted toward the far end. The roof creaked under her added weight, and she prayed it wouldn't collapse.

"Stop," a man yelled.

His voice ripped through her, making her heart beat faster. She turned, raising her hands as she did so. Six men, all in electronically distorted blackout suits faced her from the opposite side of the building. Their plasma rifles pointed right at her. She knew who they were. There was no proving it, but she knew.

Immortals. Caliphate spec-ops.

"ETA ten seconds, India," Mike-Seven-Echo said.

She let her face go slack, betraying no emotion. She just needed to stall for a few seconds.

"Danger close," she replied back.

They fired.

Nadia threw herself to the roof a split second before the beams of superheated gas flashed through the air above her.

The thunderous roar of the Corsair's plasma engines filled the rooftop as the dropship went from the speed of sound to a hover in a few seconds. Exhaust from the engines propelled snow across the roof, forcing the combat team to crouch. They angled their weapons up, firing at the Corsair. Nadia curled up in a little ball, making herself as small a target as she could.

Plasma splashed against the dropship's skin. Armor ran down the side like burning tears. For a moment, everything on the roof stood motionless; then the nose mounted multi-barrel chaingun roared to life. The gunner strafed the roof with ten-millimeter rounds fired from the coilgun. Ceracrete, roofing, and men all vanished in a pink spray of exploding matter.

"India, let's go," a deep baritone ordered.

Stifling her fear, she pushed herself up. A dark-skinned man hung from the side hatch, reaching out for her. The name BONDS emblazoned his chest on one side and MARINES the other. He pulled her in effortlessly, holding her tight as the doors closed.

She didn't mean to, but she rested her head against his chest, catching her breath. For a moment, she had thought they were going to be too late.

"Thank you," she whispered.

"If I didn't have swabbies to rescue, I wouldn't have a job, ma'am," he said. He pushed the comm button. "Chief, back to the embassy."

Nadia's head snapped up. "Belay that. We're going orbital. There's a ship up there that I need to be aboard ASAFP. Copy?"

"Yes, ma'am, I do." He turned to the intercom again. "Change of plans, Chief. Emergency orbit."

There was a pause before the comms crackled in response.

"Lieutenant, I don't have the authority to violate ATC," the pilot said.

Nadia disengaged from the big man and stepped up to the intercom. "I do. Command override Alpha-one-mike-bravo. Codeword: Dagger. Do it, Chief."

Another pause while he verified her credentials. "Aye, aye, ma'am. Better strap in."

She turned to the passenger compartments and dropped into the first seat.

Bonds dropped into the seat facing hers.

"Mind if I ask what all the fuss is about?" he asked.

She pulled out the data stick and held it in her hand, turning it back and forth. The next second, the plasma engines wailed, and she grunted from the gs.

"It's... above... our... pay grade," she managed to get out.

CHAPTER THREE

TWO MONTHS LATER – 21AUG2935

Vice Admiral Wit DeBeck leaned against the curved, bulkhead-height display of Alexandria, looking down on the planet he'd spent most of his life protecting.

All his work, all his blood, sweat, and tears, only to fail so spectacularly.

It had taken USS *Alexander* fifteen long days to return home from Zuckabar. Months later, and they were running the government from the ship, holding in geosynchronous orbit above what used to be Anchorage Bay, the craters of the city acting as visible gravestones to the millions dead.

All his spies, all his assets, the secrets he held... and he hadn't heard a whisper of the Caliphate's plan or the Guild's secret weapons.

He wanted to resign, but President Axwell already made it clear he wouldn't be accepting anyone's resignation. "All hands on deck," Fleet Admiral Villanueva had told him.

Wit closed his eyes, praying for all those who had perished —something he'd done repeatedly since returning home. He glanced at the report on his screen, and he prayed anew. Prayed that the weak-minded fools in Congress wouldn't win. But he knew the answer already.

"Admiral," his assistant said via the comms.

"Yes, Alicia?"

"The fleet admiral is here to see you, sir."

"Send her in."

Wit turned to face the hatch as it hummed open. While both admirals were older than they appeared, they both appeared far older than they had a few months before. Stress was like that.

"Noelle, thank you for seeing me before the hearing," he said.

Fleet Admiral Noelle Villanueva's smile didn't touch her eyes. Her uniform's immaculate appearance was offset by the sheer exhaustion etched on her face.

"We don't have much time," she said. "The president has put together the Congress pro tem, and we need to prepare to see them and get the official declaration of war going. I've had my aides preparing briefings and charts, putting together all the evidence."

Despite the absolute horror of the attack, the most the president could do without a formal declaration of war was expel all Caliphate citizens, businesses, and ships, which he had done without hesitation. President Axwell did his best, shifting funds to help kick-start a new era of rebuilding for the navy, but there were limits... as there should be in a constitutional republic.

"I know, and while I'm hopeful they will do the right thing, they're also terrified. Scared people make bad decisions," Wit said. He walked over to the coffee dispenser and poured himself a cup in silence.

After a moment, Noelle responded. "Wit, do you know something I don't?" she asked.

"Nothing I'm at liberty to say. You know as well as I do, we've already waited too long to respond to this... *atrocity*." He sipped his coffee, frowning at the bitter taste. Good coffee was one of the casualties of the attack. It seemed... *selfish*... to complain about it. Millions dead and he was worried about coffee.

Noelle let out a long exhale, deflating with the escaping air. "I'd hoped you had better news for me when your assistant called. Are you saying that the new Congress won't move forward on the declaration?"

Despair threatened to engulf Wit. He didn't want to believe there was no hope, but there were days that it seemed inevitable. His lips tightened as he pressed them together. He felt his control slipping, his perfectly crafted exterior failing. Decades of spycraft spilling out the airlock as his emotions were the most obvious he'd ever allowed them to be.

"I—I don't think they're going to," he said. He activated the holographic display on his NavPad, showing the fleet admiral the report his agent had sent him.

"They can't be serious. No one is going to believe that nonsense. Even the Guild—"

Wit shook his head. "What I know and what I can prove are two different things. We gave the Caliphate months to construct their cover story. Technically, virtually everything they say in this report is true. It was a Guild ship; it was a Guild crew. The Guild lied to the Galaxy for hundreds of years. Of course the Caliphate is going to blame the Guild for the attack."

He could see her struggle. The same struggle he'd had all morning.

"I..." She closed her mouth. There was nothing to say, and they both knew it. The Guild had denied everything, but after the discovery of Wonderland, they had zero credibility. At the same time, what possible motive could the Guild have to bomb Alexandria?

"They're both a pack of liars, and if it were up to me, I'd go to war with both," Wit said.

"But you don't think we are," Noelle replied. "We can't declare war on a galactic corporation, especially not one that resides out of the Terran Republic. And if we don't go to war with them, and we don't go after the Caliphate..."

Wit nodded his agreement. "We need a response, Noelle. If the new Congress doesn't declare war, we still need a response. Something that punishes the Caliphate and makes them pay for what they did, as well as showing them the gloves are off. Otherwise, they will be emboldened."

Noelle shook her head. "It would take a battle group to do that kind of damage. Without a declaration, we couldn't even begin to plan it."

He sat on the edge of his desk, nearly touching her, and a slow smile spread across his face. "You're right, of course. But there are other ways to send a message. Other ways to force their hand."

She looked up, staring directly into his eyes. One of the things Wit loved about the fleet admiral was that she never shied away from conflict. She would have made a formidable spy.

"Wit, in ten minutes I go before the president to show him my strategy for a war that you're telling me isn't going to happen. I don't have time for games. You and I both know you already have a plan. Lay it on me," she said.

Wit knew they approached the solutions to their problems in two different ways, and he knew that her bluntness served her well. Navy types weren't known for their subtlety—unless they were ONI. "Tell me, Noelle," he said with a knowing grin, "how are the repairs on the *Interceptor* going?"

CHAPTER FOUR

With one hand holding onto the console above him, Jacob reached as far as he could into the comms array's central panel. The offending optical board was pushed against the far bulkhead, nestled between a frame and a corner.

"I swear, whatever engineer designed this should be shot out the airlock," Jacob muttered. Protruding edges and sharp corners scraped his hand as he tried to bend his wrist in a way God never intended for the human body to bend.

"Sorry, sir," Spacer First Class Gouger said.

Jacob winced at the young man's reply. "Don't be, Felix," he said, using the young man's first name. He sensed Gouger perk up. Addressing them as people had that effect on most of the crew. It was one of many reasons his crew would go to hell and back for him.

Jacob bit his lip, holding back the wave of emotion washing over him. Too many of his people had gone through hell for him and had *not* come back. He shook his head, trying his best to push those thoughts back.

Interceptor was docked at Utopia Shipyards on the surface of

Alexandria's moon. The largest non-planetary body in the system.

Utopia's footprint spanned a hundred square kilometers on the surface. Mines, quarries, and factories covered another ten percent of the moon's surface, making it the largest city by area in the entire system. Maglevs connected the various buildings and terminals, allowing for the population to transit the massive complex with relative ease.

The docks included shipbuilding berths—huge wire-framed hexagons where automated drones and space-suited engineers worked on new construction—but *Interceptor* wasn't new construction. Her anchorage had her parked on the farthest port from the main section, connected to Utopia's power and support but otherwise forgotten.

Normally, ships only stayed in the temporary docking while a berth was found, but the port commander, one Commodore Naomi Tut, had made it clear to Lieutenant Commander Jacob T. Grimm that she had no spare room for a destroyer that was "consuming valuable supplies when it should be sent to the breakers."

Which left Jacob with very few options and only his official "refit and repair" orders to assist him. He received about a third of what he requisitioned, and unless he timed it just right, none of the ports engineers were ever available to work on the ship, turning a two-week repair into a month's long exercise in frustration. The only saving grace was their proximity to Alexandria.

Once they were on a reliable schedule, he made sure Kim rotated everyone on a four days on, three off for the first month, then back to a more normal schedule to expedite the repairs.

"Got it," Jacob said as his hyperextended fingers found the chip. He yanked it free and handed it to Felix. "Get this to Chief Redfern and see if he can refurbish it." Jacob heaved himself up, reflexively dusting off his work coveralls. He couldn't remember the last time he'd worn an actual uniform.

"Aye, sir. On it!" Felix Gouger snatched the chip and practically ran off the bridge, heading for engineering.

They'd completed 90% of the repairs and even cajoled the yard into manufacturing the sections of the ship the Guild's secret weapon had pulverized. There were some things, though, no amount of hard work could fix.

They had no ammo, no Corsair, no Mudcat, and their food stores were nonexistent. The crew lived on-base, and only a few people stayed on *Interceptor* twenty-four seven—Jacob being the one person who never left despite his home and father on the planet below.

He leaned against the comms panel, closing his eyes at the painful memory of the last time he'd seen his father. The shame in the old man's eyes had been too much to bear.

Of course, his dad had believed the navy and the media about Pascal. Even if he hadn't, everyone else had. How could anyone handle the weight of those accusations? Especially when Jacob's mom had heroically sacrificed herself?

Even after the first incident in Zuckabar—and despite the Navy Cross pinned to his mess dress—Jacob's name was still mud to most people. Outside of those few who knew how he earned it, no one was swayed by a medal. Civilians, and that included his father, had no idea what went into earning one, or the cost in blood to wear it. The details of the mission were still classified, even if he wanted to tell his dad, he couldn't.

"Skipper?" Marine Sergeant Jennings said from the bridge hatch. She had one hand to her ear, listening to a call.

He jumped, having honestly forgotten she was even there. Jennings hardly ever spoke and would give a shadow a run for its money on stealth.

"Yes, Allison?" he replied.

A slight downturn of her lips met him. Her dislike of her first name amused him no end. Almost as if she hated anything that reminded her she was human and not some kind of Alliance Marine robot.

"Sir, orders for you to report to the USS *Alexander* with all haste," she said.

Jacob stiffened, his muscles tightening. He could only think of one reason to report to the admiral directly.

He wasn't ready to give up his ship. Everyone knew they were going to war with the Caliphate. The congressional declaration was per-functionary—which meant the navy would need all her resources to fight them. Resources they could no longer afford to waste on a forty-year-old destroyer. Once *Interceptor* was decommissioned, Jacob was out of the navy.

"Right. Better not keep the admiral waiting." He brushed past her to his quarters. The orders were run, don't walk. No officer reported to an admiral in work coveralls, though. He only needed a few minutes to change.

Ten minutes later, he exited the ship through the boarding tube attached to the mess deck's emergency airlock. Sergeant Jennings trailed behind him, and Chief Vivienne Boudreaux brought up the rear.

From the port, they grabbed a mag-train to the center spire. For the fifteen minutes it took to go the three thousand kilometers, Jacob stared at his NavPad, willing orders to come through that would change the fate he knew awaited him. Allison stood opposite, gripping the hand loop, the other clasped behind her back.

"Skipper," Chief Boudreaux said from beside him. The train car was empty since *Interceptor* was the only ship that far away from the central docks.

He glanced over at the pilot with a raised eyebrow.

"Whatever happens, Skipper, the crew is with you," she

said. Unconsciously, she rubbed her prosthetic leg—another reminder of the price his people had paid for his decisions. Decisions that saved lives, no doubt, millions most likely, but it didn't make his crew's pain any less.

Boudreaux's naturally friendly, buoyant personality had vanished after she returned to the ship. Her features had hardened in the last few months. Gone was the "party-girl" image she had portrayed when he first met her. The wound to her psyche was almost as bad as the one that took her leg.

He smiled down at her, a look of weary resignation gracing his features. "Thanks, Viv, I appreciate it. You'll all be fine, though. I made sure there would be no punitive measures against anyone on the boat."

She nodded. "Tell that to NavPer, sir. *Interceptor* is a roach motel—we check in, but we don't check out."

He sighed. She wasn't wrong. In the almost year he'd served aboard *Interceptor*, only Lieutenant Bonds and Gunnery Sergeant Hicks had transferred off. And they were Marines, outside the domain of NavPer. It was like someone higher up had decided *Interceptor* was a one-way trip.

"We're here, sir," Jennings said.

The train hummed to a halt, and the doors opened. The walk from the train station to the spaceport proper only took a few minutes. All Jacob had to do was show his orders for the Corsair they had temporally requisitioned to them.

USS *Alexander* dominated the display as they approached. A massive battleship almost a kilometer long and five hundred meters tall, it had enough weapons to bombard a planet back into the Stone Age if needed.

Thankfully, a steward met them in the boat bay and took Jacob and Jennings right where they needed to go—the fleet admiral's office. Two Marines in dress uniforms stood outside, snapping to attention as he approached.

"Lieutenant Commander Grimm to see Admiral Villanueva," he said to the gunnery sergeant.

"One moment, sir," the Marine replied. He turned to the panel and pressed the call button.

Jacob glanced over at Jennings. Boudreaux had stayed with the Corsair, keeping the ship ready. "Stay here," he said.

"Aye, sir," Jennings replied. She took up post opposite the admiral's men. Doing her best to look superior to them.

"She's ready to see you, sir," the gunnery sergeant said.

"Here we go," Jacob muttered.

The hatch slid open with a hum, and he marched straight to the admiral's desk, snapped to attention, and saluted.

"Lieutenant Commander Grimm reporting as ordered, ma'am."

Jennings watched her skipper disappear behind the closing bulkhead. Something bothered her. Deep within her heart, she knew the skipper was done wrong by the navy and the service in general. There was nothing she could do about it, though. He'd already done more for her career than anyone else had.

She'd skipped a full rank; even though it annoyed her at the time, she realized it was exactly what she wanted. A chance to prove herself. As far as Jennings was concerned, Commander Grimm should be in charge of the navy.

When they eventually kicked him out, and the crew all knew it was coming, his absence would be wrong. An unnatural void in the heart of the service. He was supposed to be a skipper. She wasn't big on destiny or fate, but having him in command of *Interceptor* felt that way.

Could she stay in? Knowing they had thrown him under the mag-train like that?

The marines had offered her a chance to be exceptional,

which she would never have been on MacGregor's World. She liked being exceptional. For the first time since she'd left her home, ever since she'd turned her back on her family, she doubted her future. She no longer desired to see distant worlds or meet interesting people and kill them.

Her chest tightened at the thought of losing the direction the Marine Corps provided. Should the captain choose to apply his expertise to the civilian trade, he would need help. Would she go with him? Resign her uniform to help him?

The hatch opened, and the captain walked out, his limbs stiff and mechanical. The expression on his face, though, betrayed the hurt he felt.

Yes, she thought. She would go with him. No matter where he went.

He walked in silence, following the steward escorting them to the boat bay. When the lift came, Jacob dismissed the man.

"I know the way from here," he said.

"Sir, my orders—"

"I'm giving you new ones. Leave me," he said, a touch of anger in his voice.

The steward glanced at the marine who was with him. She just shrugged.

"Aye, sir. Have a nice day."

Jacob entered the lift, followed dutifully by Jennings. "Boat bay one," he told the computer. It repeated back to him his destination to make sure it was correct before moving along on magnetic rails.

Jennings remained silent, and he was thankful for her stoic nature at the moment. He couldn't face any questions or, worse, pity.

He'd lost it all.

Okay, maybe not everything. He *had* managed to restore his mother's good name. Which was the most important thing he'd wanted from his time in the navy.

He'd hoped and prayed it wouldn't end, though. He had known it was possible, even likely, from the moment he arrived on *Interceptor*, but the reality of it still hit him like a brick. Pascal had thrown all his plans in a bin and lit them on fire, effectively ending his career, even if it took a few more years to happen.

His heart ached at the thought of what they were going to do to his ship. They'd just got the damn thing back up and running, and her fate was plasma cutters and salvage drones tearing her apart. It was enough to tempt him to alcohol, and he never drank. Not ever.

After all his crew went through, they would be burdened by their time on *Interceptor*. The navy operated on prestige credit. What ships did you serve on? What actions did you see? It bothered him that his crew's time on the *Interceptor* would be a black mark on their record.

He loved that little destroyer and the people who served on her. Orders were orders, though, and he needed to find a way to tell the crew. Clearly, they needed to know sooner than later, but... it felt so anticlimactic to just tell them. What he didn't want was them finding out through scuttlebutt—which left him very little time since the grapevine was FTL capable.

The doors opened on the gargantuan boat bay, one of two on *Alexander*. He could literally park *Interceptor* inside and not touch the walls.

Jennings trailed behind him as he twisted his way to where the Corsair was berthed. Chief Boudreaux waved from the cockpit.

Jacob climbed into the boat and hit the comms button. "I'm gonna ride down here, Chief. Take off when you're ready."

"Aye, sir," her voice crackled over the speaker.

He took the first seat, mechanically pulling the harness over his head and clicking it into place. Jennings went to the bench below the cockpit and strapped in.

A few seconds later, engines whined to life, lifting the ship and thrusting her toward space. A tremble ran through the hull as she passed through the Richman field.

"Thrust in three-two-one..." Boudreaux said over the internal comms.

He crossed his arms and held onto the harness as the *g*s from the gravcoil kicked in, eliciting a grunt from him. After nearly a minute of acceleration, the gravcoil's compensation activated, and they only felt the one *g*.

"Your aviator knows her stuff," a familiar female voice said.

The cabin disappeared—the whole world vanished—as Nadia stepped around the forward chairs and sat next to him. His heart banged away in his chest, and his mind reeled. He reached out to touch her, but his harness restrained him. Then he tried to unbuckle but couldn't get his fingers to cooperate. Finally, he decided to shift in his seat as far as he could to look at her.

She sat next to him, as graceful as ever, her big brown eyes gazing adoringly at him. She completely overwhelmed his sense, pushing away his foul mood. Her presence alone was enough to make his day bright, and he found he wanted to lose himself in her eyes.

"What? Uh, what are you doing here?" he asked as his brain started to work again. Instead of a navy uniform, she wore ship's pants, a tank top, and her signature leather jacket. Her hair fell a good seven centimeters lower than he'd last seen her.

"I'm here to see you, handsome. I thought that was obvious?" she said. Before he could register what she was doing, she leaned in and placed a soft kiss on his lips.

Her embrace sent him through another wave of emotions that made him feel like he could fly without the Corsair. He clenched his hand on the armrest to regain something akin to control.

"Your timing is awful," he said.

"How so?" she asked with a raised brow.

He opened his mouth. What should he tell her? What could he tell her? "You know what? It doesn't matter. I'm just happy to share a ride with you. Why are you going to Utopia?" he asked.

She smiled at him, her eyes twinkling. "I'm not," she said as she pulled out her NavPad. With the click of a button, she sent a message.

"Skipper." Boudreaux's voice came over the internal comms a second later.

Jacob glanced at Nadia. She shrugged. "Better answer her."

"Go ahead," he said, not taking his eyes off Nadia.

"New orders just came through, sir. I'm to take you planet-side. Doesn't say why—just coordinates."

"Is this your doing?" he asked in a whisper.

"Yes and no."

He shook his head. She was as cryptic as ever.

"Are they confirmed?" he asked Boudreaux.

"Yes, sir. Today's codes."

"Set a course, Viv. Take us down."

Admiral Wit DeBeck sat on the hood of his ground car, a big six-wheeled civilian version of the Mudcat. He'd driven himself out to the remote ranch, a luxury if there ever was one. As a vice admiral and the head of ONI, he never went anywhere alone and certainly never got to drive himself.

He heard the scream of plasma engines long before he saw the predatory shape of the Corsair overhead. The ship circled the rough cross of rocks he'd thrown together to mark the landing position.

It flew by one more time before rotating its wings until the plasma engines pointed down, killing her forward thrust. Graceful as an Alexandrian fire-hawk, it set down on the exact spot he'd marked. The landing struts sank into the soft ground.

The side doors opened, revealing Commander Grimm and Dagher. Grimm jumped out first, then turned and offered her his hand.

Wit smiled at the old-fashioned manners of the commander. Dagher's skills made her his most effective intelligence asset, yet there she was, taking his hand and hopping to the ground with a giggle.

He shook his head. It pained him what he was about to ask of the commander. What it would do to him. If Wit had any other choice, he would leap at it. He just didn't see another way around.

Jacob took off his dress jacket and tossed it behind them onto the Corsair. This close to the equator, the temperature hovered around twenty-five degrees centigrade. They were about as far from the devastation of Anchorage Bay as they could be and still be on the same land mass.

"Skipper, I'll stay here with the Corsair and Chief Boudreaux," Jennings said.

"Good call," Jacob replied.

He undid the top two buttons of his shirt as he made his way to the waiting admiral, a man he recognized but had never met.

"You brought me *here* to see your boss?" he said over the din of the winding-down Corsair.

"Hear him out, Jacob. Trust me?"

He smiled. "Only you," he said. He did trust her—and his crew—but after today, no one else.

"Admiral Wit DeBeck, Lieutenant Commander Jacob T. Grimm," she said with an introductory gesture.

Jacob held out his hand. "It's an honor to meet you, sir," he said.

"The honor's mine, Commander." DeBeck's grip was firm, and there was no tug-of-war—which Jacob was grateful for. Just shy of two hundred centimeters, Jacob was used to the height disparity leading to shows of dominance. However, the admiral was a man he stood eye to eye with.

"How can I help you, sir?" he asked.

"Right to the point. I like you, I can tell. First, though, let's go for a little ride. I don't want to risk any aerial surveillance."

CHAPTER FIVE

Rashid Al-Alami concealed the navy-issue plasma pistol behind his back as he waited in the shadows of the dingy bar on Casan.

Hash hung in the air, along with a spicy-sweet smoke from the local brand of cigarettes. Every debauchery one could hope to find was readily available on Casan. Nominally, the planet was part of the Caliphate of Hamid, but on Casan there was as much enforcement of the Caliph's rules as there were police on the street. Which was none.

Rashid was no fool; he had two men stationed outside, ready to come in and back him up if his meeting proved to be a trap. He hadn't survived four years of banishment and exile because he was lucky.

His contact had arranged for him to meet an ISB agent named Nafir in the run-down bar. Normally, Rashid would have nothing to do with the dreaded Internal Security Bureau. However, they were the only ones who knew where his sister was. It wasn't like Rashid could go door-to-door on Medial and find her—when he went, he would need to know exactly where she was.

However, Nafir was late.

Rashid gripped his pistol tighter, sweat making the rough polymer frame shift under his hand. His spine tingled with anticipation and trepidation.

"Rashid, he's here, and he's not alone," Abeit said over the comms.

Instinctively, the ex-Caliphate Navy captain stepped deeper into the shadows and brought his gun around to the front. The door opposite opened, and bright sun and hot wind fought the haze for a moment before three figures stepped in and the gloom returned.

He recognized Nafir from the holo he had acquired. The two men with him screamed security detail. They split up, each taking a corner of the room and checking for threats.

Something was wrong, and Rashid didn't want to die finding out what it was. "Abeit, Muhad, plan two," he whispered into the comm fastened to his throat.

"Understood," they chimed together.

Nafir approached the centermost table, the one under the skylight. Rashid frowned as the feeling of wrongness was reinforced. A brightly lit table was the worst one to pick for a covert meeting.

Rashid's form melded with the shadows in the back, unseen even to the clientele. He debated walking away—his instincts told him it was a trap, and his nerve endings screamed at him to run.

But could he? Four years of planning, pirating, and paying bribes had led to this moment. He couldn't walk away. Decision made, he slipped his pistol into its hip holster, pulled the hood back, and strode confidently toward the man sitting in the light.

Nafir smiled widely as Rashid appeared. "I heard you were a sneaky bastard," Nafir said. "For a navy puke," he finished.

"I heard you had an epic beard. I see we are both disappointed." Rashid sat opposite the man, one hand on the table but the other hovering, ready to jerk his pistol and go to work.

Nafir's eyes narrowed, and Rashid saw something dangerous in them. A man who wasn't used to insults or any disagreement with his authority.

"For a man coming to me for a favor, you have a glib tongue. Perhaps I have my team cut it out."

Rashid glanced left and right, eyeing Nafir's security. "You only brought two?" Rashid asked, as innocently as if he were asking about the weather.

"You only see two," Nafir corrected.

Rashid let out a breath, tiring of the game, the intricate move and countermove he had to constantly play. He decided to speed things up. Reaching carefully into his pocket, he pulled out a neat stack of hard currency and placed it on the table between them.

"I'm not here to ask a favor, but to bribe a corrupt official in exchange for information he neither cares about nor can make money from. Other than through me, of course."

Nafir's eyes narrowed, only breaking contact for the instant the bills appeared. The conflict between his pride and the money was obvious. Rashid had played this game more than once over the years since he was exiled. Move and countermove, bribe and blackmail. The people who had the information he needed were hard to come by, and the money to bribe them harder still.

Greed played out on Nafir's face as his beady eyes flickered back and forth between the money and Rashid. These were the most dangerous moments in a transaction. Was the cash worth breaking the law? Was the reward for turning Rashid in worth more than the tax-free donation on the table? Or would Nafir decide the risk wasn't worth the reward? Worse, would he try for both?

"I think you know the game well, Rashid." Nafir's hands shot out and scooped up the wad of bills, shoveling them into his pocket.

Rashid wasn't out of the woods yet. Just because the man took the money didn't mean he would give up the information.

"And now that you've taken the money..." Rashid let his voice trail off.

"You want the information. Right. Well, I have it." Nafir placed a small chip on the table. The kind the ISB used to secure data.

"Do you want me to kill you right here?" Rashid asked. His hand hovered over his plasma pistol.

Nafir jerked back, eyes going wide as he feigned surprise. The two men stared across the table for a long moment. "You wound me, Rashid. Why would you say such things?"

"Because that's an ISB tracer chip. The moment I open it up, I'm found. I might as well put a gun to my head now and pull the trigger. Did you think you could collect the bribe *and* the reward?" he asked.

"The thought had crossed my mind... but you are incorrect. It's an ISB chip, but it won't broadcast your location," Nafir said.

"Prove it."

With a huff, Nafir lifted his sausage-like fingers to hover over the chip before pressing down on it.

A green light flickered, scanned his finger, and vanished.

"File unlocked," a voice said.

Rashid swiped the chip while standing, making sure it was securely in his pocket before heading for the door.

"Be careful out there, Rashid. You know not what is coming," Nafir said to his back.

Elsa opened her eyes and felt two things. One, she hurt. From her toes to the top of her head, her muscles throbbed with the ache of the beating she had taken. Two, she couldn't move. Not even a little. The only thing that seemed to work were her eyelids.

She scrambled to remember how she came into a dark room with only silence to greet her. Memories of the beating followed by the horrible collar assaulted her.

Did Jor know the pirates were Caliph? If he did, then her father would come for her. If he thought them pirates, though—well, her father would exterminate every pirate in the Iron Empire and then some. But he still wouldn't find her.

Her heart hammered in her chest, and she fought desperately to move her arms, to cry, something. But she stood frozen like a statue. She screamed inwardly, but her body wouldn't respond.

Light flickered in the dark, and a door opened. Not a hatch, but a door. The room's overheads sprang on, bathing the area in light bright enough that she had to close her eyes.

After a few moments of seeing red, she tentatively opened them. She could see, at least. The small room had sandstone-colored walls, with a single, meter-wide window three meters up, near the ceiling. A toilet and a lone bed with silk tasseled pillows were the only other objects in the room.

Either someone had gone to great length to convince her the Caliphate had taken her, or she was indeed in Caliphate space. She stood in one corner like a statue, waiting to come to life with a command.

At first, she thought the person who entered was a man, but she could only follow them with her eyes, and whoever it was stayed out of her range.

"Hello," a feminine voice said from beside her. Elsa jumped inwardly, but still did not move.

An older woman appeared in front of her, wearing a black robe covering her from the shoulders down and a thin gauzy veil over her brown eyes. "I see you're awake, that's good. I'm Abla. You will say my name."

Elsa opened her mouth, and to her horror, "Abla," came out.

"Good," the older woman said. "I wasn't sure if my language skills were up to date. No one speaks your crude tongue here but me. Your first task will to be to learn our language so that you may fulfill your destiny in service to Allah and the Caliph. You may move."

Elsa's muscles convulsed, and she collapsed. The pain she'd felt earlier was nothing compared to the agony that assaulted her.

However, the children of the Iron Emperor were not spoiled brats, they were expected to train and serve their government. Abla knelt to help, and Elsa slammed the crown of her head into the woman's face. The soft cartilage of Abla's nose crunched under the blow, and the older woman wailed. Elsa shoved her back and ran for the door.

Two steps later, her motor system shut off, and she flopped to the carpeted floor, bouncing once before rolling onto her back.

Not only couldn't she move, but her chest refused to rise; she couldn't breathe. Panic set in, and she fought with every ounce of her willpower to force her body to do as she commanded.

But it wasn't enough. The woman appeared over her. The friendly visage vanished. She held a rag over her bleeding nose while she peered down at Elsa.

"And I thought princesses were refined, delicate. Not barbarians. No matter. When my husband returns, he shall decide what to do with you. Until then, you *will* behave. You may breathe."

Elsa's chest heaved as she gulped for air. She rolled over, coughing, her body racked with tremors.

"What did you do to me?" she said between heaving breaths.

"It is the will of Allah that you serve. You will soon learn the true way," she said. The woman walked away, shutting the door behind her. There was an audible click as it locked.

Elsa tried to stand, her muscles quivering with effort, but to no avail. She collapsed on the plush carpet, gritting her teeth and forcing herself not to cry.

A moment later the door opened, and Abla returned, this time with a large, muscular, bare-chested man. To Elsa's amazement, he had no hair—not just shaved or trimmed, but none. He wore only a pair of skintight pants and... a small silver collar around his neck. Similar to the one she wore.

"Restrain her if she tries to hurt us or run," the woman said.

"Yes, mistress," the man said.

"Get up. Stand," Abla ordered.

Elsa opened her mouth to scream at her when she found her body doing exactly what Abla commanded. Her equilibrium fought with her, causing a wave of nausea that threatened to make her vomit.

"It will pass if you stop fighting," Abla told her. "Give in to the commands and you will feel nothing but joy and fulfillment."

Once Elsa stood, Abla moved directly in front of her, the top of her head only coming to the base of Elsa's throat.

"Or don't, and give our husband that much more pleasure as he breaks you."

Her head pounded in time with her heart. She struggled to no avail. No matter how much she wanted to, she couldn't move.

"If you would stop fighting and accept this as the will of

Allah, it will go easier for you. For now, though, do not attempt to hurt me again. You may speak," she said.

Elsa's throat clenched, and her mouth went dry. "I am Princess Elsa Faust of the Iron Empire. I *demand*—"

"Silence," Abla barked.

Elsa's next words died in her throat.

"You don't demand anything. You, my dear, are no longer Elsa Faust; you will soon be a wife to the great Caliph." A stupefied gaze came over Abla, her hands going out worshipfully as she looked up at the ceiling, "You will bear him many sons, and one day, those sons will claim the Iron Empire, and the greatness of Allah will spread across the galaxy like a cleansing fire!"

Elsa wanted to wake up from her nightmare. The fervor in Abla's eyes, though, made it far too real to be a dream. The evil woman glared at Elsa as if seeing through her thoughts, and a satisfied smile spread across her face.

"You have not accepted the hopelessness of the situation, but don't worry. You will come to savor your position beneath the Caliph, as do all his thousand wives."

CHAPTER SIX

The civilian Mudcat bounced along the rough ground, its six wheels deftly covering obstacles any smaller vehicle would have to go around.

Jacob recognized his childhood home, of course—he just didn't know why they were there. He'd grown up on this ranch, roaming the land as a boy and finding every rock, cave, and critter he could. He knew every square meter.

"Sir," Jacob said, breaking the silence, "I don't think you brought me here so my father could meet my girlfriend. Mind telling me why?"

Admiral DeBeck glanced at Nadia, who stifled a laugh. "No, I didn't. I'll get to the why. But first, I need to tell you what transpired an hour ago," DeBeck said.

To Jacob's ears, that sounded ominous. Was there anything left the Caliphate could do that was worse than what they already had?

"Admiral Villanueva walked into a trap today—we all did. The president formed a Congress pro tem via the constitution. It took some time, because nearly all the people he normally would have called on were killed when the Caliphate bombed Anchorage Bay.

"We had to wait for packets to reach all the planets and for them to send reps. The last one arrived here yesterday. With the information we had, we assumed voting to declare war would be a slam dunk."

DeBeck looked through the window at a pair of dirthogs wrestling with a thornberry bush. Their tough exteriors and mouths were immune to the berry's poison-covered spines.

"Are you saying they didn't?" Jacob asked in shocked disbelief.

"They did not. The Caliphate has always had the upper hand on propaganda. They've spread the word far and wide that it was all a Guild operation designed to frame them. The Guild denies it, of course, but they don't exactly have credibility, do they?"

Jacob shook his head. He tried to wrap his head around the idea of Congress not voting for war after what the Caliphate did. Didn't they know this would invite further attacks?

"So you can see why Noelle wasn't in the best of moods when you saw her," DeBeck said. "Half the new Congress wants to call witnesses and investigate what happened." He barely hid the disgust in his voice. "The other half wants to go after the Guild. We're a victim of the politicization of the *last* Congress."

Jacob leaned back, letting the revelation wash over him. "My *entire* life, they have spent blaming the navy for the Great War, ignoring the danger of the Caliphate when I'm sure they knew exactly what was going on," he said in a burst of insight. "They put on such a good outward show, everyone believed it... and now..." Jacob shook his head, hands trembling as he balled them into fists. "I can't believe they are going to do nothing."

Nadia patted his arm, giving him a soft, sad smile.

They rode in silence as the path turned into a packed-dirt

road that ran parallel to a sturdy fence—one Jacob had played on as a kid. DeBeck turned the Mudcat through the main gate labeled *Melinda May Ranch*.

For the first time in years, Jacob saw his mother's name posted on the gates, as if time stood still here, even though the boy who used to swing on them was long gone.

The ranch was how he remembered. Automated machinery parked in a line awaiting maintenance. A beat-up cargo aircar next to the house's main entrance. And the one-story house itself—seven bedrooms with an attached barn twice as large as the house.

"Sir, I haven't spoken to my father in... a while. I don't think—"

DeBeck raised his hand to stop him.

"Jacob, we're here for a couple of reasons. One, I needed to speak to you somewhere no one would think was out of the ordinary. And two, your father needs to know what happened to you." Without a further word, the admiral climbed out and walked toward the house.

A warm hand encircled Jacob's. "Let's go," Nadia whispered.

His legs refused to move. The shame on his father's face haunted him. His heart ached from the memory of the last time he saw him. Jacob closed his eyes. He had spent years trying to banish those emotions, to put them back in the box from whence they came.

Now the admiral shows up with a box cutter, tearing it all to pieces.

But Jacob wasn't one to back down from his duty. He could no more refuse an order from an admiral than cut off his own arm. He sighed, pushing open the door and stepping out into the mud.

Nadia stood beside him, her arm wrapped in his, urging him forward. The time they had spent together in Zuckabar after his last mission seemed like it had been years ago. He wanted to go back to those days, but reality approached, and it looked pissed.

The front door banged open. A man—almost as tall as Jacob but with salt-and-pepper hair and a weather-beaten face—stepped out, holding a cup of steaming tea. Jacob's father looked exactly as he remembered.

It dawned on Jacob that here on the ranch the sun had just come up, which meant his dad was going on three hours into his day. The only people who worked harder than the military were farmers and ranchers. Maybe that was why so many of their children ended up in the armed forces.

The admiral navigated the mud, stopping short of stepping foot on the porch. Jacob and Nadia followed suit, coming to rest behind him.

"Mr. Grimm?"

Jacob's father's eyes narrowed. "Ben... Unless you're from the bank, and then it's none of your damn business," he said before taking a long, slow sip of his tea.

"No, sir, I'm Vice Admiral DeBeck, Alliance Navy. This"—he turned and gestured to Nadia—"is Commander Dagher, ONI. And I believe you know your son."

What would have made anyone else smile elicited a dour nod from Jacob's father. "Son," Ben said.

The coldness of that one word chilled Jacob, and he found himself feeling like a little kid again. Like the day the navy showed up with a message and a flag to let them know his mom was never coming home.

"Dad," Jacob replied.

"Sir, I'm here because—" Ben turned and walked back into the house, the door shutting behind him, leaving Admiral DeBeck in mid-sentence, his mouth hanging open.

Jacob shook his head.

"What happened between you two?" Nadia asked in a whisper.

"It's a long story. One that won't ever change. Some people don't," Jacob told her.

Admiral DeBeck, as if he were expecting this response, pulled out an actual paper envelope and set it on the porch.

"Mr. Grimm, please read this," he said, loud enough for Ben to hear. Then the admiral turned and walked to the barn.

Baffled, Jacob followed, with Nadia in tow. It all happened so fast he hadn't time to process it. He had lost *Interceptor*; he was out of the navy; then he was home... what was going on?

Once in the barn, the admiral closed the door behind them and looked at Nadia. "Commander, if you please."

Nadia squeezed Jacob's arm before disengaging, and removed a small circular object from her pocket. She twisted the top halfway, like she was unscrewing a lid, and placed it on the ground between them. Blue light flashed, then vanished.

She pulled her NavPad out and checked the screen. "Area secure, sir."

Jacob, the solid navy officer he was, stayed silent. Baffled, but silent. If there was a reason the admiral wanted him here, he would have to wait to find out. They stood in the main room where his dad kept the machinery that needed to be repaired by hand. Along the east wall was the workbench. Jacob walked over to it and leaped up to sit with his feet dangling off the end like he had so many times growing up.

"We can talk privately now," Admiral DeBeck said.

"I'm listening, sir," he said.

"With the war effort off and Congress divided, there's nothing the navy can do to defer or dissuade the Caliphate from taking advantage. I know they are massing their fleet near the Consortium, but they're saying it's a defensive response to the wormhole. We all know that's a bunch of crap; the Alliance and the Consortium weren't the aggressors in the last war. Once again, though, their propaganda machine is ten times better than ours."

Jacob clamped down on his angry retort. The Alliance government knew full well the Caliphate wasn't peaceful or benign. Through Jacob's actions they had uncovered a human-trafficking ring and an ISB spy outpost in, well, not exactly Alliance space, but close enough. Each and every time it seemed like they discovered irrefutable proof of their aggression, they always managed to spin it by the time the news reached Congress and the media as a whole.

"With all due respect, sir, that's a bunch of crap."

"I know," Admiral DeBeck said. "If it's frustrating for you, imagine how I feel. I've got soft intel on a dozen Caliphate operations running in the Alliance. When the president gave them the official boot, my people rounded up *hundreds* of Caliphate agents. We've spent weeks interrogating them. Unfortunately, they were all compartmentalized. We still don't have the full picture."

Jacob picked up a discarded tool, examining it for a moment before hopping down off the counter. "I appreciate the briefing, sir, but I'm more than familiar with their tactics."

"Yes, you are. In fact, you have more combat experience than any other active-duty skipper in the fleet."

Jacob's mind went blank for a moment. He literally couldn't think of anything. "Sir, I... surely there are more experienced ship commanders than I?"

DeBeck chuckled, and Nadia covered her mouth to suppress her own.

"Yes, more experienced commanders. But none with more *combat* experience. Even if you count the anti-piracy patrols—and that's hardly real combat—you're it, Jacob."

Jacob let that sink in for a long moment. He turned around,

facing the rest of his barn, losing himself in his thoughts while he tried to wrap his mind around what they were telling him. The Alliance was in worse shape than he thought. It was no longer a matter of reinforcing the navy or following core values. With the Caliphate willing to bomb habitable planets from orbit against all galactic convention, it was about the survival of his people.

He turned around suddenly, his anger getting the better of him. "Then why are you kicking me out?" he asked, louder than he intended, punctuating it with a pointed finger. "I did everything you asked and more. I served the Alliance with honor. I know she said that it would only be for as long as *Interceptor* was in service, but why throw me out now, when we're about to fight a war for survival?"

Nadia looked at the admiral for permission.

"You tell him," he said.

Jacob suddenly felt like he'd walked into a trap.

"Because, Jacob, we need you to steal the *Interceptor*, fly to Medial, raid the slave pens, and destroy everything on your way out," Nadia said.

He wasn't sure which part of the answer was more absurd. His attempt to respond ended with his mouth hanging open and his hand in the air. "Okay, wait a second," he finally answered. "You're the head of ONI. Why not just give me a mission?" he asked.

"We're not at war with the Caliphate," the admiral answered. "We're not going to *be* at war with them. The next time I have proof the Caliphate did something wrong will be when they've blown up another one of our planets. Congress is full of cowards who won't do what is necessary.

"I know you love our nation and you love the navy. The question is, how much? Medial is only nominally part of the Caliphate. They have no permanent navy, no military base, and only the one city. They buy and sell their slaves in one central, easy-to-raid location. If we were at war, she would be the first place we hit. If we were at war."

"I... I need a minute," Jacob said.

Nadia put a hand on his shoulder. "Jacob, time is—"

"Nadia." He gently pushed her away. "I need a damn minute."

He'd walked this barn a million times in his youth. More than a million. He put his feet on autopilot and strode to the back of the barn, where his father's to-do list hung over the workbench.

Time had stood still at his home. He half expected his mom to come calling and force him upstairs into the bath. His dad certainly hadn't moved on. A large picture of his mother from their wedding hung from the wall. Like a small shrine, the desk below her picture was decorated with a hairbrush, her favorite tea mug, and a silver necklace with a cross on it. Dead twenty years, and she still meant more to him than his own son.

Jacob understood what they wanted—needed—him to do. He pleaded with her ghost for some sign, some idea of what he should do. In the end, he knew exactly what he had to do. Exactly what she would say for him to do.

His duty.

Duty, honor, courage. It's what the navy is about. Her voice rang out so clearly—for a second, he thought she was next to him. In a way, she was.

He didn't want to do it, he *needed* to do it. Worse, he was the only one who could. His career was over. He had nothing to lose.

Jacob turned; his heart hardened as he walked back to the two very out-of-place people. Admiral DeBeck pretended to examine some obscure piece of equipment while Nadia leaned against the wall, looking as beautiful and radiant as ever.

He stopped, scrutinizing her for a long second. Did she maneuver him into this? She was a spy—a very good one by all accounts.

No, he decided. She genuinely liked him, and he liked her. Not that they saw much of one another. What they asked of him was because of who he was.

"Okay, Admiral, tell me exactly what you want me to do."

DeBeck's shoulders slumped, and the admiral seemed both elated and full of dread. A show of emotion Jacob hadn't expected from the head of ONI.

"You understand that even if you succeed, you'll return home a criminal? Court-martialed and likely jailed for the rest of your life?" DeBeck asked him.

"Oh, is that all?" Jacob's flippant retort shielded his stronger emotions. "Will I get to receive visitors?" he asked with a glance at Nadia. She blushed in response.

"I'll make sure of it," DeBeck said.

There was something else he needed, something he had to have in order to do this. "I need one thing in return. This is nonnegotiable. I want my crew exonerated. Not even a whiff of this in their jackets. Officers too. Whip me up some official-looking orders. Make sure they are something I could create on my own, with my fingerprints all over them. When they investigate this, I don't want any doubt as to who ordered it. Me, and me alone. Understood?"

Admiral DeBeck took Jacob's hand in a firm shake.

"Son, you would have made a hell of a spy. I'll make sure none of this blows back on your crew."

Jacob shook his hand in return, letting it go after a second, then looking past the admiral to the open door where his father stood.

Admiral DeBeck watched the Corsair lift off. A gust of wind created by the plasma engines washed over him. He kept watching until the little ship disappeared over the horizon. Was it fate, or just bad luck on Grimm's part that he was the only option they had left to play? The man seemed to have a talent for bucking the odds and cheating death. Would it last, or was he sending that brave man and his people to their deaths?

"Tell me," Nadia asked from the other side of the Mudcat, "did you have Admiral Villanueva kick him out just so you could orchestrate this mission?"

He turned to look at her, once again marveling at how she switched between carefree to lethal in the blink of an eye.

"I would have, in a heartbeat, if I thought it would save us." DeBeck opened the door and climbed in, stopping only to knock the mud off his boots before buckling up.

Nadia climbed into the driver's seat. "Villanueva seemed to like him. Why did she suddenly kick him out?" she asked.

"It was her idea. She thought it might guarantee he would do what we wanted. The boy's got a streak of duty, honor, courage, in him a mile wide. It's almost enough to make me ashamed of my actions... almost. He would have made a hell of an admiral."

Nadia closed her eyes for a moment, the impact of what was about to happen washing over her. "There are days I hate this job," she said.

He turned to her, putting one hand on the dash. His features softened. "If it were easy, anyone could do it."

CHAPTER SEVEN

He didn't speak the entire trip back to the ship—not that Jennings wanted a conversation. He rode in the back, head down, going over what he had agreed to.

Insanity. It's pure insanity, he told himself over and over again.

His NavPad beeped, alerting him to a message. He ignored it.

Boudreaux signaled their approach, and he glanced up at the mission clock. The trip had taken an hour and a half, but it seemed like barely five minutes had passed. Jacob leaned back, stretching his aching muscles and back, pressing forward on his harness as much as it would allow.

What was he doing? He'd be a pirate. No better than the scum he'd fought in Zuckabar. Worse, he would risk his crew for a mission they could never tell anyone about. There would be no returning as heroes from this one. No medals. No promotions.

If he went through with it, his life was over. If he didn't, the life and freedom of millions more would be over.

Chief Boudreaux touched down seamlessly, hardly bumping the ship in the process. Jacob jumped up, stopping at the side hatch to slam the comm button flat.

"Boudreaux, keep the Corsair here. Call the port and let them know we need it for another seventy-two hours," he said.

Jacob leaped off the Corsair, not waiting for a response. He hastily snapped a salute at the ship's flag as he marched for the exit.

Lieutenant Kimiko Yuki waited for him by the double-sized cargo hatch leading to the rest of the ship. "Welcome back, Skipper."

"On me, Kim." He gave the unusually curt order as he passed.

She followed him out the hatch, up the ladder, then past the mess and up the next ladder. All the while, he said nothing.

The admiral had left him no options. His desire to do his duty outweighed everything else. They weren't quite ordering him to do it, but Jacob knew what the consequences were for failing: a war they could never win.

A few minutes later, they ascended to the O deck and the bridge. Lance Corporal Naki started to come to attention when Jacob emerged from the ladder.

"As you were," he said with a wave of his hand before heading aft.

He keyed open his quarters, taking off his uniform jacket and tossing it on the bed, then starting to unbutton his shirt.

"Uh, Skipper?" Kim asked from the hatchway. She held the hatch frame with one hand and looked at him with a raised eyebrow.

He glanced at her, then himself, and for the first time since he woke up that morning, he cracked a smile.

"Sorry, my head is in a place. One sec." Jacob grabbed a

civilian sweater from his drawers and moved to the head, closing the hatch behind him. He bumped his elbows pulling his shirt off, and hit his hands on the overhead when he put the new one on. It normally bothered the hell out of him; this time he barely noticed.

He opened the hatch and tossed his uniform jacket on the deck before collapsing to the bed with his back against the outer bulkhead.

"Sir, I'm guessing things are not well?" she asked with a glance at his out-of-character disorder.

"That's an understatement, Kim. Please call me Jacob for reasons that will soon become apparent."

Her eyes went wide, and a hand flew to her mouth. "Oh no. They kicked you out? Wait, what about *Interceptor*?" Her words flew out on top of each other.

Jacob held up his hand, motioning for her to slow down.

"To answer your question, yes. I'm out. As for the old girl, well, she's out too. As soon as the orders are processed, a breaker crew will come aboard, and she'll be scrapped for whatever... well, whatever they use scrap for."

The news hit Kim like a hammer. Jacob had processed it for over an hour, and he still couldn't wrap his head around all the implications.

She came forward, sitting down next to him in a serious breach of protocol, which he ignored.

"Why? After everything we did, everything we gave... why?" she whispered.

Jacob took a deep breath, letting it out slowly as his mind ran over every event since he took command of *Interceptor*. If he were anyone else on any other ship, he'd be in command of a heavy cruiser, and every single one of his people would be promoted to the maximum rank their age would allow. Instead, he was out of the navy, and his people were almost two years behind their peers. All because of the Caliphate's cowardly attack in Pascal.

He sat in silence, not responding to Kim's question, staring at the open hatch to his quarters. Deep down in his heart, he had to believe it wasn't for nothing. It wasn't. They had saved lives, uncovered a massive conspiracy... twice... and brought the Guild's criminal behavior to light.

"Doing the right thing. Acting with honor. Doing your duty to your fellow spacers... is its own reward," he said to Kim. "My mom used to say that. She was right then, and she's right now. As for the why..."

How did he tell her the next part? The news hadn't broken yet. As far as everyone in the navy was concerned, they were five minutes away from a war with the Caliphate.

"But the war, Skipper? I mean, won't the navy need every ship?" she asked.

"They do, but not us," he said. "Not *Interceptor*."

She let it sink in and, after a moment, nodded.

"Listen, Kim, there's more to this than our decommissioning. I—" He paused for a moment, glancing at the hatch. Standing, he took a few large steps and hit the secure button. The hatch whooshed shut.

"Skipper?" she asked at his unusual behavior.

"Jacob," he corrected. "What I'm about to tell you is off the record. Do you understand?"

"Okay... uh... Jacob," she said.

"Sounds weird when you say it," he said with a smile. "Regardless, here it is. ONI wants us to go on a black-book mission into the Caliphate and rescue prisoners held on Medial —their forward slave market distribution center."

She blinked several times. "Wait, what?" she asked. "I don't... what?"

He empathized with her. Today was a day of dichotomy. Her

reaction reassured him that his wasn't unusual. At least her career would continue without interruption.

"What I'm about to tell you isn't public knowledge yet, but it will be soon. Congress has chosen to hold the Guild, not the Caliphate, responsible for bombing Anchorage Bay. There isn't going to be a war. Which means the Caliphate will be emboldened in their action. Which means..." He trailed off.

Her face went white as she realized the implications. "Which means," she continued for him, "they'll do it again."

He sucked in a deep breath. He hadn't said it out loud, and hearing her reach the same conclusion comforted him in a weird sort of way.

"Exactly. The obvious response would be to attack the Caliphate immediately, show them we are strong, capable, and won't back down. War is never a desirable outcome, but sometimes—"

"You've got to poke the bully in the eye," she finished for him again.

He bowed his head, placing a hand on his stomach. "I can't tell you how relieved I am to hear you agree," he said.

Silenced stretched out between them for a long moment.

"So," she said, "is ONI going to issue us orders to do something mundane as cover?"

Jacob shook his head. "No, Kim. No orders, official or otherwise. If we do this, we're going to have to go rogue. I've taken steps to make sure no one will be implicated but me. Anyone who comes with us will be protected."

"This is a little much to process in one go," she said. "I know one thing, *Skipper,* I go where you go, consequences be damned."

Jacob looked up sharply, pride welling in his heart. He had wanted her to say that, willed her too, but it had to be her decision.

"Thank you, Kim. Call a staff meeting of all the officers and CPOs. We'll hold it in the mess. I want everyone to know this is voluntary, from the newest spacer's apprentice to the COB," he said.

"Aye, sir. I'm on it."

Thirty minutes and one lengthy explanation later, Jacob looked out on his officers and chiefs. He could see the same questions on their faces that he and Kim had.

"I want you all to know, this is one hundred percent voluntary. No action will be taken, in any way, to convince you to come. Everyone *must* choose to do this."

Chief Suresh pshawed him. "That's a helluva thing to say to us," she said.

"Excuse me?" he replied.

"We've all been through hell for the navy, for this ship, and for you, Skipper. You think any one of us would sit on the sidelines while you went out to do something truly epic? You're out of your damned mind, son," Suresh said.

The informality of her tone struck him. He wasn't in uniform, though, and he'd made it clear at the beginning this wasn't an official meeting.

"Uh, thank you for your honesty, Devi," he said. "Anyone else?"

Kim sat off to the side, quietly observing the command crew. She had decided not to tell them what she was doing until they had made the decision for themselves.

"Sir, uh... Jacob," Mark West asked with a raised hand. "What do we do with the crew who want to stay behind?"

He opened his mouth to respond when Chief Redfern jumped in. "There won't be any, Lieutenant West. Not one."

Jacob smiled at the chief's confidence. "I think we're getting ahead of ourselves. First, we need to discuss your decisions. As the senior staff, I—"

"Bullshit," Jennings interrupted him.

"Sergeant—" Carter Fawkes jumped up, but Jacob cut him off.

"Everyone gets to speak freely without reprisal, Carter." He nodded to Allison to continue.

Jennings pushed off the bulkhead, raising her hand. "By show of hands, who's coming?" she asked. Everyone raised their hands but Kim. The marine shot her a look.

"Oh, I'm going," the XO said. "I wanted to make sure you all made the decision on your own." She raised her hand.

Jennings nodded. "It's settled, then. Marines should run your damn meetings—they would take thirty seconds." She returned to her position by the hatch.

Jacob, along with the rest of the senior crew, looked on in stunned silence.

"Well, oo-frigging-rah," Bosun Sandivol said.

A spattering of chuckles broke out.

"Okay, that's settled. Kim?" Jacob asked.

She stepped forward, taking over the meeting. "We have a lot to discuss, so let's get to it. First, how do we tell the crew? Second, what steps do we need to take? Bear in mind, we won't have any orders or permissions for what we do next."

"We can meet with our sections and ask them individually," Ensign Owusu offered.

"Uh, sir," Roy Hössbacher said, "however we do it, I think we should tell them all at once. If anyone wants off, we can figure out what to do with them, but—and I don't think this is likely—if someone says they'll stay but then reports it to the navy, there's no way to stop them if we aren't prepared."

That hadn't occurred to Jacob. Could they keep them from reporting while in spacedock?

"What do you suggest, Roy?" Jacob asked.

The ensign blushed as all the attention turned to him. "Uh, well." He stopped to think for a minute. "I can put up the ECM shields and route all wireless signals through central comms. If anyone tries to call out, I'll know who it is."

"Anyone who doesn't want to go," Devi said, "we can detain in the rec room. They'll be comfortable and far enough from any airlocks to keep them from escaping until we're ready."

Chief Redfern cleared his throat. "I want to reiterate, no one is going to say no," he said.

"Be that as it may, Chief, a failure to plan is a plan to fail," Jacob said.

"Aye, sir, I just don't see anyone opting out."

"I like your optimism, Chief. I hope you're right." Jacob looked around the room, taking care to meet everyone's eyes. "Your support means the world to me. We have a plan—let's execute it."

Nadia looked out the side window as the aircar circled Fort Icarus, thousands of kilometers south of the equator of Alexandria. The barren wasteland, made up of ancient volcanic rock and pillars that climbed hundreds of meters into the sky, was the perfect location for a high-security detention facility.

The three-winged prison sat atop the highest pillar, a kilometer high and almost five hundred meters wide. Even if someone managed to escape the three perimeters and avoid detection by the geosynchronous observation satellite, there was nowhere to go. And nothing could approach within a hundred klicks without the proper authorization.

Authorization Nadia didn't actually have. Her cover ID, Lieutenant Commander Sara Mitchel, had it, though. As a high-ranking JAG officer assigned to Terrance DeShawn's piracy case, she could have a one-on-one interview with the former pirate.

"Aircar Oscar four-four-one, state your authorization. You have ten seconds to comply," a bored voice said via the comms.

"Lieutenant Commander Sara Mitchel, JAG. Case number three-three-five-alpha-seven-bravo," she replied, mimicking the bored tone of the comms man.

"Maintain current approach while we verify. Do not deviate, or you will be fired upon."

"Roger. Maintain current approach," she replied.

The center of the three-tiered complex housed the landing pad and main tower that controlled the prison and the guards. She gently adjusted the controls to bring the aircar to a hover as the prison's security took control. Once the computer confirmed they were flying, she leaned back and let it happen.

The car came to rest on one of the sub-pads on the north side of level fifteen. Twenty floors above her, the giant pad for the official prison transports blotted out the system's yellow dwarf star and cast a deep shadow over the smaller pad.

She keyed the door open and stepped out.

"Commander Mitchel, present your ID, please." The man asking was an army MP with *Irwin* on his name tag.

She pulled out her leather briefcase and fetched out her official ID. He scanned it with his ArmPad, the army version of the NavPad she carried. Or would have carried if she were a legit JAG officer instead of an ONI plant. Her actual Pad did much more than the standard navy issue.

"Clear. Welcome to Mount Doom," he said with a dark smile.

"Thank you."

Security in the prison was no joke. Automated systems scanned her ID, biometrics, and DNA at every door. Armed guards in body armor were stationed at regular intervals, and she even caught a glimpse of army Raptor suits patrolling the internal perimeter.

They emerged inside a hall with a series of rooms, each with an alcove to observe whoever was inside the rooms. Nadia frowned. It would make her mission more difficult if she had to do this loud.

"In here," Irwin said.

"Sergeant," Nadia interrupted him, "this is an interrogation room, not a private conference room."

"Sorry, ma'am. Some prisoners have to be watched at all times. You can file a complaint with the commandant if you like." The way he said it told her there would be no point.

She nodded, letting him leave, then took her seat on the opposite side of the only table and pulled out her NavPad. Setting it in the center of the table, she activated the recording function.

A moment later, the door slid open, and two guards escorted Terrance DeShawn in. His bright pink jumpsuit showed his name on one shoulder and his number on the other. "Who are you?" he asked.

Irwin slapped the man in the back of the head and pushed him into the chair. "The prisoner will only speak when spoken to," the MP said.

DeShawn bristled but said nothing. Nadia understood the attempts to dehumanize the prisoners, to keep them from hope. The men and women who arrived at Fort Icarus would only leave when they were dead—executed for heinous crimes, like DeShawn—or dying of natural causes. While the facility had top-notch medical care, they didn't receive the genetic anti-aging treatments available to the rest of the population.

"Sergeant Irwin, do not mistreat my client," she said with a stern look at the army dog.

"Yes, ma'am," he replied. They took position behind DeShawn, one on each side of him.

Nadia looked at both men for a long moment, but they didn't move.

"This is privileged discussion, gentlemen. You may leave now," she said.

"No, ma'am. Commandant's orders," Irwin replied.

Nadia sighed. There were rules about this sort of thing. Why were they breaking them over a low-level pirate scheduled for execution?

"Sergeant, if you don't leave this room immediately, you'll have bigger problems than the commandant." She glared at them to make her point.

"Ma'am, I can't—"

"Call General McAdams," she said.

"Calling General McAdams," her NavPad's computerized voice said.

Sergeant Irwin blanched at the name of the army commanding general. "Uh, no need, ma'am. We'll exit." He grabbed the other guard, shoving him toward the door. Nadia reached over and canceled the call.

Once the men were out, DeShawn smirked. "Nice. You my new lawyer?" he asked.

"Not exactly." She pushed a button on her NavPad. "State your name for the record," she said.

"Terrance DeSha—" Nadia's NavPad flashed, scanning DeShawn with a blue shimmering light, then blinking three times. "What the hell was that?" he asked.

"That was my NavPad creating an electronic doppelgänger of you. For the next five minutes, their computer system will see and hear what I want them to."

He cocked his head and clicked his teeth. "Prove it," he said.

Nadia reached into her bag and pulled out her deadly, armor-piercing sidearm, pointing it directly at DeShawn's face.

"What the fu—" She clicked the safety off. "Okay, I believe you!" He raised his palms as far as he could with the magnetic clamps holding his wrists to the table.

"Good. Because I could shoot you—blow your brains all over the observation window—and no one would know till I was a hundred klicks away. Do we have an understanding?" she asked.

"Crazy, psycho bitch," he snarled. "Yeah, I get it."

"Good." Nadia put the pistol away in the hidden compartment. She folded her hands in front of her and glared hard at DeShawn.

Her emotions swirled like a hurricane. While DeShawn hadn't had anything to do with *Dagger*'s boarding, he was a pirate. He'd contributed to the Caliphate's nightmarish human trafficking. Which made him partly responsible for the hell she had endured.

Her heart pounded as the memories of what happened to her aboard the little ship flashed back through her mind. The slave collar, the abuse, the pain when the collar was taken off, and the loss of her friends... she clenched her fists until her knuckles hurt.

DeShawn shrank before her, a terrified expression on his face as he looked at the door. "What do you want?" he whispered.

"You sold slaves on Medial, correct?" she said between clenched teeth.

He shook his head. "They never proved that I—"

She slammed her cybernetic fist down with a bang, denting the metal table.

"Don't lie to me." Her voice dripped with venom.

DeShawn noticeably paled. "Yes, I did. Since y'all are executing me, I guess there's no point in hiding anything," he said with a sigh.

"Good. How did you approach the planet and let them know you had product to sell?" she asked.

This was the crucial point. When they arrived in Medial, they had to make orbit, and it was doubtful they could do that randomly. The pirates had to have a way to let space traffic control know they were authorized.

"There ain't no codes. You have to know them. Someone has to have vouched for you," he said.

She leaned back, absorbing the information. That was a problem. Nadia figured they handed out a code or access card—something she could fake or copy.

"How does it work? How do new people come in?" she asked.

He jerked his hands against the restraints as if he forgot he couldn't cross his arms. "No," he said. "Do whatever you want to me, I'm done talking. If you're going to kill me, kill me."

Nadia ran through the list of her options, and it came down to just one. "Oh, I'm not going to kill you," she said. "I'm going to offer you a deal."

"What kind of deal?"

"I'll have your death sentence commuted, and you can live out the rest of your natural life behind bars."

"No deal. I'd rather die than help you," he said.

"Oh, you're going to help," she said. "You're going to help because your only other option is death. I *know* you, Terrance. You're a coward. You want to live. You would do anything to live. So you'll do this."

He glanced up, unable to meet her eyes for more than a few seconds. "Even *if* I said yes, you don't have the power to get me out of here."

She smiled. She had him. "Not officially, no. But unofficially, I can do anything I damn well please." Nadia reached inside her bag and pulled out the other gun.

"Wait," Terrance yelled, jerking back as far as he could. Nadia fired, hitting him in the chest.

CHAPTER EIGHT

Sweat ran down the small of Jacob's back while he paced back and forth outside the boat bay. Bosun Sandivol stuck his head out the hatchway, "Skipper, the crew's assembled and ready for you."

Jacob stopped, swallowing several times to lubricate his throat. All the speeches he'd given in his life, and he'd never felt so nervous before. "Roger, Bosun, thank you. I'll be there shortly," he said.

"Aye, sir." Sandivol disappeared behind the bulkhead.

Jacob bowed his head and said a quick prayer. He needed help and strength to do what he was about to do—to ask a hundred men and women to come with him on a renegade mission they might not return from. He shook his head. How would he ask them?

One word at a time, came the response. He clenched his jaw, straightened his shoulders, tugged on the bottom of his uniform jacket, and marched in. Initially, he'd decided not to wear his uniform, but Kim convinced him all that would do was lower morale.

As he marched into the boat bay, Chief Suresh snapped to

attention. "*Interceptor*, attention!" The crew snapped-to like a well-oiled machine, the clap of their boots echoing in the chamber. As the chief-of-the-boat, she was responsible for the formations of the petty officers and spacers. It was odd, not having any of the other officers in the room, but he felt strongly about the crew making this decision for themselves. If there were officers present, it would unduly pressure them to go along.

The only senior NCOs in attendance were the COB and the bosun. Since both were seen more as the mentors and friends of the enlisted than as authoritarians, it didn't hurt to have them handy.

Jacob noticed Jennings standing by the door. He hadn't told her not to come, but he'd assumed she wouldn't be in the room. The sidearm on her hip made him frown. Of course she was armed.

Walking through the room, he took a good, long look at the crew. Pride welled in him. Despite their months-long repair stay at Utopia, their uniforms were clean and sharp. It helped that he had given them weekend leave so they only had to stay on the ship the night before duties. It helped even more that most had served together for the better part of two years.

"As you were," he said as he stepped up on a small platform to be seen and heard even by the spacers in the back. They were lined up by section, left to right, tallest to shortest. Engineering anchored the back and Ops the front, with everyone else in between.

"Thank you for coming," he said. A light sprinkle of chuckles rippled through the crew. As if showing up to a formation the captain ordered was optional. "I know this is a little unusual. I want you to know, there are no officers here other than me. Everything said in this room, by me or by you, will be kept in strictest confidence. No reprisals, no repercussions." He took off his watch cap and slipped it under the epaulet on his left shoulder.

A few of the crew looked around in surprise, and Jacob heard a few whispers. He let them settle down before continuing.

"We've been through a lot together. When I took command, you were having some trouble—" More chuckles as the crew remembered the shape they had been in when the captain came aboard. "Then the pirates. We lost good people. PO Kirkland and his crew, who manned their stations to the end. DT Trevors, who died along with Commander Stanislaw." Jacob had to stop for a moment. While the crew were new at the time, each loss still stung. "All to stop pirates, corrupt officials, and Caliphate spies. We had no idea what we were walking into when we faced down a frigate that out massed us three-to-one. Because of your courage, we brought justice to the dead and saved countless lives." He paused for a moment, letting the memory of what happened in Zuckabar—the fear of dying, followed by the elation of victory—replay in their memories.

"After that was Wonderland. We, this ship, discovered the largest conspiracy ever perpetrated on the human race. The Guild hid from the entire galaxy what they were truly capable of. Until *Interceptor*"—Jacob pointed at the shark-faced emblem painted on the bulkhead—"showed everyone who they really were. We paid the price in blood for that discovery. Look around you. The men and women next to you, they have your back. In reality, there is no one, not a living soul in the universe you can trust more than your shipmates."

Jacob looked around the room. The faces of the spacers he served with etched into his memory. He realized it wasn't just a speech. He could trust everyone here, from the newest apprentice to the seasoned spacer. A few ratings he knew personally caught his eye. Gouger, McCall, Mendez. The POs. Collins,

Tefiti, Oliv, and the rest. They weren't just his crew, they were his friends. His family.

"We didn't do this for a paycheck. Or for the glory. We did it because it was our duty to do so. We did it because we have a responsibility to honor. We succeeded because we are courageous."

"Damn skippy," Private Cole shouted.

Jacob let them settle down before continuing. "That is why I've gathered you today. We have a new mission—"

"About time!" someone shouted.

"Yes, it is," he said. "However, it's not an *official* mission." This was the hard part. His throat went dry, and he had to swallow. "The Caliphate bombed Alexandria, but..." It was up to Jacob to deliver the bombshell. "Congress has decided *not* to pursue action against them at this time."

Silence enveloped the boat bay as if the exterior doors had opened, letting all the air out. The unnatural quiet lingered before someone swore, breaking it open, and the crew all started talking at once.

"Cowards," Spacer Whips said with a scowl.

"I lost family in the attack, Skipper. Why aren't we going after them?" Beech asked.

Jacob let them talk. They needed to get it out, ask their questions. He motioned for the POs to let them be, even though they had to be as upset as the spacers. In any crew, the vast majority were the eighteen-to-twenty-two-year-old *kids,* just out of school, with almost no life experience. They were the ones with the most to lose, and more often than not, the ones who paid with everything. The POs were barely a minute older, but with much more experience.

"Sir," PO Tefiti asked, loud and clear from the front.

"Yes, PO?" Jacob asked in an equally loud voice.

"If we're not going to war, then what's the mission?" he asked. All eyes turned to Jacob.

He took in a deep breath, letting it out slowly. "Not everyone in the navy concurs with the decision to stand down. They believe, and I agree with them, that every day we let go by without a decisive response is a day that emboldens the Caliphate further. They did it once. If they get away with it, then they'll do it again. Maybe not right away, but soon. I, for one, can't have that on my conscience. I'm asking all of you to go with me and help me show the Caliphate who they are messing with."

Fists flew in the air as every man and woman aboard cheered. Except PO Tefiti. He frowned, looking around.

Jacob motioned for the crew to quiet down for a moment.

"PO?" he asked.

"Sorry, sir. I know I have a lot of questions—"

"Tefiti," Jacob interrupted, "you're the best grav-man in the fleet. I'm happy to answer any questions you have." He wasn't falsely flattering Tefiti; his ability to detect gravity waves had literally saved the ship multiple times during their last battle.

Tefiti's dark skin deepened a shade from the compliment. "Uh, thank you, sir. If FleetCom is giving the orders, why the cloak-and-dagger?"

"Because," Jacob said, "there are no orders." He let the consequences of those words sink in. "If we do this, we'll be off-book. No authorization, no backup, no support. I can't tell you where we're going until I know you're with me, but I want every single person in this room to know they can decline with *no consequences*.

"I'm asking a lot. I'm asking you to possibly throw away your careers, even your lives, for something that may fail. Even if it does succeed, we might come home and face dire consequences." They met this proclamation with more silence. "But, if we succeed, we'll have given the Caliphate a black eye they won't soon recover from, and we will have saved countless lives."

He stopped, meeting as many eyes as he could. "Now, I'm going to leave the room. You discuss it among yourselves, and I will respect whatever decision you come to. I—"

Tefiti stepped forward. "Sir, you don't have to leave the room." He looked behind him, and every head nodded, from PO Desper to Spacer First Class Mendez. "We're with you, sir. To hell and back if need be."

The rest of the crew punctuated his statement with a roaring cheer. They broke into a chant of *Inter-cep-tor. Inter-cep-tor!*

His heart welled. From when he'd first come on board to that moment, nothing he'd done gratified him as much as the show of support of the crew. He scanned his people, trying to find anyone who looked as if they were just going along. Not one did.

He raised his hand, and the crew quieted down. "All right then. We have our mission. We need to prepare *Interceptor* for departure. Unlike a normal departure, we have to do it without telling anyone. As of this moment we're on radio silence. Messages to your family need to go through Ensign Hössbacher. Speak to your immediate supervisor about any questions, and..." He let out a long sigh. "Thank you."

Kim jerked her head back and forth. They were going on two hours into their planning meeting, and the senior staff was getting nowhere. The captain sat at the head of the table but remained silent, letting her run the meeting and letting his officers solve the problems.

She held up her hand to stop the second impending argument between Chief Redfern and Lieutenant West. Generally, the meetings were segregated, but they were short on time. They needed answers, and soon.

"Chief," Kim said to the older engineering CPO, "why don't you lay it down for us in a way we can all understand."

He tapped his finger on the table. "It comes down to this. Whenever a ship is sent on a deployment, they receive authenticated orders from command. That same transmission can be used to disable the ship before it leaves the system. In fact, the moment they know something is wrong, system protocol sends out a signal, querying the ship's orders. If we don't have the correct authentication, the next signal is the automated recall. They will shut us down. No flight, no mission, no victory."

"Okay. And Mark, you think we can override it locally?" Kim asked. She tended to side with Chief Redfern. A ship's computers had a certain level of flexibility, but the core systems were hardwired, not software. This prevented an enemy from remotely controlling a ship or a spy from sabotaging the software—unless they replaced key components, as had happened before.

Mark leaned forward, folding his hands on the table. "If we run silent, our EM shield will prevent any such transmission from reaching the ship—"

"*If* the EM shield is up when we receive the message. We're going to need communications, not to mention radar and lidar, to see where we're going. None of which is possible when we're running silent," Chief Redfern said.

Kim nodded, agreeing. "I see what you're saying, Mark, and if it wasn't for us having to navigate, we could do it. But I think Chief Redfern has a point."

Mark shrank back as he realized his mistake. "Ug. Sorry,

Chief, I was thinking we could point ourselves in the right direction and punch it."

Redfern broke into an instant smile. "No worries, sir. The advantage of serving longer. Of course, I'd be lost if you needed me to actually manage a department. I'll leave that in your capable hands."

Kim questioned the chief's *compliment,* at least mentally. No one ever said, "what a great manager you are."

"We have to forge orders, then. There's no way around it. Suggestions?" she asked.

"Any chance ONI could do it for us, Skipper?" Mark West asked.

Jacob shook his head. "None. They are helping in other ways, but we're on our own for most of this."

"How are orders created in the first place?" Lieutenant Carter Fawkes asked.

"That's an excellent question. Anyone care to guess?" Yuki asked.

"I don't have to guess," Chief Suresh said. "Fleet admirals don't issue orders, NavPer does. They go to the admiral for authentication, then from there out to FleetCom for distribution."

This was Kim's understanding as well. She nodded for the COB to continue.

"We don't need orders, just authentication codes to leave the system," Suresh said.

Kim felt lighter as Chief Suresh spoke. It was genius, really. Authentication codes would give them the clearance to leave. But how to get them?

"You can't just walk into Admiral Villanueva's office and ask for the codes," Ensign Hössbacher said. "They're daily codes, issued by FleetCom, and only to ships that already have orders to move."

Kim let his words sink in for a moment before speaking. "The chicken and the egg, then," she said.

"Aye, ma'am. You can't get the codes without already having authenticated orders," Hössbacher said. "You can't get the orders unless FleetCom has the authorization from the admiral."

The XO let the silence stretch out. Giving people time to think, allowing them to problem-solve. Herself included.

"I have an idea, but I'll need to go aboard *Alexander* to know if it will work. Let's circle back around to this later," she said. "Chief Boudreaux? You wanna get with Spacer Mendez and figure out the food situation?"

Chief Boudreaux stood against the far bulkhead, next to the hatch.

"Yes, ma'am," she replied in her French-Cajun accent. "I suppose we can take the Corsair over to fleet HQ and visit the main distribution network. I know a few people..." She let her voice fade away, replaced with a grin.

"I won't ask, Chief," Kim said with a matching grin. "That covers food. Our water stores are topped off here, as are the scrubbers. That leaves ordnance. We're going to need a lot—maybe more than we usually carry. I know this is normally Ops, Mark, but you've got your hands full. Suggestions?"

When a ship departed on deployment, armory shuttles would attach and deliver the ordnance needed. In *Interceptor*'s case, that consisted of ammo crates for the Long Nine, boxes of 20 mm rounds for the turrets, and several dozen 240 mm MXII torpedoes. Small arms and the like were kept up by the ship's master-at-arms and the marines. There was more than enough small-arms ammo aboard, but all the supplies for the ship's weapons had been unloaded upon entry into drydock.

Lieutenant Carter Fawkes raised his hand. "Ma'am, there's

just no way we can trick the fleet into resupplying us. Not just in the time available, but at all."

Kim frowned. She didn't like the idea that they couldn't figure it out.

"Explain?" she asked.

"Do you know about the incident on Vishnu?" Fawkes asked.

Something rang a bell. A half-forgotten memory, but there were twenty-two-star systems in the Alliance. She shook her head negative.

"I'm not surprised. It's not something the service wants to talk about. An officer, about my age, snapped and commandeered a Corsair loaded with munitions. Flew it right into the light cruiser he served on. Thankfully, the idiot ended up as the only casualty. However, Navy Logistics Corps changed how they moved munitions around after that. You could be an admiral, and they wouldn't hand you a single round for a sidearm without six different verifications. Let alone deliver the thousands of rounds we need here on *Interceptor*."

Kim marveled at the ease with which they spoke of their impending treason—for that was what it was. "The captain ordered me to do it" would only carry them so far. Any one of the plans they discussed would result in a court-martial and likely prison if FleetCom found out about it. In a way, stealing the ship proved an easier task than stealing the supplies needed to make her combat-ready.

"You don't have to go through NavLog for ammo." Jennings spoke up from the back of the room. She stood ramrod straight, with her arms behind her, forming a perfect triangle connecting at the base of her spine.

"Oh? Please educate us," Fawkes said. Kim picked up on the smug tone in Fawkes' voice. She'd have a chat with him later about that, in private.

"My pleasure, sir. It's a marine's duty to straighten out officers."

Fawkes chuckled along with the rest of the officers in the room, making Kim think maybe he'd joked with Jennings and wasn't acting superior. "All we need to do is stop by Fort Kirk Proving Grounds on our way out. It will take some muscle power, but we can grab enough pallets of what we need."

Kim opened her mouth to protest. The proving grounds wouldn't just have ammo lying around, would they?

"Holy crap, Sergeant Jennings," Fawkes said. "Of course!"

"You care to enlighten the rest of us?" Kim asked.

"Sorry, ma'am. The proving grounds have ammo to spare available for any ship's captain to requisition for a live-fire exercise. Sure, the skipper has to sign for it, and technically they need to stay within the proving grounds to use it, but..."

In a lot of ways, running a ship was like running a small business. They budgeted for fuel, ammo, even crew leave times. The captain and XO personally signed for perishables, then dispersed them to the lower ranks. Technically, if they showed up at the proving grounds and signed for a few tons of ammo, the local commander would give it to them. The captain would eventually have to account for it or risk court-martial. Something Grimm was going to face, regardless.

"Oh boy. I might have to transfer to the Corps for that," Kim said with a mocking smile. "That's amazing. Well done. Ensign Owusu, plot us a least-time course to Fort Kirk. I think we're going to end up going through Zuck regardless, but best to cover our bases. Also, keep it updated hourly. If we have to go, seconds *will* count."

"Aye, aye, ma'am," Ensign Owusu replied. He tapped away at his NavPad, beginning the precise calculations required to go anywhere in the galaxy.

"Authorization, food, ammo... am I missing anything?" she asked.

Jennings nodded.

"Yes, Sergeant?"

"When we came to port and put in here at Utopia, Bravo company's el-tee came aboard and *transferred* the Raptors off the ship. He said we didn't need them, ma'am."

Kim leaned back in the squeaky chair, clasping her hands behind her head. "That's a problem," she said.

"Yes, it is, ma'am," Jennings replied. "We've got our space armor, but the Raptors are our force multiplier. If we're seriously going to be hitting the Caliphate where it hurts the most, we're going to need our battle suits."

The captain raised his hand. "I actually know exactly how to handle this one, Allison. Like Chief Boudreaux," he said, shooting the pilot a look, "I know a guy."

CHAPTER NINE

Elsa decided her father wasn't coming for her. Thirty days had passed since her arrival, each day worse than the last. If he knew, a fleet would have already arrived and bombed the planet back to the Stone Age. No, he either didn't know where she was... *or he thinks I'm dead,* she thought with a shudder.

Her sparse living quarters were large enough for her bed, a closet, and an open-air toilet. When the horrible woman left her alone, Elsa could move around but could not leave the room without permission and an escort.

After the first time she'd set a trap for her captor, the woman started sending in servants first. Elsa didn't want to kill an innocent held by the evil collar. Just the ones who put it on her.

In a perverse sort of way, she had a privileged position. As a princess of the Iron Empire, she was set aside for the Caliph. The other slaves captured in raids weren't quite as lucky.

However, if they thought she was helpless, they had badly miscalculated. Children of the emperor were expected to work for the Empire. Her older brother headed their security services.

Elsa served in counterintelligence. She had killed men with her bare hands in the past and would do so again in the future. In this situation, she needed her intellect. She needed a plan.

The only thing she couldn't do was remove the collar. The one thing that stopped her from escaping. She looked out the small window set high above her bed. The architecture mimicked some long lost pre-electric society. The walls weren't really made of sandstone, but they looked and felt like it—enough that she was able to climb up using her fingertips and toes until she could see out the meter-wide cubed window.

From that view, she could tell the structure sat on a hill overlooking a large city. Aircars and transports constantly flew overhead. A giant arena, with walls a hundred meters high, was at the center of the city.

She wasn't great at estimating populations, but there had to be a few hundred thousand people. How many of those were slaves, she had no idea. Everyone she had met—with the exception of the horrid woman—wore a collar.

From the people who brought her meals, to the children who cleaned her room, as far as she could tell, the entire infrastructure was built on slave labor.

A noise outside alerted her to a visitor. She dropped the three meters to the floor, flexing her knees and using the momentum to roll onto her bed.

The door beeped, and a servant walked in with a carafe of water, followed by the horrid woman who controlled her.

"Elsa, no fight today? Excellent," Abla said.

Elsa turned her head away from the woman, rolling over to face the wall.

Her servant set the carafe down and departed. The door shut, and Elsa was alone again. She had to escape. Had to communicate with her father. How many citizens of the Empire languished as slaves in the Caliphate? Despair welled up in her, though. The collar. The damned collar prevented her from using violence against her captor. She couldn't remove it and couldn't escape. They didn't let her out of the room and barely fed her.

There had to be a way to signal for help, but who could she signal when she didn't even know where she was?

The door beeped again. Else assumed it was her jailer back to taunt her.

"Hello?" a small voice said.

She whipped around to face the new person. It was a girl, perhaps sixteen... her dusky-colored skin, dark eyes and dark hair marked her as a native of the Caliphate. The silver collar around her neck marked her as a slave.

Elsa's eyes went wide with confusion. Of course, if they had no problem enslaving others, they would enslave their own. The girl moved about the room, wiping down the spare furniture with a white rag.

"What's your name?" Elsa asked in Caliph.

She hesitated for a moment. "Zahra al-Alami," she said fast, as if just answering was against the rules.

Elsa reached out to her, and the girl jerked away.

"I'm sorry," Elsa said. "I won't hurt you."

Zahra's wary expression spoke of many such broken promises. She finished her task in silence, then fled the room. Elsa sat up, leaning against the wall. What kind of people enslaved their own children?

A plan formed in Elsa's mind. Perhaps her prison wasn't inescapable after all.

CHAPTER TEN

As she swiveled her borrowed Corsair around to port, Chief Warrant Officer Vivienne "Viv" Boudreaux eyed her exterior camera. Warehouse eleven flashed by for a brief instant before the rain and wind swallowed her up. A sudden gust slapped the ship to the side, and she jerked the controls back against it, pushing down on the pedals to maintain the turn.

"Hang on, Mendez," she shouted over the internal mic. She cut the plasma engines and let the ship fall two meters onto the reinforced landing pad.

Mendez yelped from below as the entire ship rocked on its landing struts.

"Thanks for the warning, Chief," he yelled up.

Viv smiled and unbuckled her harness with one hand while flipping the rear ramp open. Of the Corsair's four entrances, the ramp offered the easiest access for cargo.

Before they left *Interceptor*, she'd whipped her boat bay crew into action, removing the forty seats normally occupying the inside of the dropship, leaving only the three crew seats and the co-pilot seat behind hers.

"PO Collins," Viv said to the coxswain in the second seat, "you take the boys and go for the food stores. I'll see about rustling up anything else we might need."

"Aye, Chief. On it," Collins said as she slid down the ladder to the lower deck. Viv slid down right behind her.

"Mendez, Zach, Perch, on me," Collins ordered as she hustled down the ramp into the driving rain.

Boudreaux opened the gear locker and removed a bulky environmental jacket. Putting it on, she hit the button to open the outer hatch. With a hum, the heavy hatch slid open. Rain pelted her, forcing her to shield her eyes. She'd picked the landing pad closest to the food stores, but she'd caught a glimpse of a Mudcat while circling to land—something they might need but hadn't discussed in their meeting.

She leaped out of the ship, hitting the ground with a grunt and breaking into a run toward the next warehouse. Between the driving rain and the wind, no one walked around the perimeter, let alone inside the fenced-in area.

She slowed to a walk as her target came into view. The Mudcat they had carried on Zuckabar had a few miles on it and was the standard navy passenger version. The one before her was rigged for command and control. Large white numbers adorned the side, *LM-115*.

Chief Warrant Officer Boudreaux cracked a smile, and her mind raced through the possibilities. As she approached the vehicle, she activated her radio.

"Collins, Boudreaux," she said.

"Go for Collins," the PO replied.

"I'm going to need a minute, PO. Get the ship loaded and button her up," she ordered.

"Aye, Chief, on it. Collins out."

Viv ran her hand down the armored flank of the Mudcat.

"You and I are going to have some fun, yes?" she purred as she went to work bypassing the electronic lock.

Petty Officer Jennifer Collins half jogged, half walked down the immense aisles of the navy's auxiliary supply warehouse. Every square inch was packed with space-saving modular storage crates.

"Mendez," she said, pointing at a manual lifter.

"On it, PO," he replied as he took off to the cargo carrier.

Spacer Perch and Zach followed him, and the three spacers managed to get the lifter started. The two junior spacers mounted the outside while Mendez drove the electric vehicle to chase down their PO.

Collins pulled her NavPad from her cargo pocket and activated a map of the warehouse. A wire frame came to life, and she typed in the first thing on her list: protein, meat, canned.

"Seventeen-b," she shouted over her shoulder. "Racks three and five. All of it."

The lifter turned right behind her into aisle seventeen. It would take them a few minutes to load up the crates.

Three more aisles down, she flagged another food section. She inwardly winced at the food they were taking. The skipper didn't want to risk what had happened to them in Wonderland, which meant filling the stores to the limit with the most calorie-dense food they could find. It wasn't going to make the tastiest meals—though if anyone could make it palatable, it was Josh Mendez.

"PO," Mendez shouted and waved to get her attention.

Collins wanted to chew him out for making so much noise, but instead just walked over to where he was. "What? And keep your voice down."

"Right. Sorry, PO. Beans and rice. I can do a lot with this. Plus it's compact. I can store it under bunks if we need to."

Collins checked her list, beans weren't on it, but he made a good point.

"Do it." She waved him forward.

Walking down the aisle, she radio-tagged two more sections for the spacers to clean out. She had everything they needed. Time to move on to the "wants."

Boudreaux shouted with delight as the door lifted up like a wing. She ducked under it, planting one foot on the step and vaulting up into the vehicle.

She was right—the antennas outside were for the C&C package installed. Capable of operating as a mobile command center and infantry support vehicle, with enough comms gear to power a planet.

"Score," she muttered.

"Hey," a man shouted through the rain at her.

She pretended not to hear as she pressed the *engine start* button. Generally, as a chief warrant officer, she had clearance to operate any vehicle. The Mudcat's limited computer checked her authorization via the transponder in her NavPad and assumed lawful use.

"What are you—"

She turned to the man, a marine sergeant with a square jaw underneath his wet-weather gear. She glanced at his name tag before addressing him.

"Sergeant Garen?" she asked.

He nodded, eyes going narrow as he stopped underneath the gull wing to shelter from the rain.

"Yes, Chief. Can I ask what you're doing with the general's Mudcat?" he half shouted over the howl of the wind.

Any story she told him wouldn't pass muster, but the truth might do the trick. "I'm a Corsair pilot. My crew is loading up on supplies, and I saw this beauty sitting here and thought I would take a look."

Warrant officers filled a unique position in the command structure—above enlisted and noncoms, but below officers. They were specialists, highly skilled in their chosen fields, and usually answered to no one but their immediate superior.

Sergeant Garen glanced at the wings on her jacket. She saw him visibly relax. "No problem, Chief, she's a beauty indeed. Unfortunately, she's sat here for a month waiting for transpo," he told her.

"That's too bad. Where is she bound?"

"Blackrock. But with everything that's happened, transporting a new Mudcat to a training facility has taken a back seat."

She nodded. A momentary sadness washed over her, and she tried not to think about what the Caliphate had done to Anchorage Bay. The sheer level of destruction boggled her mind. She'd spent more than a few nights crying herself to sleep over it.

"Yeah, I know," she said, looking away. The shared pain was too great, too recent. She didn't know if they would ever heal from what had happened. "She's a nice truck," she said to change the subject.

He seemed to accept her reasoning and the compliment. "Indeed," he said.

Using the grab handle, she heaved herself onto the running board.

As she climbed down, she reached over and depressed a single button under the dash. Between the rain, wind, and Boudreaux's physical presence, Sergeant Garen missed the dull thud of transport magnets deploying.

"Anytime you wanna come by and look, let me know," he said. "I'd be happy to let you in. Maybe even bring you some coffee?"

"Thank you, Sergeant, I might just take you up on that."

Collins leaped off the lifter as Mendez drove it down the Corsair's ramp, jogging a few feet before stopping.

"Perch, Zach, clamp everything down. Magnetic and manually," she added.

The spacers groaned in unison at the extra work.

"Mendez, return the lifter *exactly* where we found it," she shouted as he drove away. His hand shot out with a thumbs-up.

Collins triggered her radio to call Chief Boudreaux, when the pilot came bounding out of the rain.

"PO, release the carry clamps, and let's get out of here," she ordered.

"Aye, aye, Chief," Collins said.

She ran around to the far side of the Corsair and knelt down to shimmy under the fuselage, then ran her hand under the belly until her fingers felt the indent, and she pulled. Six clamps jutted out on springs, each one powerful enough to hold an exterior cargo pod—or a Mudcat.

Collins went back around the other side and waited for Mendez to return.

"I'll be glad when we can get out of the rain, PO," Zach said from the top of the ramp. She gave him the evil eye; she was waiting in the rain, and he wasn't. Sheepishly, Zach turned and went back to securing the load.

A few minutes later, Mendez came out of the warehouse at a full run, waving frantically for her attention.

"PO, a sergeant saw me return the lift. He's right behind me," Mendez shouted over the driving rain.

Collins jerked her thumb toward the ship. "Finish securing the load and get strapped in."

Mendez ran past her as she keyed her radio.

"Chief, Collins. We might have trouble," she said.

"I'm here, PO," Boudreaux answered. "Strapping in right now."

Collins glanced at the warehouse entrance just as a heavyset army sergeant came huffing out the door. He wore a standard uniform, no rain gear, and he stopped as soon as the drops hit him. Backing up, he waved his hands at her, yelling something she couldn't hear.

Collins waved and smiled before turning up the ramp. Electric motors hummed to life, raising the cargo hatch and leaving the protesting noncom out in the cold.

A gust of wind blasted the side of the Corsair, sending her horizontal with her tail swinging around. Viv fought the stick, pushing the pedals to rotate on her central axis while pulling up to gain altitude. She glanced at the rear monitor, making sure to miss the fence as the wind pushed the dropship up and over.

A crash from below echoed up, followed by a scream of pain. She heard it distantly, refusing to shift focus as she fought to bring the ship under control.

Plasma engines roared as she gunned them, bunny hopping the dropship forward against the wind. Engineering overcame nature, and the ship shot off in the direction she commanded.

A squawk from the intercom caught her attention. "Chief," Collins said, "Perch broke his arm. We need to get back to the ship ASAP."

A twinge of guilt ran through her. If she weren't in such a hurry, she could have taken off smoother. She keyed the mic.

"We just have a quick stop to make. Can you man the panel on the side hatch?"

A pause preceded the reply. "On it."

Viv looked down past her feet where the canopy's translucent hull allowed her to keep an eye on the ground as she slowed down to overfly her target.

Through the rain and wind, she saw her objective: one brand-new Mudcat, parked with docking clamps extended.

"Collins, when I make the connection, secure the clamps, then shut the hatch," Viv said over the intercom.

"Roger," Collins replied.

Viv eyed her panels while glancing down at the ground. Under normal circumstances, making the connection with the Mudcat would be a piece of cake. With the fifty-knot gusts and heavy rain, it would prove more challenging.

Red lights flashed on her screen in a proximity warning. The landing gear button lit up, angrily demanding she lower them. Sweat ran down her spine as she put every ounce of focus on the exact movements of the stick. One wrong turn and she could slam into the vehicle or, worse, the ground.

A sudden gust hit her from the other side. She pushed the stick over, banking to starboard to keep her place above the Mudcat. Collins yelped from below.

"One more second," Viv muttered. The gust died down, and she evened the ship out and put her down on top of the command-and-control vehicle.

Metal clanged as the two came into contact.

"Connection secure; closing the hatch," Collins said.

"Get strapped in!" Viv yelled over the intercom. "We're going vertical in five seconds."

Silently, she counted down in her head from five. At one, she goosed the throttle, lifting straight up with the Mudcat secured underneath the tail. At five hundred meters, she pulled the stick back, lifting the nose and rotating the engines to fixed position. Plasma engines screamed as she burned through the air with her stolen bounty.

Lieutenant Senior Grade Kimiko Yuki stepped off the navy transport shuttle. They weren't as fast or spacious as a Corsair, but far easier to build and far more cost effective to operate in the close proximity of ships in orbit.

USS *Alexander*'s welcome area spanned nearly twenty meters, with three armed marines manning the hatch and a navy purser behind a small podium checking clearance.

Kim's mouth went dry as she approached the purser's desk. She clasped her hands together behind her to keep them from fidgeting.

Navy security was tight since the attack, but she wasn't doing anything wrong—no one was going to jump out and arrest her. Well... they didn't *know* she was here to do something illegal.

Three spacers were ahead of her, each as bored as she should be but couldn't quite make herself.

The PO manning the purser's desk glanced at each ID and verified it on his own screen before waving them through with a rote, "Welcome aboard."

He perked up when he noticed her rank. Kim's short stature brought her eye level with the PO's chest, something she was used to—especially serving a captain who had to duck when he walked through a hatch.

"Lieutenant," the purser said, snapping to attention. "Welcome aboard the *Alexander*. What is the purpose of your visit?" he asked.

She held up her NavPad, which automatically transmitted

her biometric security code, proving her identity. If anyone else tried to use that Pad, it would alert the purser and the marine guards.

"Twenty-four-hour pass, visiting a friend," Kim said.

"Name and department of your friend?"

Kim panicked. Last time she'd visited the ship, they hadn't asked any follow-up questions. Of course, that was before Anchorage Bay—before the attack. She should have accounted for it. "Uh, I…" She racked her brain. Did she even know anyone on the ship?

"Ma'am?" the purser asked.

Sweat beaded at the small of her neck, and she felt an overwhelming urge to run. This was stupid. They would investigate further and find out what the crew was up to, and everything would be undone because she couldn't think of a name. The nearest marine started to move, one hand hovering over his sidearm.

"Kim?" a woman's voice said from the hatch.

She glanced over, seeing a woman with light brown skin and dark eyes staring back. The last time she'd seen her, the woman was in sickbay aboard *Interceptor*—and wasn't at all a commander. It took her a moment to overcome her shock.

"Commander Dagher?" Kim asked out of reflex.

"I'm so glad you could make it." Nadia Dagher turned to the purser. "She's with me, PO Ralston."

"Aye, ma'am, make sure you check in if you're staying longer than twenty-four hours," he said to Kim.

Nadia grabbed her arm, pulling her along even though Kim's feet wanted to stay put.

"Uh, will do, PO," Kim said. She kicked herself in gear, following the commander through the hatch. They walked in silence down the corridor for a moment. Nadia looked back for a second, then pushed Kim through a side hatch. She stumbled, maintaining her balance by slapping the bulkhead.

"Sorry," Nadia said. Closing the hatch, she pivoted to Kim. "What are you doing here?"

Kim fought against the trapped feeling welling up in her gut, doing her best to maintain her calm. Did Nadia know what was going on? The captain hadn't mentioned her specifically, only briefly touching on ONI's request. She knew, though, that they were an item. She'd only officially met her the one time back in Zuckabar when she had gone to the skipper's hotel room to tell him about Anchorage Bay.

"Listen, Lieutenant Yuki, I know what you're thinking, and you're right to think it. However, you can trust me," she said, pointing to her ONI badge, a spaceship wrapped in parchment with the words *semper vigilantes* beneath the name tag.

Kim weighed her options. If the captain trusted Dagher, she did too.

"Kim," she said. "If we're friends, you should call me by my first name."

Nadia cracked a smile. "Excellent. Are you here for departure orders?"

A warm feeling welled in her stomach. The kind that came from knowing she had an ally. "Aye, ma'am. I am. The skipper told me you had the trail covered, but we still need a way out without triggering the automatic recall or having to disobey a direct order. I thought maybe I could get into the admiral's office and copy the daily authenti—why are you shaking your head?"

Nadia smiled, taking Kim by the shoulder and leading her down the side hatch to a secondary passageway.

"Won't work," she said. "Security procedures have changed in the last few months. But not to worry. I have a plan."

Kim glanced behind her as they walked away, her nerves

getting the better of her. Spies and secrets were never her cup of *saké*.

"Do you want to tell me the plan, ma'am, or should I guess?" Kim asked. They entered one of the personnel lifts running the length of the ship. Aboard *Interceptor*, she would never use one unless there was an emergency. However, *Alexander*'s kilometer-long hull prevented the crew from using ladders. Many passageways weren't even physically connected.

"Yes, I do," Nadia said. "But I have to ask, did the entire crew go along with Jacob's plan?"

Since she decided to trust the commander, there was no reason to hold back. "Every one, ma'am. Every. Last. One."

Nadia's eyes sparkled. "I knew they would. He has a way about him—"

"Yes, he does," Kim agreed.

The lift came to a halt, opening onto deck seventeen blue, the tertiary computer core. Nadia headed for the stern of the ship.

"I have this," she said, holding up a small memory chip. "It will grant us access to FleetCom for thirty seconds. Do you think that's enough time to navigate their systems and fabricate a departure key?" she asked.

Kim ran through a hundred options as they walked. Thirty seconds wasn't a very long time. Hell, she'd never even seen the FleetCom interface. Pursing her lips, she decided she couldn't. "I need more time," she said. "Thirty seconds hardly gets me time to log in and—"

Nadia spun on one heel, held her NavPad to the hatch labeled *FleetCom: Authorized Personnel Only.*

"Wait, what are you doing?" Kim asked.

"You're going to have to figure it out, because this chip"—she held it up—"is only good for ten more minutes. Come on."

The hatch slid up with a hum. Nadia grabbed her shoulder and pushed her through.

"Wait, what?" Kim said as she stumbled through. "I just told you—"

The hatch hummed closed behind them.

"Kim, I've read your file. You can do this," Nadia said with an encouraging smile. "And if you can't, well, we're in trouble."

Nadia handed the chip to the XO and pushed her toward the console.

Kim's nerves doubled down on her. Her hands shook as she pushed the chip into the console. "Uh, what's this, um, do?" she asked. The screen flashed, and FleetCom's interface opened with administrative access. "Oh," Kim said.

She went to work, typing as fast as she could.

"Fifteen seconds," Nadia said.

"Not helping," Kim replied. "Found it... and..." She tapped a few more keys, her erratic breathing making it difficult to hit the right buttons. "Almost..."

"Three seconds!" Nadia said.

"Got it," Kim yelled, slapping the fabricate key. The machine next to her hummed to life, spitting out a hand-sized data stick with the authentication codes built into it.

Nadia grinned at the junior officer. "Any problems?"

"One. It's only good for the next twenty-four hours. It was the best I could do."

CHAPTER ELEVEN

Jennings adjusted her gray and white ship's uniform. Like most things marine, its Spartan nature prevented anything from standing out and presenting a target. On the left of her chest was *MARINE* and over her right, *JENNINGS*. Her sergeant stripes adorned her sleeve in a throwback homage to an era long gone.

She hopped off the Corsair onto the deck of the USS *Crane-Shark*, a Marine Orbital Combat Carrier, the cream of the Marine Corps force. A five-hundred-meter-long, two-hundred-meter-tall fighting platform capable of delivering a thousand marines and their support craft anywhere the Alliance needed.

The last time Jennings stepped foot on one, she held the rank of private. She felt a certain level of esteem coming back aboard the *Crane-Shark* as a sergeant.

Cold air greeted her as she hopped down from the Corsair. "Chief Boudreaux, stay with the ship. I'll be back shortly," she said.

"Aye, aye, Sergeant," Chief Boudreaux said.

Jennings marched past a pair of spacers attaching fuel hoses to the just-landed Corsair. A young marine lieutenant with the name tag *VERACRUZ* stood on the other side of the embarkation line. Jennings stopped on her side of the line, snapped to attention, and fired a parade-ground salute at the deck officer.

"Sergeant Allison Jennings, USS *Interceptor*, here to see Lieutenant Bonds, sir."

The officer's square jaw clenched as he looked down at his NavPad. Like most Marines, he had the *look*. Something no civilian could ever hope to mimic.

"Jennings," he said in a New Austin accent. "You the crazy marine who counterattacked a dropship from the *outside*?"

Still holding the salute, she stood a little taller.

"Aye, sir. I am."

He snapped to attention and returned the salute. "Well, oorah, Sergeant," he said.

"Oorah, sir." She lowered her hand to her side.

"Carry on," he told her.

She walked past him onto the ship, a buzz in her stomach. She didn't do what she did for praise, but she spent so much time among navy types, it felt good and right to be among Marines who appreciated her skills.

Crane-Shark's ship's time synced with Anchorage Bay, and that meant the lieutenant was likely in the gym. In combat, marines were anything but predictable. However, a life of order was a successful life, and she found her former commanding officer where she expected—working out in the officers-only gym.

A bored navy PO3 manned the hatch, reading a book on his NavPad. He only looked up when the computer beeped, alerting him.

"Sergeant, the noncoms' gym is two decks down and—" Jennings' crystal blue eyes turned on him with an intense gaze capable of blistering paint. "Uh, I mean how may I help you, Sergeant?" He straightened up, putting the NavPad down.

"I'm here to see Lieutenant Bonds," she said with no further explanation.

"Uh, you see, Sergeant, only officers are allowed in the gym. You can use the comms panel to signal him." He pointed back the way she came.

She glanced behind her. If she wanted to comm him, she would have sent him a message. The captain wanted to avoid electronic communications whenever possible—the less they used the official channels, the better.

Jennings pointed at the very large black man pushing up a hundred and fifty kilos on the bench press.

"I'm going to go see him." She immediately headed for the weight bench.

"Uh, Sergeant?" the PO called out. She ignored him. "Sergeant, you can't go in there!" he shouted louder.

The commotion caused Lieutenant Bonds to look her way, a big grin splitting his face as he recognized his former lance corporal. "Hot damn! *Sergeant* Jennings? Congratulations," he said. Bonds slammed the weight down, then leaped up from the bench.

"Yes, sir," she said. Two other marine officers, a shorter man with fair skin, and a rail-thin woman with skin darker than Bonds, stood behind him.

"El-tee, noncoms aren't allowed in the officers' gym," the man said from behind Bonds.

Jennings stopped in front of her former lieutenant, snapping to attention and saluting. Despite him wearing his marine tank top, he was still "in uniform," and he returned the salute.

Bonds glanced over his shoulder. "Yes, sir, I know," he said. Jennings didn't miss the twinkle in his eyes and suspected what came next. Bonds turned to the two marines. "Tell you what, let's hold a little contest. Inverted push-ups. If I win, the sergeant stays; if you win, I'll buy you a case of that sludge you call whiskey."

The dark-skinned woman let out a throaty laugh that echoed around the room. "I want in on this. Captain Lepke," she introduced herself with a nod.

"Alright, let's get it on. Captain Ferro," the fair-skinned man said by way of introduction.

Ferro walked over to the bulkhead, falling into a handstand and putting his feet against the metal bulkhead.

Bonds leaned over to Jennings. "He can do about ten more than me," he whispered.

Jennings dropped into parade rest and watched as the man's muscles rippled with each push-up.

"Then why did you challenge him?" she asked.

"Because I'm not the one doing the push-ups," he said with a smile.

Heat flushed through her as she realized what he intended to do. "Sir," she whispered, "I can't do more inverted pushups than you."

Bonds kept himself close to her as he spoke. "You and I both know you never wanted to," he said.

She frowned. During her time on *Interceptor* Jennings had carefully avoided breaking Lieutenant Bonds' inverted pushup record. Apparently, though, he'd seen through her ruse.

Allison reached up and deliberately and precisely unbuttoned her tunic from top to bottom.

Captain Ferro finished, flipping on to his feet with a flourish.

"Fifty, Bonds. Beat that," he said with a cocksure smile.

"I think I hurt my shoulder on that last set," Bonds said, feigning pain as he rotated his shoulder around. "Jennings will stand in for me."

Ferro smirked, eyes narrowing as he examined his competition. Jennings shrugged out of her uniform tunic, revealing her chiseled arms and oversized neck and shoulder muscles. She pulled her shirt off, leaving just her sports bra and her very obvious six-pack.

"Oh, you are screwed, Ferro," Lepke said, containing her laughter by the slimmest margin. "Damn, girl, you can bounce a coin off that stomach."

Jennings took a moment to stretch out, loosening her muscles.

As she twisted, the four-centimeter circular scar came into view. Bonds reached out, waving his finger at it. "That's new."

"Wonderland," was all she said. The mission from their last tour was mostly classified. Even so, almost everyone knew about Wonderland—if not exactly what had happened there.

She bounced up and down a few times to limber up, then nodded, letting him know she was ready.

Ferro frowned. "I'm starting to think you set me up," he said.

"If you didn't, I wouldn't respect you as an officer," Bonds replied.

Jennings cracked her neck. Letting her mind go blank, she dropped into a traditional push-up.

"Uh, Sergeant, the bulkhead is over he—" Lepke began.

Jennings spread her feet and raised her hips. She took a deep breath and rocked forward into a handstand, her body perfectly aligned with the bulkhead.

"One," she said as she went down until her nose brushed the deck.

"Son of a—" Ferro stopped himself from finishing.

A crowd of officers formed around her as she hit ten. By thirty, they were chanting her name. When she hit fifty, they started screaming, "One more!"

Jennings was hyper-focused. An easy calm entered her

mind, even as her arms shook from the strain and her muscles rippled from head to toe as she finished the next one.

"Fifty-one!" the crowd cheered.

With a deep breath for strength, she let gravity take her down, then heaved back. Arms strained as she hit fifty-two. Then, because she could, Jennings lifted one arm up and held it tight against her side.

"Oh, for the love of—" someone said. Another cursed. She thought maybe it was Ferro, but she couldn't take her focus off her next move.

She went down, which was always the easy part. Sweat broke out on her brow as she stopped with her nose touching the deck. Pushing back up? Damn near impossible.

Jennings was a Marine; she could do three impossible things before breakfast.

Her neck and shoulder muscles flexed and shook as she cried out.

"Oorah!"

"Fifty... THREE!" Captain Lepke bellowed.

Jennings figured she'd made her point. Without losing balance, she lowered her feet and stood. Sweat ran off her neck and shoulders, dripping on the deck.

Lepke handed her a towel. "Oorah, Marine."

"Thank you, ma'am."

"Any time you want to stop hanging out on a tin can and join recon, you let me know," Captain Ferro said.

"Aye, sir. Will do."

Fifteen minutes later, Bonds handed her a cup of coffee from the dispensary. The two marines found a corner table with a view port overlooking Alexandria. The deep blue of the ocean shimmered up at them, and the height made Jennings uneasy. She wasn't afraid, exactly, just uneasy as she stared at the planet hundreds of kilometers away. With the crater site coming into view, she decided to sip her coffee as a way of avoiding it without looking like she was avoiding it.

"It's like a fresh wound every time it comes around," Bonds said. "I know you're not from here, but damn if it isn't on everyone's mind every second of the day. It'll be good to get some payback. That is, if Congress will get off their ass and do their job," he growled.

Along with the unease, a new feeling hit her. She worried the el-tee would think less of her if he knew she was lying to him. She couldn't do that. Not to him. "Sir, I have to be honest —" She glanced around, making sure no one was even remotely close to their table. Leaning in, she said, "We're not going to war with anybody, sir. Not the Caliph, not the Guild, no one."

Bonds' face split into his trademark grin. But then he saw she was serious. Anyone else he might think they were joking, but Jennings went AWOL the day God handed out humor.

The skin around his knuckles tightened, and she could see him fighting for control.

"I don't know how you came about this information, but let's assume I accept it as truth. Why are you here?" he asked. "When I saw you walk in, I thought maybe you wanted me to pull some strings and get you reassigned—"

Jennings jerked back like he'd slapped her. "And leave the captain? No, sir. I like *Interceptor*."

Bonds relaxed slightly. "Then what is it?"

Jennings decided she never, ever, wanted to work for or with ONI if at all possible. The kind of line-walking doublespeak required here, even though it was to protect Bonds' career, infuriated her. She put her coffee down. With one hand, she started tapping her forefinger on the table.

After a moment, Bonds said, "I'd say this is unlike you, but you're always quiet. Usually though, it's for a purpose—" He trailed off as she continued to tap the table.

A pattern emerged. A long-forgotten message system, taught to marines as an exercise for improving memory, formed with her repeated taps. She watched him follow along through one whole cycle, then his eyes went wide, and she knew he understood.

"You've gotta be kidding me..." was all he could say.

Utopia Shipyard's interior design didn't look at all like a shipyard to Petty Officer First Class Prisca Desper. Her medical training left her woefully unprepared to judge things like spatial architecture.

Utopia's designers wanted to let in as much natural light as possible, hence the hundred-meter-tall atrium acting as the central complex for the barren moon's base. While it had started out as a small mining station two hundred plus years ago, over that time it had experienced steady growth, making it the largest population center in the system outside of Alexandria herself. She might not know anything about building design, but the atrium alone took her breath away. She tossed her empty medical bag over one shoulder and picked up the one resting at her feet as the train stopped and the doors opened.

Main Atrium. Command, medical, and engineering services, a pleasant female voice informed the passengers.

Prisca stepped off the train. Lines painted on the deck, an age-old method of directing traffic, told her where to go. Red for command, leading to the upper levels, yellow for engineering, blue for medical.

She followed the blue line past a pair of bright red maple trees, their leaves fluttering in the breeze. From there, the line intersected with an escalator. She didn't wait for the stairs to carry her, instead jogging up to rejoin the blue line at the top.

Time was short, and she checked her NavPad, hoping for an update. When they finally departed the system, they would do so in a hurry. She couldn't believe what they were doing. In all her time in the navy, she would never have thought she would participate in stealing her own ship.

Stepping off the escalator, she headed for the infirmary. The blue line split in three, each one in a different direction. She followed the one to the right with the sign *Pharmacy*. When she queried the computer, it had told her the middle of the day just after lunch was the least busy for the pharmacy.

The pharm techs worked behind a reinforced bulkhead, divided into six stations. All but one was empty.

"Prisca?" a freckled-faced ginger-haired man said from behind the counter.

Her knees shook and her heart quivered as she saw him. If she had a weakness, his name was Lieutenant (SG) Bartholomew Johansen. They'd dated on-again, off-again for three years. When her duty brought her home, they ended up spending every waking moment together. He had the luxury of a semipermanent duty station because of his naval specialization. Back in Zuckabar, when she'd learned about the attack, she'd spent the entire trip home submerged in her work to avoid thinking about if he'd survived. After all, he lived on Alexandria—it could have hit him just as easily as the next person. The relief she'd felt when he messaged her carried her through the following months of backbreaking work repairing the ship.

"Hey, Bat," she said, using his pet name. He smiled ear to ear. It wasn't like they hadn't said goodbye over breakfast that very morning.

Her face faltered, followed by her chest tightening. So much had changed—it felt like a lot more than four hours. She stopped at the counter, putting her bags down and leaning over to kiss him on the cheek.

"You know, if you keep seeing me off-duty and on, people are going to talk," he whispered to her. Despite the disparity in their ranks—him being an officer and her an NCO—fraternization wasn't strictly prohibited. They were both consenting adults and in different chains of command. As long as they were never in direct duty with each other and they filed the paperwork letting command know, they were fine.

"Well, Lieutenant, I wanted to see you and..." She glanced left and right. "I need a favor."

The weariness in his eyes washed over her. He hid it well, but he was from Alexandria. His sister lived—had lived—north of Anchorage Bay. The bombing hadn't killed her, but as with so many millions, over the following weeks, the radiation did the job. There just weren't enough meds for everyone, and by the time there were, the casualties were high. Too high.

"My assistant will be back in a minute," Bat said. "Then I'm all yours."

She shook her head. "Actually." She lifted the bags up and slid them across the counter. "It's better if no one else is here."

Two kilometers away, in fuel depot five, Chief Redfern looked for his own contact. The lanky engineer cracked his knuckles one by one as he and Spacer Beech hung out in the seedy underbelly bar known as "Short-timers."

"How do you even know about this place, Chief?" Beech asked.

"Time and experience, kid. You ever wonder why I'm the second-highest-ranking noncom on *Interceptor*?" Redfern asked.

Beech lifted the semi-clean glass to sip his smooth beer. "I just figured you liked tin cans, Chief."

Redfern drank down the rest of his dark lager, letting the last tasty bit drop into his mouth. "I do, Beech, but I also may have had dealings with the 'wrong kinds of people,' as my NCIS jacket reads."

Beech looked like he was about to fall out of his chair. "Chief? You? You're kidding?"

"You stay in the navy long enough and you learn there are times you follow the rules, and times you don't." Redfern tapped the table, then pointed at the disheveled power tech with a shaved head who walked in. The coveralls he wore were standard issue, but had clearly seen better days.

Redfern slid his NavPad over the table reader, paying for the drinks. "Let's go see what we can get," he said.

Beech leaped up, trying not to fall over as he trailed behind the engineer. "What *are* we trying to get?" he whispered.

Redfern waved his NavPad in front of the kid. "About two hundred kilos of nano-matter. Enough to fuel the fabricators for several deployments."

Parts aboard ship were always a problem. No ship, not even one as massive as the kilometer-long USS *Alexander*, could carry spare parts for every eventuality. With the advent of enhanced nanotech a century earlier, they didn't need to. From hull plating to optical boards, if the fabricator had the blueprints, they could make any part they needed.

Like the rest of *Interceptor*'s perishables, they would normally be refilled by the Utopia Shipyard umbilical. With no deployment orders, though, they couldn't get more than what they needed for specific parts. Of course, Redfern knew of a few alternate sources.

"Echo?" the gruff-looking man said, jumping to his feet as the lanky engineering chief approached him.

"Mason!" Redfern clapped the man on the shoulder. "Mace, this is Beech. I'm breaking him in to the sweet life of a space engineer."

Beech held out his hand, which Mace engulfed. Beech had the distinct impression the rough-looking man could crush him like a grape.

"No finer tutor than Chief Echo Redfern," Mace said with a big grin. He motioned for them to sit.

"Thank you, Mace. I was sorry to hear about—"

Mace held up his hand. "Please. Don't. I appreciate it. But what's done is done, and there's no going back. At least when the war breaks out, I've enough pull to... What?" He stopped midstream. "I can see it in your faces. What?"

"You should tell him, Chief," Beech said.

Redfern hesitated, the decision contending on his face. "It's not public knowledge, Mace. You can't repeat this to anyone."

"This isn't like you, Echo. You're not here against your will, are you?" Mace asked, glancing around.

Redfern let out a sharp laugh. "I'm out of the game, Mace. No black market for me—at least, not normally."

Mace nodded. "Okay then, I won't tell anyone. Now, what is it?"

Redfern glanced away, picking at his sleeve for a second. "Mace, we're not going to war. Congre—"

The power tech slammed his hand on the table. "You're full of—"

Redfern grabbed the man's hand and squeezed. Redfern knew what Mace had lost in the attack... what so many who served in the navy had lost. Especially those stationed on Alexandria and her system. "From what I know, Congress is going to investigate further while laying the blame at the feet of the Guild."

"No. You're wrong. But..."

Redfern shook his head. "I wish I were. You can't ask me how I know, but we've known each other a long time, Mace. You know I wouldn't lie to you, especially not about this."

"How can they not?" he pleaded with Redfern. The sudden fragility in the stocky spacer caught Redfern by surprise. He eased his chair closer, draping an arm over his suffering friend. He then proceeded to whisper in his ear, and by the time he was done, Mace had a grim smile on his face.

CHAPTER TWELVE

On a small destroyer like *Interceptor*, space was always at a premium. Jacob's "desk" folded out from the bulkhead and allowed him to set up his NavPad to use it as the primary communications tool it was. He never used the desk as such, since he had to cram himself into a folding chair that was far too small for his frame. He preferred to write in the mess, but what he was doing needed to be private.

Dear Admiral Villanueva...

He hated that opening. It felt like the start of a breakup letter. He wanted her to understand the why, not just the what. The old-fashioned letter with its official "Dept. Of the Navy" seal sat unopened next to him. It had arrived an hour before, and he didn't have to open it to know that it contained his separation orders.

He could, he supposed, call her and tell her directly. But

then she would be forced—duty bound—to report him. He couldn't put her in that position, even if he suspected she was in on the secret mission.

Admiral,

Thank you for your kindness, respect, and encouragement. It's with a heavy heart I tell you of what I'm about to do. You have to know, or at least I hope you know, that it was not the Guild, but the Caliphate that bombed Alexandria. They are masters of subterfuge and misdirection, and they manipulate the media the way a toddler does his parents. I have firsthand experience with the way this works. Unless we respond with strength, they will feel victorious—and they will repeat their attack. Since I am to be resigned and my ship scuttled, I feel it is my duty, and mine alone, to respond. My crew thinks I am acting under orders, and have no knowledge of what I'm about to do.

The trick, he decided, lay in sounding a little bit insane, but still plausible. If the fleet bought his "renegade captain" act, then maybe they would go easy on his crew. Admiral DeBeck swore they wouldn't bear any of the blame for the act of piracy they were all about to commit, but Jacob didn't want to bet their fate on a man whose job description literally involved *lying to everyone.*

"Captain, Gouger, sir. Private communications from the planet."

Jacob waved his hand over the holographic interface of his NavPad. The letter he was working on vanished, replaced by the last person he expected to see.

A square jaw and dark brown eyes stared back at him, a face

that was eerily similar to his own, but not quite the same. Seeing his father's face pressed the weight of his past on his shoulders. He pushed back from the desk, putting a few more centimeters between them.

"The man who was out here with you, he a friend?" his dad asked.

Jacob didn't know what to say. His throat tightened, and his mouth went as dry as the desert. Those few words were the most his father had spoken to him since Pascal. Jacob couldn't bring himself to speak, just nod.

His dad looked off-screen. "He said some stuff to me, made me think I'd misjudged you. If I did, I'm... well, I'm sorry."

Sergeant Jennings could take lessons on laconic speech from his father. The man's infuriating lack of verbal engagement drove Jacob nuts. All these years he'd wanted to hear this, and his dad had to go and say "*if.*"

Jacob's mind stalled, refusing to compute what words he should put in his mouth next. Instead, he tried to say several at once and ended up sputtering out an incoherent mess. Years had passed, and his father still made him feel like a kid. He closed his eyes and focused for a moment. "Dad, thank you. I... uh, I don't know what to say."

His father rubbed the stubble on his face. "It's late here, almost three a.m. What time is it there?" he asked.

"About the same."

"You look so much like your mom," his dad whispered. The connection died, and Jacob found himself staring at a fading holographic image of his father.

Some commanders would work their crews to the bone, keeping them exhausted and on edge at all times. Those kinds of commanders were ready to flip out over any perceived infraction or dirty deck plate. Jacob liked a tidy ship as much as the next CO, but he would never take his people to task over an open hatch or a bit of grime on the bulkhead. After all, *Interceptor* was forty years old and then some. He wasn't even alive when she came off the assembly line, nor was the majority of her crew.

Still trying to figure out how to tell the admiral, he exited his cabin, NavPad in hand, and noticed the hatch to the briefing room half-open. Despite months in the yard, there were a few... quirks... *Interceptor* couldn't shake. Chief among them the malfunctioning briefing room hatch. With the entire aftersection above deck three and behind the bridge rebuilt over the last three months, he often felt privileged that anything else had received attention at all.

Which struck him as odd. Why scrap the *Interceptor* after spending millions repairing her? Yes, she was old, but she still had fight left in her. Why—

The realization hit him like a cold bucket of water. Villanueva knew. She knew before he was ever in her office. Had she planned it with DeBeck, or was it happenstance?

If he was right, then he knew who waited for him in the ship's only briefing room. He strode to the hatch, peeked his head in, and smiled at the dark-haired woman who made his heart pound whenever he looked upon her.

His eyes narrowed when he noticed a man a few meters away from her. He was thin and pensive, with eyes like a trapped rat. Not military, Jacob was sure. As much as he liked Nadia, it annoyed him that she had brought a stranger onto his ship without permission—or at least someone notifying him.

"Do you really think I couldn't sneak him on board?" she said with a smile, as if she read his mind.

"You can't read thoughts, can you?" he asked.

She moved in to hug Jacob, something he happily accepted.

His curiosity piqued as she moved away to the man with her, and Jacob swore as he finally recognized him. He took a step closer, fists balling. Nadia placed her hand on Jacob's chest, holding him back.

"Easy there, tiger," she said.

"Give me one reason not to have him thrown out the airlock," Jacob demanded.

"We need him," Nadia said. "Where we're going, you can't just show up and park where you want. He's our in."

Jacob fought to maintain control. There was nothing in the galaxy that disgusted him more than human-trafficking pirates. "What's your name?" he spat out.

"Terrance... Terry DeShawn," the prisoner said, not willing to meet Jacob's eyes.

"He's been to Medial, Jacob. He knows who to talk to when we arrive. We need him."

A bitter tang filled his throat, and he had trouble swallowing. His lip curled in disgust, and Jacob marched past the flinching man to the commander's chair at the head of the table. He punched the built-in comm button. "Man-at-arms, please come to the briefing room. And bring your sidearm."

The computer routed the call to the appropriate personnel, and moments later, Petty Officer Green entered.

"Green, this man is a prisoner. Find a place to keep him. If he gives you any trouble, shoot him," Jacob said.

"Aye, aye, sir," Green said with a vicious smile. He grabbed DeShawn's arm and dragged him out of the briefing room.

Nadia frowned, seemingly not pleased with the reaction, but at the same time, what else was she to expect.

Once he was gone, Jacob turned to Nadia. His anger subsided when the despicable piece of trash was gone.

"Why didn't you tell me you were coming with us?" he asked.

She slipped into the chair closest to him, running one finger over the painting of the shark on the table. "We didn't one hundred percent have a plan when we approached you," she said.

He raised an eyebrow, a ghost of a smile on his face. For some reason, Jacob assumed ONI would have a plan for everything—including using an old destroyer to strike at the heart of their enemy.

"I have a plan," Jacob said.

Surprise flashed across her face. He enjoyed it. "Strategy and tactics are part of the job description," he added.

Jacob slid his NavPad forward between them. Lights flickered to life, projecting a hologram of the United Systems Alliance logo for a moment before morphing into a map of their space.

"Before the wormhole, the fastest way to Medial from here would be to go through the Corridor, skirt Consortium space, and enter Caliphate territory here—" Jacob highlighted a system marked with a glowing red aura.

"That's not exactly a plan," Nadia said. "Unless your plan is to get blown up."

"No, not today. Like I said, *if* we were going the traditional way, this would be it. However, we have an alternative." He hit another button, bringing up *Praetor,* the Consortium's end of the wormhole. "We use the wormhole to bypass the Corridor and then—"

"It won't work," Nadia said. She frowned, pulling out her own NavPad. "This is the latest intel from our sources in and around the Consortium. It's only seventeen days old instead of the more than two months it would have been before the wormhole. Our intel shows the Caliphate Navy massing near the border. They were careful to tell the Consortium ambassador about it, assuring him it is just a training exercise."

Jacob let out a short bark of laughter.

Nadia hit another button on her Pad, morphing the map into a spreadsheet showing the breakdown of the Caliphate fleet. "It's at least two-thirds of their entire navy, and it's five days from the wormhole."

The massive fleet on the virtual doorstep of the Alliance changed the nature of their mission. Jacob sat up straighter, his mind hyper-focusing on the problem. "This is actually good news," he said.

Nadia was taken aback. "A giant fleet between us and the target isn't good news," she said.

He waved his hand over his NavPad, activating the navigational function, showing a yellow line spreading out from Zuckabar through the wormhole, then toward Medial, bypassing the fleet.

Nadia shook her head. "That course doesn't exist—there are no starlanes on that route." Her breath caught sharply. "Where did you get this?" she whispered.

"When we took the Guild ship. I had Kim make a copy of the navigational database, just to see if they had any other hidden planets. With everything that has happened, I don't think NavCom has gotten around to exploring them. We'll have to verify each lane individually as we go, but it's a lot better route than through an unstoppable fleet."

Nadia gestured to the map. "For all you know, these lanes don't exist," she said.

A small pit formed in his stomach. "It's possible, but"—he held up his hand—"unlikely. The Guild ship we captured from Wonderland had this in their navigation system. I don't think it's fake, and it leads us exactly where we want to go and from a direction no one will suspect. From the notes on the charts, it also appears to be mostly unknown to the Caliphate Navy." Jacob deactivated the NavPad. "Sneaking to Medial will be the easy part. *Interceptor* is built for speed and stealth. As soon as they see us, though, we'll be outgunned—unless the admiral thought I would nuke their planet. Which I won't."

"No, he wouldn't think you would. Nor would he want you to. I'm glad you figured out a route, because I have the way in." The image on her NavPad shifted to show a bulk freighter.

Recognition hit him. "This is the freighter that ran from us in Zuckabar... *Komodo*, I think?" he asked.

"Yes, it is. The naval commander of Kremlin Station impounded her. But between your discovery of Wonderland and the attack on Alexandria, they've been occupied with other things. She's still parked in orbit above Zuck. We can take her and tuck *Interceptor* inside her shadow—"

"A Trojan horse," he said. Jacob's skin practically buzzed as he slapped the table. Between the deviousness of the beautiful woman across from him and his good old-fashioned navy know-how, they were going to get this done. "We've got a plan, then—"

Nadia interrupted him. "Let's execute it."

———

Time counted down on *Interceptor*'s main viewer. A clock on Jacob's MFD attached to his squeaky command chair mirrored it. Commander Dagher and Lieutenant Yuki flanked his command chair for the impending departure.

"Ensign Owusu, time to exit system?" Jacob asked.

"From departure, eight-point-six hours, sir," Owusu replied.

Hellcat bridges weren't large to begin with, and in order for him to see every station, it required a bit of leaning. Nadia could literally reach out and touch Lieutenant West's shoulder with one hand while holding onto the grab bar above her head with the other.

"That's going to cut it close, Skipper," Lieutenant Yuki said. "If fleet suspects something wrong, they may try to override the computer before we can exit but after the passkey has expired."

He knew the risks. Fleet procedure would authenticate the ship on departure, and not again after leaving the relative orbit of Alexandria, but a lot had changed since the attack. A jumpy tech might decide the *Interceptor* needed to check in before departing the system, and that could wreck their whole day.

"Is the Corsair still aboard *Crane-Shark*?" he asked Spacer Gouger.

"Aye, sir. Chief Boudreaux signaled five minutes ago that they were loading the last Raptor."

Nadia let out a whistle. "I would love to know how a sergeant managed to requisition four Raptor suits with no authorization."

"You know marines," Yuki said. "Improvise, overcome, adapt."

"Felix, would you please remind the chief we're on a tight schedule?" Jacob asked his comm tech.

"Aye, aye, sir," Gouger replied. "Charlie-One-One, this is Indigo-One-Zero. The skipper would like to remind you of the time."

Jacob didn't need to hear Chief Boudreaux's scathing reply —he read it in on Felix's face. As the comms person on duty when the captain had the center seat, he spoke with a certain amount of authority. At the same time, the poor kid had just turned twenty-one. He still had to face speaking to people of considerably higher rank than himself.

"Sir," he said, gulping. "Uh... the chief said she'll be back ASAP."

Jacob nodded at the young man. "Thank you, Felix. Though I'm fairly sure those were not the words she used."

Felix turned bright red, shaking his head.

"Suggestions, Kim?" he asked.

Lieutenant Yuki unsealed her boots, circling behind him to lean over Astro's console. As the XO, she was a little bit of everything, from pilot to engineer. It was her responsibility to learn all the jobs so she would know what she could ask of her people when she took command.

While Yuki consulted with Ensign Owusu, Jacob pulled up the status of the departments. Everyone aboard had busted their butts, from the lowest spacer to his senior staff, to get the ship ready.

The officers had been surprised when not a single spacer or noncom asked to stay behind. Chief Redfern had correctly predicted their loyalty and took great delight in reminding them of the esprit de corps the enlisted felt. Their captain moved heaven and earth for them; they would do the same for him.

It was the highest compliment his crew could give him. He would do no less than his very best for them. Speaking of which, he pressed the comm button on his chair. "Mess, Captain," he said.

"Spacer—uh, PO Third Class Mendez, sir. Go ahead," the newly promoted young man said.

Jacob wanted to promote everyone on board. God knew they all deserved it. However, NavPer, in their infinite wisdom, wasn't approving promotions or transfers. He'd received a handful of spacer's apprentices when they returned to Alexandria for repairs, but no crew were transferred away.

As the captain of a warship, though, he had a few strings he could pull, and he'd promoted the truly outstanding spacers up a rank. Mendez met the requirement and then some. During their last tour, the spacer's resourcefulness with his cooking skills had literally saved the lives of everyone aboard.

"Josh, listen. I want to start with your outstanding stew this time. No rationing, but I want us to keep an eye on the stores," Jacob said.

"Aye, aye, sir. I won't let you down," PO Mendez replied.

"Good man." Jacob eyed the clock, worry clawing at him. As the skipper, he kept it cool, portraying the collected captain to a tee. It would all be for naught, though, if they weren't on their way to Zuckabar when the clock hit zero.

"Got it, Skip," Yuki said. "If we keep our acceleration down, we can get underway and swing closer to *Crane-Shark* without raising any suspicion. It will shave fifteen..." Owusu tapped her sleeve, pointing at his latest calculations. "Sorry, twenty-three point seven minutes."

Jacob admired Yuki's cleverness, and her solution filled him with pride. Sitting a little taller in his chair, he gestured at the helm. "XO, take us out."

Kim nodded. "Chief, course one-three-zero mark zero-one-five at one-zero gravities for three-zero minutes," she said.

"Aye, aye, XO. Setting one-three-zero mark zero-one-five at one-zero gravities for three-zero minutes," Suresh replied expertly.

Yuki pressed the "all hands" button above her station. "Now hear this, set condition Yankee, prepare for underway. I say again, set condition Yankee." Her voice cut through the ship like a knife. Crew, from deck six to right outside the bridge, stopped what they were doing and rushed with deliberate precision to their departure stations. Airtight hatches were dogged, seals double-checked, and umbilicals severed.

Less than thirty seconds later Gouger signaled *ship secure for departure.*

"Coxswain," Kim said, heedful of the weight of what she was about to say, "execute."

Chief Suresh's fingers danced along the controls. The engines hummed to life as the gravcoil along the keel of the ship pulled power from the fusion reactor at its core.

Jacob could never figure out if it was by design or a by-product of the way ships maintained gravity, but as they accelerated, he felt the undeniable pull "behind them," forcing the crew to lean back as if they were climbing up a hill. The variance in gravity when maneuvering created the need for near-constant restraint, from the most common—magnetic boots and grab bars—to the five-point harnesses that held them in their chairs.

The exception being the Pit. In addition to the harness, its sunken controls had the pilot cradled like a glove as a second line of defense against sudden gravity fluctuations. Plus it allowed the ship's commander to see their course at a glance.

"We're underway, Skipper," Yuki reported.

"Good job, Lieutenant. Once we've recovered the Corsair, please execute our course with all haste," he said. "In the meantime, you have the con. I'll be walking the ship."

Jacob found his feet, heading for the hatch to follow his tradition. He couldn't let a little thing like piracy end his practice.

CHAPTER THIRTEEN

Fleet Admiral Noelle Villanueva pushed back from her desk for the first time in hours. She rubbed her hands together, blowing some heat back into them. The constant balancing inside a ship for heat versus cold nearly always left her cabin five degrees too cold or too hot, depending on the day. Today it was too cold.

She pulled on her uniform gloves with the fur interior, flexing her fingers. She yawned, far more from her near-constant state of worry than from physical exhaustion. "Switch to audio," she told her NavPad.

A pleasant baritone sprang to life in her ear, continuing where she left off on the report.

They were spread too thin, with too many avenues needing defense. With the Caliphate fleet massing near the Consortium side of the wormhole, the logical move would be to defend Zuckabar... but what if they were feinting?

She couldn't help but second-guess herself. Not even Wit had seen the destruction of Anchorage Bay coming. Every planet or base she left unguarded could be destroyed.

The Guild swore they only had the one prototype stealth ship, but it wasn't like she could verify—or believe them. Not after discovering their fingers in almost every computer in the Alliance. That alone had taken billions of dollars to undo.

In her heart, she knew Wit DeBeck was right about their response. One swift, decisive strike would set the Caliphate back on their haunches and delay—if not outright stop—a war. Congress' refusal to do just that was emboldening the Caliphate even more. Despite thousands of years of civilization, bullies were still bullies, and tribes were still tribes. At its core, the Caliphate was tribal.

If they could just—

"Incoming priority message from Lieutenant Commander Grimm. Shall I play it?" the virtual assistant in her NavPad asked.

Grimm? "Play it," she whispered. "Secure mode," she added in a hurry.

Each word from the young man was a punch to her gut. He had carefully constructed his letter to make sure all the blame fell on him.

Her stomach tilted. She dropped her head into her hands, overcome with a sudden revulsion at her own behavior. She'd sent good men and women to die before, but this was different. She knew how hard he had worked to recover his mother's reputation after Pascal. How much his crew had overcome.

Now she hadn't just killed him, she had ruined him. If there was one person in the entire navy whom they needed more than ever, it was an officer like Grimm. If only there was some way to remove some of the obstacles he might face in Medial?

She turned to her tactics board, where all her fleet data shined like little jewels against the night sky of their region of the galaxy.

For the moment, though, all she could do was wish him Godspeed.

Elsa huddled in the corner of her small room. Her mornings consisted of a meager meal for which they left her alone, followed by language instruction. Abla forced her to learn the tongue of the Caliphate by using the collar. After language, they made her do stretches and calisthenics. Apparently, the Caliphate liked his foreign wives tall, thin, and blonde.

Bad news for Elsa, who had hair like her mother's, as pale as straw in the summer. Since her father required his children to serve the state in both the military and government services, she kept herself in shape and weighed seventy kilos. Which at one-point-eight meters made her normal by any standard.

She took a deep breath and threw herself at the wall, scrabbling up until her fingertips met the lip of the window. Grunting and panting, she pulled herself up the rest of the way, her arms quivering from the strain. It was getting noticeably harder—which meant the food they gave her wasn't nutritious enough; the weight she lost came from her muscles. As a citizen of the Iron Empire, weakness didn't sit well with her.

Through the small window, she could just make out the bright sun as it rose over the horizon. It took up a massive amount of sky. The planet had to be on the very inside edge of the habitable zone for the sun to appear so large.

To protect the indoors from the too bright sun, the windows were like tunnels, a meter long, giving her a very narrow view of the outside.

The city looked like it stepped out of the past. Sandstone structures, open markets, and the giant arena. Nothing appeared different from any other day she looked.

Ships took off daily from the spaceport in the city. She heard the rumble of plasma engines every hour. However, the main source of noise and activity in the city was the arena.

A roar of applause rose from the coliseum like thunder. Even from a kilometer away, she could hear the chanting. She didn't know if all the slaves were there, or just the ones they couldn't sell.

Intellectually, she always understood that the Caliphate enslaved people. Looking on from the Empire, though, it was a very distant idea, not an immediate concern. Now, faced with the brutal reality, she wanted to kill everyone on the planet who wasn't wearing a collar.

Footsteps alerted her to an approaching servant. She pushed off the wall, dropping to the bed with a grunt but managing to scramble to a seated position before the door opened.

Zahra entered with a carafe of water and a plate with bread and the usual mealy soup. Elsa's stomach rumbled with thoughts of a juicy, rare steak. The young girl placed the tray on the small stand, then refilled the clay cup of water and turned to leave.

"Don't go, Zahra. Can you stay and talk?" Elsa asked in perfect Caliph.

"You... you speak my language? I thought they were still teaching you?"

Elsa smiled as she reached out and took the bland soup bowl and sniffed it tentatively.

"I know many," Elsa said.

Zahra wavered—as if she wanted to stay but couldn't decide. Elsa offered her the food, and that did it. The girl placed the carafe carefully on the uneven floor and sat next to Elsa on the bed.

Elsa gave the bowl to her and then tore off half of the rough, bread-like biscuit and offered it to the girl.

"Do they not feed you much?" Elsa asked.

Zahra shook her head. "I'm to be sold soon, and they expect me to... be fit."

"Sold? Aren't you already..." Elsa didn't want to say "slave," so she pointed at the collar.

Zahra nodded. "Since I was twelve. I have worked as a servant in the mistress' house for that time. However, I've... matured... and she can sell me for a small fortune to one of the —" Zahra closed her mouth, looking down.

"I'm sorry," Elsa said.

Zahra nodded. "I've had a long time to come to terms with my fate. I guess, in a way, I'm lucky. I still have my mind."

Elsa took a small bite, trying to make the food last and trick her body into thinking she wasn't hungry.

"What do you mean?" she asked.

Zahra pointed at the collar. "It affects people differently. I've seen strong men go mad and kill themselves, women turn into mindless puppets. Some people retain their personalities and knowledge, but not most. The longer you wear it, the more you lose—until you are just a shell. The stronger your will, the more you keep, the more valuable you are to... buyers."

Elsa's eyes stung as she thought about home, her mother and father, her brothers, and how she would likely never see them again. Which was bad enough... but to lose herself, lose all the things that made her who she was? That wasn't acceptable. She couldn't... *wouldn't* kill herself, but she had to escape.

"Zahra, how many people on this planet wear these?" she asked.

"I don't know how many. Do you not know where we are?" Zahra asked back.

Elsa shook her head. She looked up at the window. "Somewhere in the Caliphate of Hamid, I suppose. But that's obvious."

Zahra smiled. Her full lips made crinkles on her face, and Elsa found it contagious.

"We are on Medial, the peripheral slave center for the Caliphate."

Medial. Elsa racked her brain, trying to remember where it was in relationship to... "Oh no," she muttered.

"What?" Zahra asked, concern evident on her face.

"It's just... I'm from the Iron Empire. My home is on New Berlin. I'm months away by the fastest ship possible, and I don't think my father even knows where I am," she said. Elsa felt it all weighing on her. She collapsed against the wall, wanting to cry but not wanting to give in.

Zahra leaned against her, patting her shoulder. "I wish I could tell you it would be okay. My brother said he would come for me. He promised. That was four years ago. Even if he showed up tomorrow, I'd never get off the planet."

That piqued Elsa's curiosity. She pushed the self-pity away and wiped her eyes with the back of her hand, focusing on what Zahra said.

"Why couldn't you get off the planet?" she asked.

Zahra fingered the collar again. "They control us individually, but there is also a central controller. With the press of a button, they can kill every slave."

Elsa put a hand to her mouth in horror. What had gone so horribly wrong with these people? "Zahra?" she asked. "Do you know where this controller is?"

Zahra shook her head. "I am rarely allowed outside the compound. Why?"

Elsa took the girl's hands in hers. "Because I refuse to be some broodmare to a pig of a man who plans to overthrow my own father. I'm getting out of here, and I want to take you with me."

Zahra shook her head, but Elsa saw something more in her eyes. Something that was in short supply with the collars on their necks. She saw *hope*.

"You can't escape," Zahra whispered. "No one ever has."

"*Kippen* is my people's word for *can't*. There is no kippen, Zahra. We can. We will." She touched her collar. "But first, I need to know more about how these things work."

CHAPTER FOURTEEN

Interceptor burst to life in a brilliant shower of rainbow light as she decelerated from multiples of light speed to a near standstill. On the bridge, Jacob blinked several times, bringing himself back to full awareness. He removed his helmet, sucking in a deep breath from the ship's canned air. The small amount of tension he always felt when entering and exiting a starlane faded away as life returned to the bridge.

His crew followed, cracking open their suits in a chorus of depressurizing air. Within seconds, the vague, unsettled feeling of falling *up* vanished.

"Status?" he asked.

"Successful transition, Skipper. All systems are responding, and no casualties reported," Yuki answered.

"Thank you, Kim," he replied. Her efficient handling of the ship and crew freed him to focus on the big picture while she took care of the details. "Comms, confirm *Komodo*'s location? Helm, give us two-five gs to clear the lane," Jacob said.

As the ship pulled away from its exit location, Jacob took a moment to check their inventory one more time. The eight-day trip from Alexandria to Zuckabar had progressed as smoothly as he could have possibly hoped. Even the stop at Fort Kirk for munitions had gone off without a hitch.

"Uh, sir, I think I've confirmed *Komodo*'s location," Ensign Hössbacher said.

Jacob frowned at the communication's officer's tone. "Is it in orbit?"

Hössbacher turned and motioned for Lieutenant West. Comms, like 70% of the ship's company, fell under operations. If officers had trouble, they went to their immediate department head first. On the bridge, that was Mark West.

West unbuckled and moved to stand behind the ensign. At the moment, *Interceptor*'s bridge housed nine crew in a space big enough for six. Mark had to hunch over the comm panel to verify what Hössbacher saw.

Jacob glanced at his XO's face displayed on the MFD. She shrugged. Something was clearly amiss, and Roy Hössbacher wanted to verify it before bringing bad news to the captain. If it was good news, he would have been happy to report it.

Mark put his hand on Hössbacher's shoulder, and Jacob saw visible relief flow through him.

"Skipper, she is in orbit, but it looks like she's going to need some work to get her up and running."

Jacob frowned. An impounded ship would be under the purview of the military governor. He'd hoped to enter the system, pick up *Komodo*, and be through the wormhole without having to speak to anyone. If they had to do repairs, it would delay them—possibly dangerously so if word of their theft reached Zuckabar before they were able to exit the system.

"Damn," he muttered. "Kim, suggestions?" he asked his XO.

She glanced off-screen for a moment. "I don't see we have much of a choice, Skipper. We need a freighter, and she's the only one."

Boots clanked against the deck as Commander Dagher

entered the bridge. She came to stand next to Jacob in the XO's usual spot.

"Trouble?" she asked.

"Looks like *Komodo* may need some repairs," he informed her.

She gave him the little half-smile he found so adorable. "Nothing your crack engineering team can't fix, right?"

Her response brought a smile to his face. He loved how positive she was in the face of adversity. Then again, her career was safe. "I'm sure Lieutenant Gonzales will see it that way."

"Got it in one," she said, patting him on the shoulder. "Mind if I talk to you?" she asked with a nod toward the conference room. She didn't wait for him to respond, walking out past Sergeant Jennings.

"Astro, set a course for Kremlin. Mark, you have the con," Jacob said. He followed Nadia off the bridge.

"Aye, sir, I have the con," West confirmed.

In the briefing room, Nadia stared him down.

"What?" he asked. He suddenly felt like a cadet on review, and he didn't like it one bit.

"You're still thinking like a navy officer, Jacob. We can't afford to do things by *the book* out here. If you try to talk to the system's OIC, our mission is screwed," she said.

Jacob leaned into the passageway, motioning for Jennings to close the perpetually broken hatch.

"I appreciate what you're saying," he said once the hatch was closed, "but there is a limit to what I can do and protect the crew. If I go too far outside the bounds, FleetCom will never believe they were 'following orders.' They'll say they should have known I was up to something." He held up his hand to forestall her complaint. "Nothing is more important than my ship and my crew. I won't risk their future with shortcuts. If we can secure *Komodo* without endangering them, we will."

Nadia held up her hands in surrender. "Okay, I got it. Message received. However, how do you plan to explain your presence to Captain Oberstein when we arrive in orbit?" she asked.

Jacob frowned. The confidence he had felt the moment before evaporated like so much water in the desert. "I..." He was unable to think of an answer. "Suggestions?" he finally asked.

Nadia's devious grin lit up her face as she hopped off the table. "Nothing. Go radio silent. Don't even acknowledge his hails. What's he going to do? You can pretend your orders supersede his, with no real issue. It's rude not to call him, but not against the regs. While he's spinning his wheels, you can go to Kremlin and talk to your former engineer—who is now the commanding officer of the station. I'll take a crew over to *Komodo* and prep her for flight. You can ask Beckett to stall Oberstein. If he says no, then we just go faster."

Jacob admired her with open-mouthed awe. She had thought the whole situation through in a way he couldn't; move and countermove, but with people and assets instead of ships. Was that what being a spy was? Applying strategies and tactics to people?

"What?" she said after a moment. Her face heated from his unadulterated smile.

"I was just thinking how amazing you are. Too bad we can't officially be on the same ship."

She leaned down and placed a hand on his shoulder, then let it slowly trail down his chest. "It would be awful," she whispered. "We'd never leave your cabin."

Governor Rod Beckett stopped his long walk to lean against the outer bulkhead of the station. He could go to the zero-*g* gym, or the gardens to bask in the open and simulated space of the massive station. However, after forty years on ships, it all felt wrong. It wasn't uncommon for retired spacers to suffer some form of agoraphobia. He decided to deal with it by avoiding open spaces.

Instead, he donned his sweatsuit—a silly baby blue outfit his gorgeous new wife had bought him—and headed for the maintenance tubes, long tunnels that circled the station, stuffed between the inner-hull and the armored outer-hull. They allowed the crew access to virtually any part of the superstructure, while also providing kilometers of walking paths for a retired engineer.

He still couldn't believe he was married. During his time in the navy, he'd never stopped to have a serious girl, let alone a wife.

Now, the part of him from a small island on Weber was happy to be married. The other part of him, the confirmed bachelor who answered to no one but the navy, chafed at the added responsibility.

It was silly, and he knew it. Short of choosing engineering as a career, marrying her was the best decision he ever made. Anya made his life worth living. Getting his old butt out of bed at 0500 to do his mandatory physical therapy hardly seemed a steep price to pay.

"Governor Beckett?" His assistant's voice broke the silence.

Rod jumped at the interruption. His people knew his workout time was blocked out, and that they weren't supposed to contact him unless it was urgent.

"Yes?"

"Sorry to bother you sir, but we've just received a signal from USS *Interceptor*. She's approaching the station, and her captain has requested to meet you."

Surprise washed over him, mingled with confusion. They

normally notified him of when a new ship was coming, not to mention how unlikely it was for a ship to be assigned to the same system for a third tour.

"Who's commanding?" he asked.

"Lieutenant Commander Jacob T. Grimm, Governor."

Rod shook his head. If he were in charge of the navy, Jacob would be commanding a frigging battleship on the Caliphate border, not a rear echelon destroyer. Of course, if Jacob were out on the border, Kremlin Station and its inhabitants would be dead.

"Invite him to dinner with my compliments. Make sure *Interceptor* has a berth. I want her fueled and resupplied," Rod said.

His time on that little ship had changed his life. Not just losing his feet—though that had certainly contributed—but the young man showing up and succeeding against all odds had made an indelible impact on him and many others.

"We can, sir, but she has no accompanying orders to do so."

Rod dismissed the man's concerns. "I'm sure they will be along. Set up the berth; make sure they get whatever they need. For the time being, issue it on my authority."

"Yes, Governor."

His assistant killed the line, and Rod wondered why the man sounded so hesitant. Kremlin Station—*hell, everyone in the system*—owed their lives to *Interceptor*. Twice over.

However unusual, he was glad for the interruption; his feet ached. Limping, he found the nearest lift and headed back for his quarters.

―――

Governorship had its privileges, Jacob noted. The dining room consisted of a single long table with settings for eight. The main entrance was directly behind him. Across from him, behind Rod Beckett and his wife, was the entrance to the kitchen. On either side of the room, smaller doors led to and from the main complex. The first course, a savory potato-based soup, was placed in front of him in an intricately carved bowl.

"Thank you," Jacob said with a smile to the server. Her bright eyes reminded him of jewels. He noticed a shiny silver brooch with a gold star pinned to her lapel. "That's very pretty. Can you buy them here?" he asked, pointing at her brooch and thinking of a gift for a certain someone.

She smiled back, shaking her head. "No, sir." Her accent marked her as a local. "It was my mother's."

"Well, it's beautiful," Jacob said.

She blushed as she finished putting his food down, departing quickly once she was done.

Rod marveled at the ease with which Jacob made the people around him feel respected and appreciated. Never in his long time in service had he seen someone more naturally in command.

Jacob wore his dress uniform. Not the highest formal uniform known as mess dress, but the middle ground—a double-breasted jacket with brass buttons and a stiff collar, complete with formal medals on his left breast and his ship's shark logo on the right.

His two hosts were formally dressed as well. Rod wore a high-necked stiff-looking wool coat with an abundance of ribbons and buttons on it. Anya had her blonde hair in an elaborate braid that left her neck bare to expose a shiny pair of dangling silver earrings. Her pale green dress sparkled when the light hit it right. Jacob was more than a little surprised by the youth and beauty of Rod's wife. Not that he wasn't a good man and worthy of marriage, it just caught him by surprise how quickly the man had married after retiring from the navy.

Sergeant Jennings stood at parade rest behind him and by the hatch. He'd tried to convince Jennings to let him go alone, but she insisted on coming. At least he'd managed to get her to wear a formal uniform, even though he knew she hated it.

Rod's wife intrigued him. She was younger than the governor, but how much younger he couldn't say. With genetic treatments to reverse aging so widespread, it was nearly impossible to be sure of anyone's age. Jacob hid his examination of her behind a sip of mint tea. The two had entered holding hands and clearly had an affection for one another.

"Commander?" Anya Beckett asked suddenly. "What was my Rod like aboard ship? He talks little of his experience before Kremlin." Her accent sounded native to Kremlin, with the crisp clip of their Russian heritage.

Jacob chuckled. There were two kinds of ex-service people: those who talked about everything, and those who talked about nothing. Considering how Rod left the service, Jacob wasn't surprised at his tight-lipped ex-engineer.

"Rod Beckett is the finest engineer I've ever had the privilege of serving with, ma'am," Jacob said. "And a good friend."

Rod blushed, looking down at his food intently. Jacob felt a twinge of guilt at his declaration. It wasn't a lie, but he couldn't help but feel like he was buttering the man up for a favor.

Anya's smile spread from ear to ear. "Now, Commander—"

"Jacob, please," he told her.

Anya's eyes sparkled. "Fantastic," she said. "Please, tell me more?"

"I'm sure the captain would prefer to talk about something else," Rod interrupted.

"Captain?" Anya asked. "I thought he was a commander. Have I been using his wrong rank?" She shrank back in embarrassment, hand coming to her chest.

Rod chuckled.

"No, ma'am," Jacob said. "I'm a lieutenant commander by rank. In the Systems Alliance Navy, we shorten that to *commander*. However, when I'm 'in command' of a ship, I'm considered the captain of that specific vessel. It's confusing," he said with a smile. "Even for spacers."

She reached out and touched Rod's shoulder, relief on her face. "I was about to be cross with my husband. Thank you for clarifying," she said.

Jacob finished his soup, enjoying the pulpy, salty flavor. Once they were done, servers entered to remove the bowls and replace them with hot plates filled with sizzling steak.

"Rod, you shouldn't have..." he protested. The cost of fresh meat on a station had to be enormous.

"I would be strung up by the locals if I didn't give you the full treatment. Everyone here knows what you did. What *Interceptor* has done," Rod replied. "The navy's treatment of you is down right demoralizing. If it were up to me—"

Jacob raised his hand, warding off the rest of the sentence. "I made my peace with it some time ago," he said.

Anya had an inquisitive expression on her face. "Treatment?" she asked.

"It's nothing," Jacob said with a dismissive wave of his hand.

"Nothing," Rod muttered. "Anya, my dear, you are looking at one of the finest officers ever to wear the uniform. Not to mention one of only four serving with the Navy Cross." Rod pointed at the golden star-shaped badge on Jacob's chest.

It was his turn to blush. From both embarrassment and shame. It wasn't his cross. It had been earned by the men and women who'd died on *Interceptor* during the first Zuckabar action. Jacob tried to hide his feelings, but he wore them on his sleeve, not the best trait for a navy captain.

"Well, regardless," he said, "it is what it is. Besides"—he sipped his tea—"I love the *Interceptor*. I wouldn't trade her for any ship in the fleet. Though, I wouldn't mind six months for a full-on refit."

After they finished the main course, the servants returned with after-dinner cocktails. Jacob raised his hand to ward off the alcoholic drink.

"One of the advantages of retirement—I can drink whenever I want," Rod said with a smile.

Anya reached over and held her hand over the whiskey glass to stop the servers from filling it.

"Light drinking only," she said with a glare.

"Whenever you want?" Jacob said with a raised eyebrow. He was glad he'd never picked up that particular habit in the service, though he'd met more than one person who said some variation of "never trust a man who doesn't drink." They just had to get over that with him.

Rod waited for his wife to remove her hand before picking up the glass and knocking it back in one swallow.

"Well, whenever it's good for me," he said. "Tell me, how is the old girl?" There was sadness in his voice and a bit of longing.

Jacob was unable to hide the pride he felt in his ship. "Lean and hungry," he said. "We did most of the repairs ourselves, without the yard. A great deal of care went into making sure the systems were functional on the rebuilt aft portion." Jacob spent a few minutes relaying the mundane details of his ship—which he knew Rod would enjoy.

"I miss it, you know, sometimes. When my feet don't hurt," Rod said.

"I know the feeling. Two years assigned to port duty had me going batty. If the *Interceptor* hadn't come along, I was ready to ship out on the first freighter that would hire me."

Another server entered, making the rounds, refilling their water.

"I'm assuming," Rod said, "that whatever you're here for, it has to do with the impending war?"

Jacob failed to hide his grimace. Much of what he needed to do would be completely unnecessary if Congress had declared war. Which was needed, even though it would have meant the end of his service. But they hadn't, and they weren't going to. When *Interceptor* had exited Alexandria, the news wasn't public. It would still be another day before the current affairs reached Zuckabar.

He shook his head. "No, I wish it were, but it isn't. Unfortunately—"

A female server entered, awkwardly carrying an empty tray with both hands. His eyes went to the gold star pin on her lapel. It was the same pin, but not the same person. Confusion froze him for a precious moment. Time slowed down as he ran through the possibilities until only one remained.

"Jennings!" Jacob yelled as he shoved himself backward from the table.

The server tossed the tray aside, revealing a wicked-looking black energy pistol.

Jennings' strong hand jerked him back. The pistol whined, spitting out a superheated beam of microwave radiation, and the table exploded, sending deadly shards in all directions.

Jacob hit the carpeted floor with a whoosh of expelled breath. Jennings knelt over him, firing her MP-17 with one hand, grabbing his lapel with the other. She dragged him toward the door while Jacob kicked with his feet, trying to help.

Someone screamed. More attackers entered, shooting heaters. Two servants burst into flames, flailing as they beat at their bodies and wailed until their lungs gave out.

Jacob rolled away from Jennings. Kicking off with his feet,

he crashed through the door. The marine used the door jamb for cover as best she could. She hit the button on her pistol that converted it to SMG, the barrel growing longer and a shoulder stock emerging as the nanites reconfigured the weapon.

Jacob peeked into the dining room. One of the real servers was pulling Rod through the kitchen door. To Jacob's horror, though, Anya huddled behind her chair, screaming as superheated beams burned through the air above her.

"Cover me," he yelled, charging by Jennings.

"Dammit, sir," she growled. Her rapid fire filled the air, and assailants screamed as the deadly flechettes found their targets.

Jacob charged into the room, one arm over his head in a vain effort to shield himself from fire. He hit the remains of the table and slid over the surface, scattering dishes and drinks until he fell off the other side to land in a heap next to Anya.

A beam of energy whizzed behind him, striking the remaining section of the table with an explosive reaction. He flung himself over Anya, shielding her from the blast. Shards stabbed into his back, and he grimaced as they sliced through his uniform, dotting his dress whites with red blemishes as he bled.

A moment later, Jacob grabbed Anya by the shoulders and jerked her up, pushing her toward the exit and shielding her with his body as he ran behind her.

A man appeared in front of them, a wicked knife in hand. Jacob lunged forward, tackling him into the wall. The knife swung his way, and he flailed out, hitting the hand and knocking the blade loose.

The man recovered and came at him. Jennings' lessons in close combat came to mind; Jacob feinted to the left, and when the assassin bought it, he charged hard—straight to the exit, pushing Anya through the door and into the arms of her security team.

Pain hit him like a hammer, and he screamed as he fell, his entire back on fire. Writhing in agony, he struggled to get to his feet. More pain struck his side, sending him spinning into the wall. He looked down to see a blade sticking out of his ribs.

As he slid down the wall, the room faded from view. The last thing he saw was Jennings shooting the knife-wielding man in the face.

Vivienne Boudreaux fought back a sense of déjà vu as she eyeballed the approach to *Komodo*. While the captain went aboard Kremlin to sweet-talk the station commander into letting them leave with the freighter, Commander Dagher led a boarding party to repair the ship and command it once they were going.

At no point did Commander Dagher act like the skipper wouldn't be able to secure the ship, which meant she was okay in Viv's book.

"Two hundred meters," PO Collins said from the second seat behind and above her.

Every approach was hazardous. Two ships moving toward another generated enormous force, capable of destroying the smaller of the two vessels—in this case, her Corsair. For that reason, and a host of others, the navy loved redundancy. Viv had her eyeballs, the instruments, and PO Collins riding herd, letting her know exactly how close they were.

At one hundred meters, she killed main thrust and used only the maneuvering jets to close the distance. It took longer, but with herself, two crew for the Corsair, and twenty members of the boarding party, she wanted to be extra careful.

Her thumb deftly adjusted the hat switch, moving the ship at a steady half-*g* laterally. She cut acceleration, rolled the ship, then counted down in her mind. She could see the approaching ship through the flooring at her feet. Holographic details lit up her HUD, giving her a frame of reference for the ship's distance.

"Twenty-meters... fifteen... we're closing fast," Collins said.

"Steady," Viv muttered. At five meters, she reversed thrust, two gs slammed down on the ship, and a cacophony of groans echoed up from the passenger section. A second later, she let up, and the ship touched the freighter with a reverberating thump she felt in her pants.

"Contact," she yelled.

"Checking the atmo," Owens said. A moment later, he signaled all clear.

Viv's job was done. She took her hands off the controls and leaned back. She loved flying, and these moments in between gave her time to reflect on what she had done right and wrong.

"Charlie-One-One, this is *Interceptor*. RTB ASAP," Lieutenant Yuki said. "I say again, return to base."

Viv jerked forward, hands flying through the prelaunch as fast as she could make them before she even responded. "*Interceptor*, Charlie-One-One copies," she said. She keyed the comms. "Commander Dagher, I have an RTB for *Interceptor*. I need your people off right now," she said.

"Roger that, Chief. We're moving," Dagher replied.

The moment the commander signaled they were clear, Viv blew the release, rotated the ship and punched the throttle.

CHAPTER FIFTEEN

As the Corsair vanished into the black, Nadia frowned through the visor of her helmet. She'd planned on having the ship available to make ferry runs to the station if they needed any equipment.

"Ma'am," Chief Redfern said from the hatchway leading to the bridge, "the bridge is that way. I'll take my crew to engineering and get the engines ready," he said.

"By all means, Chief, get it done," she replied. It was useful having people with her who had been on the ship before.

Nadia watched him go, admiring the discipline and dedication of Jacob's crew. He'd done a great job, forging them into what she considered the best crew in the fleet. One willing to risk their careers, even their lives, because they trusted their captain.

Nadia knew the true reason Jacob hadn't been promoted. It had nothing to do with Pascal—though that was the beginning. Jacob was too valuable an asset. Admiral DeBeck needed an asset with nothing to lose, and when he couldn't find one, he made one.

Interceptor's crew—at least the noncoms—had to suspect something was afoot. No one stayed a destroyer skipper forever.

She shook her head in amazement that he could inspire that kind of loyalty and at the same time be the kind of down-to-earth man that he was.

Following the chief's instructions, she started up the narrow staircase. Freighters weren't known for their wide-open spaces or large cabins, and this one was no exception. Her shoulders brushed the metal walls as she climbed the decks to the bridge. Nadia wrinkled her nose; burnt ceramic and melted plastic assaulted her senses.

"Geez. What happened here?" she muttered. A black spot on the deck marked where a maser had fired continuously at something or someone. Warped deck plating stuck out an angle that would make an engineer cry.

Nadia went about the long process of bringing her up to working status. There were a hundred things to check and very little time to check them all.

Muffled sounds reached Jacob's ears as he gently floated from sleep to a dim awareness of his surroundings. The memories of the attack flooded back, and he snapped awake, trying to jerk upright, only to find he couldn't move. His heart raced a million miles an hour in response to the flood of images.

"Skipper, it's okay," PO Desper said. Her distorted voice reached his ears through a liquid medium. He was under water... no, he was *in* water. Completely immersed. If it weren't for the paralysis affecting his limbs, he'd be splashing for the surface. After a moment, though, the panic of submersion passed, and he realized he could breathe. As his mind cleared from the painkillers and the shock he realized he was in sickbay.

"It's okay, sir. You were burned pretty badly. Immersing you in a perfluorocarbon-nanite solution was the only way to repair your skin fast enough to save the tissue underneath. I'll go get the doc," she said.

A moment later, she returned with Dr. Krisper in tow. He had his MedPad out, reviewing the situation. Krisper glanced up and smiled at the captain. "Skipper, I know the first thing you will want to know is that Mrs. Beckett is fine. You got her behind the door before the maser hit you."

They knew him well.

"One sec, sir," Desper said. She manipulated controls on the side of the tank, and a moment later Jacob's limbs jerked awake.

He gave them a weak thumbs-up.

"The good news, sir, is that we staved off any nerve damage or permanent scarring by getting to you so fast. We can thank Chief Boudreaux for her, uh, *efficient* flying," Krisper said with a smile.

Jacob could only imagine. As he continued to wake up and his mind cleared, an intense itching that quickly turned to pain bloomed along his back.

He tried to speak, but with the liquid in his lungs, all he could do was open and close his mouth wordlessly.

Desper was ready, though. "Don't try to talk, sir. Just breathe normally."

He showed her a weak smile and another thumbs-up.

"Now for the bad news, sir... we're going to have to keep you here and in a coma for a week," Krisper said.

Jacob jerked alert. A week? He couldn't be out of commission for a week on the most important mission—the final mission—of his career!

"Lieutenant Yuki is in command, sir, and she concurs. She said she'll come down and see you as soon as the *Komodo* is up and running. In the meantime..." Krisper held up his MedPad and started a video of Rod Beckett.

"Jacob, I can't thank you enough for what you've done. Anya is as grateful as I am. Listen, I wish I could do more, but the word just arrived from headquarters. Your ship is to be detained, and you arrested."

Jacob wanted to growl. It couldn't end like this, not after everything they had done. He missed what Rod said next and had to force himself to calm down so he could hear.

"Regardless of the consequences, I can only give you twenty-four hours. Then I have to inform Captain Oberstein. You saved our lives, Jacob. I can do no less. Good luck."

The transmission ended. Jacob blinked several times, trying to reconcile the whiplash of emotions. Could they make the twenty-four-hour deadline?

"I've already notified the XO and Commander Dagher. I need you to focus on healing," Krisper informed him. "I'm going to put you back in a coma. We'll see you when you're well, Skipper."

He couldn't afford to be out of commission for a few *hours,* let alone days. Jacob tried to wave Krisper off, but he lacked the strength to raise his arm. Then darkness took him, and he fell again into blissful unconsciousness.

Lieutenant (SG) Kimiko Yuki strode onto the bridge, her crisp uniform snapping as she walked. The crew focused on their screens with unnatural calm, as if looking her way would confirm the captain's awful condition.

Kim stopped next to his chair, putting her hands on the back and swiveling it lightly. Her bone-dry mouth refused all attempts to speak. After a long moment, she was able to will it to work.

"As you know, the skipper is hurt... bad. Dr. Krisper is confident he will make a full recovery... but we're going to be without him for a bit." The tension in her chest eased somewhat as she looked at each station. "Meanwhile, we will continue the mission. We've come too far to quit. We still have a long way to go. Carry on."

Kim turned the chair, sitting down and swiveling to face front. There were a million things to do before they could leave the system, and they didn't have the time to do the majority of it. She tapped the command chair, unconsciously mimicking Jacob's nervous habit. Memories of the last time she commanded the ship haunted her.

"Spacer Gouger, make a note in the ship's log that I am assuming command until the captain is medically capable of continuing," she said.

Gouger turned to look at her. "Ma'am? In the *log*?"

Kim understood his hesitation. If he noted in the log that she had taken command, then she would burn right next to Jacob. There was no possible way she could convince the admiralty she wasn't in on it. It was more than just being in charge—she would have access to the same information Jacob had. She would know there were no official orders. However, if she didn't formally take command, it would cast the entire crew's knowledge about the piracy into question. If her skipper could throw himself on a grenade for the crew, so could she.

"Yes, Felix, in the log," she reassured him. Odds were, she wouldn't have made it out with her career intact anyway. If she had to go down, there was no finer reason than fighting for the homes of her ancestors.

"Aye, aye, ma'am. Note made," Gouger replied.

Rod Beckett had bought them time; Kim needed to capitalize on it.

"Mark," she said, turning to face Ops, "once our supplies from the station have arrived, I want us to break umbilical and head for *Komodo*. It will make things easier if we're right next to her."

"Aye, ma'am. I'll stay on top of it. As soon as the bosun tells me we're topped off, I'll let the COB know," Mark said.

"XO?" Lieutenant Fawkes called her from the weapons station. He took the three steps to the center seat and knelt down next to her chair, a courtesy she appreciated. The only person shorter than her on the whole of the ship was Sergeant Jennings, and that was only by a slim margin. The captain's height never presented a problem for her, but that was because she almost always stood in Carter's current position. Now, sitting in the center seat herself, if not for the uniform, she could be mistaken for a teenage girl

"Yes, Carter?" she asked.

He leaned in closer to keep their conversation private—a near impossibility on a ship as small as *Interceptor*.

"XO, I just talked to Commissar Pechenkin, the head of station security on Kremlin," he whispered. "He's falling all over himself trying to apologize for what happened. Mr. Beckett refused his resignation, so I'm guessing he trusts the man."

The attack on the skipper and Mr. Beckett's family had stunned them all. It wasn't clear whom the assailants were working for, or whom they were targeting, but regardless, her captain was floating in a tank of healing liquid in a medically induced coma to keep him from feeling the pain of the burns—something she understood well.

Fawkes continued, "He thinks they were local separatists, loyal to the previous regime. However, he's also found some evidence their funding was extra-solar."

Kim hated the heavy feeling falling on her shoulders. She shouldn't be shocked, but there it was. "Caliphate," she spat out.

"Aye, ma'am, that's his guess too. We knew they had a vested interest in the system before the wormhole. It has to be doubly important now."

It was a miracle no one had marched in and taken the damn thing from them yet. Galactic politics were above her pay grade, but she supposed no one wanted an all-out shooting war if they could avoid it. Since the Caliphate believed they could bomb Alexandria and get away with the crime by blaming the Guild, they probably felt like they could get away with anything.

"Good to know, Carter. Let's double security on the gangplank. Also"—she tapped his arm as he stood to follow her orders—"let Sergeant Jennings know. She might want to make her own changes to ship security."

"Aye, aye, ma'am. On it," he said.

Kim added separatists to her list of worries, causing her brow to furrow. She understood Zuckabar had a long, proud tradition of independence, but the last regime had *literally* sold people into slavery. How could they resent the people who put a stop to that?

She knew how. No one cared until it happened to them or their family. The vast majority of victims came from the Terran Republic, where massive overpopulation, poverty, and generally poor conditions meant there were plenty of people who wouldn't be missed.

She sat a little taller, a little straighter. She was part of the crew who put an end to the slave trade, and no matter what happened next, she would always be proud of that accomplishment.

CHAPTER SIXTEEN

In eight hundred years of space travel, there were two simple reasons no one had discovered a wormhole before: One, the anomaly emissions hid within the gravity noise of a binary star system. Two, the only other emissions presented by the wormholes were short bursts of intense gamma radiation—similar to what a black hole might produce.

Space explorers, and their computers, were understandably wary of approaching anything remotely connected to the idea of a black hole—which was why her every instinct told Kimiko Yuki to turn the ship around. Instead, she tugged at her ELS helmet, pulling it over her watch cap.

"All hands," she said as the ship-wide broadcast began, "helmets on, helmets on, helmets on." Yuki didn't care how safe the science people said it was to travel through the Bella Wormhole; she would do exactly as the captain would, and make sure the crew took every precaution.

She glanced over at Ops as he recorded every response coming in. After a moment, he shot her a thumbs-up. She wiggled in the unfamiliar command chair, regretting Commander Grimm's injury, knowing he would have loved to see what they were about to do. His loss was her gain, though, and she was going to take full advantage of it. Besides, it was his own fool fault for risking his neck, she thought with a smile.

To her surprise, some industrious employee of the station leaked video of the attack to the media, and they had played it twenty-four seven since. Seeing Jacob risk his life and take the heat blast in the back before being stabbed made him look every inch the hero she knew he was.

After that, it was easy for Governor Beckett to arrange handing over *Komodo* to them. No one questioned it. Or if they did, they kept it to themselves. The only caveat he gave them was to be out of the system in twenty-four hours. After that... he couldn't stop Captain Oberstein and his heavy cruiser from seizing *Interceptor*. Which they were about to avoid, with a little time to spare.

"Distance from *Komodo*?" she asked.

PO Tefiti checked his screen, tapped a button, then turned to her. "One-three-five-one klicks, directly to the stern, ma'am."

Wormhole command had warned them to keep at least one thousand klicks separation. Something about matter annihilation if two massive objects went into the wormhole at the same time. Which, in her mind, begged the question: what if something came through the other end?

Her MFD showed the departments' green readiness lights. *Condition Zulu: Action Stations* flashed in a yellow band at the bottom of every screen. Action stations wasn't exactly the right fit, but better safe than sorry.

Having never traveled through a wormhole before, she didn't know what to expect. A dotted line on her display showed the threshold to the maw of the anomaly. A countdown next to it gave her the time until entry. "Coxswain," she said as the ship approached the coast point, "thrust to zero."

"Thrust to zero. Aye, aye," Chief Suresh replied.

"Close the aperture," Kim ordered.

Suresh took her hands off the controls, placing one palm on the scanner and depressing the aperture control switch with the other. The ship shuddered as the metal hatch sealed off the bow portion of the gravcoil. "Aperture closed, aye," she replied.

They coasted along at a lazy crawl of twenty meters per second.

"Ops, drain the can."

Mark West punched the code into his console, and a half second later air hissed as it was pumped into pressurized canisters.

"Can drained, aye," West said.

Without atmo, her own breathing was all she heard.

Don't be nervous. Don't be nervous. Don't be nervous, she repeated as a mantra. A large flashing yellow alert notified her of the approaching Rubicon. "Full power to radiation shields," she said.

"Aye, aye, full power to radiation shields," Lieutenant Fawkes said.

"Gamma radiation spike detected," Ensign Owusu said.

Wormhole Command allowed daily traffic through the anomaly, but they were keeping it down to no more than one ship an hour, and only a few ships a day, while they made sure it was safe. They were making an exception for *Interceptor* and *Komodo*, though, allowing them to go through one after the other.

"Shield status?" she asked. She knew Carter would report anything unusual, and she didn't have to ask... other than to calm her nerves and reassure everyone else that things were perfectly normal.

"All readings nominal," he replied.

Kim tapped her fingers on the armrest, letting her nervous

energy out as the ship drew inexorably closer to the wormhole's maw.

"All hands, we're about to cross the threshold. Take a deep breath and let it out slowly. Focus on your stations and your duty. We got this. XO out."

Taking her own advice, she inhaled till her lungs felt like they would burst, then slowly let it out.

"Five seconds," Chief Suresh said.

Kim counted down in her mind. On the "one," she let out the rest of her air.

As they approached, space bent in front of them. The edges were thick like the bottom of a bottle, while the inside was as if a magnifying glass appeared in front of the ship, showing them stars no one from Zuckabar had ever seen. Around the bottle, a thicker, more condensed field of stars swirled counterclockwise relative to the stars within.

The "edges" shimmered. For a brief moment, all the light from every star on the other end of the wormhole warped in a kaleidoscope of color. "Bella" fit like no other name she could imagine. It truly was beautiful.

As they approached the center, the view shifted, and *galaxies* suddenly appeared. Stars no human had ever seen shone through the other end, a perfect sphere of light reflected from millions of parsecs away.

"Contact," Chief Suresh whispered. Tremors rumbled through the ship. Gravity shifted, pulling them in different directions.

"All hands, we're in the wormhole. Stay calm and report anything unusual," Kim said over the ship's general speaker.

Light flickered as they passed through the event horizon. Photons flashed and swirled around them as they shot forward.

Unlike the gravcoil-powered starlane, there was no feeling at all; one second, they were in normal space, then... hyperspace. Starlane travel showed nothing on the viewer but a point of light in front of the ship and blackness behind. This was wildly different.

"Good God, it's beautiful," PO Tefiti muttered.

Kim couldn't agree more. They were in a tunnel of condensed space; in the distance, a ring of orange light showed them Praetor. The tunnel "walls" were shifting waves of light and particles. The view outside the wormhole distorted space, but Kim thought she could make out the individual stars as they passed by.

"XO, how long until we're through?" Lieutenant West asked over their direct line.

"You had the same briefing I did, Mark. More than a minute, less than an hour," she replied. There were a lot of variables, and not enough solid information to give them a specific time. One of the reasons they were limiting ships was to experiment with different factors to see what impacted travel times. Despite what they had learned so far, there were still no exact predictions.

Kim decided she could watch the lights of the wormhole dance forever.

"Bridge, Engineering. Lieutenant Gonzales." The interruption pulled her gaze down to the MFD, where Gonzales' face appeared.

"Go for XO," she said.

"Ma'am, we're getting some really strange readings down here. I... is this real?" he asked.

"Welcome to the new world, Lieutenant," she said.

"Aye, ma'am. I feel like I'm going to have to go back to school. Gonzales out."

Kim looked up from her screen, marveling at the kaleidoscope of color before the ship. If it was going to take an hour to get through, she would enjoy every second of it.

Locked in her ELS suit, magnetically sealed to the hull, Jennings watched over her captain. Despite Dr. Krisper's vocal protest—and his assurance that Commander Grimm would be fine in a few days—Jennings refused to leave his side.

There would be a marine present everywhere the captain went. As far as Jennings was concerned, that marine would be her. She owed him. She should have been the one to charge across the fire and save Mrs. Beckett. But that damn fool of a man was determined to risk his own life instead of hers.

Should have been me. It was a bitter pill to swallow. As a marine, it was her job to risk her life, especially for her captain. It was his job to give the orders so that more lives weren't lost.

When he woke up (she refused to believe it was an *if*), they would have a conversation he wasn't going to like.

"All hands, we're in the wormhole. Stay calm and report anything unusual," the XO said. Two of her marines, Owens and Cole, were at their damage control stations. Lance Corporal Naki held the bridge watch.

Anything unusual? Jennings laughed. They were going through a wormhole, wasn't that unusual enough? The ship shuddered in multiple directions. She glanced at the med tube the captain floated in, making sure the nano-reinforced glass held. Theoretically, it was as strong as steel.

Theoretically.

Aboard ship, efficient use of space took priority in design. Sickbay consisted of four beds and an isolation room—which was where they also treated burn patients. In an emergency, they could expand into the guest quarters.

From where she stood, Jennings could just make out the main sickbay. However, with everyone locked into harness, there was no moving around. Something floated in her peripheral vision, and she snapped her head over to look, hand going to her sidearm.

For a moment, she thought a water pipe must have burst; what looked like a globe of water floated through the ship, light shimmering from within it.

"Hello," she muttered as it moved closer.

She was pretty sure this was defined as "unusual." As her own department head, she didn't have to report it to anyone. The globe floated toward her, reflecting her visage back.

In a moment of uncharacteristic curiosity, Jennings reached out. Her fingers brushed the globe, sending a jolt of electricity through her. Where she touched, the globe shimmered, deforming around her hand. She understood something monumental was happening. Something no other human had experienced.

As fast as it had appeared, it was gone, and she wondered if she had seen it at all?

On the *Komodo,* Nadia watched as *Interceptor* vanished into the globe of distorted space. One second the little destroyer orbited the entrance; then she moved faster and faster, like a Ferriseagle skimming the surface of the water before submerging. Except unlike the predators roaming the skies of Alexandria, *Interceptor* didn't emerge with her prey clamped in her beak.

Nadia stiffened in her chair, glancing over at PO Oliv and Collins. The two navy women sat side by side, one flying the giant freighter, the other manning the gravitic sensors.

"Status?" Nadia asked.

Unlike *Interceptor*, *Komodo* didn't have flight stick controls or a Pit; the bridge was laid out in parallel. The captain's chair sat on a pedestal against the stern bulkhead, and the stations were arranged in two rows up against the forward hull.

Collins' delicate fingers danced across the helm, slowing the ship to a crawl. "Thrust to zero. Velocity steady at two-zero meters per second."

"Six-zero seconds to point Rubicon," PO Oliv said in her accented voice.

"Roger that," Nadia replied. "Close the aperture."

"Aye, aye," Chief Redfern responded from his station in engineering.

The hull rumbled as the aperture ground closed over the front of the gravcoil. Gravity shifted as the secondary gravcoils took full control. "Aperture closed and sealed," Redfern reported.

"Okay," Nadia said, "it's out of our hands now."

Nadia shifted in the uncomfortable chair. Civilian freighters were a lot like military ships in that regard—no extra money spent on anything that wasn't absolutely necessary. The spartan nature of the ship reminded her of home. Not the planet she was born on—she'd only lived there until she was eight—but her adopted planet of Providence, where the people lived on as little as possible.

She shook her head, forcing those memories away. They led to a path she didn't want to go down. Making a fist with her flesh hand, she squeezed until it hurt.

"Ms. Dagher?" PO Oliv asked.

Nadia's head shot up. "Yes?"

"Rubicon," she informed her.

The large globe hovered in the viewer, growing larger and larger. She could make out other stars reflected in the center, but on the outer edge of the sphere... light swirled, counter-clockwise.

"My God," Oliv said. "It's beautiful."

When they were less than a klick away, it took up the whole screen. Entire galaxies reflected through it from the other side. An entire universe of cosmic glory condensed to a tiny celestial area.

Komodo shuddered, her angle shifting as the ship accelerated toward the anomaly. In Nadia's mind, she imagined the ship diving like a surface attack craft setting up to strafe targets.

Collins closed her eyes. There was literally nothing for her to do. The wormhole controlled everything now. Oliv's lips moved as she prayed.

Komodo heaved to one side as she struck the outer edge of the wormhole, her internal gravity fluctuating as new forces arrayed against her.

"Contact," Oliv said.

CHAPTER SEVENTEEN

Senator Talmage St. John leaned back in his chair in sheer amazement, his face frozen between a grin and a frown like some kind of bizarre Picasso. He fully expected the admiral standing in front of him to break into a smile and tell him this was some kind of elaborate prank. Talmage even glanced at the calendar, half expecting it to be April 1 on Earth.

"Are you serious?" Talmage asked.

"Yes," was the admiral's laconic response. "And you can't tell anyone," he added.

Talmage didn't know whether to thank the man or have him tried for treason. He stood, his muscles so full of energy he had to do something. "You gave one of the navy's ships an *illegal* secret mission, hung it all on the captain of said ship, and you don't want me to say anything? Why did you tell me in the first place?" he demanded, pounding one fist onto his prefab table.

"No, I did not 'give him a mission.' I suggested the target, and he decided to go after it. No orders, no missions, no formality. As far as the law is concerned, Lieutenant Commander

Grimm stole his ship and is heading for Medial of his own free will. Nothing more than an act of piracy."

Talmage pressed his temples, trying to stave off the coming headache. He might as well try to stop Alexandria in orbit.

"Admiral, you—" Then it dawned on him. "You're playing by their rules..."

DeBeck smirked at the senator. "My only rule is 'win,' Senator. You know that. There is no silver medal in this race. We either beat them, or they wipe us out, with every Alliance planet bathed in nuclear fire, and the survivors sold into slavery. When that is the cost of losing, then there is no price I'm not willing to pay to win."

Talmage believed the admiral. He'd seen firsthand what the Caliphate was capable of—atrocities so horrific most people wouldn't believe them, even with evidence. It was easier for the House to believe the utter destruction of the Alliance capital was due to a renegade faction than to accept that it was the deliberate act of a power-crazy empire.

He'd hoped the new politicians would galvanize and grow a spine, but it was a vain hope. Enough of the old way of thinking survived that they were paralyzed with fear, paralyzed long enough for Caliphate propaganda and their own pathetic concerns to override good sense and duty.

Shameful as it was, the lowly lieutenant commander had more sense of duty in his pinky finger than the entire House and Senate combined.

The admiral was right, of course. The Caliphate weren't playing a game. They believed, truly believed, they had a moral duty to cleanse the universe of infidels. Normally, their sort of tribal government would never have flourished to become a galactic power, but a cruel accident of fate had given them dozens of worlds with vast resources. The only thing stopping them from spreading like wild fire was their lack of manpower.

Their slave trade had always involved sex trafficking, but it didn't take long for them to expand into forced-labor camps. For generations, they had preyed upon the galaxy like a plague, stealing the one resource they couldn't manufacture fast enough: people.

Talmage had read a book or two, and he knew that empires built on slavery fell in revolution. The collars changed that, though. Suddenly, their camp laborers would literally work until they dropped. No rebellions, no deadbeats. Turn the collar on, and the higher functions of the brain were suppressed.

Alliance scientists had gotten their hands on a few and were trying to figure out a way to neutralize them, but the reports weren't hopeful. There was no way to inoculate the population against them.

"What now?" he asked DeBeck.

"We prepare a brief disavowing Lieutenant Commander Grimm's actions as those of a renegade captain. It should be easy—the government propaganda arm did it once before." DeBeck said.

Talmage winced. They had unfairly sold Grimm out for Pascal, and here they were doing it again. Once was bad enough. They owed that man an unpayable debt. To do it again felt wrong on so many levels.

"And he knows that even if he succeeds, he will spend the rest of his life in prison? He knows that, right?" Talmage asked as he sank back into his chair.

"He knows. If there's one thing Commander Jacob Grimm has in spades, it's his sense of duty. He's doing this because, like me, he knows it's the only way to stop a war we can't win."

Talmage nodded. He'd seen the naval estimates. In sheer tonnage, the Caliphate Navy could out-throw them three to one. If they weren't too clever for their own good, they would just bulldoze their fleet into Zuckabar and take it. Maybe they were worried about an all-out shooting war as well. Who knew?

He hated himself for agreeing with DeBeck. Hated himself for going along with it. But most of all, he hated the corrupt politicians who lacked the intestinal fortitude to resolve the situation once and for all.

"Okay, let's assume he succeeds—"

"Based on his past performance, that would be an excellent assumption," DeBeck said, with the first hint of a smile he'd shown since the meeting started.

"Right, okay then. He strikes at the heart of Medial and rescues a few people. What then? How do we spin that as a success comparable to the nuking of our capital? I don't see the comparison."

"You're not thinking like them. This strike—it was the most they *could* do. They consider it a devastating blow, made more so by our unwillingness to counterattack. They don't think we *can* counterattack. They believe that if we could, we would."

Talmage shook his head. "That makes no sense. People are pissed. Angry and afraid. We didn't declare war by the slimmest of margins. In six months, though, that could all change."

DeBeck waved his hand away. "That's how we see things, not them. They have a doctrine similar to all tribes throughout history. They hit us; if we do nothing, they hit us again. Simple as that. They are emboldened by our lack of action.

"Just like you, they believe we think like them. If the tables were turned and they could strike back, they would. They assume that we cannot. When Grimm assaults Medial, it will show them we can and will hit back. I don't think it will permanently stop them from hitting us again, but it will delay them. Isn't that what we need? Time?" he asked.

Talmage found himself agreeing with DeBeck's philosophy, if not his execution. "Couldn't you have sent your spies? Blow up something on the border world and loosely connect it to us?"

"If spies had detonated a nuke on Alexandria, then yes. However, they sent a warship. We *must* respond in kind," DeBeck stated definitively.

Talmage considered the man's words. It didn't really matter if he agreed or disagreed, though, it was done. *Interceptor* would be through the wormhole already, and nothing he did could change that. They were out of the Alliance's reach; the only thing he could do was pray. "I'll get to work on a statement. You'd better inform the president. He's going to want to know about the details."

Talmage inwardly cursed himself for a coward. If not for his unregenerable wound, he would still be in the marines, fighting this war. Instead, he sat at a desk, disavowing the very men and women he should be fighting shoulder to shoulder with.

Since the Great War had ended, relations between the Alliance and the Iron Empire were chilly, to say the least. With the Terran Republic acting as a buffer between them, there was no direct trade—nor conflict. Which was why, when Wit DeBeck received an official message from the ambassador of the IE, it intrigued him. It was too much of a coincidence for them to contact him after he launched a mission to Medial.

He sincerely hoped Commander Grimm and the *Interceptor* could pull off the raid, but he was no fool. As the saying went, putting all one's eggs in one basket was a quick way not to have any eggs. Regardless of how well *Interceptor* performed, as long as Nadia reached the surface, then the real mission had a chance.

His aircar landed on the roof of the Imperial Embassy. Due

to its location far to the south of Anchorage Bay, it was one of the few to survive the bombing. Even the Caliphate wasn't stupid enough to make enemies of their former ally.

The car touched down, green lights flashing around the pad, letting him know it was safe to exit the vehicle. At the roof entrance, two Kriegsmarines in flat-black power-armor snapped to attention.

"Herr Admiral, the ambassador is waiting for you downstairs, if you will follow me," one said.

Wit nodded. "Thank you, Leutnant," DeBeck said, imitating their inflection and making sure to pronounce the rank correctly.

DeBeck didn't recall ever having entered the embassy before. Most of the different governments would hold galas or dinners, but the Imperial Embassy was strictly behind closed doors.

Thankfully, the stairs were brief, leading to a small hall lined with paintings of the House of Faust going back six generations. There was something efficient about the way they passed power from parent to child. A series of weak rulers could leave such a power diminished. Faust, though, made sure their children were strong and ready to rule, putting the people of their empire before all other concerns.

There was no denying their achievements, of course. The powered armor of the two men flanking him was far more compact than anything either the Alliance or the Consortium could build. From the reports he received, he knew their ships were just as advanced.

"In here, Herr Admiral." The Kriegsmarine Leutnant opened a door and gestured him inside.

The door closed behind him. For a moment he couldn't see, and he wondered if he'd walked into some elaborate trap.

He almost laughed aloud at the idea. He was spending too

much time planning moves and countermoves against the Caliphate. If the Empire wanted to go to war, they would mass their fleet and hit like a hammer.

The lights flared to life, briefly blinding him.

"Sorry for the theatrics. One can never be too careful when dealing with the greatest spy the Alliance has ever produced," a man with a light Imperial accent said.

A young man, or at least someone who appeared young, sat behind a utilitarian desk empty except for a gray tablet resting under his fingers. Wit knew from intelligence reports that the tablet was the Empire's version of the Alliance OmniPad. However, what really interested Wit was the man.

"Theatricality is part of the life," Wit replied. Clearly, they were fishing for something. He was more than willing to wait and let them get to their point in their own time. After all, the crown prince of the Iron Empire wouldn't have visited the Alliance covertly without a very good reason.

"I take it you're not surprised to see me?" Heinrich Faust said. A bemused smile played on his face.

Wit let a trace of a smile grace his marble-like features. A lifetime of lying allowed him complete control of his expressed emotions.

"Surprised you're on Alexandria, Your Highness. Not surprised by who you are," he said in a moment of frankness. He could give a little.

"My father doesn't like his children's movements to be well known. The cost of having any of us taken would obviously be high," Heinrich said.

Wit filed away that piece of information. "I would expect no less, Your Highness. Please give my regards to your father. After all, it takes an artist to truly appreciate fine art," Wit said.

Heinrich smiled. "I'm going to like you. I can tell about people—it's a gift."

Wit hid his surprise at the revelation. "My thanks, Your Highness."

"Henry, please. We are both men of action—can we dispense with the formalities and subterfuge?"

"By all means," Wit said.

"Good. You have a destroyer captain who uncovered a human-trafficking ring. I would like to speak to him." Prince Henry wasn't asking.

Wit folded his hands in front of him, keeping his body language as neutral as possible. If they wanted to know more about the ring, then they had begun to suspect what really happened to their princess.

"I'm afraid he's not in-system." Did he have more intelligence on what was going on along the borders of the IE than Henry did?

Henry frowned. "I thought we agreed to dispense with the subterfuge? I know he is here. We have—"

Wit held up his hand to interrupt the prince. "Pardon, Your Highness. I'm sure you have solid intelligence."

"I do. I trust my agents implicitly, which is why I know you're lying."

"*If* his current whereabouts were part of an official mission, then you *would* know, and therefore would be right to suspect I was lying. I also would never dream of trying to deceive you." How much could he share? The two countries weren't enemies, but they certainly weren't allies. Then there were OpSec considerations. Even an innocent use of the information could lead to a disaster.

"Then he's not in-system?" Henry asked.

"No, I'm afraid not. Nor will he be back for some time."

Prince Henry leaned back. The first glimmer of his true emotion flashed on his face, and it wasn't pretty.

Wit debated his next move. He would leap at the chance to

bring the Empire in on the side of the Alliance, even if it burned all his bridges with the Terran Republic. Which it would. The two nations bumped up against each other and had such ideological differences as to be irreconcilable. If he had to choose one, though, it would be the Iron Empire and their massive fleet.

Silence stretched out between them as the two men fought a subtle battle of wits, trying to calculate moves and countermoves before speaking a single word.

Wit decided to roll the dice and hope for victory. "I will take the first step," he said. "Nothing I say can be *officially* verified by my government, understood?"

Prince Henry tapped a button on his Pad and turned it over. "I understand," he said. The look on his face told Wit he would be skeptical of any offer to help.

"Hypothetically speaking, if I were aware of a certain government's efforts to ramp up their purchase of human cargo —" At this, Henry's face turned to stone, further entrenching Wit's suspicion. "—From the Terran Republic and other nations to the *east* of my own, then what would you like to know?"

Henry growled, hands clenching into fists. The temperature in the room increased dramatically, but Wit stayed cool. Yes, he was completely at their mercy in the heart of their embassy—essentially imperial sovereign soil—but Wit DeBeck was no snot-nosed midship. He was a professional spy.

"Please, Your Highness, I would be blunter if I could, but while we're being honest, I would like to point out that the last time our two sovereigns came into contact, it resulted in a massive loss to my fleet."

"You attacked us," Henry said through clenched teeth.

"We allied against you, yes, but we didn't launch the war. Regardless, in the decades since the end of that war, the IE has all but closed their borders. Forgive me for not leaping to help with all the knowledge at my disposal... unless you're prepared to formally ask for such help?"

If the Empire were willing to request formal support, it would force the Caliphate to rethink whatever plans they might have.

"No," Henry said with a shake of his head. "Not yet."

"I understand. Then I've said all I really can—" Wit stood.

"Wait!" Henry said. The anguish in the young man's voice was genuine. There were plenty of agents who could mimic such emotions, but Wit didn't think Henry was one of them—or that he was simply acting now.

"Go on?" Wit asked.

"You don't make this easy," Henry said.

"What makes you think I want to?"

"My father would give a great deal to have a man like you as the head of our intelligence apparatus," Henry said. The ghost of a smile lit up his face from the darkness consuming it a moment before.

"Thank you for the compliment."

"A... citizen... of the Empire is missing. She was taken by pirates during a sting operation designed to capture them. The pirates got lucky, and now we are trying to find this citizen," Henry said.

Wit took a deep breath and let it out, returning to his seat. "Thank you for your honesty," he said, knowing the prince hadn't shared everything. "What would you like the Alliance to do?" He kept his expression as pleasant as if he were asking about the weather.

"I am not used to the uneven footing I find myself in," Henry said to himself as much as Wit. "I wanted to speak to Commander Grimm. To seek his insight on where we might find our missing citizen."

"Is that all you're interested in?" Wit asked.

"Yes," he said.

Wit made another note in his own mind about the nature of the royal family. Given time, he could foster a relationship with the prince. In a year, or maybe five, he could be the path to forming an alliance with the IE.

If only they had such time.

"Henry, I understand your concern. If one of our citizens were missing, I would like to think we would do everything in our power to bring them home safe." Wit toyed with the idea of stringing him along, trying to get more out of him. However, he knew whom they were looking for, and if it came out that he knew but had not helped—it would end in disaster. He wanted allies, not enemies.

"Your citizen was taken by the Caliphate Navy posing as pirates and operating out of Omega-Centauri Four—"

Henry's face turned into a mask of rage as he slammed his fist down on the table, and he stood abruptly.

"They're not there," Wit interrupted.

"What do you mean?"

"Your citizen isn't there," Wit repeated. "After their last op, the Caliphate Internal Security Bureau folded their FOB on Omega and fled to Medial." Wit stopped, letting the information set in, waiting for the prince to react.

"How do you know this?" Henry asked.

Wit wasn't prepared to go into full detail regarding his own intelligence services, but he needed the prince to believe him. Which meant he had only one card to play.

"Your Imperial Security Services are very good in matters of state security. My office's primary job is to gather intelligence that will assist us in defending our home. For the last twenty years, I've prepared for the war that's about to begin. Believe me when I tell you, I know your schedule better than you do," he said, finally revealing his true knowledge. "Just as I know it was your sister who was taken and not some random citizen." Wit's sudden revelation put truth to the lie of them dispensing with the subterfuge. He was playing a dangerous game, but he was almost certain they wouldn't kill him. He waited, letting his opponent work through his own solutions. Wit was never one to shy away from long silences—or the secrets they could reveal.

"While we're being frank, do you know what weapon the Caliphate suddenly possesses that allowed them to destroy a light cruiser with a single hit?" the prince said.

That was news to Wit. Not the weapon, but the loss of the ship. "I'm sorry about the ship. I didn't know. My condolences to your Empire and the crew."

"You mean that, don't you?" Henry asked.

"Of course. We're all spacers, regardless of uniform."

"Not everyone would share your viewpoint," Henry said thoughtfully.

"The weapon is likely one the Guild devised. It uses a ship's gravcoil to create a coherent beam of concentrated gravity, like a lance. A direct hit is capable of obliterating most ships."

"The Guild?" Henry spat out between clenched teeth. "I'll see they pay for that."

"We've seized all their assets here and anywhere else we've found them, and we tried to spread the word as best we could, but they have an infrastructure that no one knew existed. I envy your government's lack of involvement with them," Wit said.

Henry motioned for someone to come in. A servant entered with two cups of heady-smelling coffee, placing one in front of the admiral. He picked it up carefully, sniffing the aroma with approval before sipping. "That's magnificent," he muttered.

"Thank you. We are not isolationists. Just unwilling to easily trust foreigners. The Guild included."

"In this case, it paid off. I'll see that a dispatch is sent here with everything we can disclose about them and their bases," Wit said.

Henry's eyes glimmered with approval. "I was right. You are a good man."

"I wish that were so, Your Highness. But I am a spy, and good men make poor spies... and poor kings. As for your sister, Medial was her last confirmed location." Wit stood up, taking a long wistful sip of the excellent coffee.

"If you come across any more information..." Henry said.

"I'll gladly send you anything we have. I'm not authorized to make any kind of formal agreement, but perhaps your ambassador could speak to ours?" Wit hung the question out.

"I'll mention it, but, like you, this isn't my area."

The guard opened the door and gestured for Wit to follow. Wit decided to take one last chance. He held his hand out to the prince.

Henry glanced down at the offered hand. It was so much more than a perfunctory gesture. They shook, and Wit felt it was the beginning of something that would save the Alliance.

"I only pray we find her in time, Admiral. The Caliphate isn't known for their gentle treatment of women," Henry said.

Wit knew. Only too well.

Elsa ran in the heat, sweat pouring off her. She would have preferred not to run in the nude, but Abla's cruelty knew no bounds, and the collar forced her to obey, running for hours while alien carrion birds circled high above, not knowing the difference between Elsa and a soon-to-be-dead creature they could eat.

All Abla had to do was tell her to run at a certain pace, and she ran. The compound had its own private track, and only the other servants and Abla saw her shame.

The cruel woman relaxed in the shade while one of the naked male servants fed her something locally grown that looked like yellow grapes. A semi-concealed gate slid open, revealing a path to the city. A robed man with a sidearm entered and made his way to Abla.

Elsa did her best to watch what was happening out of the corner of her eyes. Her legs shook with each step, body quivering from both the exertion and the heat. The only refuge from the too-bright sun was a pair of goggles they gave her to keep her from going blind.

The newcomer leaned down to speak to Abla.

"You may stop," Abla said to Elsa.

Elsa collapsed onto the coarse sand surrounding the field. Nothing green grew under the brutal light, though some local plants hid under the sand, some kind of native cacti, ready to stab anyone foolish enough to go digging for water.

From the corner of her eye, she saw Zahra step forward, holding a carafe of water. Elsa shook her head, waving the girl off. It was important Abla didn't know of their friendship if they were both to escape. The man left with a bow, and Abla ordered Elsa to her next class.

Several hours of language therapy later, Elsa returned to her room to collapse in exhaustion. She had to escape soon or she wouldn't have the strength left to run, let alone fight. Zahra rushed in, closing the door behind her and sitting down on the bed.

"Elsa, we have to go. I can't wait any longer. They brought buyers in to... inspect me. The monthly auctions are in a few weeks. I can't be sold off as a piece of meat!" The poor girl shook, and it was all Elsa could do to lift herself up and hold her tight.

"Zahra, we don't know where the collar control station is. Or how to get off the planet when we do. I've barely completed my sketch of the compound. I can get us out of the building, but unless we can turn the collars off, we won't make it very far."

Zahra pushed away. "We can't stay. I'd rather die than be sold off… can't you do something?"

Elsa believed her sincerity, if not her will to see it through. They still had hope. The very thing that made Abla value them so highly was also what kept them going. Elsa wouldn't surrender, and she wouldn't let Zahra surrender either.

"Zahra, I can work out how to get us out, but you have to find where they control the collars from. Think. Is there a part of the house you've never seen? A door you're not allowed through?"

Elsa could see the girl working through her memories. Then her eyes lit up.

"There's only one room I've never entered. It's so obvious—why didn't I see this before?" Zahra said.

"And?" Elsa prompted.

"Abla's private quarters. They're off-limits to slaves other than the ones she brings for her own use."

That had to be it. A control freak like Abla wouldn't allow anyone else such access. No, she kept it in the room or on her person. *Which means,* Elsa thought with a wicked grin, *killing Abla and escaping are the same goal.*

Elsa had a problem, something to work through. Her mind played out a hundred different scenarios as she leaned back on the hard bed. Zahra departed quietly, leaving the princess to her machinations.

CHAPTER EIGHTEEN

Interceptor's bridge crew stared with held breath at the light codes blinking on the main viewer. Whether through fate or just dumb luck, they had transited almost on top of a Caliphate patrol. Three systems and nearly a week deep into Caliphate space, with the skipper still in sickbay, the last thing they needed was a fight.

"Status?" Kim asked in a voice barely louder than a whisper. She sat in the center seat, helmet racked next to her. She was frozen in the act of pulling off her ELS gloves.

"They are accelerating at two-five-zero gravities at a course of one-eight-zero away from us. I don't think they saw us, XO," PO Tefiti said.

Kim let out a breath of relief. Two Caliphate light cruisers had appeared out of nowhere, just at the edge of their sensor range. If it weren't for the fact that *Interceptor* was motionless in space with zero emissions, the mission would have ended before it began. Light cruisers would eat the destroyer for breakfast. No amount of luck could have saved them. Maybe if they caught one by surprise they could kill it, but two?

As they closed on their objective it was only going to worsen.

"Confirmed, they're moving away, ma'am," Tefiti said. "Gravwake weakening. If they saw us, I doubt they would be continuing."

Kim let out the breath she was holding. She watched their tags—Tango One and Two—fade out of range. While their gravwake would register for some time, after ten million klicks, the readings were less useful.

"Do you think they're on a set patrol pattern or passing through?" she asked the officers on the bridge.

"They look like they came from the Theodosia starlane and are heading for El-Alamein. The course is spot on a for a starlane transit. Either they're using it as a reference point, or they are passing through."

Kim leaned back, glancing from her MFD to the main viewer as a dozen tactics leaped into her mind. "If I were patrolling a system, I'd want it to look like I was on my way out. Keep monitoring the passive sensors, and we'll play hide-and-seek."

"Aye, ma'am," Tefiti said.

This was the tricky part. Kim pulled up the star charts. According to official maps, this system had three starlanes. However, the Guild's charts listed a fourth. She transmitted the coordinates to Ensign Owusu.

"Plot it, Ensign," she said.

"Aye, aye," he replied.

If the Guild's charts were wrong—or fake—then they were going to end up in the middle of nowhere with no way home. Logically, there was no reason for the Guild to carry fake charts, especially when they had a standing order to blow up their own ships rather than be captured. Then again, they shouldn't even have access to starlanes the rest of the galaxy knew nothing about.

"Coxswain," Owusu said, "come three-two-three mark one-one-five. Accelerate at two-five-zero gravities for two-two-three minutes."

"Aye, aye, Ensign," Chief Suresh replied, repeating the course back to verify. "Course laid in."

Kim leaned forward. "Execute." *Interceptor* surged forward as her gravcoil powered her through space. "Drop the towed array," she ordered.

A second later, they felt the thrum of the cable unspooling behind the ship for thirty seconds before it thumped to a stop. The long cable was lined with passive sensor pickups and expanded the ship's ability to detect electromagnetic emissions across a broad spectrum.

"Unspooled," Lieutenant West reported.

With three hours to turn over, then another three for deceleration, Kim grabbed her helmet and headed for the hatch.

"Mark, you have the con. Stand down from Condition Zulu," she said.

"Aye, ma'am. Stand down from Condition Zulu," Mark replied.

Kim stopped at the ladder leading to deck one, leaning against the railing for a moment until her hand stopped shaking. She was certain she was ready for command, but had never felt the monumental pressures until the captain was incapacitated on Kremlin. With over a hundred lives depending on her every decision, she understood like never before.

"XO, Dr. Krisper," the doctor said over the comms.

"Go for XO," she replied.

"The captain's awake, ma'am."

Jacob pulled his black uniform sweater over his head. His back ached from the exertion, his skin feeling like it would pull right off him. Dr. Krisper had informed him it would pass, that the new skin would take time to gain flexibility, but it still felt odd and stiff.

Checking the mirror, he made sure his uniform was perfect and his watch cap sat level on his head. He needed to show the crew that everything was okay—even if he didn't necessarily feel that way. And boy, he sure didn't feel that way.

At least he had managed to save Rod's wife, which was what really mattered. How many times could he cheat death? From the ambush on Kremlin, to Gamma-7, and then Kremlin again... too many.

He shook his head. Each time he had Jennings watching his back. *Jennings,* he mused. The marine sergeant stuck by his side through thick and thin. He hadn't failed to notice how she was always on duty when he was, standing outside his cabin or the bridge. She was a rock. A deadly rock.

His cabin hatch whooshed open as he approached. Outside, Jennings snapped to attention. While it was the marines' duty aboard ship to protect the captain, they didn't normally wear sidearms. Seeing the MP-17 belted to her side, he nodded at her approvingly.

"Allison," he said as he walked by, "from now on I want all *Interceptor* marines armed, aboard ship and on shore."

"Oorah, sir." She fell in step behind him, taking up the position outside the bridge's double hatch. "Captain on the bridge," she said in her way of shouting without shouting.

"I have the con, Lieutenant West," Jacob said.

"Aye, sir, captain has the con," West replied as he stood up from the center seat and took position next to it.

"Status?" Jacob asked as he sat in his chair.

"Good timing, sir. We're ten minutes out from the jump into Medial."

Jacob examined the charts. They didn't name any of the systems they discovered, only gave them designations. So far, *Interceptor* had traveled through four Guild-discovered starlanes with no trouble. Not to mention the wormhole.

He suppressed a sigh. The time he had spent in a coma had cost him some truly amazing sights. This was it though; they were nearing Medial.

"Any signs of other ships?" he asked.

"Yes, sir," Tefiti replied. "A few small freighters, some corvette-sized ships. Nothing with a military signature or flying a Caliphate flag. It seems the Guild wasn't the only one who knew about these… back doors… to Medial. It makes sense though," Mark said.

"How so?"

"The Caliphate can't officially trade with pirates, and they can't have open borders, so it makes sense they have a few *unofficial* paths to their trading hubs. I'm not sure how far these Guild lanes go into the Caliphate, but they will get us to Medial —mostly unseen."

It would never occur to Jacob to allow pirates access to one of the Alliance planets. Pirates were scum who pillaged and raped their way through the galaxy. They provided no use to any civilized nation.

He stomped on that line of thought. It was all too easy thinking of his enemies as ignorant savages. That was a mindset that led to mistakes. In his line of work, mistakes cost lives.

"Skipper?" Spacer Gouger said. "Incoming message from *Komodo*."

"On my screen," Jacob said.

Nadia Dagher's smiling face appeared. "Commander Grimm, I'm so glad you're up and about," she said with a full smile.

He tried to keep his expression professional instead of the goofy grin threatening to expose his feelings to the entire bridge.

"Me too. I was catching up on where we are and what's next."

"Oh, good," she said. "I was speaking to our source about how to approach Medial."

"I have some thoughts on that. What about tucking inside the *Komodo*'s sensor shadow as we discussed?" he asked.

"I'm afraid new information will make that impractical." Nadia gestured off-screen.

"Captain Grimm?" a man said. Nadia touched a button, and the screen zoomed out, showing Terrance DeShawn next to her.

"Yes, Mr. DeShawn?" He couldn't keep the ice out of his voice. Nor did he want to.

"Uh, sir, that won't work. Medial doesn't have a navy presence per se, but they do have a fleet of corvettes—at least a dozen. Even if we signal Medial that we're friendly, they will still do a flyby of the ship. They won't board for an inspection, but their corvettes are more than enough to destroy a dozen freighters in a short amount of time."

Jacob frowned at the revelation. That would teach him to assume like that. No *official* navy presence wasn't the same as no presence. Hiding in a ship's shadow was a reliable way of stealthily passing detection, but it wouldn't stand up to a close inspection.

"Could we magnetically secure her to the side and conceal her?" Jacob asked.

DeShawn shook his head. "I don't think so... if they saw it...

well, I know your crew is on point, but could you take them from a cold start without risking *Komodo*?" he asked.

It irked Jacob that DeShawn was asking the strategic questions, somehow prickling his pride. Jacob had no doubt that *Interceptor* could take a dozen corvettes, but not while defending *Komodo*.

"That only leaves us one option. Leave the *Interceptor* on the outskirts of the system and go in with the *Komodo*... but that will leave us uncovered for..." He turned. "Ensign Owusu?"

Owusu jumped in surprise at being brought into the conversation. He consulted his computer, embarrassment clouding his ability for a moment. "Uh, sorry, sir. One moment," he muttered. "At Medial's current orbital station, which is on the opposite side of the system, it will be twelve hours from the starlane vector. If we want to stealth in, it will be at least twenty-four."

Jacob tapped his fingers against the well-worn armrest. He glanced down at the display to look at Nadia.

"That's a long time to wait for backup. There has to be a way to bring the ship in closer without tipping our hand," he said to her.

PO Tefiti waved to get his attention, one hand on his gravity headphones, a look of focused concentration on his face.

Tefiti turned to Jacob. "Possible contact, two-seven-zero relative. There's a ship ahead of us. She's not hiding, just sitting at the entrance to the starlane. I only heard her because they didn't power down their gravcoil—they just aren't accelerating. If we were running civilian detectors, we wouldn't hear a thing."

"Let's table this discussion for now while we figure out what's going on here." Jacob keyed the comm, "All hands, Condition Zulu, battle stations."

The klaxon wailed, alerting every crew to the situation. Jacob turned to Ops. "Mark, rig us for silent running."

"Aye, aye, sir. Silent running. We can't hide the *Komodo*, though."

"I'm aware." He looked back to the monitor. "Nadia, full stop while we check this out."

CHAPTER NINETEEN

Rashid al-Alami checked his Pad for the tenth time, making sure he had the time and date right. The ISB agent, Nafir, had sold him the data, but there was still a chance he was being double-crossed.

His small ex-Caliphate corvette hovered less than a million klicks from the area of space where ships coming from Medial's general location would exit the starlane.

Normally, he spent his days terrorizing the pirates connecting the Consortium to Medial—which had earned him the nickname *"Marauder."* He was careful, though, to limit his attacks to the pirates who frequented uncharted space. He might no longer be a member of the Caliphate Navy, nor a citizen, but he still had his dignity. He wouldn't attack a civilian ship under normal circumstances.

It just so happened that today wasn't normal.

"Rashy, I have something..." his navigator, Bin-al-Shied, called out.

"Bin, what is it?" This was no time for trouble, no time at all. If Nafir were to be believed, one of the crew on the freighter they were about to take would know the exact location of his sister on Medial.

"For a moment, I thought I detected a gravwake..." Bin said.

Rashid sighed. "We are expecting a rather large freighter."

"That's the thing, Rashy, it's coming from the wrong direction. It's the right time, but..."

That made him stand up and pay attention. His information network monitored all the starlanes coming and going, but space was big, and ships were missed. "I didn't see any traffic on the register this morning," he said as he walked to Bin's station.

"I know, but... it's not like there is a lot of traffic to begin with. And the wake the computer detected was minimal, like a ship coming to a stop after a long deceleration."

Rashid hunched over Bin's shoulder and punched a few codes in himself. It was a poor captain who didn't have at least some familiarity with his ship's systems.

The screen brought up the detected gravity-wake and showed him the different angles at which it had passed through the lasers mounted inside the ship's hull. Freighters had powerful gravcoils to move their mass, but compared to military ships, which had to accelerate three times as fast, they were feeble.

"I think it's military," Rashid muttered.

Bin shook his head. "The Caliphate Navy never comes out here. It's the wrong direction for Medial's system patrol."

"I know, but look at the wave density. It's an order of magnitude higher than anything that should be here—" He pointed at the thick line displayed from the computer's interpretation.

"It could be two ships. The gap there," Bin said, zooming in on the line, "might indicate a trailing ship."

Rashid frowned. A glance at the clock told him they only had a few minutes before their intended prize came through. Did they have time for a second ship? If he engaged the first, would the one he really wanted run away while he was busy dealing with the newcomer?

Rashid al-Alami had survived on his wits and luck for most of his life. Events that would have broken or killed another man simply redoubled his efforts. His instincts told him to stay silent... but if it really was two freighters decelerating, they would never be able to outrun his ship and get out of range of his plasma turret in time. He could force a surrender. Worst case, he could disable the new ships and still pursue his primary target. No matter what, though, he needed the one coming from Medial. If he were in the middle of taking the ship coming from one direction, he would be a sitting duck for the other two. If they were pirates and armed, then his little adventure would come to a swift and fruitless end. He couldn't leave his six exposed like that.

"Go active on the radar, bring the plasma turret to bear, and turn the ship around. I want to see what we're up against."

Tefiti jerked back in his chair as the gravcoil of the ship he monitored went hot. "Contact. Bearing two-seven-five relative. Range, thirty-five thousand klicks! Designation Tango-Zero-One, possible corvette or—"

Ensign Owusu cut him off. "Radar. They've gone active, Skipper."

Jacob signaled Spacer Gouger. "Send it, Felix," he said.

"Aye, aye, sir, sending."

A small smile played on Jacob's lips. It was partly good

planning they'd gotten in so close, and partly luck. If Tefiti hadn't heard their gravcoil on idle, they might have flown right by and never seen them until it was too late.

"Carter, light 'em up," he ordered.

"Aye, aye, sir, activating close-range targeting lidar," Lieutenant Fawkes said with a smile. It wasn't often they got to have the upper hand on another combat ship.

Bin flinched in his seat like he was slapped.

"What?" Rashid asked.

The navigator's mouth worked, but no words came out. "It can't be," he finally muttered.

A pit formed in Rashid's stomach. The ship's comm beeped, and he pressed the receive button.

The large screen at the front of the bridge lit up with the smiling visage of a square-jawed officer wearing a black turtleneck sweater and a red watch cap—the uniform of the Alliance Navy.

Not a life suit, not a battle outfit, just his regular day uniform. The implication of this hit him like a fist, and he felt physically ill. He shook his head, trying to focus on what the officer was saying. His understanding of standard wasn't the best, forcing him to wait for the computer to translate the message.

"Heave to and prepare to be boarded. I say again, unknown vessel, this is Commander Jacob T. Grimm of the United Systems Alliance destroyer *Interceptor*. Heave to and prepare to be boarded. Any resistance will be met with the destruction of your ship. Please acknowledge."

"Rashy, they're hitting us with targeting lasers. At this range, we are dead."

Marauder indeed, he thought bitterly to himself. "Signal our surrender," he ordered, "before they annihilate us."

A moment after they surrendered, the freighter Rashid had paid dearly to find appeared from Medial's starlane, flying away without ever knowing how close it came to destruction.

Rashid kept his head up as the two navy personnel marched him into the small room to meet the captain. All his planning, every move he'd made over the last four years, was utterly wasted by a single moment of bad luck.

What the hell was an Alliance destroyer doing this deep into Caliphate space anyway? Worst of all, he lost his best chance to rescue his sister. That bitter pill stuck in his gut like acid.

The two spacers escorting him stopped him in front of a large table painted with a grinning shark. A circle around the shark proclaimed the ship's name and designation, but he couldn't read the motto. To Rashid, it was quintessential Alliance bravado. He couldn't fault them for their procedure, though. He had participated in his fair share of naval disciplines and hearings, and the captain of this ship obviously ran a tight crew.

"State your name for the record," said the navy man next to him.

"You know my name," Rashid replied without looking at him. "What is yours?"

Across the table, the ship's captain watched him with shrewd eyes—eyes that told Rashid this man would not be intimidated or bullied.

"I'm Commander Jacob T. Grimm. And we do know your

name, Rashid al-Alami. How did a pirate come into possession of a military-grade corvette?"

Nor was he a bully. There was something about him... a sense of... trust. Something Rashid wasn't used to seeing in his own circles. It felt foreign, like oil on his skin.

"How do you say... It fell off the back of a freighter?" Rashid chuckled at his own joke, and to his surprise, the captain did as well.

Grimm cocked his head to the side, as if seeing through Rashid, who found it unnerving to be examined like a worm on a hook.

A small device next to the captain beeped, startling Rashid. A sure sign of his emotional state despite his attempt at humor.

"Skipper, Jennings. No sign of human cargo," a distorted female voice said from the device.

"Acknowledged. Good job. *Interceptor* out," Grimm replied. He examined Rashid with an appraising eye.

After a long moment of silence, the urge to speak grew until Rashid blurted out, "By what legal right did you seize my ship?"

Grimm's confidence didn't go away. Instead, he leaned back and tapped one hand on the arm of his chair, shifting his weight to the side.

"No right. Other than the four turrets trained on your vessel. I have no legal authority here. The Systems Alliance Navy can't interfere in foreign ports unless specifically requested by the appropriate authorities." He sounded like he was quoting chapter and verse. "Something I doubt the Caliphate would ever ask us for."

Rashid closed his mouth, biting off his retort. It was a stupid question to ask—of course they had no authority here. Several things occurred to him at once. Rumors had flown around for months that the Caliphate was responsible for nuking

Anchorage Bay. While he would never have pulled the trigger on a civilian population, as proven by his exile, there were plenty of captains who would. A fact that left him no doubt that the rumors could be true.

"You're here for revenge... aren't you?" Rashid asked.

Captain Grimm leaned forward, clasping his hands together, his unshakable air of confidence growing stronger. "Now, what makes you say that?"

Rashid glanced around the room. This wasn't the tone of the conversation he had expected when brought aboard at gunpoint. He was trapped, nothing he did would change that, but, if Commander Grimm was going after Medial, maybe they could both win. Then again, they could just duck into the system, fly by Medial, and blast it with nukes. Even if it cost him his life, he couldn't allow that.

"You cannot nuke Medial. Whatever your plans, you can't," he said, surging forward. The short woman with the many hash marks on her sleeve hooked his elbow to hold him back. Rashid didn't resist, but he would throw himself on the deck and beg if it would stop the captain from killing his sister.

Grimm's face turned sour, as if he just ate a bug. "I don't know what you've been told about the Alliance Navy, *Mr. Al-Alami,* but we abide by the Treaty of Okinawa-Deruta. Not to mention the sheer idiocy of escalating violence between our people." Grimm stood, walking around the conference table. He didn't quite have to stoop, but he did anyway, as the red watch cap on his head almost brushed the overhead.

"They're not my people," Rashid said, recovering somewhat. "Caliph Hamid is a madman. I didn't see it until it was too late. He butchers and enslaves his own people, keeping them starving in the streets." He resisted the urge to spit in distaste.

Grimm raised an eyebrow at his declaration. "I understand these three systems aren't *officially* part of the Caliphate of Hamid, but you must admit that you're nominally under their jurisdiction."

"You misunderstand, *Captain*. I'm *mahjariyy*," Rashid said.

"Forgive me, I don't understand," Grimm replied.

"I am exiled. My name erased, my family executed, and my sibling sold into slavery. It is why I'm here. It is why I'm asking — begging you not to bomb Medial from orbit. My sister is on that planet, and I've spent the last four years of my life trying to find and rescue her. Please, Captain Grimm, do not destroy Medial. Do not kill my sister."

Jacob liked to think he was a good judge of character. Rashid certainly had sincerity. Something in his eyes, the way he held himself, told Jacob he could trust the man. Or at least, trust his intentions. If Rashid truly wanted nothing more than to rescue his sister, it was possible for them to work together.

Grimm motioned for Rashid's cuffs to be removed, which were. Rashid rubbed his wrists, surprise clear on his face from the gesture.

"Mr. Al-Alami, I think we might be able to help each other," Grimm said.

Rashid mentally ran through everything he knew about the Alliance. The tidbits of history, the interviews, the officers he'd met. He wanted—*desperately* wanted—to believe this captain. Could he, though? With his sister's life in the balance?

"Captain Grimm, I"—he glanced around the room as if it had ears—"am not in a position to make an informed decision."

"I understand your hesitance. If our situations were

reversed, I would feel the same. You're right, we are here to attack Medial. However"—he raised his hand to calm Rashid—"not in the way you think. My orders are to raid the planet, destroy the slave infrastructure, and free as many of the enslaved people as we can find."

Rashid let out a sharp bark of a laugh before he could stop himself.

"Now I know you are lying. No one would be foolish enough to send a single destroyer to attack an entire planet. They have a squadron of state-of-the-art corvettes piloted by their best. On the planet itself are two battalions of light infantry. Fifty thousand people live on Medial, all rich traders and merchants with their own private security staff, all concentrated in the only city.

"Assuming you somehow managed to defeat all of them and seize control of the planet, there are thousands of slaves on Medial at any given time, just awaiting auction or pickup. Then there are the ones who live there. The servants, the workers, the *companions*." He bit back the last word with bitter regret.

Captain Grimm seemed to take it in stride, his expression not changing from the friendly "enemy with honor" persona he had affected since Rashid entered the room. Either the man's proficiency at lying matched the ISB, or he truly meant what he said.

"Thank you for that. We have precious little intel on the planet. Most of what we know comes from a single pirate who had dealings there. We brought him along to get us in, but we've run into a problem—he failed to tell us about the corvettes guarding the system until after we arrived. Now, I have no doubt my ship can take a few corvettes"—he ran his hand along the words painted on the table, *First to Fight*, as he spoke—"but not while we're protecting our civilian assets. Nor could we destroy them in time to prevent them from calling for reinforcements."

"You give me a lot to take in, Captain."

"Commander, actually. Lieutenant commander. I'm only a 'captain' in the context of the ship." He shook his head, waving his hand. "Never mind about all that. Just call me Commander Grimm."

Grimm pressed a button on the desk. "Mess, briefing room."

"Mess. PO Mendez here, Skipper."

"Josh, can you send up some coffee?" Grimm glanced back at Rashid. "Black, no sugar, for our *guest*."

Rashid nodded, indicating it was indeed how he liked his coffee.

"On the way, Skipper," Mendez said.

Grimm was happy to speak no more until the coffee arrived via a man who seemed far too happy for such a menial task.

"My thanks," Rashid said, taking the brew.

"I don't expect a cup of coffee to make you trust me, but perhaps we could break some barriers, right here, you and me. I have no siblings, but I would do anything to rescue my parents. I understand your noble desire. If you help me get to the planet —and I pledge this to you—if your sister is alive and down there, we won't leave until we've found her."

Rashid's hand froze with the coffee halfway up, unable to believe the earnestness of the commander. Every instinct in him said he could trust the man, but his upbringing and education fought with him, telling him not to believe the infidel.

In truth, his mind was numb from the sudden turn of events. In the span of a few hours he had gone from commanding his own ship to becoming a prisoner of the Alliance, to being offered the one thing he wanted. The *only* thing that mattered to him.

"If you're going in, you couldn't have picked a worse time," he finally said. "It's a good thing you illegally seized my ship."

"I guess that makes *us* the pirates. COB," he said to the woman with all the hash marks on her sleeve, "hoist the Jolly Roger."

She snapped to parade-ground attention. "Hoist the Jolly Roger, aye, sir."

CHAPTER TWENTY

Nadia glowered hard in the mirror, sweat dripping down her brow as her grim reflection gazed back. The small head attached to *Komodo*'s bridge barely had room even for her lithe form. She bent over the sink, alternating between drinking the potable water and splashing it on her face. She forced back the memories of her time under the influence of the Caliph's accursed collar technology. The things they'd made her do and say—

Her fist smashed down on the steel sink. She'd tried so hard to move on, to convince the admiral—to convince herself—that she was fine. That those events hadn't affected her. Even with her fantastic acting skills, she couldn't lie to herself. And here she was, heading for a planet full of people who would gladly slap a collar on her and sell her to the highest bidder.

From within her coat she took out a small pill known only to her. A pill that would guarantee she would never again fall under the influence of the collar. All she had to do was pop it in her mouth, and within three seconds she would be dead. A knock on the hatch interrupted her thoughts. She hastily slid the pill back into its secret pocket.

With the risk they were about to face, Jacob had sent more of his crew over. He wanted to make sure *Komodo* could run fast if she needed to. There simply was no way to sneak *Interceptor* into orbit, not while defending the *Komodo*.

However, the hold was more than large enough to fit the Corsair, its Mudcat, and the marines with their powered Raptor armor. They were down there currently, disguising the dropship and the Mudcat to look more like something pirates would operate.

Once in orbit, *Komodo* would know the location of every enemy and, when the time was right, transmit it to *Interceptor*.

She exited the head onto the cramped bridge, making sure she stayed to the side of the video pickup. Rashid al-Alami occupied the captain's chair, and DeShawn stood to his right. The rest of the bridge crew were male ratings from *Interceptor*. PO Oliv and Collins stood off to the side like Nadia to avoid the camera.

"Time to orbit?" Rashid asked.

Spacer First Class Albert manned the ship's con. "S-six minutes-thirty-two seconds, sir," he stuttered his answer,

Rashid nodded. "Drop the 'sir.' You all already look like military—you don't want to sound like it too. One or two of you, I can explain, but a whole crew? They'll just blow us up to be safe."

"Aye, s—yes," Albert said.

Rashid nodded.

Nadia approved of his command style. Whoever he was before piracy, she would bet money he had spent time in the Caliphate Navy.

"Commander, we're being hailed," Lieutenant West said.

Rashid pushed a button on his command chair, causing the central screen to flicker and change to an older man with a thick, bushy beard.

"Unknown ship, identify yourself or be destroyed," the man on-screen said with a bored expression.

"Prize ship *Komodo*, taken from the Corridor," Rashid said.

The man narrowed his eyes as he typed in something off-screen.

Nadia hoped Rashid's bluff worked. Since the discovery of the wormhole, Corridor traffic had all but vanished. Even waiting months to use the wormhole ended up being more cost effective than risking the Corridor between the Consortium and Alliance space.

"It's been six months since a prize ship came from there. You must be eager to land," the man said.

Nadia glanced at Rashid. The way the person on the line spoke sounded like a challenge phrase.

"Not eager enough to die," Rashid returned the challenge.

DeShawn let out an obvious sigh. Nadia could strangle the ex-pirate. If he were really here as a pirate, then he'd have nothing to worry about. Thankfully, the man on the other end seemed oblivious.

"Orbit Traffic Control will send you parking instructions. Follow them to the letter, or you will be destroyed. How much time do you need?" he asked.

Rashid lifted his chin. "That's new. Can't we stay until we're done?" he asked.

"You can have up to a week at a hundred thousand per day," the official responded.

"*Per day?*" DeShawn interrupted. "That's outrageous. Last time we were here for a week and only paid the sales tax!"

"You are welcome to pay nothing and forfeit your ship, cargo, and lives. You have two minutes to decide," the man said, then cut the line.

Rashid looked over at Nadia. "Do you have the funds?" he asked.

She nodded. "I have a hard-coded account with enough."

"Good, because they aren't screwing around. They will destroy this ship," Rashid said.

DeShawn gulped. He'd avoided death in prison; he wasn't keen on dying in the black. Nadia made a mental note to keep an eye on him. She wouldn't put it past him to turn them in if he thought he would survive. She tapped her NavPad. "Bravo-Two-Five, we're in orbit. Prepare to drop on my arrival."

Sergeant Jennings' radio-distorted voice answered immediately. "Aye, ma'am."

Nadia handed Rashid a chip as she walked for the hatch. "This should cover it. Call them back. Once it's settled, we'll head for the planet. West," she said, pointing at the lieutenant, "you have the con."

Nadia winced as the Corsair buffeted down through the atmosphere. The dropship's angular hull was made less aerodynamic by the addition of the command Mudcat slung under the tail.

Four marine-issue Raptor suits were crammed into the back of the compartment, their cockpits wide open for immediate embarkation. Sergeant Jennings, Lance Corporal Naki, PFC Owens, and Private Cole were strapped into passenger seats, as were Rashid and Nadia. The only other person was DeShawn, but she had strapped him into the electronics seat under the cockpit where she could keep both her eyes on him.

It was impossible to make the marines look like civilians, but hooded cloaks and full-face masks to protect their eyes from the extreme brightness of the sun did enough to obscure their features.

"We shouldn't take them with us," Rashid whispered to Nadia.

"It was nonnegotiable. Commander Grimm would never have signed off on this if we didn't have security," she said.

"I can handle myself, and I think you can as well, yes?" he asked.

She glanced at him. The sly half-smile on his face made her want to flatten his stupid nose with her cybernetic fist.

"Do not mistake our shared ancestry for any kind of kinship. I am loyal to the Alliance. Nothing and no one else."

"Of course. I didn't mean to imply you weren't. I just... well, you know how our people treat traitors and thieves. Me, they will just kill, but the woman." He nodded to Jennings.

Nadia clenched her jaw, pushing back against the memories and the pain. She would spare anyone that, but there was nothing to be done. Jennings would sooner cut off her own arm than disobey an order from *"the captain"* as she constantly called him.

"We're just here to recon. We need their expertise and protection. Once we've located the holding pens, we can call in the *Interceptor* and start the rescue—"

The Corsair shook as the wings extended, grabbing the atmosphere, followed by the howl of her plasma turbines.

"You really think you can rescue your people?" Rashid asked.

She shook her head. "It doesn't matter what I think. Only what my orders are. As long as we rescue someone, blast enough infrastructure, and make enough noise, the job will be done. You know as well as I do what cowards *our* people are." She shot him a sideways glare.

Rashid recoiled from the venom in her voice. "Not all of them. I don't know what happened to lead you to think this way of our people, but just because the current government is bad doesn't—" He stopped talking when she turned her withering gaze on him.

"Don't give me that *just following orders* bullshit," she spat. "The fish rots from the body up. If the people of the Caliphate wanted change, they would get change. Instead, they live off the labor of others. They wouldn't know what to do with freedom if it kicked them in the face. Don't tell me about the *noble spirit* of your people. Tell that to the millions of men, women, and children they have enslaved and murdered."

Nadia deliberately turned her body away from him, staring at the NavPad in her lap.

"If you hate us so, why not just bomb the planet from orbit?" he whispered.

Nadia turned her hate-filled eyes on him. "If it were up to me, I would. But I'm not in command. I have my orders. Right now, those orders include helping you find your sister. Don't think for one second I trust you, though."

The unending blackness of starlane travel came to an abrupt halt as *Interceptor* re-emerged into space on the outskirts of the Medial system. The bright white-blue of the massive primary was barely visible at their distance.

"That's one bright star to see it this far out," Jacob remarked.

"Aye, sir," Owusu agreed. "The computer shows it as a red supergiant. Very big, very bright."

"Update our astrogation, and let's see where we are," Jacob ordered. Astrogation charts were updated whenever ships traversed systems. They shared with friendly ships automatically. With no friendly ships within a hundred parsecs, the only data on Medial was from the original survey almost six centuries earlier.

"Seven-planet system," Owusu said. "Six moons, two on Medial. I'm picking up a healthy amount of in-system traffic, plus some industry in the single asteroid belt."

A map of the system appeared on his MFD, and Jacob took a moment to study the orbital bodies. He pushed down the part of him that longed to explore—that wasn't his mission. It would likely never be his mission. Still… looking at a system no one in the Alliance Navy had seen before sent a thrill up his spine.

How would his life have differed if the Alliance Navy still had an exploration mission?

"What are you grinning about, Skipper?" Kim asked from beside his chair.

"For just a moment, I imagined we were explorers on a voyage of discovery," he told her.

"You mean traveling through unknown starlanes only to find ourselves trapped with no way home?" she said with a shake of her head. "I'll pass."

"Where's your sense of adventure, XO?"

She turned serious eyes on him. "We went through a wormhole on our secret mission to rescue slaves from an evil empire. I'd say my sense of adventure is fully occupied," she deadpanned.

"Point taken." He certainly couldn't fault her reasoning, nor suppress his own desire to see things no one else had ever seen.

"Immediate area clear, Skipper," PO Tefiti reported.

"Outstanding. Ensign Owusu, I think the asteroid belt will be an excellent place to hide. Plot a parallel course to Medial. It's close enough we should be able to intercept the planet without much trouble. Do the math, please."

"Aye, aye, sir," Owusu said.

"Bosun Sandivol, rig us for silent running," Jacob ordered.

"Silent running, aye," Sandivol said from where he manned Ops. The lights on the bridge flickered from white to red.

"That's my cue. I'll be in DCS if you need me, sir," Yuki said.

"Dismissed." Jacob waved her away.

"Course plotted," Owusu stated. "Helm, set course two-five-one, mark three-four-three, ahead two-five gravities using interval acceleration."

Suresh repeated the course and plugged it into the computer. When running silent, they kept their acceleration to a minimum. Thermal radiation from the ship's activities routed to the heat sink, minimizing her infrared signature. By the time they needed to change it out, they would be safely in the asteroid belt.

"All stations report ready, sir," Sandivol said.

"Thank you, Bosun. Chief Suresh, execute course."

"Executing course, aye," Suresh said.

Jacob leaned back and watched the numbers flash by as the ship changed direction toward the asteroid belt. *Interceptor* accelerated at twenty-five gravities for ten seconds, then the gravcoil shut off for ten seconds. Suresh alternated the activation to keep the gravwake sporadic. It slowed down their overall progress, but in situations where stealth was key, they had to do everything in their power to avoid detection.

"Burst signal from *Komodo,* sir. They've achieved orbit," Ensign Hössbacher informed him.

He wished he could return the signal, let them know they were not alone. The next time he would talk to them would be when they were both in orbit.

CHAPTER TWENTY-ONE

Jennings pulled her hood down low as she leaped off the disguised Corsair. Boudreaux had worked overtime painting her in a series of mismatched colors and removing all the insignia. The twin tails bore a faded Jolly Roger instead of *Charlie-One-One*. Scratches, scrapes, and dents covered the keel, and she had even removed some nonessential paneling.

Even the Mudcat looked the part. One of the tires hung limply from the back. A single window on the passenger side had spiderweb cracks that reflected light. Both the Corsair and the Mudcat looked old and worn out. There was no mistaking their military nature, but no one would look at them and think they were current.

Her boots crunched in the sand of the civilian landing pad. They weren't allowed at the main spaceport, but a secondary site reserved for unofficial visitors. AKA *Pirates*.

The landing pad was surprisingly empty. Besides the Corsair, there were only two other ships, both far enough away to avoid prying eyes. Jennings motioned for the remainder of her people to disembark.

"Cole, stay with the ship. Keep Chief Boudreaux safe," Jennings ordered.

"I don't need anyone to—" Boudreaux started to say.

"Chief, this isn't Alliance space," Commander Dagher interrupted her. "An unescorted woman isn't safe. Period."

"Fine," Boudreaux replied, clearly not happy with the situation.

"Owens," Jennings motioned forward, "take point. Naki, follow up the rear. DeShawn, surgically attach yourself to my hip," she growled.

DeShawn visibly gulped, but he agreed.

Rashid and Dagher wore a hodgepodge of robes—the only difference between the two was the hadji. Jennings, however, simply wore what the rest of her squad wore. With her thick upper body and combat gear, no one could tell at a glance she was anything other than a short man—for which she was thankful. She didn't think she could pull off the obedient, compliant-woman act Commander Dagher had assumed.

A mishmash of sandstone buildings and modern structures spread out before them. They couldn't see much from the secondary spaceport other than that it was hot and bright. Rashid led the way to a low-rise control tower that acted as an arrival gate for their specific class of "traders" who frequented Medial.

"No one brought any weapons, right?" Rashid asked as they approached the gate.

Jennings smirked. "Nothing they're going to find."

"I'm serious. They don't allow us to carry weapons in the city," Rashid said. He turned to them, an alarmed look on his face.

"Will they search us or scan us?" Jennings asked, but she already knew the answer.

"Scan. Why?" Rashid asked.

"Then we aren't carrying any weapons," she assured him. Naki chuckled softly from behind.

The sandstone-colored metal door swooshed open. Two men with thick black beards and wearing tan uniforms stepped out. Jennings glanced at the powerful short-range plasma pistols they carried. More for intimidation and brutality than sustained combat.

The larger of the two soldiers said something to Rashid in their native tongue. Jennings didn't understand the dialect, but she knew enough to recognize it. Rashid laughed, then pointed at the Corsair. For a second, she thought he was going to betray them, and she prepared herself to kill the three men before they could raise an alarm.

DeShawn fidgeted, drawing Jennings' attention. Her fingers brushed the three throwing knives concealed in her cloak. If either of them was going to betray the crew, now was the time. She sympathized with Rashid's efforts to free his sister, but he might attempt to turn them over in exchange for her freedom. Or DeShawn could betray them in exchange for his own freedom. Jennings would make sure neither man lived long enough to achieve his goal.

After a tense moment, though, the larger guard broke out into a laugh. Rashid joined them while handing over a sack of coins.

Jennings might not have understood the language, but she recognized a bribe when she saw one.

The soldier in charge nodded, holding out a hand scanner and pointing it at each of them in turn. Satisfied, he said something else before returning to the air-conditioned building.

"What was that all about?" Naki asked.

Nadia answered him. "They wanted to know our business —and of course collect a fee for using the spaceport," she said.

Rashid glanced at her, more in confirmation than surprise.

Jennings realized that the commander was just reminding Rashid that she spoke the language.

"A bribe?" Naki asked. "I thought you paid the fee up top?"

Rashid grinned, letting out a chuckle. "Such naivete, my young friend. The *fee*, as you say, was a bribe. This is a bribe. And if we had cargo, a bribe to sell it would also be needed."

"Bizarre way to do business," Naki muttered.

Rashid shrugged as he turned to the trail leading down to an aircar station. "Such is life on the rim. No one is safe; no place is safe. Had we not bribed them, they would have arrested us, seized our ship, and our mission would be over."

They walked in silence, making their way down the well-worn path. At the bottom, a shaded building housed a call button, which Rashid pressed. Jennings' head moved constantly, taking in the area, checking attack angles, making sure they were safe. Something provoked her danger sense. She was sure there was something wrong, but having never been on Medial before, she couldn't quite put her finger on it.

"They must not get a lot of traffic if this is the kind of infrastructure they have," Owens said.

Rashid did a slow turn for a moment, nodding his agreement. "Something has changed in the last year, that is of no doubt."

DeShawn interrupted, "Last time I was here, we landed our ship at the main port. We paid the bribes, of course," he said, pointing back the way they came, "but the port bustled with activity. I hadn't realized it was all piracy from the Corridor."

"Where to next?" Nadia asked.

"I have a contact in the city," DeShawn said. "A broker. If Rashid's sister is here, they will know where. Nothing happens."

A few minutes later, an aircar landed in a cloud of sand. The side doors opened, and the six people crowded into the passenger section. DeShawn fed it an address, and a moment later the automated taxi lifted off.

"The city's bigger than it looks," Owens said, motioning with his hand to the spread-out suburban area.

"Low population density, though," Naki added. "I can't imagine anyone wanting to live here."

Jennings could. Her homeworld was far more inhospitable than Medial. "I've seen worse," she muttered.

"Gravity is about the only thing tolerable here," DeShawn added. "If it weren't for the black-market and slave trade, no one would ever come." The man suddenly looked around, remembering whom he was with. His throat bobbed as he gulped. "I'll just keep quiet," he muttered.

"You do that," Nadia hissed at him.

The aircar banked as it took off, climbing to a hundred and fifty meters before shooting away toward the main city. At that altitude, the city was more visible. The hills around were dotted with expensive residences, while the valley itself had the more modern-style buildings and businesses. A coliseum and large hotel dominated the middle of the city.

"How many people live here?" Naki asked.

"Around fifty thousand, spread out through this valley. Mostly merchants, traders, and buyers," Rashid explained.

Naki let out a whistle. "Look at that," he said, pointing toward the spaceport proper. "I've never seen a ship like it."

The sleek vessel's triangle shape, huge gravcoil, and large landing struts made it stick out beyond the smaller ships.

"I didn't know ships that large could land," Rashid said. "Who would build such a thing?"

Nadia leaned against the window as she looked down at the ship. While the Caliphate Navy had done their best to remove all the markings and repaint her, she recognized it instantly. "It's a Schnell-class liner. Rich people in the Iron Empire use them when they want to bring their luxury hotel with them," she said.

"What's it doing here?" Jennings asked.

Nadia shrugged. "I wouldn't know."

Jennings narrowed her eyes behind her mask. She wasn't exactly a people person, but she had a decent sense for when they were lying to her.

"Right," she said flatly. As long as it didn't endanger the mission, she would let the commander have her secrets.

A few minutes of silent flight passed, and the aircar descended, landing on the roof of one of the many multistory buildings that all looked the same.

"I can't take you all in there," DeShawn said. "Me and three others, tops."

Jennings pointed at Naki and Owens. "Go with them, keep them safe."

Naki didn't like the mission or the two men they were escorting, and he flat-out hated the planet. The only saving grace was the enviro mask he wore, which kept him nice and cool in the hot sun. The marines all wore the faceless masks, making them look more like robots than people.

Naki and Owens followed Rashid and DeShawn down the stairs. The lenses in their masks automatically adjusted to the dim light levels. Naki's hand itched for the butt of an MP-17; only carrying knives somehow felt wrong. The narrow walls and steep stairs made his skin crawl. If he were setting up an ambush, this would be the place.

"Stay frosty," Owens said over their silent and secure comms.

"I know," Naki said. A brief flash of annoyance passed over

him to have the PFC tell him, a lance corporal, to stay cool. Owens was no crayon-munching recruit. The four-person fire team, led by Sergeant Jennings, were all combat veterans. If Owens said something, it was because he sensed Naki's nerves.

Naki gritted his teeth, his jaw aching as he choked out a response. "Thanks, PFC," he replied. His pride was a bitter pill to swallow.

The mic clicked twice in response, a universal acknowledgment without words.

The door at the bottom whooshed open, letting in bright light. His visor dimmed to compensate, and his hand went to the combat knife concealed at the small of his back.

Back on the ship, when they were going over their kit, Boudreaux had asked, "Knives aren't exactly dangerous. What are you going to do with that?"

"Marines are dangerous, Chief. Naked, a marine can kill quickly and efficiently. Give us a knife? We'll overthrow a planet," he'd replied.

She hadn't seemed impressed, but didn't say anything else. Despite his bravado, he wasn't wrong.

"DeShawn, my friend, It's been some time." A woman's voice from the other side of the lit doorway spoke.

"Hafsah, you are well?" DeShawn replied.

"Very. Come in, please."

Everything sounded like code to Naki. At least it was in Standard. He had no idea how to speak Caliph, and checking his NavPad for a translation wasn't an option.

Rashid followed DeShawn through the portal.

"Owens, stay here, stay alert," Naki whispered.

"Oorah," Owens replied.

Naki stepped through the door, checking angles and keeping his head swiveling as he followed the two men through. He didn't trust them for a red-hot second, but he would follow his orders unto death.

Hafsah, as DeShawn called her, stood in a round room with no windows. Naki wasn't sure what he had expected, but an older woman with salt-and-pepper hair and wearing plain clothing wasn't it.

The air inside the room registered at a cool eighteen degrees centigrade. In the center of the room, pillows were placed for a comfortable area to sit or lie down. Naki, however, did neither. He stepped to one side of the door and placed his back against the wall. Eight realistic, naked blue mannequins of Consortium people surrounded the room. It was an odd decoration, but everything about Medial was odd. He found himself staring at one in particular, a beautiful Consortium woman with blue skin. The details were so lifelike, he half expected them to start speaking.

His arm bumped something soft. Naki shifted to the side, thinking he'd missed another person, but there was only a mannequin.

His eyes went to her very naked chest, and he saw the slight rise and fall as she breathed. *God almighty, they aren't mannequins,* Naki realized as bile welled up in his throat.

The girl he'd jostled didn't say a word, but he saw a tear well up and fall down her blue face. She was young, he thought. In the age of genetic treatments that froze or even reversed age, it was almost impossible to guess accurately, but she couldn't be more than eighteen, he decided, and obviously from the Consortium. He averted his gaze, looking away and avoiding eye contact.

His hands formed fists and shook with impotent rage. Intellectually, he knew they had slaves, but seeing it was a whole other thing.

"Are you here to buy or sell?" Hafsah asked as she motioned

for the two men to sit. She went to the corner and poured three cups of coffee. "And who is your handsome friend?" she asked with a gesture toward the pirate captain.

"This is Rashid. He's my new captain," DeShawn said.

"Ahh, the life of a pirate is dangerous," Hafsah said.

"You have no idea," DeShawn muttered.

She returned with their drinks, bowing as she served them. Cups in hand, all three retired cross-legged to the pillows, facing one another.

Naki throbbed with pent-up rage. He used the cloak to disguise it as best he could. It helped that Hafsah didn't seem to pay attention to him. He tried to let it go, but it was against his oaths as a marine to walk out of this room without freeing these people.

He looked at the girl again. Her eyes flickered to him, and he could see her pleading with him for help. How many men had walked in and examined her? Looked at her like a piece of meat? How many came in and bought the men as if they were machinery. Mere digging machines to use until they were all used up?

"Hafsah, we are looking for a specific person. She would be sixteen. Probably served as a house slave or personal servant to someone wealthy. Her name is—"

Hafsah raised her hand. "I don't deal in that kind of merchandise. It's more trouble than it's worth. If you are not buying or selling, then leave." She stood up, turning her back on them.

Rashid and DeShawn looked as if they were going to give up. Naki would have none of that. "Charlie, this is Bravo. Weapons hot," he said to Owens.

"Roger that. Weapons hot."

Naki moved with a purpose born of fury. The six-inch-long, nano-hardened steel blade appeared in his hand.

"What are you—" DeShawn shouted. The sudden outburst

alerted Hafsah. Rashid slammed one arm across DeShawn to prevent him from interfering.

The slaver turned just as Naki reached her. He palmed her face, swept her feet out from under her, and forced her down. Holding the knife to her throat hard enough to draw blood, he moved his face until it was almost touching hers.

"You're going to do two things," he said to her in a low whisper. "First release these people, and then answer his question."

Her eyes went wide. She heard death in his voice.

Parked on the roof, Nadia stayed in the aircar with Jennings while the rest of the team entered the building. She took out her NavPad and went to work.

"Okay, Commander, what are we really doing here?" Jennings asked. She knew something was going on, and knew it wasn't something the captain was aware of.

Nadia looked up at the marine. "Astute as always, Sergeant," she said, then looked back down at her NavPad.

"Does it have something to do with that fancy liner we saw?" Jennings asked.

Nadia shook her head, fingers flying across the screen. "I'm trying to break into the network, so if you could let me focus for a moment, that would be great."

Jennings leaned against the side of the aircar, closing her eyes and forcing her body to relax. Whatever the spy was doing, she would share it in due time. For now, it was enough that she knew someone was onto her.

"The mission is still the same," Nadia said as she worked. "Rescue as many prisoners as we can, blow up as much as we can, and escape."

Jennings snorted. "Right. What else?"

Nadia held up her NavPad and turned it around for Jennings to see. "This," she said. A picture of a thin, young, blonde woman appeared. She wore the uniform of the Iron Empire and had the regal look of someone who wasn't to be trifled with.

"She doesn't look like a native," Jennings said.

"Because she's not. This is Princess Elsa Faust, daughter of Emperor Faust. She was kidnapped by pirates several months ago. They took her from a disguised Schnell-class cruise ship while she was leading an operation to capture pirates. The irony wasn't lost on me. Unfortunately for her, it wasn't pirates but Caliphate raiders. I tracked her back to here but wasn't able to do more from Alliance space."

"Are you telling me that the entire reason for this mission is to rescue one missing princess?" Jennings asked.

Nadia pressed a button on the NavPad, and the picture shifted. It was the same girl, thinner, if that were possible, and darker skinned, but with the same straw-colored hair and wearing very little.

"Yes. Right now, we have no allies against the Caliphate, Sergeant. The Terran Republic isn't in a position to provide for their own people, let alone come to our rescue. They might even join against us. The Consortium has their hands full protecting their border. If the Caliphate promises them a nonaggression pact, they might just agree. We need an ally. Someone the Caliphate won't want to mess with. If we can bring the princess back *and* punch the Caliphate in the nose while we're at it, then we win. Period."

"And you didn't tell the captain this because you're a spy?" Jennings let the question dangle.

"Because it's 'need to know.'"

Jennings raised an eyebrow. "Then why are you telling me?"

"Because you need to know." Nadia turned around and punched in an address on the aircar's command console.

"I'm not leaving my men behind," Jennings said.

"Order them to stay with Rashid and DeShawn. They can call another aircar and go back to the ship and wait for us."

Jennings' muscles tensed as the car lifted off. She didn't like it, but she had no choice. "Bravo, this is Alpha. Come in," Jennings said.

Naki replied instantly. "Bravo, go ahead."

"Remain with package and RTB LZ, confirm," she whispered into the mic attached to her throat.

"Alpha, say again?" Naki replied.

She repeated herself.

"Roger, but... Alpha, we have a situation here..."

"Deal with it, Bravo. Alpha out," she said.

As the aircar lifted away, leaving the building behind, Nadia buried her nose in the NavPad. Jennings had no choice but to follow the commander wherever she went. Hers was not to question why, hers was just to do or die.

Lieutenant Mark West occupied the captain's chair on *Komodo*'s bridge, his feet up on the console in front of him. PO Collins manned the helm, and Oliv sat at astrogation. A handful of ratings worked the other stations.

Every launch from the planet was recorded, every ship in orbit cataloged. In less than forty-eight hours, *Interceptor* would charge in; he wanted to have detailed intel for his captain well ahead of time.

"Lieutenant," PO Oliv said. Her accented voice always sounded odd to his ears, but then so did everyone who was from one of the planets that maintained their own language. He probably sounded odd to her.

"Yes?" he asked.

"Sir, I'm... there's something big coming. I'm picking up some heavy gravwake interference. This high up in orbit, it's either a nearby ship moving fast, or a very large ship approaching."

Mark frowned. They couldn't use active sensors without drawing attention to themselves. *Komodo* was a civilian ship with limited passive sensors, but it was all they had.

"Could be a freighter. An M-class? Can you tell me anything more?" he asked her.

She shook her head. "No, sir. Not until it passes us or the angle of the wake changes to such that—" She froze, one hand going to her earpiece.

He resisted the urge to prompt her. In the days before Commander Grimm, he would have. He would have impatiently pestered her until she told him what she'd heard. The captain wouldn't, though, and he respected him too much to revert to his old ways the moment he was off the ship.

Oliv's normally light brown skin paled as she pushed herself back. "Sir... I..."

"What?" Mark asked, putting his feet on the deck.

PO Oliv looked at him with an expression of dread. "Sir, it's a heavy cruiser, an hour out and making for orbit," she whispered.

Mark stood, unable to reply for a moment. They might as well shoot blanks as go to battle with a heavy cruiser. The entire mission was predicated on the intel that Medial didn't have a navy presence. Only corvettes the *Interceptor* could easily destroy if need be.

"Will *Interceptor* see it before...?" he asked.

Oliv shook her head. "No, sir. They're too far out of range. By the time they pick it up, it will be too late."

He couldn't warn them either. Any signal powerful enough to reach the captain would be picked up by the local authorities.

"What do we do, sir?" PO Collins asked from the helm.

"I... I'm working on it," Mark replied. In truth, he had no idea. *Interceptor* would walk right into a trap and be destroyed before they even knew what hit them. He couldn't let that happen...

Even if it meant *Komodo* and the ground team were killed.

CHAPTER TWENTY-TWO

Jacob sipped his orange drink in the mess while he read the latest crew reports from the department heads. He chuckled at the irony of having to do paperwork even though he was technically in command of a stolen ship. However, he couldn't deviate from his routine lest the admiralty find a way to blame his crew: *"Why didn't you ask the captain why he stopped checking his daily reports or signing off on repairs?"* they would ask.

"Refill, Skipper?" PO Mendez interrupted him, holding a carafe of orange juice.

"Thanks, Josh, I'm good." He covered the top of his cup. Mendez nodded and moved on to the next table.

The chatter of spacers filled the room as they moved in and out, rotating through their mess schedule. A quarter of the ship took meals at any given time, almost enough to fill up the large compartment.

"Penny for your thoughts, Skipper?" Suresh asked. She sat down with her tray. It was the daily special, from what Jacob could tell: *beef in sauce with vegetable*. Along with something that could generously be called mashed potatoes.

As the skipper, he got to eat what he wanted, within limits. He preferred sandwiches to almost anything else, a food that was easy to make and hard to screw up. If they were running low on stores, he would eat what the crew ate, but otherwise PO Mendez kept him fed with a steady diet of ham and cheddar sandwiches.

"I'm afraid they're not worth that much, Devi. How about yours?" he asked.

"Me, sir? I'm just waiting for the Sierra to hit the fan," she said.

Jacob laughed. The navy prohibition on swearing was well enforced, and everyone aboard found great delight in finding ways around it.

"I've planned for that," he said with a smirk. They were in an enemy system, with no backup, in a ship that could outrun —but not outfight—most other ships. Sierra had hit the fan the moment they entered Caliphate space.

"Good to know, sir," she said as she nibbled at her food.

"I hate being out here, though," he said. "I would much rather have gone right in, guns blazing." He made pistols with his fingers and mimed shooting.

"Ha! Wouldn't we all. Rashid was right, though, sir. This is the best plan. Once we do go in, we'll have intel on enemy locations, and we won't give the groundside people time to do anything rash."

By *rash* she meant kill the slaves they held. Rashid had warned them that it was a possibility. Given time, the Caliphate slave owners would use the collars to kill their slaves rather than see them freed. Jacob couldn't risk letting that happen.

He refused to leave Medial without rescuing as many people as he could. If the Caliphate pushed him, though, and murdered the slaves, he would bomb them back to the Stone Age in retribution. He would have no choice.

"Let's hope it doesn't come to that," he told her.

"Aye, sir. Let's hope."

"Are you out of your mind?" DeShawn barked. Rashid stood with one foot on the pirate's chest, preventing him from rising. Meanwhile, Naki knelt on the slaver, knife pressed against her throat.

"Answer the question," he ordered her again.

Hafsah's eyes looked at Naki with raw hatred. "If you kill me, they die," she said between clenched teeth.

Naki's internal resolve wavered for a heartbeat. He didn't let up the pressure on her throat, though.

"You'll still be dead," he told her. "Now answer." The knife cut a millimeter deeper. Fear replaced the contempt in her eyes. She expected the threat of killing the innocent to stop him; when it didn't, the realization of her own mortality hit her.

In truth, Naki would hate himself if they died because of him. But at least the person responsible would be gone and no longer able to hurt more innocent people.

"I'm looking for my sister. Zahra al-Alami. She would have come here four years ago from the capital. Do you know where she is?" Rashid asked.

Naki counted to five in his mind. If he got to one, he was going to hurt the woman. Thankfully, he didn't have to.

"You are Rashid al-Alami?" she asked, eyes wide.

"Yes," he replied.

"Kill me, then. I will never help you—traitor." She tried to spit, but the knife prevented her from swallowing.

Naki glanced up, and Rashid just shrugged. "But you know where she is, don't you?" Naki asked. He placed his knee in her solar plexus, cutting off her air. She began to gasp, face going red as she struggled to breathe.

"Answer him," Naki ordered her. He let up for a moment. She coughed and choked. Her eyes glared at him as she tried to regain her composure, but she said nothing.

"Rashid, do you know how to use these collars?" Naki asked as an idea formed in his mind.

Outside the door, Owens did his best to blend into the shadows. He held his four-inch karambit curved blade underneath his cloak. Marines were encouraged to train with as many weapons as possible—knives being a favorite.

"The alarm went off. She must be in trouble," a man said from the top of the narrow stairs.

Owens braced himself, listening as the footsteps descended on the sandstone. If he timed it right, he could surprise them.

When the first one turned the corner, Owens exploded into action, vaulting up the stairs three at a time. The first guard held a pistol with both hands extended out in front of him. As the man fired without aiming, Owens threw himself to the side and dragged the curved blade across the guard's hand, then up his arm and hooked the sharp blade under his jaw. His scream of pain turned to a gurgle as the edge bit into his jugular.

The second man fired blindly, shooting his friend as well as Owens, whose body armor absorbed the ballistic rounds. The marine shoved the dying man into his friend while grabbing the still hot pistol. He pulled, yanking the second man off his feet—right into his blade. He gashed the man's throat, spraying blood against the wall. Both bodies fell, twitching for a moment, then settling still.

Owens sucked in air, remembering to breathe after the action. It wasn't the first time he'd seen combat, but some things were hard to overcome. "Bravo, Charlie. Two Tangos down," Owens said.

"Charlie, Bravo. You need help?"

"Negative. Now I've got a pistol. Charlie out."

Owens scooped up both guns. Once he was sure he could use them, he searched the men for ammo and found spare magazines for both.

"Excellent," he said to himself as he reloaded both weapons.

"You know what that sound was?" Naki asked. "That was the sound of your guards dying. Last chance. Where's the girl?"

Hafsah snarled at him.

Rashid approached from the side, a shiny new collar in his grip. "One way or the other, you're going to tell us," Rashid said. He reached out for her neck—

"Damn you to hell," she spat out. "I'll tell you."

Naki grinned under his mask. "Where is she?"

"It won't do you any good to know. She's already sold. I brokered the deal. To be honest, I was surprised anyone wanted the sister of a traitor. But on a ship, who cares, right?" she sneered.

Naki hesitated for a moment, not sure what she meant. "Where?" he asked again.

"She's at the Caliph's plaza, up on the hill. *He* knows where it is." She jerked her chin toward Rashid.

"Do you believe her?" Naki asked.

"Yes, I think I do. It makes sense."

Naki grabbed a fistful of her robe and hefted her up and slammed her against the counter.

"Free them," he told her.

"How do I know you won't kill me once I do?" she asked.

"I will absolutely kill you if you don't," Naki said, holding up the knife to remind her.

She reached over and pressed a button behind the counter. One by one, the collars sprang free and dropped to the ground. The eight slaves fell as well, collapsing as each collar was deactivated. The blue-skinned woman Naki had noticed before curled up in a ball and sobbed.

"DeShawn, find them some clothes. Rashid, go up top and call us an aircar. Something with enough room for everyone," Naki ordered.

"You want to take them all?" Rashid asked.

"I'm not leaving this planet with anyone wearing any of those damn collars if I can."

"You might find that impossible, my friend," Rashid said quietly.

Naki looked the man dead in the eyes and channeled his inner drill instructor. "I'm an Alliance Marine. We do three impossible things before breakfast." He jerked his head toward the door.

Unwilling to argue the point, Rashid shrugged, then moved past him and out the door.

"Allah!" Naki heard him say as Rashid went up the stairs.

Owens came in a moment later, carrying two pistols. He handed one to Naki, who checked its load out and slipped it into his belt.

"Thanks," he said. "Any problems?"

Owens shook his head. "Nothing I couldn't hand—" His eyes went wide as he took in the sight of the eight slaves. DeShawn had found robes and was dropping them on each of the former captives.

Naki put a hand on Owens' arm to keep him from raising his gun.

"You're going to let her live?" Owens asked.

"We had a deal," Naki informed him.

Movement caught his attention, and Naki stepped sideways to avoid the blue girl who rushed by him. She'd grabbed a lamp and smashed Hafsah in the head with it. Porcelain shattered, and Hafsah went down. The girl leaped on the broker, slamming her hand on the woman's face as the slaver screamed and tried to slap the girl's hands away.

Naki wrapped one arm around the girl's stomach and yanked her off, pushing her toward Owens, who secured her.

Hafsah's face bled from a gash. Her eye hung uselessly out of its socket. She screamed in agony, holding the wound while simultaneously trying to stand. A piece of the porcelain had sunk deep into the slaver's neck, and blood squirted out of the gash.

"Naki," Owens said, "she's dead if we don't call an ambulance." Hafsah collapsed to the ground, spasming, near death.

Lance Corporal Naki looked down at the writhing form of the slaver, then at the former slaves as they tried to make their limbs work. He pulled the stolen pistol and fired two rounds into Hafsah's chest. She stopped moving.

"Let's go," he said.

———

Jennings knelt down at the edge of the space platform on the wrong side of a powered security fence. On the platform, the Schnell-class star cruiser was guarded by a three-man team who walked the perimeter every fifteen minutes.

Beside her, on her belly, Nadia held a receiver that showed her the view from a micro-drone camera as she navigated it around the ship.

"What do you think?" Nadia asked.

Jennings glanced back and forth from the control tower to the guards. "Can do," she said.

Nadia dropped her head in the grass where they hid. "Yes, with fire support and space superiority, I'm sure you could. I need just us to do it. Undetected."

Jennings glanced down at the spy. "You know I'm a marine, right?" she asked.

"You're more than just a marine, Allison. You're an operator. I know you think you're a blunt instrument, but you're more than that. You're fast, stealthy, and capable. Can you get into that ship without anyone seeing you... and no one dying?" Nadia asked.

Jennings frowned. She felt slightly uncomfortable, as if she were being asked a personal question she wasn't prepared to answer. She clenched her fist in frustration. This wasn't the kind of thing she normally dealt with from a superior. "What are you trying to do?" she asked.

Nadia pressed the return button on the drone controller. It buzzed back, landing next to her. She pocketed the device, then rolled onto her side to look up at Jennings. "There's more to you than what you present to people, and I want to know what it is."

Jennings shook her head. "There really isn't."

"Come on," Nadia said as she stood. Turning her back to the ship, she stepped down into the culvert to avoid detection. Hunched over, the two women made their way down the drain to the main road where their aircar was parked.

Once inside, Nadia directed the vehicle back to the Corsair.

"Think of it as a tactical exercise, then. How would you get aboard that ship without killing anyone or alerting them to your presence?"

Jennings leaned back, her mouth tight with suppressed dissatisfaction. She preferred to understand the "why" before coming up with the what, but she also preferred a straight-up fight to all this sneaking around. "Bait and switch," she said after a few moments of thought. The aircar banked over the landing field, coming to hover next to their disguised Corsair.

Nadia leaned forward with a raised eyebrow, waiting for more. When it didn't come, she prodded. "Care to explain? And please use more than three syllables."

Jennings opened the door and leaped out, falling the one meter to the ground. The aircar settled down behind her. Nadia stepped out and followed the marine to the side entrance of the dropship.

"A diversion on the other side of the port would allow us to infiltrate undetected," Jennings said as she pulled herself up into the Corsair.

On the deck next to the behemoth armored suits, Cole knelt arm deep in the primary magazine storage. Several large munitions boxes were scattered around him.

"Hey, Sarge, I'm just reseating the ammo boxes. You know how the suits get jostled," Cole said.

Jennings waved her hand at him. "Fine." She found a chair and sat down with her back to the hull.

Nadia leaped in behind her, slapping the button to close the door. "What kind of diversion?" she asked.

"Fire or explosion."

Nadia sat down next to her, pulling out her NavPad and activating the holographic function. She used the drone to map the area and projected it for them both to see.

"Here." Jennings pointed to a spot on the opposite side of the starport.

"Why there?"

Jennings traced the road that ran from the main port to the

cargo area. "If there's an emergency on this runway here"—Jennings pointed at the original location—"then they will move people along this road. The landing pad with the Schnell is far enough away to give us time, but close enough that the guards should respond to the alarm."

"Excellent," Nadia muttered. She made a note on the hologram to show exactly where Jennings had pointed. "Thank you, Sergeant. I can work with that."

The ship vibrated as another aircar flew over the Corsair. Jennings leaped up, grabbed an MP-17 from the chair next to her, and ran over to the controls. She hit the outside view button.

"What is it?" Nadia asked.

"Bravo and Charlie are back." Jennings triggered the door to open, revealing Lance Corporal Naki, PFC Owens, and eight freed slaves, along with Rashid and a fidgeting DeShawn.

"I brought friends," Naki said. He motioned for the blue-skinned Consortium natives to hustle onto the ship. One girl refused to leave his side as they climbed aboard.

"What's the plan here, Corporal?" she asked, gesturing to the former slaves.

Naki placed the girl in a seat, took off his coat, and covered her with it. He murmured something Jennings didn't hear, reached out to touch her face but then thought better of it and let his hand fall awkwardly to his side.

Hot air gusted through the open side hatch as the rest of the team finished loading.

"Sorry, Sergeant, no plan. I just couldn't stand by and let them remain behind. It wasn't right."

Nadia leaped up, standing in front of the marine. "Are you out of your mind? You would jeopardize this entire mission to rescue eight people? What if her body is discovered? What if they sound an alarm and lock down the planet? She glanced at her NavPad. "We still have twenty hours before *Interceptor* starts her run and—"

From the ladder leading up to the cockpit, Chief Boudreaux cleared her throat. "Sorry, ma'am, but we've got bigger problems than that."

Nadia spun around, a frown on her face.

"What happened, Chief?" Jennings asked. Partly to know and partly to get the commander off her marine.

"*Komodo* contacted me via tight beam while you were gone. A heavy cruiser came into orbit right after we disembarked. We're not going anywhere as long as they have the high ground."

Jennings gripped her pistol until her knuckles turned white. A Caliphate Navy ship wouldn't park in orbit unless they were planning on being there for a while.

"Which ship?" Rashid asked from the back. Every eye turned to him.

"Uh." Chief Boudreaux fumbled as she pulled out her NavPad and called up the data. She turned the Pad so he could see the screen. "I don't know how to say the name," she admitted.

"Oh no," Rashid said. "That is the *Glory of the Wind*. My old ship. I know why she's here." Rashid stumbled back. Cole jumped up and stopped the man from falling. Jennings took a step forward. DeShawn moved away to give them space.

"Your old ship?" Nadia asked. "As in you were Caliphate Navy?"

"Yes. I... I refused to bomb a civilian target from orbit. When the local imam found out, he had me flogged and imprisoned. My parents were executed, and my little sister... sold into slavery," he whispered.

"Man..." Cole said from beside him, one hand on his shoulder for support. "That sucks balls."

Rashid managed a small smile. "Yes. Yes, it did."

Movement caught Jennings' eye, and she instinctively turned, raising her off hand to ward off a blow.

DeShawn hurled a collapsible gurney at her from the storage next to the side hatch, forcing her back when it hit her upraised arm. He slid out the side, hitting the dirt landing pad and running as fast as he could, away from the port, toward the outskirts of town.

"Get him," Nadia shouted, pointing her hand at his fleeing back.

"We'll draw too much attention running through the port after him," Owens said.

"He's right," Jennings said.

"I don't think we need to worry about him," Naki said with a grim smile.

"Why is that, *Corporal?*" Nadia asked, her tone dropped several degrees.

"Because we killed his contact. If he goes to the authorities, he'll be implicated, and I'm pretty sure they'll just kill him."

Nadia raised her hand to argue, then stopped. "You're right. He's a survivor, he'll do anything to live. He would never jeopardize his own life like that."

"Ma'am, if it's all the same to you, we still need to figure out what to do about the heavy cruiser in orbit," Jennings said.

Boudreaux let out a laugh, leaning against the bulkhead and shaking her head. "There's nothing *to* do, Sergeant. It's a heavy cruiser. When *Interceptor* charges in, she'll either have to run or be destroyed. There's no tonnage comparison there. The best we can hope for is she runs, taking the cruiser with them. Otherwise, she'll blow *Komodo* out of orbit the second they think something is up."

CHAPTER TWENTY-THREE

Jacob watched the clock tick down on his MFD. He tapped the arm of the command chair in pace with the seconds.

They were ready. They had to be. The crew had drilled and practiced for the last twenty-four hours. He made sure they were well fed and rested. Once they began, there was no turning back.

Rashid's intel from the last time he visited the system would prove invaluable. However, having *Komodo* in orbit to relay the exact location of the Caliphate corvettes on patrol—plus the orbital defense and any other threats *Interceptor* would need to disable—was a stroke of genius.

He wished he'd thought of it.

The only downside to the plan, a significant downside, was going in blind. By the time *Komodo* could transmit to *Interceptor*, there would be no time to cancel. His ship would be committed to the fight, no matter how tough it ended up being. Jacob pushed up and took the two short steps to kneel beside Chief Suresh.

"Skipper?" she asked without looking up from her controls.

"Devi, I know we talked about this in our planning meeting, but what are our realistic options if we need to break off?"

She shifted in her seat to better see him. Devi Suresh's thick black hair was wound up in a bun so tight, he imagined it took a machine to do. Her dark skin crinkled around her eyes as she thought about her answer.

One of the things he appreciated about her—had from the moment he came on board—was her forthright attitude and willingness to tell him like it was. It made her a fantastic chief-of-the-boat. Essentially, she acted as his first officer, but for the enlisted. Someone they trusted, who they knew had the ear of the captain. Which she certainly did.

"Not good, sir," she whispered low enough for just him to hear. There was no need to alarm the crew. "If anything does go wrong, we're going to be at a low relative velocity... unless you want to do a flyby, but that has its own set of problems."

He'd considered it. However, if they missed anything, it would take time to turn around and come back. Rashid had mentioned the possibility of mass executions of the slaves, and that wasn't something Jacob wanted to risk. Unforeseen casualties were a part of any mission. It sucked, but there was no way around it. He wouldn't, though, turn that into a blatant disregard for life.

"If we do run into trouble, I trust *Interceptor*'s speed more than her brakes," he said with a grin.

"Aye, sir. Me too," she said.

Jacob patted her on the shoulder. Standing up, he made the rounds, starting with weapons and Lieutenant Fawkes. As his tactical officer, he was the most important piece in any battle strategy.

"Carter," he said by way of greeting, "how are the gun crews?"

"Lean and hungry, Skipper," he said.

"Good. Make sure they rotate out. Once we go, it's four hours and change to Medial. I don't want them sleeping in the turrets."

Carter gave him a thumbs-up. "Will do, sir."

"Good man." Jacob visited the rest of the stations before exiting the bridge. He had a tradition to maintain. While he couldn't always know when action would take place, in this instance, he did. He felt the pull to walk the deck and visit the different compartments manned by his crew. Let them see his face and know he was with them.

Nadia shook her head as Jennings laid out her plan to simultaneously take both the compound and the general slave quarters housed at the arena.

"We shouldn't split our forces," Nadia insisted.

Jennings pointed at the 3D holographic map of the sprawling city. In the center stood the arena: an eight-story coliseum with a twenty-story hotel attached to it. "Ma'am, the skipper said not to leave anyone behind. This is the best plan for that," Jennings said.

"If the alarm is sounded before we rescue Zahra and Elsa, then this is all for naught," Nadia said. She felt trapped in the Corsair, with four marines, an ex-Caliphate Navy captain, and eight freed slaves. Leaning against the wall, she folded her arms across her body and tried to relax.

"What do you mean?" Jennings asked.

"If we fail to rescue Elsa, our mission can only be a partial success. To that end, I can't sign off on any plan that doesn't make retrieving the princess and Zahra a priority."

Jennings frowned. "Ma'am, there are two things you need to come to terms with," Jennings said. She held out one finger.

"One, this is our area of expertise." She held out a second finger. "Two, we're the ones who are going to die if this all goes wrong. Let us plan and carry out the mission. Trust that we know what we're doing... ma'am."

Nadia wanted to look away, but she knew it was a battle of wills, and she refused to lose.

Jennings must have sensed her indomitable will. She sighed. "Okay, Commander, what do you suggest?"

"The minute the *Interceptor* signals us, we go in hard. The five of us hit the compound, using the Corsair as CAS. We go in, get the girls, get out. Shoot everyone in our way... just the way you like, right?" she asked.

Jennings shook her head. "Normally, yes. However, the captain wants us to rescue *everyone*." She turned to Rashid. "What are the chances your sister and the Imperial princess are the only ones being held there?"

"Zero to none," Rashid answered.

Jennings looked back at Nadia. "We can't go in fast and hard, as much as I would like to. We need to identify where everyone is in the compound, enter tactically, and take out Tangos as they present."

Nadia knew *tactically* meant with care. Two, maybe three people could enter the building without alerting the guards. Five? Not without risking undue attention.

"With the Raptor armor, you won't need surprise, though. You can mow down anyone who gets in the way," Nadia said, gesturing to the armor.

"That's true, ma'am," Naki said. He sat cross-legged on an ammo box. The blue-skinned girl he had rescued was glued to his side. Nadia wasn't sure what had happened, but he'd certainly made an impression on her.

Jennings sat back, staring intently at the map. She manipulated the controls, zooming in on the compound and rotating it clockwise to look at the building from all angles. "I can't believe I'm going to say this, but... what about a compromise?" she asked.

From the expressions on the other marines, Nadia suspected those words might never have escaped the sergeant's lips before. "What did you have in mind?"

On the hologram, an icon appeared, representing the drop ship. It moved from their current position to the mansion where both girls were held.

At first, Nadia had thought it dumb luck that both their primary packages were in one place. That was before Corporal Naki told her exactly who Rashid was. A captain in the Caliphate Navy committing treason was normally punishable by death. He must have had some high connections to avoid execution. Two high-profile women being held in the Caliph's personal residence on Medial wasn't a coincidence.

In Jenning's hologram, the dropship hovered as one figure leaped out; then it moved to the north and paused as two more jumped out. From there, it turned and headed for the city.

"You go in first, since stealth is your area," Jennings said. "You locate the barracks where they hold the house slaves. Once you know their location, you find the packages, lock them down, and we come in."

Jennings pushed a button on her NavPad, and the camera scrolled over to zoom in on the spaceport. "Bravo team and Rashid, who we'll designate Romeo-One, will hit the spaceport. My marines will create a diversion while Romeo takes the liner. Once secured, he flies it to—"

"You're assuming I can fly it?" Rashid said.

Jennings glanced at Boudreaux, handing the question to her.

"Can you?" the pilot asked.

Rashid rubbed the back of his neck. "I... yes. I think I can."

Jennings continued as if he hadn't objected. "Once secured, he takes it to the arena. Bravo"—Jennings pointed at Naki—"will fire the IPB. Then Bravo team assaults the arena. Charlie rendezvous with Alpha back at the compound. Romeo and Bravo use the liner to rescue as many people as we can."

Naki raised his hand. "We've only got the one bomb, Sarge. Are you sure you don't want to use it on the compound?"

"Negative. From what Rashid has told us, there's maybe five thousand people in those pens. If I know the skipper, he won't be happy unless we rescue as many as we can. That bomb should free them all at once and fry every power system for three square klicks."

"Wait," Rashid said. "What's an IPB?"

Naki replied like he was quoting from a manual: "Ionized Pulse Bomb Mark Two. It sends out an E3 pulse that shorts out power systems. Like an EMP, but much harder to shield against. Should work on the collars, lights, plasma rifles—you name it."

Jennings continued: "Once that's done, Bravo goes in, takes out any resistance—which should be light, but don't count on it—and loads people up."

She stood up, brushing her hands off on her legs. "The Corsair will rendezvous with *Interceptor*. Our alternate RP is *Komodo*. Rashid, you take the liner and make a run for the starlane exit vector. Wait for us there, but no more than twelve hours. I'll make sure you have the codes needed to get you into Alliance space."

Rashid frowned, shaking his head as his arms tensed. "I'm not leaving without my sister," Rashid said. "I'll wait for your dropship, and you can hand her off to me."

Jennings shook her head. "No. We need a second ship, and only you can fly it. There will be no time to stop and do a prisoner exchange. You're going to have to trust us... the way we've trusted you."

"I have a lifetime of learning that tells me the Alliance can't be trusted. I'm not leaving here without my sister. You want someone to fly the liner, use your pilot," he said, pointing at Boudreaux.

Before Jennings could answer, Nadia stepped in. "Rashid, you want your sister to live. We want our mission to succeed. I swear I'll get your sister out of there. However, you know the kind of weapons a heavy cruiser has. You know that if we stop to swap people, they will have a window to take us down. Trust us. Please," she said.

He looked like he would argue more... but deflated, falling back against the hull. "I've spent so long trying to get her. Don't let me fail," he said in a whisper.

"We won't," Nadia whispered back.

"Settled," Jennings said. "We'll leave the Mudcat here with her full jamming suite on remote. Boudreaux, once the shooting starts, activate it. Don't wait for the order."

Nadia went over the plan in her head, looking at it from different angles. Jennings was good. All their bases were covered. Even if the starliner didn't make it, Elsa, who was the priority, would. Plus, with Rashid out of the way... if a tough decision had to be made, she could make it without having to contend with him. Despite what she had just promised. Of course, this all assumed *Interceptor* would find a way to deal with the heavy cruiser.

"All right, Sergeant. You have my go-ahead," Nadia said.

Jennings looked around, making eye contact with every person in the room. "We have a plan. Let's execute it."

CHAPTER TWENTY-FOUR

Elsa collapsed in agony on her bed. Her muscles screamed for rest. Her feet hurt, and her hands were on fire.

Silently, she prayed for relief. Every day they made her run for hours in the hot sun until she dropped. Her muscle tone was almost completely gone. What was their plan? Hand her over to the Caliphate as a stick figure? Her ribs stuck through her skin already—she didn't have anything left to lose.

Except her mind.

They were trying to break her. Using hunger and exhaustion, they were trying to break her will. She laughed out loud as she realized that was their goal. They were in for a surprise if they thought the daughter of the Iron Empire would break from mere physical exertion. Not to mention, if Zahra confirmed the location of the control unit, then tonight was the night.

If.

None of the other servants spoke to her. She only picked up bits and pieces from the masters during her *training*. Elsa suppressed a shiver of fear at the thought. She'd seen with her own eyes, and heard with her ears, what the other female slaves were forced to endure. For some reason, Zahra was spared the worst of it, as was Elsa. No one would dare violate the Caliph's next wife.

Her fist clenched at the thought of subjecting herself to a lifetime of abuse at the hands of a monster. Not to mention facilitating the downfall of her father's empire. With a grunt, she pushed herself up to a sitting position. If they had to go tonight, she needed to be ready. The door slid open with a whoosh, and Zahra entered, holding a carafe of water.

Elsa struggled to lift her arms to accept the carafe, not bothering to use a cup.

"Are you okay?" Zahra asked.

After she gulped down all she could, she replied, "I'd be better if you told me that the control unit is in her quarters."

Zahra looked down, the ghost of a smile on her face. "It is," she whispered.

Elsa felt adrenaline surge through her. It was about time. If only she had more to eat, but "beggars can't be choosers," as her father would say.

She glanced up at the small window. Only a faint amount of light came through. "We need to go tonight, Zahra. Can you come back when the moon is up?" she asked.

"Yes, I'll see you then." The girl took the empty carafe and exited the room... and almost slammed into a guard who was taking up station outside Elsa's room.

"What are you doing here?" he asked.

"D... delivering water," Zahra said. The collars compelled an answer from the wearers. To some degree, it compelled the truth, but the truth could be flexible, and the longer she wore the disgusting device, the more she figured out how to circumvent it.

"Go on then," the guard said.

Elsa frowned when she saw the uniformed guard. It wasn't

just any uniform, but that of the Caliphate infantry. He also wasn't wearing a collar. In the past, they hadn't stationed a guard anywhere near her. Why now? With the collars, there was no need for guards. As far as she knew, she would do anything demanded by an authorized user. She racked her brain, trying to remember if she'd let anything slip about their escape. She was sure she hadn't. They couldn't know.

Something else was going on, then. Groaning, Elsa struggled to her feet. Weeks had gone by since she last was able to climb up to the window. Her once strong arms were reduced to spindles.

Elsa focused her mind, drawing on her inner reserve and taking several deep breaths. She needed to see what was going on outside. It was the only way to know if they could really escape. For Zahra's sake, they had to.

Nadia held onto the grab bar installed next to the sliding hatch of the Corsair. The dropship flew mere meters above the desert floor. Hot air circulated through the open hatchway keeping the cooling circuitry in her suit working over time.

"You good on weapons, Commander?" Jennings asked over the radio. The four marines were in their Raptor powered armor, for all the world looking like four-meter-tall, bipedal dinosaurs carrying rapid-fire coilguns mounted on articulating arms.

"Yes. I don't need much," she said, pointing to her gun belt. She carried her old-school, five-point-seven-millimeter slug thrower with integrated silencer. Powerful enough to pierce soft body armor, but quiet enough that she could kill stealthily. There wasn't anything she could carry that would penetrate hardened armor. Not anything that was quiet, anyway.

"Coming up on Alpha drop," Boudreaux said over the radio.

Nadia reached up and pulled her blackout suit hood over her head. Light shimmered and swirled around her as she vanished, replaced with an odd visual distortion as the Ruthenium nanites blended her suit into the background. Like the Raptors' adaptive camouflage, the blackout suit worked best if she wasn't moving.

"Drop," Boudreaux said. As she spoke, the Corsair tilted up, coming to a near halt only a meter above the ground, stirring up dust devils of sand and bushes.

Nadia leapt out, hitting the desert and tucking into a roll. She stayed down as the Corsair's plasma turbines roared, lifting the ship off into the distance.

Nadia watched until it was gone, then slipped goggles over her eyes, allowing her to use her NavPad's mapping function to navigate as well as see in the dark. A light blinked showing her Point Hotel, the compound.

Once oriented, she took off in a sprint. If she managed her breathing, keeping it even and controlled, it would take her less than five minutes to run to the compound a klick away.

Nadia trusted the marines, trusted they would do their job, but that heavy cruiser orbiting above them nagged at her. There was nothing to be done about it, not by her. She had a lot of tricks in her repertoire, but none of them involved shooting a ship out of orbit.

Her NavPad blinked, warning her of the proximity to her target, and she skidded to a halt, ending on a knee at the base of a small hill. Staying low to avoid detection, she climbed up to the crest.

The compound spread out below her, butting up against a natural cave system where an underwater river disgorged, feeding the house.

To the west was an exercise field with a track. To the east lay a pool connected to the aqueduct. Nadia cocked her head to the side, trying to change her perspective. Something about the compound didn't feel right.

There were walls everywhere. Every section had a wall and limited entrances. It wouldn't provide an obstacle for the Raptors, but it made her job much harder. "Bravo-Two-Five-Actual, India-One in place," she whispered using her call sign. It was the only communications she would have with the marines until they joined her. By then, the shooting would have started, and COMSEC would allow more communications.

The desert ground proved a challenge to her footing as she worked her way down, placing each step with care. The blackout suit prevented any of the possible array of electronic security systems from detecting her—she was invisible—but if she slipped or disturbed a rock, it could be seen and heard.

She reached the base of the three-meter exterior wall and froze, taking a moment to recover her breath and listen for any sounds. There were no second chances here; if she failed to rescue the princess, that would kill any chance of the Empire coming into the eventual conflict on the side of the Alliance.

Once she was ready, Nadia leapt as high as she could. Her hand gripped the edge of the wall, and she pulled herself up with ease. The other side held a small garden with a path around a pond. She doubted there were any goldfish in the pond—the weather of Medial wasn't conducive to life from the outside.

She jumped down, making the barest whisper of a crunch as her sound-absorbing boots hit the gravel. When she was sure no one was coming, she gingerly moved to the entrance.

Nadia held up her special ONI NavPad, scanning the door. While the faux-sandstone construction made them look ancient, they were actually quite advanced, including hidden sensors that read biometric data. After a moment, the NavPad tricked the locks, and the doors opened.

The inside led to a comfortable study of some kind. The NavPad sent out an ultrasonic pulse that bounced its way around the house, creating a map Nadia could see on her HUD.

It took several undetectable pulses for the NavPad to show her a completed map. There was no key, no way of knowing what each room was, but she could guess based on the size, layout, and number of occupants.

She examined the map until she decided on a direction. On the second floor, there was a row of small rooms, all of them empty except for one. The hall itself had a single person standing outside the room, which made Nadia think it was a guard.

The radio in her ear squawked twice, letting her know the marines were in position. Every second she delayed was a second she or the marines could be discovered. It was time to go.

Nadia made it to the south hallway, ever so slowly peeking her head around the corner. A Caliphate soldier stood outside the door she wanted. He wore the uniform of the Immortals—elite, ship-based soldiers who were usually attached to important missions or people. The same cadre who had boarded *Dagger*, murdered her crew, and tortured her.

Nadia placed one hand on the wall, pushing against it, desperately trying to suppress the memory of what the Immortals had done to her. Her chest hurt, limbs growing heavy while her eyes burned, making it difficult to see.

Stop it. Stop it. Stop it! she screamed at herself. What they did to her wasn't her fault.

It's not my fault, she recited.

That thought steeled her resolve. Her eyes stopped burning, and she could breathe again. She pushed off the wall, moving silently toward her target. Even silenced, she couldn't risk the gun.

Raqib (Sergeant) Muhunnad Salib stifled a yawn. He hated guard duty. Every soldier hated guard duty. Standing alone for hours on end, expected to keep alert even though he was on a planet the Caliphate controlled. It wasn't like the slaves could start trouble, much less hurt him.

His commander met with the Caliph's local *wife*. She was the mistress of the compound and spoke for the Caliph when he wasn't there. Salib knew the package behind the door was valuable, and the secret VIP the ship carried was there on official business. None of that knowledge helped him stay alert through guard duty.

Pressure wrapped around his throat. Salib's eyes went wide as he tried to breathe, but he couldn't open his esophagus to do so. He flailed at his neck, only to discover an arm wrapped around his vital points. He hit, scratched, and desperately tried to find some leverage. There just wasn't enough time. His vision faded, turning red, then black, until finally—

Nadia held the man with her cybernetic arm hooked around his neck. The sudden crack startled her when it broke, and his body went limp. She braced him on her hip and let him slide down her to the ground. Her NavPad showed no pulse, no breathing. He was dead.

She used the NavPad on the door. It slid open, revealing the sleeping form of Princess Elsa Faust, daughter of the Iron Throne.

Oh, thank God, she thought. There was always the chance her intel was wrong, and she had *really* needed it to be right.

Nadia hooked her hands under the dead man's arms and hauled the body through the door. He weighed close to a hundred kilos, and it took an effort to drag him out of sight.

"Who's there?" Elsa asked, her soprano filling the room.

Nadia punched the deactivation on her NavPad, turning the camouflage of her blackout suit off. Elsa gasped, pushing herself away until her back was against the wall in the small room.

Nadia pulled her hood off, then held her hands up. "It's okay. I'm here to rescue you. I'm Alliance ONI. I've got marines outside and—"

Elsa's eyes went wide with alarm. She shook her head, muttering, "No-no-no."

Nadia moved forward, reassuring the girl with open hands. To her surprise, Elsa didn't seem afraid of her, but there was something else.

"It's okay." Nadia pulled her mask down and goggles up to fully expose her face. She needed the princess to trust her, and seeing her face would go a long way to doing that.

Elsa shook her head. "You don't understand," she said, pointing to the collar. "They'll kill me."

Nadia understood all too well. "I can remove it," she said, holding up her NavPad.

"This collar is different. If you try to remove it, I will be killed."

For a moment, Nadia entertained the idea that Elsa had succumbed to some kind of brainwashing, but no, she wasn't trying to stop her escape—just do it correctly.

"Do you know where I need to go to deactivate it?" Nadia asked. She pulled her mask and hood back on; she was going to have to go searching.

"No—but Zahra does. She's supposed to come here soon. We were planning on escaping tonight."

Nadia reeled at the luck fate had given her. "You know Zahra?" she asked.

Elsa nodded. "She's a young girl who's getting sold off to someone tomorrow. It's tonight or never for her."

Nadia went over her options. She could wait for Zahra to show, or go blindly searching for a device she had no idea how to find. "Okay, we'll wait here for a few minutes," she said.

Desert turned to city underneath the Corsair. Chief Boudreaux held their flight ceiling below a hundred meters to avoid detection. At her current altitude, conventional radar and lidar wouldn't be able to distinguish her from the background. However, satellites looking down would pick her up easily. There wasn't a lot she could do about it other than fly fast.

"Thirty seconds," she said over the comms.

The blue-skinned girl, Sakura, clung to Naki's side, refusing to let go. He'd managed to get her to just stand or sit next to him while he and Owens finished prepping the Raptor suits and loading the IPB. She didn't seem skittish at all around the Raptor suit, which impressed him; the suits were downright intimidating. With the Corsair about to hover over their target, though, he needed to climb in.

"Sakura—"

"*Hai*," she said.

"No. I mean..." He didn't speak Consortium standard, and from what he knew, it was a mix of old-Earth Asian dialects. *I need to invest in some language skills,* he thought. He'd already decided to stay in the Marine Corps for life. Learning some languages other than his own native and Standard couldn't hurt.

"I have to go," he said, pointing in the suit. "You have to stay here." He pointed at the row of seats the other freed prisoners occupied.

She shook her head, clasping his newly donned Alliance Marine combat uniform. It ripped at his heart what these poor people had endured, what Sakura had. He wanted to help them beyond just rescue, but he still had a mission to accomplish. Walking her over to the seats, he sat her down and knelt in front of her.

"I have to go save more people," he said. He took her hands and held them together.

She shook her head, saying something he didn't understand, but he picked up the gist of *"don't go."*

He smiled softly at her. "It's okay. I'll be back." She pulled him into a fierce hug, which he returned. After a long moment, he disentangled himself and turned and climbed into his Raptor. Owens already waited in his own Raptor and gave Naki a thumbs-up.

"Ten seconds," Boudreaux said over the comms.

Naki finished clamping himself in. With the flick of his thumb, the Raptor activated. The canopy disappeared, giving him a full one-eighty view. Green lights flashed across his field of view, each system signaling its status. He manually checked the connection to the Mudcat, making sure he could activate the jamming on a moment's notice.

"Bravo ready," he said.

"Charlie ready," Owens said.

He stomped over to the side door, using the Raptor's built-in controls to remotely activate it. The door hummed open, revealing the city as it flashed by underneath.

"Romeo-One, in position?" he asked.

"Ready to go," Rashid said.

Naki checked the map of the area on his HUD. A blinking yellow dot showed where Rashid was, opposite the liner in a culvert running parallel to the starliner.

"Roger. Starting our diversion." Naki leaped out of the dropship, falling the twenty meters to the hard concrete below. He hit the ground with a crunch. Owens landed a few seconds after him, leaving a series of spider-webbed cracks.

"Bravo team, weapons hot."

Owens swung his five-millimeter coilgun over to a row of parked, long-range aircars and opened fire. Light flashed, not from the coils firing, but from the burning air as the rounds screamed at their targets.

The effect was as dramatic as it was immediate. A line of explosions ripped through the air, sending smoke and fire leaping up into the sky.

Naki clicked the selector switch on his grenades to *thermite* before launching them at a cluster of hangars. A siren wailed over the explosions and raging fire. "I think we diverted them, Bravo," Owens said.

"Roger that. Activate camo and go stealth," Naki ordered. Active camouflage rendered the suits difficult to detect. It required tremendous amounts of power to baffle thermal output, but they only needed it for a few minutes as they exited the airfield, heading for the arena.

Once he was sure security forces were responding, he activated the link to the Mudcat and flooded the area with ECM. They were blind and burning; time to start the real carnage.

CHAPTER TWENTY-FIVE

Nadia perked up as footsteps echoed down the hall. The door to Elsa's chambers opened. Her gun went up, pointing right between the young girl's eyes.

Elsa leaped forward, grabbing Zahra and pulling her into the room before she could scream.

"Zahra?" Nadia asked.

Elsa nodded. "Zahra, this is a friend who's going to help us escape," she said.

The young girl's eyes went wide at the dead guard on the floor, his face discolored from asphyxiation.

"Who are you?" Zahra asked.

Elsa told her.

"I just need to know where the device is, and I can go deactivate it," Nadia added.

"I think it's in Abla's suite."

Nadia examined the map her device had built of the compound. There were three rooms on the second floor that could be master suites; which one was this Abla's? If she went up there blind, it would increase the likelihood of being discovered.

Vibrations filled the walls as they shook. A thunderous sound echoed overhead, rising to a crescendo, then falling.

"What's that?" Zahra said. Her eyes going wide with fear.

"An explosion?" Elsa asked

Nadia nodded. Ejecting the mag from the pistol, she jammed a fresh one home, but careful not to let either of the girls see that it was empty. "You're not the only reason we're here. We're out of time. Stay here," she said. Nadia flipped her pistol around and held it out to Elsa, butt first.

She shook her head. "I would love to, but I can't hurt anyone here, and it would be too easy for them to order me to shoot you," she said.

That answered the question of whether the woman was brainwashed or not. She ejected the empty mag and put a full one in.

"A trick?" Elsa asked.

"A test," Nadia replied. She saw approval in the princess' eyes. Nadia racked the slide, holstered the pistol, then activated her camo and vanished.

Zahra gasped. From her point of view, the door opened itself.

Nadia stuck her head out, made sure it was clear, then moved. Light stepping, she headed for the stairs. She heard people moving about upstairs. Someone yelled, and more doors whooshed open.

Stopping at the bottom of the stairs, she made sure no one was coming down. Once clear, she double-timed it up, taking them as fast as she could. On the second floor, she stepped into the hallway and froze. Two men wearing Immortals uniforms ran right by her. Nadia frowned.

Whoever Rashid's enemy was, he had enough clout to warrant elite guards. Perhaps it was a twofer; they were here to get Zahra for the ship *and* to deliver the princess to the Caliph.

The door at the end of the hall opened, revealing a man in Caliphate Navy pants but with his hairy chest bare. Beyond him, two girls were kneeling on the floor, the red stripes on their backs matching the whip in the man's hands.

Nadia's pulse pounded in her ears. Her vision narrowed, and for a moment she was back on her ship, wearing the collar.

She ran down the hall, pistol out and firing. The two Immortals dropped, heads perforated. The man reacted without hesitation, leaping behind the wall next to the door.

Nadia fired until the pistol clicked empty, forcing the man to keep his head down while she tucked and rolled through the doorway.

He swung the whip where her head would have been, missing her by a meter. Nadia leaped up and hit him with all the strength her cybernetic arm gave her.

The crack of his jaw filled the room. He flew back, slamming into the wall. She was on him before he hit the floor. Pummeling his head and face.

Her last blow cracked his skull, ending his life. Movement caught her eye, and she dove as a man she hadn't seen stepped out of the shadows and scrambled for his sidearm hanging on the arm of the chair against the wall.

In one swift movement she dropped the empty mag in her pistol and loaded another one. He had one hand on his gun when she fired.

The first round shattered his shoulder, the second took him in the lower back, followed by the third and fourth. He tried to scream, but his mangled jaw and broken face couldn't form the sounds. Instead, he sank to the carpeted floor, dead.

Nadia didn't move, heaving breaths as the world vanished around her. She knew she needed to move, but her mind refused to do so.

"India, this is Two-Five-Alpha. The compound is going nuts. Are we go?" Jennings asked over the radio.

The sudden voice in Nadia's ear snapped her out of her daze. "Negative, Alpha. Wait one," she said.

With her wits back about her, she gave one look to the girls, who were frozen like mannequins. She would come back for them once the collars were off. She didn't bother with hiding the bodies when there were bullet holes in the wall and blood splashed around like a macabre painting.

There were only two rooms left. She keyed the next door. It opened into an opulent bedroom. A fat, older woman stood in front of an open cabinet. A complex electronic device with multiple controls lay within.

"Don't move," Nadia said.

The woman looked in her direction, squinting, as she couldn't make out who spoke.

Nadia raised the pistol, deactivating her camo at the same time.

"Who are you?" the woman asked.

Nadia jerked the pistol to the side, indicating what she should do.

The woman looked at the pistol, then back to her panel. Nadia sensed what she was about to do and acted.

A single five-point-seven-millimeter chemically powered projectile took Abla in the head, puncturing her skull and killing her instantly.

Nadia pulled her NavPad out and scanned the panel. It was some kind of master control—exactly what Elsa and Zahra had said. Several fail-safes and coded traps appeared on her screen as the ONI-issued Pad hacked its way into the computer.

After a moment, it beeped, and the lights on the panel went dark. A second later, a girl's scream split the night as the collars were deactivated.

"Two-Five-Alpha, India. Go loud. I say again, go loud."

———

Rashid watched from the shadows as the guards ran away toward the explosions and fires in the distance. He waited five more seconds before moving in. The fence yielded to the laser cutter, splitting open in a flash of red light. Running as fast as he could, but careful to keep the liner between him and the tower, he crossed the field.

The hatch opened without issue. Inside, he followed the NavPad the spy gave him. She hadn't told him she was a spy, but Rashid had known his fair share of ISB agents; they all had a look and manner to them. He believed she had every intention of trying to save his sister, but she was a spy.

He had his own plan.

———

Jacob pulled on his ELS helmet. He hated the dang thing, but they were approaching the point where they would receive the tight beam from *Komodo*. If anything went wrong, he wanted to be combat ready.

Bosun Sandoval's voice rang out over the comms. "All hands, Condition Zulu, battle stations. Prepare to drain the can!" He repeated his warning several times. The computer showed anyone who didn't have their helmet on, but on the off chance of error, it made sense to broadcast it.

Jacob split his MFD display into four screens. One showed the farthest scan resolution of everything directly in front of *Interceptor*. The second displayed his velocity, acceleration, and current heading. His third screen mirrored the helm. The final screen showed Lieutenant Yuki. They were in constant contact. Everything he saw and heard, she did as well.

"Roy, all hands, please," Jacob said.

"Aye, aye, sir. All hands." Hössbacher pushed a series of command keys, then pointed at Jacob.

Jacob took a deep breath, letting the moment wash over him. This was it. The moment they had worked for since they had left Alexandria.

"Crew of the *Interceptor*. Over the next two hours, we are going to engage in the fight of our lives. We have the intelligence, we have the initiative, and we have the heart. Even so, some of us might not make it. But know this... we are fighting back. Not for revenge, nor out of pride or arrogance. We are fighting back to show the Caliphate we will not go quietly into the night. We will not roll over and die. If they want to take us, they are going to pay for it. That's why we're here. Our battle may not prevent the larger conflict. However, if, by our actions here, we can delay that war, we can give the Alliance, our homes, and our families a fighting chance."

Jacob let that hang for a moment. His chest swelled and tightened as he continued speaking. "I'm proud to be your captain. I'm proud to have the best crew in the entire Alliance. No officer in the navy could ask for more."

He stopped to look up at his bridge crew, taking a moment to make eye contact with each one. They had to know how much he valued them.

"As a child, my mother spoke to me of duty, honor, and courage. Until I came aboard *Interceptor*, those were mere words. You, all of you, have taught me what these words mean.

"I read a poem once, written long ago, long before humanity even had space flight.

> To every man upon this earth
> Death cometh soon or late.
> And how can man die better
> Than facing fearful odds,
> For the ashes of his fathers,
> And the temples of his Gods.

"I think it was true when it was written, and it's true today, here, a thousand light-years from home. If we must die this day, then we will do so defending the homes of our families and the beliefs of our people."

Every word he spoke was the truth. He had spent his life preparing for this moment. Living by the words *duty, honor, courage.* If they were to die this day, they would do so with the greatest of company, each other.

"You know your jobs. Trust your training. Look out for one another. We will be victorious. Captain out."

He leaned back, rubbing his gloved palms on the arms of his chair, hoping he'd said the right things.

"Skipper," Yuki said in a whisper, "that was pretty good."

He smiled down at her. "Thanks, Kim. I meant it."

"Aye, sir. That's why it was good."

CHAPTER TWENTY-SIX

Sergeant Allison Jennings skipped her Raptor suit along the desert floor, reaching a hundred kph. The heavy war-machines shook the ground as they hit every ten meters. Private Cole's own suit mirrored alongside her.

"Delta, weapons hot," she ordered.

Cole replied, "Roger that, Alpha. Weapons hot."

The two armored suits were a hundred meters apart when they came upon the compound. The sky beyond glowed orange with the spaceport fire. On her HUD, Jennings found Charlie-One-One circling in behind them, ready to extract.

"Alpha, contact front," Cole shouted.

A Caliphate IFV hovered in front of the compound. A single-barreled plasma turret rotated on the top, firing green bolts Jennings' way.

Jennings jerked her suit to the side as the plasma bolts ripped through the air she'd occupied a second before. Her onboard computer tracked back the fire, and she squeezed the trigger without hesitation.

The cannon spun, spouting flame as five-millimeter rounds screamed through the air at hypervelocity.

Her projectiles struck home, ripping through the thin-skinned vehicle. It rocked to the side, then exploded in a shower of fire and shrapnel.

"Tango down," she said.

"Roger," Cole replied. "Three Tangos, second level, small arms."

Jennings swiveled her armor as smaller green bolts hit her. The handheld plasma weapons weren't capable of penetrating her armor, but luck could always swing their way.

"Concussion grenade," she said. The suit clunked as the grenade launcher rotated, changing the load. She could annihilate them with sustained coilgun fire, but she didn't want to risk anyone inside the building.

Once the grenade blinked green, she touched the firing stud. A pop and a moment later the five kilograms of explosives detonated above the three men firing at her.

She leaped the Raptor off the cliff side, half sliding, half running down the incline before she smashed through the barrier surrounding the compound, shattering the faux sandstone in an explosion of debris.

"India-One, Two-Five-Alpha. Status?" she said.

No response from Commander Dagher.

"Alpha, I'm picking up aircraft coming our way," Cole said.

"Weapons free," Jennings said. Kneeling her suit, she used the clawlike hand to smash the interior wall. "India-One, this is Two-Five-Alpha. Come in?"

"Alpha, the situation has evolved. We need to hold the compound for as long as possible."

"Say again, India? Hold the compound?" Jennings asked.

"Roger. India out."

Jennings suppressed a curse. This was supposed to be in and out; they didn't have the force to hold a position for long.

Damn spies.

Naki leaped through the low city buildings, beelining for the arena. His display showed Owens a hundred meters to the west, on a mirror approach. His radio crackled to life, startling him.

"It's awful quiet," Owens said.

"If you were a local, would you come out and face us?" Naki asked.

"Hell no. Not even if I were drunk," Owens said.

Two klicks from the coliseum and he could go up and become an easier target for long-range ordnance, or stay low and risk an easy ambush in the high canyons of the city.

"Owens, go weapons hot."

"Say again, weapons hot?" Owens asked.

"Yes. I don't like the idea of civilian casualties any more than you do, but we're in the sticks here. We might only have a second to respond. Our safeties might cost us our lives. Understood? All targets are valid targets. Over."

Naki clenched his fists for a moment, using an old trick to loosen up his hands. It didn't help. All he could imagine was the worst case; if they were in a firefight, surrounded by these buildings... hundreds—maybe thousands—of civilians could die. Raptor suits could be outfitted for different missions, but on small ships like *Interceptor,* there wasn't the space to carry all options. Instead, they were given the RPT-25 Combat, General Purpose.

"Two-Five-Bravo, this is Alpha. Sitrep?"

Naki slowed the Raptor down to a trot as he passed a pyramid-shaped building. "Alpha, Bravo. We're zero-five mikes from target. Over."

"We've got a situation here. I need you to—"

The shrill whine of air-to-surface missiles filled the air. By reflex, Naki hit the jump jets. Raptors couldn't fly, but they could jump forty meters straight up.

"Contact front," Owens said. His calm tone was at odds with the adrenaline pumping into Naki's veins. However, the marines drilled constantly to keep their cool in combat.

Twin contrails sliced through the air from the missiles, striking the building and imploding the front façade. Naki swiveled his cannon around and fired a long burst. Five-millimeter rounds stitched a line through an aircraft. The engine exploded, it lost altitude, and slammed into a building.

Green bolts flashed around him as ionized plasma rifles fired from an elevated position. His computer tagged the source, and he spun, firing a pair of HE grenades into a loft three stories up. There was no time to watch the results of the twin explosions.

"Charlie, stay moving. If they know we're here—"

A roar blasted through the air as two Dhib assault dropships burned through the atmosphere, a trail of fire behind them.

"Alpha, we're in trouble here. Over," Naki called out.

CHAPTER TWENTY-SEVEN

Interceptor decelerated as they approached Medial's primary moon. They wouldn't stop, but they also couldn't blow by at a thousand KPS. Jacob had calculated their speed to give them enough time to fire each turret twice.

"Sir," Hössbacher said, "tight beam message from *Komodo*. Relaying to your screen."

"We're still an hour out. Why send it now?" he asked.

"Unknown, sir. It's brief and holds targeting info for Lieutenant Fawkes, sir."

Jacob leaned forward. The audio would come through his suit, but the picture was on the MFD.

"Receiving targeting information," Lieutenant Fawkes reported.

Lieutenant West appeared on-screen with a sour expression. "Sir, we're risking sending you this early due to a new arrival. PO Oliv tells me if you shut the gravcoil down immediately, you can sail past Medial undetected. We'll do our best to get out of the system and rendezvous with you at RP Foxtrot-One-Three. West out."

They were still far enough out that any signal he replied with would be unduly risky.

"Anyone know what he's talking about?" Jacob asked.

"I'm afraid I do, Skipper. A moment if you will," Fawkes said.

Jacob unbuckled his harness and made his way to tactical. Leaning over, he froze, hand going tight on the back of Fawkes' chair. His chest felt like it was going to collapse. *No. God, no. It's not fair,* he thought.

There was no standard definition of a destroyer or cruiser in the navies of the galaxy. They were more a distinction of armor, firepower, and the role they played. Small, maneuverable ships like *Interceptor* were destroyers. Larger ships could have multiple roles, like the light cruiser Jacob had served on previously. They were often used as support ships during massive fleet engagements. In those battles, destroyers and light cruisers focused on defense. Light cruisers could also patrol and perform similar deployments to destroyers, but since they weren't as agile, they were most often used in more populated systems.

Then there were the heavy cruisers. Absolute battlewagons, designed to pummel the enemy with an array of weapons. More maneuverable than a battleship, but almost as heavily armed and armored. Fighting a heavy cruiser with a destroyer was suicide.

That fact tormented Jacob. There was no mistaking the Caliphate heavy cruiser orbiting Medial.

Jacob took a deep breath. His heart ached at the sight of that monster. He turned away from Carter, taking up position behind his chair and grasping the leather back with both hands, squeezing as hard as he could.

His ground team would have already started their assault. The whole idea was for the rescue to be underway when *Inter-*

ceptor rolled in and started blasting the opposition. The corvettes would be forced to engage her at point-blank range, which favored the fast, agile destroyer.

But a heavy cruiser? There was no fighting it. Even if *Interceptor* survived to close the range, even with a broadside hit with the Long Nine, the most they could hope for was a disabling shot.

"Kim, I..." he said over their private channel.

She looked up from her own tactical display, a mirror of Fawkes. Her hollow eyes and tight jawline told him what he already knew to be true.

If *Interceptor* attempted to engage the cruiser, his ship would be destroyed. If she went silent, coasted along, then maybe they would make it—but the ground team would be outnumbered. There would be nowhere for them to go. The best they could hope for would be death. Having witnessed the atrocities the Caliphate committed, no one would want to be their prisoner.

As captain of an Alliance ship, he was expected to make the tough calls. Sometimes that meant sending spacers into situations where they could die. He had done it before. He might do it again. Hope, though, was the best weapon in a captain's arsenal. If he could give his people hope, then they might just achieve some kind of victory.

With a heavy cruiser ready to obliterate *Interceptor*—where could he find hope? They had fought larger ships before, but there had been mitigating circumstances. The stolen Consortium frigate's crew were pirates; they had no idea how to use their warship properly. A heavy cruiser, staffed by experienced spacers, wouldn't have such a weakness.

If he coasted, saved his ship, then his ground forces were wide open to attack from above. It wasn't just her guns, either. Heavy cruisers carried entire companies of ground soldiers.

Even with the Raptor suits, his *four* marines couldn't hope to defeat over a hundred Caliphate regulars.

"I don't know, Skipper, I... I just don't know," Kim said. The look on her face mirrored his own.

He gave her a choppy nod through tight muscles. Their plan relied on timing and surprise. Timing and surprise.

An idea came to him. Maybe it would work, just maybe. "Chief Suresh..." Jacob closed his eyes, begging God for help, and for forgiveness if he were wrong. "Kill the gravcoil."

"Two-Five-Alpha, Charlie-One-One. Hostile air force is—" Boudreaux cut out.

"One-One, how copy?" Jennings said.

More static filled her ear.

"Delta, what do you see?" she asked Cole, who maintained overwatch outside.

"Charlie-One-One is turning and burning with a couple of dropships, Alpha. They're moving pretty fast—they have to be short-range attack craft."

Everything was going to hell. Jennings charged through the rubble of the wall to reach the outside, then back up the hill.

Alarms wailed from EM beams hitting her suit. She spun around, following the yellow pip that told her where they came from. Down the hill, toward the city, a pair of four-wheeled vehicles with manned turrets climbed the road.

Jennings brought her chain gun down until the crosshairs wavered over the lead four-wheeler. She squeezed the trigger twice, sending two bursts of three rounds into the first one. It exploded a half second before she fired the third burst, which obliterated the second vehicle.

"All teams, I say again, all teams, this is Two-Five-Alpha, go loud. We are blown. I say again, go loud."

She didn't have time to tell every member of the ground party to use whatever means required to defend themselves. The "go loud" order would have to do.

"Alpha," Cole said, "I've got two Dhib-class dropships coming down over the city and heading in our direction. One minute out."

Jennings crested the hill, setting her Raptor to brace and turning her EW suite to full. Electromagnetic noise filled the airwaves, hopefully buying them some time to deal with the incoming aircraft.

"Roger, Delta, I see them. Fire at will."

Both Raptor suits opened up, filling the air with five-millimeter rounds as they tried to nail the fast-movers.

"Hang on down there," Boudreaux yelled into her mic. She couldn't spare any more thought to warning the eight passengers strapped into their chairs. Pulling the stick hard up and goosing the throttle, she led the two attack craft into a loop.

They were more maneuverable than her and built for air-to-air combat, where her dropship was not. The computer screamed a warning, and she did the only thing she could, twisting the stick to send the Corsair into a corkscrew.

Green plasma rounds flashed by the cockpit.

"Come on, baby," she muttered as she pulled hard on the stick, coming out of the spin in a random direction. She looked up through the canopy to see where the enemy was; they guessed wrong and shot past her.

"I can do something you can't do," she said. Because of her sudden change in direction, her velocity bled off. Throwing the variable switch, her wings rotated until the engines pointed down.

In the blink of an eye, she came to a full hover. Using her foot pedals, she spun the ship on her central access, opening fire with the multi-barrel ten-millimeter chain gun mounted under her nose.

Tungsten balls roared out of the barrel at fifteen hundred meters per second, stitching a line across the engines of the first craft. It shook, dipped, then broke apart like a cracker in a child's hand, disintegrating in midair.

She lost track of the second vehicle. The Corsair rocked as plasma struck her starboard engine. Alarms wailed in her ear as the dropship faltered.

"Mayday, Mayday, this is Charlie-One-One. We're hit. I've lost the starboard engine."

She pushed the nose down, letting the automatics deal with the fire while she rotated the engines back to forward propulsion. She could still fly with one engine—the military loved its redundancy—but she was slow and unable to maneuver.

CHAPTER TWENTY-EIGHT

Naki leaped through a faux-sandstone wall, shattering the molded concrete and falling on his side.

The explosion behind him blasted through the hole, peppering his suit with shrapnel and debris.

"Owens, how many?" he asked over their encrypted radio. He struggled back to his feet, taking a moment to make sure his armor wasn't breached.

"Fifty? How the hell should I know? They're lighting the street up like it's a damn fireworks show." Owens returned fire from his position ten meters behind Naki.

Another explosion rocked the building around him. It wasn't going well. Under this kind of fire, they couldn't rescue the hostages—or bring in the starliner to pick them up. A single shoulder-mounted rocket would obliterate the civilian ship.

"We need air cover," he said. "Charlie-One-One, Two-Five-Bravo. We need CAS ASAP."

"Negative, Two-Five-Bravo." Boudreaux sounded distracted as she answered.

Naki took aim with his grenade launcher and fired a smoke barrage that concealed him physically and thermally. The second the cloud shielded him, he charged out of the building. The concrete shattered under his clawed feet as the suit accelerated to fifty kph.

A parking garage for air and ground cars lay at the end of the street. He triggered his jump jets, launching into the sky in an arc. His HUD showed multiple soldiers running out of the buildings behind him, firing their plasma rifles through the cloud of smoke at his former position.

"Screw this," Naki muttered. He hit the top floor of the garage, skidded to a halt, then jerked back the way he came. He triggered the full auto with his thumb. At the ledge, he aimed his cannon at the mass of soldiers and pulled the trigger.

Nano-hardened tungsten balls blasted through flesh and bone, tearing up the street behind them. In a second, a dozen men lay dead on the ground. The rest scattered, running back to the buildings.

Owens followed up with a cluster of grenades. Explosions rippled down the street, blasting soldiers to pieces and shattering the street.

Overhead, the two dropships Owens had spotted roared past, shooting toward the hilltop compound.

"What's going on there that they just ignored us?" Owens asked.

"I have no idea, but it gives us a minute. Let's take advantage of it."

The two Raptor suits took off toward their intended target.

―――

For a seized vessel, the Schnell was in remarkably good shape. Rashid had expected to find it stripped for parts, but they hadn't touched it. Perhaps they were intending to offer it as a gift, along with the princess.

Regardless, it made his job easier. All the doors were open, and the bridge was easy enough to find. It was the type that rested on the central keel, with giant bay displays that showed the front of the ship. Certainly not a military-built ship, it was clearly designed to impress the passengers.

The bridge lit up, and the consoles came to life as the computer detected his presence. Rashid pulled out the data stick Commander Dagher had provided for him to access the encrypted computers. Lights blinked on the device, and within sixty seconds, the computers granted him full access. He moved to the pilot's seat and took over the station. The controls were different from what he was used to.

The first thing he needed to do was to seal the ship. Which he couldn't do from where he sat. He looked around, locating the internal security station.

"Don't move," a man said. An older man in a spaceport security uniform held a plasma pistol pointed right at him. Rashid raised his hands immediately. He should have known the distraction wouldn't pull everyone. Just his bad luck.

"Who are you? What are you doing here?" the security guard asked.

Rashid ran through a couple of options and decided on a bluff. "I'm securing the ship for Captain Bitar of the *Divine Wind*," Rashid said. He gambled that his former first officer had inherited command of the ship and was the one coming to collect his sister for revenge.

The guard lowered his weapon. "Sorry. I wasn't told anyone in the navy was coming. With the firefight going, I—"

Rashid used the man's momentary confusion and charged him. Screaming, he tackled him to the floor. The pistol whined, and a bolt of plasma blasted so close to Rashid it burned hairs off his head.

He grabbed the barrel, bending it backward until the guard

cried out in pain. Rashid kneed him in the stomach, ripped the gun from his hands, and fired two shots into the man's chest. Smoke from the burning flesh filled the air, disgusting Rashid.

"I'm sorry," he muttered. He had no room for mercy, not with his sister's life on the line, but he didn't relish killing a man doing his duty.

He dragged the dead man's body clear of the hatch. It only took a moment for him to seal the large door and lock it to avoid any more unwanted guests. He checked his side—his clothes were singed, but he wasn't hit. All that was left was to figure out how to fly the ship before someone blew it up.

Jennings raised her multi-barreled coilgun into the air, following the limping form of the Corsair with her crosshairs.

"Charlie-One-One, this is Two-Five-Alpha. We're following your progress. When I say dive, dive."

"Roger, Alpha," Boudreaux said. Her voice was strained, and Jennings imagined the pilot fought for control as smoke and fire belched out of the starboard engine.

"Cole, move five hundred meters to the west; fire at the fast-mover when I fire."

"Roger that."

They had one chance: if they could use the Corsair to lead the fast-mover into a crossfire, they could take her out. The dropship would never make it to the ground with a dedicated air-to-air combat ship dogging her. Jennings was shocked Boudreaux had managed to take out one of them. Her respect for the flier's ability shot up several marks.

"Sergeant, those Dhibs are almost on top of us. Thirty seconds," Cole said.

"I know. Be ready," she replied. Standing still, the active

camo in their Raptor suits made them all but invisible. When they fired, they would glow like flashlights on the Dhib's sensor panel.

The fast-mover arced around, leaving a contrail as it made a wide circle back to the Corsair. The enemy pilot flew with caution, not wanting to fall for a trick like his wingman had.

Jennings' computer showed the distance falling fast. She had to make sure the enemy was at the exact right range. "Charlie-One-One, angle up; then cut your engines," Jennings ordered.

Boudreaux responded without hesitation. The nose of the ship jumped up, then the port engine died. For a moment, the dropship hung like a leaf in the wind—before it fell like a stone.

As Jennings had planned, the fast-mover pulled up, rolled and prepared to follow the ship down to finish the job.

"Now!" She squeezed her trigger.

The pair of coilguns fired full auto, spraying hundreds of rounds in an X pattern in front of the fast-mover; the pilot never saw it coming. His ship exploded as red-hot tungsten balls ripped through fuel cells.

"Cole, move!" Jennings shouted as she sprinted away. The Dhib closest to her opened fire a second later. Green plasma bursts peppered the ground around her, exploding the sand and rock in superheated fury. She kicked in her jump jets, leaping forty meters forward then down the other side of the hill as the ground behind her exploded with each deadly hit.

Checking her map, she swung around the side of the hill, away from the compound where Commander Dagher was. The last thing she wanted was for the Dhibs to disgorge their soldiers and overrun them.

"Cole, shoot, move, hide," she said.

"Roger that," he replied.

"Head away from the compound until we're clear," she added.

After two hundred and fifty meters, she turned and popped up over the hilltop. The Dhib circled above, its nose-mounted plasma turret swiveling for her. Just like the Corsair, the ship could hover slowly, which it was doing as it searched for the two marines.

"Frag out," she said. The suit bucked as it launched a frag grenade. The projectile flew through the air in a lazy arc that ended in an explosion right in front of the small ship's cockpit.

The dropship tipped forward, the engines roaring to life as the pilot died and slumped into the throttle. It accelerated straight into the ground, exploding on impact.

"Tango down," she said. "Status?"

"I'm getting worked, Sarge," Cole said. He was calm, but she heard the strain in his voice.

Jennings checked the map. He was three kilometers away and moving fast. She tied into his feed to see what his suit's cameras saw.

The Dhib was right behind him, firing plasma as fast as it could. The area around Cole offered no cover, no concealment, nowhere to run.

"Turn toward me; we'll meet in the middle," she ordered.

Her Raptor suit took off in an earth-shaking run. Within ten seconds, she hit her top speed of one hundred kilometers per hour. All she really had to do was clear the next hill and she would have a perfect line of sight on the Dhib's tail.

Cole's feed went wild, jerking from side to side before it cut out. She willed Cole to be alive. "Ten seconds, Cole, hang in there," she barked.

Her suit cleared the crest in a leap that carried it fifty meters above the ground. Alarms wailed at her, warning her of both the active radar hitting the armored suit and that she had exceeded the suit's maximum jump height.

Three hundred meters away, the Dhib hovered ten meters off the ground. Soldiers leaped out the back in twos, rushing to surround the blackened, smoking Raptor suit.

Jennings brought her crosshairs in line with the Dhib, and at the apex of her leap, she fired. The suit bucked; vibrations from the sustained full-auto made her fight to keep the weapon on target.

Hundreds of tungsten balls rained death on the disembarking soldiers. Bodies exploded; others flew back into the ship. Then the rounds hit the ship itself, stitching a line through the open bay doors and right through the center of the cockpit.

The suit screamed at her as she hit the ground, overtaxed synthetic muscles collapsing under the strain. She rolled, doing her best to absorb as much of the impact as possible. Swaths of red damage alarms appeared on her internal display, including her cannon and grenade launcher.

The Dhib lurched sideways, tilted, and hit the ground, crumpling the starboard wing before rolling on its back. The superstructure collapsed like a house of cards, folding in on itself as fire leaped from the fuel cells, engulfing the ship.

Jennings struggled to stand up. Her emergency backups were kicking in, and even though she had no weapons, she could walk... maybe.

Soldiers streamed over the burning wreckage, yelling orders. The whine of plasma rifles split the air. They were shooting at her. She rolled to the side. Unable to make the suit stand, she had only one option. A tingle of anticipation ran through her. "Eject, eject, eject," she said in an even tone.

The front of the suit exploded outward. She dove out, keeping the wrecked suit between her and the enemy. Plasma rounds filled the air around her.

Jennings knelt behind her suit, pulled out her MP-17, and took in a deep breath, letting it out slowly. She had counted at least ten hostiles. Her fingers tapped three buttons on the pistol-sized weapon, converting it to a battle rifle. She shouldered the rifle, closed her eyes, imagined where the targets were, and waited. After a few seconds, the barrage let up.

Jennings opened her eyes, swung the rifle around, and stood up. Plasma rifles were powerful—capable of burning through solid steel—but they heated up fast, and they needed a few seconds to cool down between bursts. The first black-clad soldier filled her sights, and she fired a burst. He jerked backward, arms flailing. Another stood next to him, and she shifted aim, firing too high. The soldier leaped to the side, but she adjusted and fired again, taking him in the chest.

Jennings dove behind the demolished suit as the others opened fire. Heat bled off the metal as it absorbed burning plasma. "Cole, you with me?" she asked over her radio.

"Sarge... yeah, banged up but alive... I think," he said. His voice was weak, unsure. If he was injured, the suit would initiate first aid. Part of that protocol was painkillers.

"I'm coming. Hang tight."

Jennings yanked a small metal cylinder from her combat harness. Depressing the button, she said, "Air burst, five meters." The light under the button blinked. Jennings rolled onto her back and heaved the grenade over the suit as hard as she could.

Five meters away—to the centimeter—the grenade detonated. A blast of air rolled over her. Shrapnel pinged off the Raptor armor.

Jennings rose to a knee, firing the second she had targets. A group of five Caliphate soldiers were approaching the suit. Two had been blown to bits by her grenade, and she methodically shot the remaining three, one at a time, as they scrambled to recover from the blast.

Her ears rang from the explosion. She focused hard, narrowing her eyes to maximize her perception, scanning the blasted, burning battlefield for a hint of movement, any sign of a threat.

When none presented, she half walked, half crouched forward. The fiery wreck of the Dhib burned like a blast furnace, and she had to swing wide to avoid being roasted. Movement in her peripheral alerted her; she turned, firing into a dying man's chest. His sidearm fell from a lifeless hand.

Beyond the brutal field of battle, she saw Cole's Raptor cracked open. Bile rose in the back of her throat. She focused on her breathing, but her normally stoic expression cracked.

Cole's left side was blackened and burned, his leg a charred ruin. His eyes were open, but the drugs in his system were suppressing the agony he had to be in.

"Cole," she said as she rushed to his side. The suit had taken a direct hit from the Dhib's turret gun. Plasma had melted steel and flesh. Cole was dying, and there was nothing she could do to save him.

"We win, Sarge?" he whispered through charred lips.

"Yes, Cole, we won. They're all dead," she replied. Kneeling beside him, she shifted her rifle to the side and placed one hand on his chest.

"Oh, good," he said. "Tell the captain I did my best." His chest shuddered as he sucked in his final breath.

"I will, Cole. I will." Jennings promised her fallen comrade, and nothing short of death would stop her from fulfilling it.

CHAPTER TWENTY-NINE

Naki had arenas on his home planet of Ohana. They were the best in the galaxy, as hi-tech as a sports arena could be. Nothing at all like the archaic structure before him.

Naki imagined it would fit just fine in an ancient epic about the old world, when swords were the weapons of choice and wars were fought over small patches of land.

"Geez, what is this place?" Owens asked.

"The land time forgot," Naki replied.

Their two Raptor suits crouched at the top of the arena, their active camouflage set to full power, hiding them from visual as well as electronic systems.

Below them, the sands of the arena stretched out three hundred meters long and fifty meters wide. He figured there were enough seats for maybe twenty thousand people. On one end, a modern hotel rose four stories above the highest wall. Giant luxury suites crowned the building with extravagant balconies. Naki imagined they were for the high-rollers.

"How much you want to bet the people in the hotel are pissing their pants right about now?" Owens asked.

Naki shrugged. "Not our concern. The prisoners in the barracks are." He glanced at his sensor suite, suppressing his building worry. The transponders for Two-Five-Alpha and Delta were offline. Charlie-One-One had issued a Mayday. And worst of all, an electronic wall of noise had clamped down on the city, blocking off all communications with *Komodo*. Taking a sip of the go-juice from the straw next to his mouth helped his dry throat, but it did nothing to ease his apprehension.

"Okay, Owens, you're the expert here. When the IPB detonates, what do we do?" he asked.

Owens' Raptor suit mimicked the man's motions inside; a long arm ending in three clawed fingers pointed at the middle of the arena.

"I'll use the center of the arena as the target. It should fry every power system for three klicks. Except us... theoretically."

Naki jerked his head up. "Theoretically?"

"That's how it worked in training, Corporal," Owens said, somehow making his suit shrug.

"Roger that. Okay, wait one." Naki pointed the range finder at the center of the arena. They were seventy-three-point-five meters from the center. He turned around—careful to go slow as not to disrupt his camo—and pointed the range finder back the way they came.

The street below them went for a good hundred meters. He moved the invisible laser up until it read three klicks. The compound was just outside the blast zone.

"Looks good. Arm it," Naki said.

"Roger that," Owens said.

Naki waited, watching his monitors for any movement. Since the two fast-movers went down, followed by the Dhibs, the sky had been silent. Somewhere up there was a heavy cruiser, but there was no orbital bombardment. Which Naki wasn't going to complain about. He knew the Caliphate Navy wouldn't hesitate to bomb a civilian population from orbit—he just hoped they valued the infrastructure here more than killing the enemy.

"Ready," Owens said.

Naki keyed his radio. "Romeo-One, Two-Five-Bravo. Are you in position?"

No response.

"Corporal, I think we've got trouble," Owens said.

"What?" Naki swore as he turned around. Rashid should have answered by now. They trusted the man to take the liner after they set the field ablaze. What if they hadn't cleared all the guards? Or if he couldn't fly it? He knew they had left too much to chance, but what choice did they have? They needed both the Corsair and the Schnell to complete the mission.

"Look."

Thousands of people were silently streaming onto the field, either naked or with very little clothing. He zoomed in to see the little silver collars on their necks.

"Well, it's a safe bet they figured out we're here," Naki said.

"IPB ready. Give the word," Owens said.

Naki muttered a curse. "Two-Five-Alpha, this is Bravo. Come in."

People continued to flood into the sands of the arena. They milled about like workers waiting for instructions. At least they were all in one place for easy pickup.

Engines rumbled in the distance. Naki and Owens turned to see the Schnell lift off. The sleek passenger liner hovered for a moment before flying away from them. Naki's elation turned to frustration as the ship went the wrong way.

"And we're screwed," Naki said. "Romeo, how copy? You're going the wrong way."

No response.

Naki swore silently.

"I think they're going to use the slaves to defend the hotel," Owens said. "We should launch the IPB now."

Naki changed focus to the hotel side of the arena. Armed Caliphate soldiers were coming out from the first floor. They weren't acting alarmed about the swarm of prisoners, which led Naki to believe Owens was right about how they were planning to use the slaves.

"How many you counting?" Naki asked.

"Prisoners or guards?"

"Guards."

"Twenty... no... twenty-three. Naki, look," Owens shouted.

Naki spun around just in time to see the guards open fire on the prisoners.

"Fire the IPB now!"

Owen leaned forward and pulled the trigger. The fist-sized bomb shot out with a dull thump. Arcing lazily through the air, it landed exactly where Owen had targeted. There was no detonation; the device simply sparked followed by a puff of smoke from burning electronics.

The impact was immediate. Collars popped off, falling to the ground a thousand at a time. Confusion spread among the private security men as their weapons failed.

"Let's go," Owens said.

The spell broke, and the slaves in the front charged the private security. The two guards closest were overwhelmed instantly and beaten to death with bare hands. The rest tried to use their rifles like clubs—it worked for the first few, but they were quickly and violently brought down and killed.

"I guess that saves us the trouble," Naki said with grim satisfaction.

Chief Boudreaux fought the controls as the Corsair plummeted toward the ground. She had kept the ship together long enough for Jennings to splash the fast-mover, but it cost her all the lift she had, and the engine had stalled.

The ship fell sideways through the air, its wings and twin tails doing little to slow it down. She pushed the pedals, forcing the rudder to turn the nose into the dive. Once she faced the ground, she pulled back on the stick, bringing the nose up meter by meter. With air blowing through the turbine, she keyed the restart.

Nothing.

"Pull up. Pull up," the computer voice warned her. Despite her success at regaining partial control, the ship sliced through the air at a forty-five-degree angle. Dropships could glide, but not from a standing start. Her only hope was to keep trying the remaining engine.

Eight seconds to impact.

She tried again.

Nothing.

Two hundred meters. Still going too fast. "Brace," she yelled to her passengers. Time slowed down in Boudreaux's perception. She watched the altimeter spiral downward.

The Corsair slammed into the ground. Metal struts buckled on impact. Emergency systems sprayed impact safety foam throughout the ship, protecting the passengers and stopping fires before they started.

Metal screeched and sheared off as the dropship dug a furrow through the soft ground, sliding to a halt.

She trembled all over, her brain refusing to believe she was alive. The foam disintegrated, leaving everything, including her, covered in a soapy white residue. She took in a deep breath, filling her lungs with tangy air, then released her harness and dove into action.

"Two-Five-Alpha, this is Charlie-One-One. We made it to the ground, but the Corsair is lost." She climbed down the small ladder to the main deck, having to duck to avoid the places where the hull had collapsed. She could only pray her passengers had survived.

Two broken and very dead bodies littered the passenger compartment. Viv's hand went to her mouth, and she bit back bile. She could only imagine they had removed their harnesses.

As an aviator, she rarely saw the kind of mayhem the marines did. It took everything she had to force herself to keep the vomit down. Thankfully, other than bumps and bruises, the remaining passengers were alive and well. She didn't speak Consortium, and they didn't speak Standard, so she motioned for them to follow her.

She grabbed an MP-17 from the weapons locker next to the hatch. It was already configured for carbine mode for easy carrying.

Rent metal and buckled supports were all that remained of the side hatch. She keyed the panel, blowing the remains off the hull with a bang.

Her passengers screamed.

"Sorry," she muttered. Shouldering the weapon, she stepped out onto the desert ground. From her last reckoning, the compound lay five hundred meters to the south. If the marines were still alive, that's where they would be. If the mission was still a go, it was the only place she could meet up with everyone.

"Follow me. Stay close and low," she said, then shook her head as she remembered they didn't understand her. She motioned them down, then crept forward.

No one moved.

Boudreaux waved them toward her and mimed walking with her fingers. They got it and huddled after her. She just needed to escort them five hundred meters on a hostile planet. In the middle of a running battle. Piece of cake.

Jennings activated Cole's nanites, preserving what was left of his body from further deterioration. After she got the green light, she picked him up and slung him over one shoulder, carrying her MP-17 in the other. "Okay, Marine, time to get moving," she whispered. *Three klicks, I can do that in my sleep,* she thought.

They would make it if the heavy cruiser didn't send any more troops to the surface. Cole's body weighed her down as she took her first step, but she wouldn't leave him behind—not to be desecrated by the Caliphate. She sneered at the thought of them getting their hands on Cole. The worthless, honorless bastards of the Caliphate could rot in hell for all she cared.

Her anger and contempt for their society fueled her march through the hot desert. She wished she still had her powered armor, but she didn't waste anything more than an errant thought on it.

Jennings angled away from the way she'd come, knowing that if a patrol came out, their first move would be to scan the wrecks. Without her armor, she couldn't hope to take out another Dhib. As weapons went, the MP-17 was far more versatile than most and completely safe to use in any environment. The versatility gave it strength, but also robbed it of power—the silicate rounds were incapable of penetrating hardened armor. She could always get lucky, but her marine training told her not to rely on luck.

Her booted feet sank an inch into the sand with every step, straining her muscles. Between the weight of Cole's body and the oppressive sun, Jennings was sweating buckets after a klick.

With enough water she could carry him forever, but it was still hot.

A grunt caught her ear. Jennings dove for concealment behind a small berm. A row of small, cactus-like plants dotted the side of it, hiding her. She waited, tempering her breathing to keep herself steady. With one hand, she reached back and drew the long combat knife, then rested her rifle on the knife arm. If there were soldiers and they wore the same kind of gear the others had, then close combat would be her only chance for survival.

Moments passed, and she heard more noise: the rustle of clothes, the steady steps of people walking in a line, the heavy breathing of those not prepared for exercise. Her curiosity piqued, she risked raising her head a few centimeters.

Chief Boudreaux stumbled along, weapon held ready in front of her, exhaustion on her face. The pilot worked to stay in shape, even aboard ship, but there was pilot exercise and then there was marine exercise.

Jennings let out a short, sharp whistle. Boudreaux's head snapped up along with her rifle, and she tried to look everywhere at once. After a moment, her eyes met Jennings', and relief washed over her.

"You're a sight for sore eyes, Sergeant," she said.

Jogging over, Jennings checked out the six people with the pilot and shot her a questioning look.

Boudreaux shook her head slightly, indicating the rest didn't make it. Jennings frowned. They both knew the captain would be unhappy about that—if they ever got back to the ship.

Not that anyone could be more unhappy with Jennings than herself. She'd lost a man in the line, and it was a new experience. One she disliked.

"Sergeant, which way? I wasn't sure we were going the right direction," Boudreaux asked. Her eyes registered what was left of Cole's body on the ground next to where Jennings had hidden.

"The second Dhib got him," Jennings said in a flat voice.

"I'm sorry..." Boudreaux managed.

Jennings looked away, not yet wanting to acknowledge the loss. "Follow me," she said.

Picking up Cole with a grunt, she slung him over one shoulder. After a moment to orient herself, she started walking.

"Too fast, Jennings," Chief Boudreaux said. "These poor people haven't had a proper meal in months. They can't run through the desert like a marine."

"Sorry," she said, and slowed down. The pace felt like a crawl to her. She was sure that a Dhib or fast-mover would spot them any second. If they were attacked, she would sure as hell take as many with them as possible.

Adjusting Cole on her shoulder, she came face-to-face with him for a moment. His dead eyes stared at her accusingly.

Why did he die and I didn't? a small, nagging voice asked.

That's a stupid question, she answered. *Combat decides who lives and dies.* "When it's your time, it's your time. It doesn't matter how fast you're running." The ancient words spoken by a fellow marine, whose name was lost to history, filled her mind.

It didn't comfort her, though. She was still alive, and he was still dead.

CHAPTER THIRTY

Nadia's NavPad scrolled through hundreds of lines of code per second to crack the computer. From the casing, she guessed it was some kind of comms equipment. It was higher tech than she was aware the Caliphate had. "I don't recognize any of this equipment," she said over her shoulder. Her NavPad continued to run through options, flashing a red light at each failed attempt.

"Do we have time for it to work?" Elsa asked from behind.

Nadia turned around, facing the man in the chair. "Who are you?" she asked.

He ignored her, instead looking blankly at the floor.

"Is he military?" Elsa asked.

Nadia circled him. Something about his profile struck a chord in her memory. He certainly looked naggingly familiar. *No, it couldn't be*, she thought.

"What? What do you see?" Elsa asked.

"I don't know what, but something," Nadia said. After a moment, she decided. "We're taking him with us."

His head shot up, and he snarled at them.

"From all the noise outside," Elsa said, "I'm not sure any of us are leaving."

Zahra's eyes went wide. "Wh—what? I can't stay, I can't. I'd rather die than go back."

"Stay calm," Nadia reassured her in a quiet voice. "We're getting out of here."

The man laughed. "You are never leaving this place. You will be my personal slaves until I tire of you. Then I will throw you out the airlock," he said in the language of the Caliphate.

Zahra broke into tears, falling against the wall and sliding down.

Nadia stared at him with a blank expression on her face. "If it comes to that," she said in Caliph, "I will put a bullet between your eyes." She pulled out her gun in the blink of an eye and pressed it to his forehead. "Or maybe I just do it now and save myself the trouble," she growled.

He looked up at her with spite in his eyes and pressed his head against the gun. "Do it," he said in Standard.

She slid the gun into her holster. "Do you know what kind of person wants you to kill them?" she asked Elsa, all trace of anger gone from her voice.

"No?" Elsa said, confusion evident on her face.

"The kind with valuable information to hide," Nadia said with a grin. "Information they don't want falling into enemy hands even if it costs them their own life."

"You were playing him?" Elsa asked. "It was an act?"

"He's military, that's obvious. It's hard to say his actual age, but that kind of commitment doesn't come to the young. He's either high ranking or… Oh, damn," Nadia said as realization dawned on her.

"You know who he is?" Elsa asked.

Nadia put one hand to her ear. "Two-Five-Alpha, how copy?"

She kept one eye on the man sitting in the chair and motioned with her fingers for Elsa to do the same.

"Two-Five-Alpha, three-by-three," came the response.

Three-by-three meant a weak and garbled signal. Their own jamming had no effect on their communications, but between difficult terrain and an enemy flooding the area with ECM there was bound to be static.

"I need you back here ASAP. We have a priority Tango. Any word from Bravo or Romeo?" she asked.

Static filled the air for a few seconds before the radio clicked back on. "India, we're minus two Raptors, one KIA. Charlie-One-One is down, but the crew and six of the passengers are with me. No word from Bravo," Jennings said.

Nadia admired the marine's flat tone. Keeping it together after a KIA wasn't easy.

"Roger that, Two-Five-Alpha. Rally point Hotel ASAP. Over."

Nadia turned back to her new friend. She reached into her blackout suit and pulled out a pair of mag cuffs.

"I don't want you running off," she told him as she slapped them on his wrists and ankles.

"Who is he?" Elsa asked again.

Nadia flashed a wicked smile. Admiral DeBeck would lose his mind when she brought home this prize.

She had worked her hypothesis through her own math. A light cruiser or even a frigate would have served much better for picking up Princess Elsa. Why send a heavy cruiser unless the person coming to collect the prize was worth protecting? After all, they weren't at war. Nothing in space short of a squadron of cruisers could take out a heavy cruiser. She pushed the thought of *Interceptor* attacking such a beast aside. Jacob's problems were beyond her ability to solve; all she could do was hope and pray he made it out in one piece.

"I'm guessing that heavy cruiser in orbit isn't here for Zahra," Nadia said.

"It's not?" Zahra asked.

The man fidgeted, trying to push his body away from her.

Nadia smiled victoriously. "No, it's here for Elsa. And it's not just any heavy cruiser, but the personal ship the *Minister of ISB*. Also known as Imran Hamid, the Caliph's oldest son and heir. Let me guess, you came here to collect the princess? Hoping to deliver her to your father, or maybe keep her for yourself?"

He didn't answer.

"I know you speak Standard. There's no use pretending," she said.

He looked away, face burning with shame and anger.

"No wonder he wanted you to kill him..." Elsa whispered. "What now?"

It was a good question. Things weren't going strictly to plan, but what could she do? "Now we get out of Caliphate space before the whole damned navy comes after us."

Jennings placed Cole's body on the sand next to her, careful not to make any noise. She turned to the group following her and motioned them down with her hand. Only Boudreaux understood the hand signal, but when she dropped, the six former slaves knelt in the sand behind her.

Boudreaux shimmied up next to her. "What is it?" she asked, pitching her voice low.

Jennings glanced at her and put one finger to her lips. "I heard a noise. Stay here."

Up ahead was the crest of a hill. They were close to the compound, perhaps a hundred meters, if she was right. The troupe couldn't hide from aerial surveillance, but so far, none had arrived. Either the heavy cruiser had engaged *Interceptor*, or they were unwilling to send more troops to their death.

Medial had its own security forces, as well. She'd taken out two IFVs initially, but that didn't mean there weren't more. There had to be at least a few thousand soldiers stationed on the planet.

It helped that the Alliance's state-of-the-art command-and-control Mudcat sat unmolested at the spaceport, jamming everything but the Alliance.

Jennings crawled ever so slowly, careful not to make a sound as she reached the edge of a small hill. Five meters below her were three Caliphate Regulars, armed with slung plasma rifles. With a few seconds of examination, she knew what she needed to know. If they were regulars, they were damn sloppy.

Decision made, Jennings shouldered her MP-17 carbine. Switching the selector to full-auto, she hosed down the three soldiers at near point-blank range. Their light-duty uniforms and helmets were no match for the deadly weapon. Three men fell dead as shards perforated their heads and chests.

The marine listened for any sounds of alarm—any sign there were reinforcements nearby. *Nothing*. She beckoned Boudreaux, then jumped down to where the soldiers had died.

The weapons were keyed to the soldiers and useless. From their position, she saw the compound and the entrance she'd made when her Raptor had crashed through the wall. With line of sight, she activated her radio.

"India-One, Two-Five-Alpha. We're north of your position, point-five klicks. How copy?" she asked over their secure radio. The one in her Raptor could reach orbit; the unit in her ear only worked with line of sight and only about a dozen klicks.

"Two-Five-Alpha, affirmative. We're ready to extract. Can you reach Romeo?" Nadia asked.

There was a long pause. Jennings scanned the horizon,

searching for any sign of the Schnell liner she knew was out there. The distant sound of plasma explosions and cannon fire echoed through the desert air. Some of it came from Raptor suits; their sound was distinctive and easy to identify—if one knew how.

"Negative, India. Wait one while I contact Bravo."

"Roger," Nadia replied.

"Two-Five-Bravo, come in," Jennings called.

"Alpha, Bravo. Good to hear your voice," Naki replied.

"Roger. Sitrep?" she asked.

"We're sitting pretty with about five thousand civilians, collars off, ready to go. I can't reach Romeo though. You?"

Jennings swore. If they still had Charlie, they could evac, albeit with multiple trips. But with just the Schnell? Everything hinged on one ship, piloted by an unreliable ally. "Wait one," she said. "Romeo, respond."

She motioned for Boudreaux to get the group to the hole in the wall. The pilot gave her a thumbs-up and waved for her six shadows to follow. Once they were past her, Jennings tried Romeo's radio one more time.

He was either dead, caught, or had betrayed them. She didn't think he would betray them and risk his sister. That just left caught or killed. If only she could have spared someone to go with him to watch his back. She didn't have time to ponder what-ifs, though. This was the here and now.

"India, sending Charlie and guests. November evac clear. I'm going to go look for Romeo." She covered Boudreaux with her carbine until the last person disappeared into the compound.

Jennings scrambled to the top of the hill. Staying low to avoid her silhouette being seen, she crouch-walked along the ridge until she could see the city directly. Pulling her NavPad out, she adjusted the power setting to amp up the signal into a directional beam toward the spaceport.

"Romeo, this is Two-Five-Alpha. Come in?" She waited, scanning the horizon for any sign of the ship taking off. Nothing.

"Dammit," she muttered. She checked the map on her NavPad. Could they move the prisoners on foot? From the explosions echoing through the city, it didn't seem likely.

They couldn't hold the compound for much longer. Certainly not if that heavy cruiser stayed in orbit. In the meantime, all she could do was guard the road.

CHAPTER THIRTY-ONE

Captain Bitar paced the command deck, stress tightening his stomach and giving him the beginnings of a headache. There was too much at stake for him to fail. If he did, he would be lucky to only suffer the same fate as his old captain. *Irony, eh, Rashid,* he thought.

"Jamal, status?" he asked his intelligence officer.

"There's a lot of jamming and counter-jamming happening on the surface, but it looks like both Dhibs are down. The commanders aren't responding, sir."

"Can you reach the minister?" Bitar asked.

"No, sir. He's not responding."

This confirmation filled Bitar with dread. His skin crawled, and he wanted to find some place quiet to go and vomit. It was bad enough to be here when the attack happened, but to lose the Caliph's son?

Medial wasn't a secret, but it was far enough behind the "front lines" that neither the Consortium nor the Alliance could have reached it to launch a counterattack—even if they knew the back door. "Where's their ship?" he asked.

Jamal displayed the orbit of the planet. "There are fifteen ships in orbit large enough to carry a substantial ground force."

Bitar ran over the possibilities in his head. They came in a cargo ship, then. Not a hidden assault force, but more of a light raid. The Consortium wouldn't risk something like this, and the Alliance was too far away. Who then? Pirates?

"Eliminate any with a Caliphate transponder," he said. Nine ships vanished from his screen. "Eliminate known pirate vessels." Three more vanished.

All that remained were three bulk freighters: *Mercury Moon*, the *Labors,* and *Komodo*. He could board each one and verify that they were supposed to be in Caliphate space, but it would be easier to destroy them in orbit.

"Helm, plus one-zero-zero-zero kilometers," he ordered.

"Yes, sir, increasing orbit from planet by one-zero-zero-zero kilometers."

The ship strained in response. Heavy cruisers were the definition of cumbersome—unlike the light, maneuverable craft of their smaller brethren. Thrusters exerted force against mass and it took time to move the ponderous beast.

"Weapons, get me a firing solution on these three ships," he said. With a flick of his wrist, he sent the ships' coordinates to the weapons station.

His weapons officer, a young man whose name he couldn't recall, confirmed the three ships and coordinates.

"How long, helm?" he asked.

"Two-five minutes, sir."

He nodded in satisfaction. With the Caliph's son on the planet, he could take no chances. Once the ships were eliminated, he would land more troops. He'd have to land them far from the central city, though. It was possible his Dhibs were out of contact from the jamming, but it was more likely they were destroyed—and whoever invaded had surface-to-air weapons.

Medial's location, plus the nature of her activities, meant she was only nominally under the protection of the Caliphate. It allowed the Caliphate to deny any involvement in the slave trade, while supplying them with a never-ending stream of cheap labor and sex dolls. It was a win-win.

"Who do you think it is, Jamal?" he asked.

Jamal shook his head. "Could be pirates, maybe Consortium, but this kind of operation isn't like them. It's hard to say without seeing their gear, sir. I imagine we'll know soon enough. After all, once we destroy the ships, they can't leave the planet. They'll have no choice but to surrender."

True enough, he decided. Once they had the infidels in the brig and under the control of a collar, he could let the crew interrogate them until they couldn't walk.

"Sir," Nazzari said from communications, "I just intercepted a partial communication from the surface."

"Play it," he ordered.

Static filled the bridge speakers, followed by a harsh voice. "... get security forces to the arena. Something shut down all the collars in the city."

"Security forces?" a man responded. "Contact that cruiser in orbit and have them send down more Immortals. The last two Dhibs were shot down with all hands," the receiver said.

Bitar sucked in a breath. He'd hoped some of his men had survived. If the city was under siege though, at least the Minister was likely safe at his secured location.

"Jamming is too intense; we can barely rea—" The frequency devolved to static, and Bitar missed what the man said next.

"Is that all of it?" he asked.

"Yes, sir. I'll keep scanning though," Nazzari said.

"Do that," Bitar replied.

The enemy forces on the planet weren't going anywhere. He

could deal with their method of escape first, then take them out at his leisure. But his throat clenched as he went over the past few hours. Two Dhibs, escorted by planetary security and loaded with Immortals, would have been more than enough to handle an insurrection or pirate attack. But military forces... he couldn't have accounted for that.

If only they had gotten the minister out first!

Then he could have just razed the planet. It would be a loss, but the Caliphate wouldn't care. With the Caliph's son on the planet, though... he couldn't risk it.

"Train all our sensors on the planet. Alert all orbital traffic to hold position or be destroyed."

Komodo hadn't missed a thing. Twelve corvettes were parked in low orbit above Medial. A central platform housed the crew and refueled the ships. It was maybe three times as big as *Interceptor*. Two detached while Jacob watched, heading down to the planet below.

"Carter, adjust," Jacob ordered.

"Aye, aye, sir. Target adjusted."

At twenty light-seconds out, they had a clear passive picture of the ships in orbit and the surrounding orbital defenses. Eighteen satellites, right where *Komodo* said they would be. Ten corvettes, no gravcoils, capable only of orbital operations, guarded from a central control platform. Had the heavy cruiser not shown up, it would have been fish in a barrel.

Jacob shook his head, refusing to go down that path. Yes, the odds were long. *Interceptor*'s 20 mm turrets could handle the satellites and corvettes without much problem. The heavy cruiser's mass permitted it to absorb much more damage than

Interceptor. There were sections the coilguns wouldn't even penetrate without a lot of luck.

"Do we have a read on the class?" he asked his crew.

"Yes, sir," Tefiti replied. "It's a Sayaad-class heavy cruiser. I'll send what we have to your screen." Tefiti did his best to keep his tone even, but Jacob knew what the man must be feeling, since he was feeling it himself.

Interceptor's weapons were nothing compared to a Sayaad-class. With her sixteen double-barreled turrets, six main guns mounted forward, and six torpedo tubes, she had a throw weight a hundred times what his little ship could do. No matter what, he couldn't get into a blow-for-blow trade with that monster.

However, no heavy cruiser ever made could match *Interceptor* for speed.

With her five-hundred-and-forty-gravity capability, his little ship was the best in the fleet. She could change course, overcome velocity, and reach max speed much faster than the tub of lard they faced.

He knew they couldn't beat such a monster in traditional combat. But who said he had to fight traditionally? Or even fair? A famous Earth warrior once said, "The only unfair fight is the one you lose."

Interceptor was traveling at a little over two hundred KPS, coasting in, running silent. On her current course, she would cross the cruiser's stern at a few thousand klicks.

If Carter timed it right, they would destroy the orbital defenses and still have time to hit the cruiser. He couldn't abandon his people on the ground or in *Komodo*. He *would not* abandon them. No doubt his crew agreed.

"Sir, the cruiser's changing orbit," PO Tefiti said. "Increasing distance from the planet."

Jacob motioned for him to put it on his screen. Sure enough, the heavy cruiser had engaged thrusters and pulled away from the planet. Why not use their gravcoil?

"Kim, what do you think they're doing?" he asked.

She looked up at him from her station at DCS. "Maybe they detected us?" she asked.

"Maybe... but if it were me, I'd engage the gravcoil, come head on, and obliterate us in a broadside," he said.

"I acknowledge it's a guess, Skipper. Maybe they detected something, but don't know what. Or..." She paused, eyes going wide.

"What?" he asked.

"They know about the ground attack... and they have to know a ship brought the troops in. If it were me and I didn't care about loss of life, I'd just blow any suspect freighter out of orbit," she finished.

Jacob's jaw clenched. It was madness—to kill that many people on the off chance one of them was involved?

"Chief?" Jacob turned to Suresh.

"Skipper?" She looked in the mirror, and he saw the thin line of her lips pressed together.

"Where do you think they are moving to?" he asked.

Suresh stared at the monitor for a long second while she worked through the problem. "High orbit? Maybe another nine hundred klicks? They're using thrusters, moving slow because she's a pig."

"Right," Jacob said. Using gravcoil in orbit wasn't practical. Thrusters were slow, though, and they took a while to move a ship any distance.

If they were planning on firing on the freighters, they wouldn't warn them first—they would just open fire. "How long?" he asked.

"Maybe fifteen minutes," Suresh answered.

"When are we in firing range, Carter?" he asked.

Carter turned to face him. "Twenty-five minutes to optimal range. We could fire sooner, but we would reveal our location, and... they could just move a few hundred meters and we would miss."

Dammit, I knew he was going to say that, Jacob thought.

He couldn't let them fire on the ships. There could be thousands of people on them... maybe more. There was little chance *Komodo* wasn't on their strike list. A dozen of his crew were aboard the freighter, plus however many went down to the planet. He would lose all of them.

And for what? If *Interceptor* sailed on without them, all he could do was return home and face the music. Life in prison for mutiny. At least if they completed the mission, he could have the satisfaction of knowing he'd punched the bastards right in the face.

He was going to have to play this one tight. They had to wait till the last possible moment to go active on the drive. He'd light the ship up like a Christmas tree. Radar, lidar, full acceleration. Hit them with everything they had as they blew through orbit. And pray it was enough.

"Chief, here's what I want to do..."

CHAPTER THIRTY-TWO

Josh Mendez rubbed his suited hands together to reduce his tension. Spacer Perch sat across from him, harnessed into his identical chair. They sat on either side of the Long Nine's loading assembly. Buckled above them in the firing station, PO Ignatius handled the controls to the stern.

He noticed Perch glancing back and forth, his lips moving silently. Josh reached up and triggered his radio. "It will be okay, Perch. The skipper has gotten us through worse."

Perch triggered his radio. "It's a heavy cruiser, Josh. I might only be a spacer, but even I know we can't beat a heavy cruiser," he whispered. Perch closed his eyes, leaned his head back, and clenched his jaw.

"I know what *the Book* says, Perch. But... it's the captain. We might have long odds against us, but we did in Zuckabar too, and we sure as hell did in Wonderland. We're still here," he said.

Perch's eyes snapped open, and he leaned as far forward as his harness would allow. "Yeah? How many aren't?" he asked.

Josh glanced at PO Ignatius for help. The man nodded for him to continue. Josh had stepped in it; he needed to clean it up.

Fear was a poison, a disease. It spread on contact. It kept good men from doing their job when they most needed to.

"You're right, Perch. Some of our friends didn't make it. Some of them won't make it this time. Maybe us..." he said, pitching his voice low. "But we signed up for this. We're doing something good out here. If we fail, so be it. But we fail defending our home worlds." Josh looked the man square in the eyes. "We save lives, no matter what happens. After this, the Caliphate will know they can't screw with us. We're going to give them the biggest middle finger in the galaxy. And if we win?"

Perch relaxed, breaking into a mild grin. "Fortune and glory?"

"Sure," Josh said. "But think of the stories you can tell once we're back in port. I, for one, think the girls back on New Austin are going to be mighty impressed, us, a pair of kids facing down the Caliphate with nothing more than an old ship and the iron will of our captain."

Perch's grin spread into a smile. "It *will* make a pretty good story, won't it?"

"Damn skippy," Josh replied. "It's OK to be afraid. There is no courage without fear. We got this, Perch. We got this."

He held out his gloved hand in a fist. Perch leaned forward and slammed his own home.

Fusion reactors were tricky beasts to run silent. Even with the ship battened down to lower emissions, it wasn't like Lieutenant Gonzales could turn the thing off and then back on. Instead, they reduced power output to the absolute minimum by reducing the fuel valve size. As *Interceptor* coasted toward

Medial, Gonzales rode the valve, giving it his undivided attention.

The computer could control it, but Gonzales found that when the flow fell below a certain level, the required amount of fuel became erratic. By riding herd, watching the output, he could anticipate the changes, increasing and decreasing flow as needed. While the reactor was an exact science, its behavior from moment to moment fell in a range, not an exact number.

Beech stuck his head into the little chamber, activating his proximity comms. "Sir, we're good to go. Do you need anything?"

Without taking his eyes off the readout, Gonzales shook his head. "Not at the moment."

Beech turned to leave, but Gonzales called him back. "If we get through this, Beech, remind me to have a long talk with you about OCS. You know entirely too much about ships and engines to be in the trenches."

Beech frowned. "The PO told you, sir?" he asked.

"Yes, he did. I looked up your parents' ship, your pre-navy record, and your naval record. You had the highest marks in engineering for your class. The only reason you aren't sitting where I am right now is you didn't want to go to OCS."

Beech closed his mouth, too stunned to reply for a few seconds.

"That wasn't it, sir," he said after a long moment. "I didn't want the navy to spend all that money only to stay for a single tour. Before all this, I didn't know what I wanted to do with my life, sir."

Gonzales pushed the slider up, opening the valve two millimeters to compensate for a drop in power. "And now?" he asked the spacer.

Beech's eyes brightened, and he stood up straighter.

"Between the captain and Chief Redfern, sir, I'm convinced. If you'll vouch for me, I'll sign up."

Gonzales clapped him on the back. "Good man," he said, using the captain's favorite compliment.

Kim was ready. She'd ordered her DCS crews to concentrate on the weapons and engineering. No matter what, those two systems were the most important.

Green lights glowed across the board, showing the status of every station with a human being manning it. They were required to ready check every fifteen minutes with a go/no-go signal. If they couldn't give a green light, she routed their station chief into the comms, and they found out why.

While she loved her job, both as exec and DCS chief, her location during combat galled her. She wanted to be up there, in the action, hearing the orders, feeling the flow, seeing her direction have impact.

That wasn't her job, though. It was Commander Grimm's. A job he was unequivocally qualified for. Secretly, and she would never tell Jacob this, she had once hoped the navy would promote him, give him a new ship, and then let her continue to be his XO.

She'd learned much since he came aboard. Not just about ship handling and tactics, but leadership—which he excelled at. In fact, she'd probably never met anyone who was more of a natural leader.

Even if they survived the coming encounter, one they had little chance of making it through, when they returned to Alliance space, he would be tried for mutiny, found guilty, and sent to prison for the rest of his life. There could be no other outcome.

The thought sobered her some. She would stand by him. Even if they sent him to a firing squad, she would stand by him. He'd returned something to her she hadn't known was missing.

Duty. Honor. Courage.

The motto of the navy, but not something she understood until Jacob T. Grimm came aboard her little destroyer. She understood it now, in orbit above an enemy planet, about to face down a heavy cruiser, with nothing more than determination and spirit.

The Caliphate would never know what hit them.

Lieutenant West anxiously watched the sensor panel aboard *Komodo*'s bridge. On it, the Caliphate heavy cruiser continued to climb in orbit.

Interceptor had to be there soon. The captain would find a way to make it all work. Even if he had to cheat death itself.

"Thirty seconds, Lieutenant," PO Oliv said, updating him on their progress.

"Thank you..." He struggled to remember her first name. Commander Grimm always knew. Like he spent hours memorizing first names before he came aboard. *Mary? Martha?*

"Marta, sir," she said without looking at him.

He flushed, feeling foolish and realizing why it worked so well when the captain did it. The fact that he memorized their names and faces meant he spent time doing it—time that equaled respect. Too bad he wouldn't live to remember the lesson.

"Sorry, Marta. Thank you for your service. It's been tremendous," he said to her.

She turned and nodded to him. "It isn't often an officer does a one-eighty, sir. I have a lot of respect for you for turning around the way you did."

West's face heated. He had tried to lie to himself about what had happened after the original captain of the *Interceptor* died, but he just couldn't hide the truth from himself. That Oliv knew, and recognized what had happened, filled him with equal parts shame and pride.

"Thank you," he said, barely able to even get that out.

He glanced at Collins, who manned the helm. She wasn't paying attention to the exchange, only watching the heavy cruiser while her hands hovered over the controls. He wouldn't sit here and die. The moment they thought the ship would fire, Collins would punch it as best she could, and Oliv would drop the beacon.

"Sir?" Olive asked.

"Yes?"

"*Interceptor* just powered up and—"

Alarms wailed as the ship's computer detected weapons fire.

CHAPTER THIRTY-THREE

Captain Bitar stewed in his command couch. In less than a minute, they would have the orbital height to take out the three ships with turret fire. Once they were expanding clouds of gas, he would send down his remaining two Dhibs loaded with the other half of his ground forces.

In retrospect, he should have done that first—overwhelmed the enemy. It was a mistake he wouldn't make again. While he had time to think, he decided that once the minister was safely aboard ship, he'd just bombard the planet from orbit until nothing remained. The Caliphate would not tolerate sedition.

"We're in position, sir," Jamal said from his console.

Interceptor was out of time. As Jacob watched, the heavy cruiser reached the apex of its climb. At any moment, the ship tagged as Tango-One on his MFD would open fire. When that happened, every freighter in orbit would be destroyed. Jacob couldn't let that happen.

"Tefiti, distance?" he asked.

PO Tefiti shook his head. "One point five three million kilometers, sir."

Too far. The freighters would be destroyed long before the 20 mm rounds would arrive.

If he ignited the gravcoil, they would know within five seconds that a warship was inbound. *Interceptor* would lose its surprise but save the other ships. He sighed, sagging back into his chair. He'd desperately wanted to sneak up on Tango-One. If they were to have a hope in hell of winning, it had to be a surprise attack. He just wasn't willing to trade the lives of those freighters, or his people on the ground, for a slim chance of victory.

With a quick breath to clear his throat, he gave the order. "Helm, flank speed. Set your zero right for Tango-One. Weapons, switch to secondary targets," he said. "Charge the Long Nine." The main gun required a spectacular amount of energy and couldn't be used without first energizing the supercapacitors.

Chief Suresh responded immediately. She flipped up the shield over the gravcoil power button and mashed it down. "Flank speed, aye, aye," she replied. Once power flowed into the coil, she pushed the throttle lever all the way forward. *Interceptor* leaped forward like a snake striking its target.

Gravity pulled at their rear, sinking them into their seats as the field keeping them oriented to the deck and the field powering up behind them fought for control.

"Firing solution Foxtrot-three-zero, ready," Lieutenant Fawkes announced. "Long Nine charging. Six-zero seconds to ready."

"Fire the torpedoes," Jacob ordered.

Interceptor shook as four gravcoil-powered torpedoes shot out in front of her, adding their own acceleration to the current velocity of the ship. They spread out, crossing the distance far quicker than the twenty-millimeter rounds fired by the turrets could.

Bitar opened his mouth to order them to fire.

"New contact bearing two-one-three, distance one-point-five million klicks!" Ensign Sabaag said.

"Classification?" Bitar asked.

"Alliance destroyer... Hellcat class? I don't know what that is," Sabaag said.

Bitar's eyes narrowed, and his mind froze for a moment. Alliance? A destroyer? By itself? Bitar wanted to laugh. Of all the bad timing for them. They had sent a single destroyer to raid Medial—a Hellcat no less—a ship that was old when the last war ended. Was this their response to the attack on their capital? Send a single, outdated, underpowered ship to deter any further attacks? Laughable.

"Launch, launch, launch," Sabaag said. The doors on the bridge slammed shut as the ship's automated programming prepared it for conflict.

The plot updated, and a measly four torpedo signatures appeared. While his ship was a good target for torpedoes, it would take many more than four to get through his defenses. And more than that to seriously hurt *Divine Wind*.

"How long to impact, Sabaag?" Bitar demanded.

"Calculating. One-three-zero seconds, sir," the radar man replied.

Two minutes. More than enough time.

"High alert. Ready stations," Bitar ordered. As the alarms wailed, he sat in his command chair, projecting calm to his command.

He motioned to his executive officer. "Jamal, we'll deal with the freighters later. Set all turrets to automatic point-defense. Helm, bring up the gravcoil."

Jamal flipped the automated defenses to the on position. They weren't as effective as a well-trained crew, but with two minutes to impact, the computer would be more than sufficient.

"Engineering reports three minutes to gravcoil power-up," helmsman Gaber announced.

Bitar weighed his options. Even if the gravcoil came up early by some miracle, they wouldn't be able to pile on enough acceleration to escape those weapons. Normally he would be worried, but it was only four torpedoes. Whoever the captain was on the enemy ship, he was a fool for firing so soon. He should have waited till the last minute.

"Computer confirms point-defense, sir. Tracking," Jamal said.

As hilarious as the odds against the destroyer were, however, he did know with absolute certainty that if the Alliance made it off the planet with Caliph Hamid's oldest son, then Captain Bitar would be better off dead.

"Comms, are they still jamming us on the planet?" he asked.

"Yes, sir. I can't get through to any ground forces."

Bitar glanced at the time, then realized something was wrong. "Jamal, why aren't the turrets firing?" They should have opened up immediately upon switching to computer control. The plasma turrets slow rate of fire and shorter range meant the computer picked targets carefully. It wouldn't waste shots on targets of no value.

"Uh, one moment, sir," Jamal said.

"A moment? Impact in sixty seconds!" Bitar said.

It was a hell of a time for a computer glitch. Even if those torpedoes couldn't reliably destroy his ship, they could do tremendous damage.

On Jacob's screen, the big cruiser began to move, lumbering to life as the thrusters filled in for the gravcoil. Not that it mattered.

"Fawkes, fire the turrets," Jacob ordered.

"Aye, sir, firing all turrets." Lieutenant Fawkes hit the button, spinning the turrets to target their prearranged objectives. It was going to be close.

"Long Nine?" Jacob asked.

"Charged and ready, sir," Fawkes said.

Jacob looked down at the plot, manipulating the controls to show the massive orbital platform where Medial parked their corvettes when they weren't on patrol and dozens of defense satellites, each one marked with a crimson code designating them as targets. They were only going to have one pass, and they couldn't miss even one.

"How long to torpedo impact?" Jacob asked.

"Four-five seconds. They should spot the trick any second," Fawkes said with a grin.

Bitar smashed the arm of his chair. His mind reeled from the surge of stress and the fake appearance of calm. His turrets weren't firing, and those torpedoes were getting closer. "Jamal," he shouted, "take them off computer control and fire them manually." Why wasn't the computer shooting at them? The entire purpose of computer control was to buy gun crews time to get in position and protect the ship from direct attack until they could exert manual control. Protecting the ship from attack was the computer defenses' primary function and—

"Oh Allah," he said as he put it together.

When the destroyer appeared, the bridge crew had left the torpedoes for the computer to handle while they focused on the sudden arrival of a ship that shouldn't be there. Now Jamal was too late. The computer was more than aware the incoming torpedoes were a threat, just not a threat to the *Divine Wind*. Ten seconds before impact, the torpedoes' flight path became obvious; they would sail far wide of *Divine Wind*, with ten thousand kilometers to spare. The computer wouldn't waste time on torpedoes that would miss.

Four Alliance two-hundred- and forty-millimeter torpedoes flashed by the ship, their gravcoils glowing as they continued to accelerate toward their true target. Six thousand klicks aft of *Wind* the corvette orbital station stood helpless.

Slush deuterium ignited simultaneously and four torpedoes detonated sending their payload of twenty-millimeter nano-hardened tungsten balls out in a cone before them. Energy equivalent to a nuclear bomb shot out from the fore of the torpedoes, turning the normally hardened tungsten into burning plasma hotter than the sun. Three hundred and twenty such orbs saturated an area less than five hundred meters cubed.

The station, ten corvettes, and all three hundred orbital defense guards were converted to an expanding cloud of superheated gas in a fiery blaze of death.

Jacob breathed a sigh of relief. Telemetry showed good hits on all targets. The first part of his plan had worked. He liked to think the captain of that ship would understand the trick in retrospect. The enemy ship was running on minimal power and no gravcoil. Here comes an Alliance destroyer, flank speed and heading right for them. Of course it didn't occur to them there were other targets. Jacob would have thought the same thing. Why he was concerned with the feelings of the enemy captain was beyond him.

Jacob traded a maybe for a win. The heavy would pursue *Interceptor*, thinking they were the reason for the attack on the planet. While he led them on a merry chase, his ground team could escape to the starlane, unmolested by the destroyed orbital defenses.

"Skipper, they're getting ready to fire," Ensign Owusu said. "Active radar and lidar tracking us now."

"Roger. Helm, twenty degrees up-bubble, fifteen degrees starboard," he ordered. Maneuvers while approaching a target were tricky. Turn at too much of an angle and they would be sitting ducks. "Continue evasive."

"All primary targets destroyed," Fawkes said. "Engaging secondary targets."

It was better than he could have hoped for. With that much damage inflicted on the orbital infrastructure, he left the heavy cruiser no choice but to chase them.

For a brief moment, the distance to the enemy ship hovered at three hundred thousand klicks before it started climbing again. He'd debated going in all the way, firing the main gun, but that was suicide. They would never survive long enough to get in range.

"Launch, launch, launch," Owusu said. "Six torpedoes in space, sir. Seven-zero-zero golf acceleration. Time to intercept, three-zero-seven seconds."

"That's just for show," Jacob informed his crew. "We're too far away and moving too fast. Engage point-defense, Mr. Fawkes."

"Aye, aye, sir." As the ship adjusted course, turrets two and three tracked, firing where the computer predicted the torpedoes would be.

Jacob leaned back, watching the numbers increase as they pulled away at an angle. All he had to do was keep them out of weapons range and they would maybe pull out of this with no casualties.

CHAPTER THIRTY-FOUR

Naki held the road from the top of the arena. His coilgun chattered as he engaged moving targets approaching the stadium.

Below him, Owens organized the massive crowd of former slaves. The PFC's voice boomed over the area as he tried to calm them down. "We are Alliance Marines. We are here to rescue you. If there are wounded, please pick them up or flag me. Everyone must walk or be carried. We don't have much time," Owens announced.

"Charlie? Status?" Naki asked.

A ground security man stepped out of a doorway two hundred meters away, shouldered a weapon, and fired. Green plasma leaped, stretching toward the arena wall.

Naki's suit warbled at him. He reacted by triggering his jump jets, sending him flying straight up. The weapon designed to take out hardened targets hit the wall with the force of a bomb, and the faux-sandstone structure exploded inward, showering the arena floor with shrapnel, dust, and debris. Freed prisoners screamed as they ducked for cover.

As Naki hit the apex of his jump, he targeted the source of

the plasma and fired three thermite grenades in rapid succession. One after another, they exploded in bright flame against the building and road.

As he fell, he used the last of his jump-jet fuel to push sideways, away from the destruction. He landed with a crunch, the veneer at his feet cracking, sending bits of rubble flying.

"Status is we're FUBAR, Bravo. Unless Romeo is about to land," Owens said over the radio.

"Roger that," Naki replied. He leaned over the edge of the roof and fired off a hundred rounds just to be sure, peppering the still burning building. "I'm zero on fuel and low on ammo. I can't hold the street. Let's trade," Naki ordered. A few seconds later, Owens landed next to him.

"I've got it," Owens said. His coilgun spun up, covering the most likely angle of approach.

Naki jumped off the roof. He stumbled as his three-toed, clawed feet scrambled for purchase, then took a moment to look out on the sea of people huddled, scared, and confused. Anger surged in him as he made the last leap down to the arena floor. He clenched his teeth, determined to keep it in check. An angry marine was a dead marine.

Once on the ground, Naki made a three-sixty of the arena. It was a fishbowl, and they were the fish; exposed on all sides. All it would take would be one soldier with a rifle to start killing the poor people.

With one eye on the towering hotel at one end, he turned his PA system on. "Attention, please form a line on that side of the arena." He pointed toward the hotel. If they were close enough to the base of the hotel, snipers on the roof would have a hard time shooting at them. "We have a transport ship on the way."

A few people moved; some looked around; others stayed on the ground, weeping or with blank expressions. How the hell did he move them if the threat of capture or death wouldn't do it? "Romeo, how copy? Bravo needs immediate evac."

Static was his only answer.

Nadia glanced away from Imran to her NavPad when it beeped.

"Keep an eye on him," she said to Elsa.

Picking up the NavPad, she studied the readout; most of it was far too technical for her. While she wasn't a slouch, she was no engineer. The software had scanned the computer top to bottom; when she reached the end of the report, she froze. Her heart thumped in her chest, and her nostrils flared at the realization of what the machine was.

She looked at Imran. He stared death back at her. If he could get free, she knew he wouldn't hesitate to kill her. Good thing for her he was never going to get free. "Is this a Conundrum Cipher?" she asked in Caliph. When he said nothing, she marched over and grabbed his chin with her cybernetic arm and forced him to look at her. "Answer me!"

When he didn't, she pushed his head away, leaving the beginnings of a bruise on his jaw.

"What?" Elsa asked. Nadia could tell the princess was tired of asking the question.

Nadia pointed at the machine. "It's a Conundrum Cipher. It would be like if your enemies got a hold of one of your EnTabs," she said, referring to the highly secure and encrypted computers that officers in the Imperial forces carried.

Elsa raised an eyebrow at the casual reference.

Nadia shrugged. "My boss likes to keep tabs on... well, everyone."

"So it would seem," Elsa said.

Nadia waved her hand as if to dismiss the concern. "Conundrum Ciphers are their quantum communications devices. There are only a handful of them. They're FTL. Limited to simple messages and only to the quantum entangled counterpart, but FTL all the same."

Imran jerked in his bindings, seething anger on his face as he swore at her in their shared tongue.

"That's not possible? We've tried for a century. How do they have such a thing and my security forces don't know of it?" Elsa asked.

"I don't pretend to understand the science, Princess, but they have it and now we have it," she said, holding up her NavPad.

"India, Charlie-One-One. I'm coming down. Don't shoot," Boudreaux said over the comms.

"Go ahead," Nadia replied.

The aviator came down the stairs, taking each one with care, holding out her snub-nosed MP-17 in front of her like a shield. She saw the three girls first, then the bound man. She stopped and looked back up the stairs, holding out her hand in the universal "hold" symbol.

"There are two IFVs at the bottom of the hill," Boudreaux informed them. "The troops look like regulars, not Immortals."

"Good, 'cause we're not staying," Nadia said. She pulled a cylindrical grenade, set the timer, and placed it on top of the Conundrum Cipher.

"What are you doing? That is irreplaceable!" Imran growled.

"Shut up, or I'll break your teeth," Nadia replied. She bent down and pressed the release on the cuff holding his arms. His wrists were still bound together behind his back, but they were no longer locked to the chair. A second later, the ones on his ankles separated, but she didn't take them off. "You try to run,"

Nadia said, "and..." they snapped together, taking his legs with them.

"Who's this guy?" Boudreaux asked.

"I'll tell you later." Nadia pushed him up, keeping one hand on his shoulder and the other hand free. "March," she ordered him. "Boudreaux, lead us back to Jennings. Elsa, take the rear."

"Aye, aye," Boudreaux said as she turned around and double-timed it back up the stairs.

"You will not leave this planet alive," Imran said.

"You'd better hope I do, oh great one. Because if I go, you go."

Things were not going well, Jennings decided. A klick away, at the bottom of a hill next to the compound, two armored IFVs disgorged troops. It was a smart move, since they had no idea the Raptor suits were destroyed. The burning hulks of their two brother vehicles served as a reminder to be cautious.

Thankfully for Jennings, her view of the troops remained unobstructed. As it so happened, she was also an expert shot with every weapon the Corps used—and a few they didn't.

With the push of a button, her pistol-sized MP-17 extended the stock and barrel until it reached ninety centimeters long. The see-through holo-dot sight converted to a 4x magnification. Already lying down, she shouldered the weapon and craned her neck to look through the scope. The readout in her vision told her the distance to targets, number of rounds remaining, and where her shot would hit.

The soldiers, like those from any nation, milled about behind the armored vehicles, waiting for the officer in charge to give the orders. They clearly weren't the fast-reaction squad she had smoked earlier, nor were they Immortals from the orbiting cruiser. They had to be Caliphate regulars or part-timers. She almost felt bad. Almost.

The last man exited the lead vehicle. Even if he hadn't immediately started yelling at the soldiers and pointing up the hill, his crisp uniform and shiny boots were a dead giveaway that he was an officer and in charge. *Too bad for him.*

When sniping, the first shot was the most important. Jennings had all the time in the world. She could make sure her first round hit exactly where she intended. After that, every subsequent shot would be made while taking fire.

The ancient battle mantra of the shooter echoed in her mind as if her drill instructor stood right next to her, whispering it in her ear. *"Slow is smooth, and smooth is fast."*

Jennings moved the crosshairs over the head of the officer, leading him a hair as he walked left to right from her perspective. When he paused to berate what she thought was a sergeant, she let out her breath and squeezed the trigger.

Since the MP-17s used electricity to accelerate silicate particles to lethal speeds, they were naturally silent. Only the hum of the discharging battery and a slight warming of the barrel signified firing.

In the middle of his shout, the officer's face exploded. Blood and bone sprayed the sergeant. The man stumbled back, speechless, wiping his face while pointing at what just happened.

Jennings squeezed off another round, taking the man in the thigh. He jumped and fell sideways, screaming and holding his bleeding leg. She got one more shot off before the troopers realized what was happening and returned fire. Their green plasma rounds sprayed in all directions—a few even flew over Jennings' head.

They could get lucky, of course, but the plasma rifles they used were short-to-medium-range weapons, and Jennings had partial defilade. She fired again, taking down the man farthest away. He fell to the ground, screaming. Only her first target was a kill shot; the rest she aimed for nonvital areas. Not that she was squeamish about killing—a wounded soldier required aid, and their screeching in pain and begging for help while bleeding out destroyed morale.

Jennings changed targets, shooting a trooper who ran to help the sergeant. Even from this far away, she could hear the shout that meant they had spotted her position. She ducked back as a dozen plasma rounds exploded against the dirt and rock cover. Heat washed over her from the near misses.

With one hand over her head to protect it from flying debris, she dropped her rifle, pulled a grenade, primed it, and hurled it with all her might.

Jennings' position was all wrong for a grenade—the only advantage she had was altitude. The weapon sailed out, hit with a thump and rolled, coming to a stop about sixty meters away, woefully short of the enemy.

Thick red smoke poured out of the grenade like it was a raging inferno. Within seconds, the firing stopped as they lost all visibility of the cliff top. Using the smoke as cover, Jennings leaped up and hauled butt over the crest and out of sight. At the very least, she had slowed their assault.

She double-timed back to the compound wall, ready to direct the prisoner, when a thunderous noise rose up in the distance. Through a cloud of sand, she made out the Schnell lifting off.

"Thank you, Rashid," she muttered, walking backward up the hill.

When Nadia peeked her head out, Jennings waved her up to join her on the hill. A man bound in cuffs followed them, and she wondered what the spy was up to.

CHAPTER THIRTY-FIVE

Rashid ducked his head as far-off explosions boomed through the hull. He ran through the preflight, prepping the ship as fast as he could. There wasn't anything he could do until the marines cleared the arena, and he couldn't fire up the engines without alerting the spaceport that something was wrong. The last thing he wanted to do was loiter in the air with his old ship in orbit, ready to blast anything that moved.

Once he completed the cycle, the ship confirmed it was ready for liftoff. While the bridge layout was extravagant, it wasn't intended to be operated by more than a few people—just one, if incase of an emergency. Most of it was for show, he imagined, to impress rich passengers. Even ships like his former heavy cruiser could be flown by a single person.

Waiting, he listened to the raging combat outside. Helping the Alliance went against every instinct, every doctrine he knew. They were infidels, murderers, betrayers. Yet... they weren't the ones who executed his parents and sold his beloved kid sister into slavery.

After his banishment, he'd hoped one day maybe he could

return to embrace his home and people. Oddly, he realized with a start, his faith hadn't wavered, simply his faith in the men who wielded their own faith like a weapon.

After this, he would have no choice but to leave Caliphate space forever. The woman, Nadia, had done it. Or at least her parents had. And to command such an assault force, she must work for the Alliance Navy in a high position. Would they accept him as well? Allow him to join their navy? Could he? Knowing that one day, possibly soon, it would bring him into conflict with his former comrades?

Possibly.

First, though, he had to survive and rescue his sister. Entranced in his thoughts, it took him a moment to realize the pops and booms of the battle had stopped. Yet no call came.

He pulled the radio out of his pocket... or what was left of it. The plasma from the near miss had turned the side to slag. He threw it against the hull, angry at himself for not checking sooner. What if they were calling, and because of his idiocy, they were killed? Firefight or no, it was time to go.

He hit the last button, and the massive fusion reactor fired the four plasma turbines that provided in-atmosphere thrust for the liner. Dust swirled around the ship as it lifted off, blowing sand up in a curtain. The controls felt like lead weights, fighting against him as he turned the ship on her axis.

"Allah, she's a pig," he muttered. Liners, even ones made to land, weren't fighters.

At two hundred meters up, he managed to clear the dust cloud. The arena appeared, and he saw a lone figure on top, firing into the street.

He made his decision. Yanking on the controls, he turned the ship further and pressed her toward the compound where his sister was held. Green lines of burning plasma reached up to the ship. They had no more effect than throwing rocks. The only thing he feared was handheld anti-armor weapons.

The ground directly below the ship was obscured, but he could see forward at a forty-five-degree angle to the ground. As the bow passed over the compound, he spotted her.

"*Allahu Akbar*," he said fervently. He'd finally found his sister.

With the ship coming to get them, Jennings needed to make sure the Caliphate soldiers at the bottom of the hill weren't approaching.

She reached her previous spot and took a knee, moving carefully to stay behind defilade and avoid her head being blown off.

Once she could just make out the bottom, she extended her head a tiny bit and then ducked back down just as fast. The soldiers were pulling their wounded into the vehicles while others fired at the liner as it passed overhead.

They could get lucky with small arms, but it was unlikely. She ducked around again and saw one of the men removing a shoulder-mounted launcher from the back of the IFV. That wouldn't require luck.

"India, do not wait for me. Take Delta with you, board the ship, and head to Rally Point Alpha," Jennings said. RP Alpha was the arena.

"Two-Five-Alpha, confirm last?" Nadia asked. "Leave you?"

"Roger. No time to explain."

Jennings prayed the spy was capable of leaving her behind, because if they waited, they would lose the ship.

She flipped a switch on her rifle, converting the sniper weapon to a full-auto battle rifle with only the barest of sights.

She wouldn't be aiming. She then retrieved her last grenade and primed it for proximity detonation.

Another glance confirmed the range. Enemy forces were five hundred meters away. She could throw her weapon a max of seventy, maybe eighty meters if she did so while running.

They were no slouches either. Four men fired at the Schnell, four tended the wounded, and four pulled security, their weapons pointing at or near Jennings' spot.

"Come on, Marine. You want to live forever?"

Sergeant Jennings vaulted off the hilltop, flying three meters through the air before hitting the ground. She tucked and rolled, letting her momentum carry her another half dozen meters before she was up and running.

A soldier spotted her and shouted, waiving his arm to alert his comrades. He fired, burning a green line of death up the hill. Either because of her sudden presence or the speed at which she moved, he hit behind and above her. She knew—from first-hand experience—that hitting a moving target was far more difficult than it seemed.

After a hundred meters, she screamed at them and sprayed her weapon in an arc. Silicate pinged off their armor, blasting sand into the air and forcing them to duck.

They returned sporadic, unaimed fire at her, unwilling to move from cover to aim. The man assembling the shoulder-fired weapon dropped the battery that powered it. He glanced up at Jennings as she continued to run down the hill, still screaming.

Two hundred meters down, a line of burning plasma brushed her shoulder. Brilliant pain lit through her, and she clamped her mouth shut to focus on suppressing the agony. She tripped on a jagged rock, forcing her to dive into a roll. Her rifle fell from numb fingers. She slammed into another rock, smashing her ribs before spinning face-first into the dirt.

A roar of engines exploded as the Schnell lifted off into the sky.

"Two-Five-Alpha, we're clear," Nadia said.

Jennings dared not answer her, knowing she couldn't keep the pain out of her voice. All her training, all the times she'd taken hits, nothing had caused agony like the plasma burn. Once again, the soldiers lifted their weapons to fire on the liner. With a grunt, the marine rolled herself over. She had two hundred meters to go.

Come on, Allison. The captain is waiting.

She pulled the primed grenade from her waist and vaulted down the hill, bounding in two-meter leaps with one hand cocked back to throw and the other out for balance. The soldiers, intent on firing on the liner, couldn't hear her through the cacophony of the plasma engines or see her through all the sand kicked up by the exhaust.

She couldn't see them either, but she knew exactly where they were. Ten more steps and she hurled the grenade blind, directly at the spot where she *knew* the soldier with the anti-armor weapon stood.

Two seconds later, the blast lit up the area, creating a sudden surge of wind outward. For an instant, it cleared the sand, and she saw her throw had nailed the intended target. He was dead, along with the two soldiers near him. The sand whipped back up, blinding her, but she ran anyway. There was no way out but through.

She stumbled and slammed bodily into a man pointing his rifle up, still trying to shoot the liner. They went down in a heap. Jennings bashed her forehead against his face. His nose exploded, and the satisfying crack of broken bones was followed by blubbering cries.

She pulled her knife and sheathed it in his bicep tendon.

Pushing off with her legs, she rolled over him, pulling her knife out as she went.

Hitting the next man she saw wasn't as easy; he heard his friend's howls, turned to see her coming, and pulled the trigger, sending a line of green plasma to slice like a knife through her abdomen. She hurled herself forward, sticking the bayonet-sized blade in his throat.

Her hand clasped the wound in her stomach. It didn't bleed —a side effect of burning plasma.

It hurt though, like someone had reached in and removed a rib without bothering to cut.

She had one chance: get to an IFV and drive it to the arena. Grunting, she got her legs under her and heaved toward where she knew the IFV was. The sand had cleared somewhat as the Schnell slid away toward the city proper. Her good shoulder hit hard metal. She'd found it.

Could she drive it, though?

Naki managed to gather most of the people to huddle against the hotel wall. There were still hundreds who couldn't walk, and more whom he classified as walking wounded. They stood staring at nothing, eyes vacant.

"Two-Five-Bravo, India. Evac inbound, ETA thirty seconds."

Naki clenched his fist in excitement. "Hell yes, I copy, India. Damn good to hear your voice."

He really didn't want to die here or, worse, get turned into a slave. If it came to it, he considered ordering Owens to follow him as they took off for the outskirts. However, it hadn't come to that. "Charlie." He keyed his radio to Owens. "You have eyes on Romeo?"

"Yes, I do. Coming overhead now," the PFC replied.

Sure enough, thunder echoed in the arena as the liner slid over the wall Owens held. Small-arms fire splashed green lines of plasma against her hull with no effect.

The liner was too large to set down in the arena. Opposite the hotel was a square with the room she needed. Naki directed them using a radio beacon. In response, the ship tilted, sliding through the air until it was past the arena and hovering over the public square.

"Come on," he yelled over his loudspeaker, punctuated with a wave. "This is your ticket out of here. Move it!"

Thousands of bodies surged forward, moving as fast as their malnourished, beaten muscles allowed. Many more simply couldn't.

"Owens, get down here and help me with the wounded," he said.

"Naki, they're still down there. If we withdraw, they'll push…"

Naki was well aware of the tactics. He also understood the skipper's orders: not one person left behind.

"I know. Get down here," he said. He flipped the switch on the radio to call the liner. "India, be advised, there are wounded in need of assistance. You'll need to hold the square."

He turned and picked up a small woman who was curled into a ball and ran for the ship. The line of slaves marched after him, moving as fast as they could.

The liner set down, and a side hatch opened up. Boudreaux waved him over.

"Chief, you lose your bird?" he asked as he handed her the woman.

"Not before I took out one of theirs," she said.

"Oorah, Chief." Naki turned back, running as fast as he could. Owens passed him carrying two wounded, though Naki was certain it wasn't a medically approved maneuver.

Several dozen people in the crowd saw what the two marines were attempting and joined in, finally waking up to what needed to be done.

Naki couldn't blame them, though, as he knelt down and picked up an old man with dark brown skin and patchy hair. They had endured so much; asking them to risk their own lives when escape was at hand was a lot.

He only hoped they could load everyone before the security forces caught on.

CHAPTER THIRTY-SIX

Lieutenant West hadn't slept a wink since the ground operation had started. Worse, he'd warned *Interceptor* off, yet they came anyway.

He watched helplessly as the heavy cruiser tagged Tango-One powered up her gravcoil at last and sped after his ship.

Interceptor had done her job, though, with a precision few ships in the navy could hope to match. Every defense satellite and every corvette and the base housing them were space dust. Nothing but debris in orbit.

"How long until Tango-One is out of weapons range?" he asked.

"Three-zero minutes, sir," Oliv answered.

"Collins, as soon as we have our ground team back on board, set course for the starlane, flank speed," he said.

"Aye, aye, sir," PO Collins said.

Mark wished there was something he could do other than wait. He felt so impotent. *Komodo* didn't have a single weapon, no ability to go to ground, nothing.

"Sir, incoming signal from India," Oliv said.

"*Komodo*, this is India. Bug out. Bravo Oscar. Rally point

Echo. I say again, Bravo Oscar, rally point Echo. India out." Commander Dagher sounded terse.

West shook himself, getting his body to catch up with his mind.

"Helm, come about one-eight-zero. Set course for point Echo. Execute when ready. Flank speed," he said.

"Aye, sir, point Echo, flank speed," PO Collins repeated.

"Sir," Oliv said, "we're still in range of her torpedoes..." She gestured to the icon representing the heavy cruiser on the big screen. Unlike fast little ships, big lumbering freighters were ideal targets for torpedoes. "Not to mention, if they see us running, they could just come right at us."

"I know, but the commander said bug out, and that means we bug out. I just pray they have their own way out."

The planet shifted in the viewer as Collins deftly turned the ship. He hoped the heavy cruiser was too busy with *Interceptor* to notice.

———

Naki breathed hard as he made his umpteenth trip carrying wounded back to the ship. Everyone had chipped in, but it was still taking too long. He caught sight of Sakura doing her part. The profound respect he had for her, the courage it took for her to willingly get off that ship and help, was nothing short of spectacular.

But it wasn't going to be enough. He handed his two off to Boudreaux and looked back at the arena. While dozens of people ran back and forth as fast as they could, there were still at least a thousand more who couldn't walk on their own.

"Two-Five-Bravo," India said over his radio.

"Go for Bravo," he replied.

"How long?" she asked.

It took two minutes for him to move two people, with the amount left... he did the math, and it wasn't pretty.

"Not long, ma'am," he said. He hated lying to anyone, let alone an officer. But the captain wanted everyone, and by all that he held sacred, he was going to give the captain what he wanted.

"Bullshit, Corporal. You've got five minutes, and we're dusting off. Over," she said.

"Aye, ma'am. Over."

That was that. He was just a corporal; he couldn't disobey an officer's orders, no matter how much he wanted to.

He lumbered over to where Boudreaux helped people and popped his canopy to speak with her privately. "Chief, I need you to find a way to stall the ship," he said to her as quietly as he could.

Boudreaux looked at him with a mix of surprise and incredulity. "Why?" she asked.

He glanced at the constant stream of prisoners. "Because we can't leave anyone behind, Chief. Not one." What were they going to do? Court-martial him for disobeying orders on an illegal mission?

Chief Boudreaux set her expression in stone and nodded. "On it, Corporal."

"Charlie, pick it up," Naki said as he closed his canopy.

"What do you think I've been doing?" Owens replied.

Nadia took cover behind a concrete barricade, her borrowed plasma rifle at her shoulder. There were three avenues of approach into the square: she held one, Rashid another, and Elsa the third. They were spread thin, but at least she had stashed Imran in the brig, locked down tight. All they had to do was get off the damn planet. Why didn't the marine corporal understand that?

Her position faced the main street, hundreds of meters long and lined with buildings. It was the most exposed of the three lanes—which was why she took it.

She had the daughter of the Iron Empire and the son of Hamid, the Caliph. Their mission was no longer about delaying the war, but ending it before it began. The Caliphate wouldn't dare attack them, not when it would risk bringing the Iron Empire into the war against them. And as long as they held the Caliph's son, they wouldn't bomb any planets for fear of killing him by accident.

Movement caught her eye, and she reacted, swiveling her rifle and squeezing the trigger. A line of green plasma burned through the air, dropping a soldier in his tracks.

"We got company," she yelled into the radio.

As if on cue, a volley of plasma fire lit the air around her. She ducked, and heat washed over her with the near miss.

"Nothing here," Elsa said.

"Clear," Rashid said.

Either this was their only assault force, or they were trying to get her to commit to an angle, then counterattack?

"Stay in position. Hold your lane," she said. "Owens, get your butt over—" An air turbine roared, followed by the sickening crunch of metal on flesh. Nadia poked her head out to see what happened.

The soldiers had staged in what looked like a blasted-out restaurant. Once they were sure where she was, they had moved out in a line, firing to keep her down. The turbo fan she'd heard belonged to an IFV that had run them down before slamming into the cafe's shattered exterior.

There were six crushed soldiers plus the one Nadia had downed. With a hiss of escaping atmosphere, the side hatch opened, and Sergeant Jennings stumbled out, her uniform marred by burn holes and covered in blood.

"Jennings!" Nadia jumped up and ran for the marine, her excitement at seeing the tough woman alive overriding her good sense. She reached her just in time to hold her up as the marine's legs buckled.

"Holy crap, you're heavy," Nadia said. She strained to keep the woman upright. Jennings was short as hell, but the woman had to weigh a hundred kilos.

"Bravo, I have Alpha at my location. Help," she said. Five seconds later, Raptor powered armor leaped over the barricade and skidded to a halt in a shower of dust and broken sandstone.

"I got you," Naki said through the PA. He lifted Jennings like a toddler picking up a doll.

Nadia watched the suit retreat to the ship. "Corporal, we're out of time. We need to dust off now," Nadia said over the comms.

"Commander," Boudreaux broke in, "there's a problem with the Schnell's inertial inverter, I'm fixing it, but we need two-zero minutes."

If the situation weren't so damned urgent, she would admire Jacob's crew and loyalty, but dammit, it wasn't time to play hero. They had to get off this planet.

"Boudreaux, you've got ten mikes; then we're leaving."

"Aye, ma'am."

―――

Somehow, it was enough. Naki hung off the side of the ship, sans his armor, helping the last person up into the hold. As time ticked by, more and more of those already aboard had woken up and rushed to help those left behind.

Lance Corporal Naki was overcome with emotion, tinged

with a little sorrow. How many more people were on Medial? How many were they leaving behind? How many more on the many worlds of the Caliphate?

Sakura had found him in the crush of bodies, managing to stay pressed up against his back as if his very presence kept her free. Maybe it did. He didn't know.

He'd joined the marines right out of school, with no direction, no idea what he wanted to do with his life—a story often repeated in the corps. But in this moment, surrounded by people he had helped rescue, he knew. He knew that he would be a marine forever. He knew that if at all possible, he would spend the rest of his life trying to free more poor bastards from slavery.

Rashid leaped out of the seat as Boudreaux arrived on the bridge, barely acknowledging her presence as he rushed by her. Four years he had waited for his sister's return; he could not wait another moment.

The cargo hold was packed with passengers. While there was more than enough room in the liner itself, most of the former slaves were too dazed, stunned, or in shock to go further.

"Zahra," he shouted. He pushed through the crush of bodies, leaping as he went, trying to get a glimpse of the child he had known. "Zahra," he shouted again.

The Alliance didn't seem to know the effects the collars had over extended duration. They would realize it soon enough when they found many of the slaves they freed unable to cope with their sudden autonomy. He hoped, no, *he prayed*, his sister's will had survived.

The two marines were out of their armor. Uniforms

soaked in sweat, they were handing out meal packets to the malnourished. The taller one in charge—Rashid couldn't remember his name—had a blue-skinned girl following him around.

But no Zahra.

"Rashid," Nadia said from the far side, waving her arm. She stood next to a tall, thin, blonde woman who he figured was the Iron Emperor's daughter.

The crowd parted for a moment, and his heart leaped into his throat. He fought back tears as his beautiful sister turned to see him. Fear, dread, and guilt all warred within him. Would she blame him? Could she forgive him?

She smiled, as big as the world and twice as bright as the sun. Tears streamed down her face as she ran for him. They met in the center, falling to their knees as they hugged. Rashid buried his face in her long black hair, sobbing.

"I'm sorry, Zahra. I'm sorry," he said. "I have tried. By Allah, I tried to free you sooner."

Her body shaking with tears, Zahra could not respond. She held onto her brother tight, not wanting to ever let him go.

―――

Chief Boudreaux finished her preflight, making sure each subsystem pinged green before she activated the plasma turbines.

"All stations, Charlie-One-One is on the move. Hang tight. If *Interceptor* missed any defense structures, this could get interesting."

She pushed the power forward, and the Schnell responded with a rumble as it lifted from the ground. A moment later, the bridge lit up as a fireball climbed into the sky from the direction of the foreign spaceport.

"Boudreaux, Naki. The Mudcat just went offline. I think they found the source of the jamming."

With the jamming off, any ground-based systems would be able to lock onto the ship and fire. Without satellites, though, they would have to rely on a radar lock; if she were smooth enough, she could get the ship out of their airspace in a few minutes. Assuming they gave her that time.

Alarms rang out, alerting her to radar and lidar beams hitting the hull. "Commander Dagher, I need you and anyone else who can operate a ship on the bridge right frigging now," Boudreaux yelled.

Schnells were fast and agile—in space. In atmosphere, the massive liner handled like a pig. Boudreaux needed the turbines to cycle up to a million impulses each. She could do that while gaining altitude, but then they would be sitting ducks a few klicks over the city. She reached over and swiveled the engines for downward thrust and jammed the throttle all the way forward.

The ship creaked and groaned as the superstructure absorbed thrust it was never meant to.

Alarms wailed at her. She glanced at the board, but without an understanding of the Empire's language, she could only guess what it meant. The wailing turned to a rhythmic siren that cycled faster and faster. "I know that sound," she muttered.

Elsa, Rashid, and Commander Dagher burst onto the bridge.

"Where do you want us?" Dagher asked.

"ECM, power, and nav," she said without taking her eyes off the controls.

Nadia pointed at Elsa. "Take ECM."

Elsa vaulted over a panel and slid into a seat on the starboard side of the ship. "Weapons lock," she shouted as she furiously punched buttons on the console.

"They won't fire while were over the city," Dagher said.

"You wanna bet?" Boudreaux said from the side of her mouth.

She needed a few more seconds. Power curves built, and the numbers climbed higher as the plasma engines cycled.

"They're going to fire in three seconds," Elsa said.

"Chief, we're not moving," Dagher said.

"I know," she replied.

"They're going to fire," Elsa said.

"I know."

"It would help if we moved," Dagher added.

"I know," Boudreaux said through gritted teeth.

One million.

"Missile launch!" Elsa shouted.

Boudreaux's deft hands moved, rotating the engines around and slamming the thrust to maximum. Plasma turbines wailed in electronic fury as they accelerated gas to hypervelocity, turning the exhaust into molten air, melting the very ground underneath the ship.

For a moment, the Schnell didn't move. Boudreaux focused on her controls, willing the ship to climb.

"Missile tracking," Elsa said.

"Wait for it," Boudreaux said.

The plasma engines found their stride, and the three-hundred-meter-long passenger liner shot into the sky like a bullet, leaving a line of burning atmosphere behind it as it accelerated to escape velocity only five hundred meters above the city. The secondary gravcoil was pushed to its limits, fighting to keep the passengers from being crushed to death by the *g* force.

Boudreaux watched the screen as the surface-to-air missile streaked after them, her vision tunneling until all she could see was the looming threat.

One thousand meters to impact.

Five hundred meters.

At two hundred meters to impact, the missile's fuel ran out, and the warhead fell out of the sky behind them.

"Wow," Elsa said. "How did you know?"

Boudreaux looked at her and blinked. "I didn't."

CHAPTER THIRTY-SEVEN

Jacob held onto the command chair's armrest as the ship shook. The secondary gravcoil did all it could to keep their gravity at 1*g* normal, but when the ship accelerated or changed course rapidly, or when the weapons fired, the two sources of gravity fought, resulting in slight disruptions.

An engineer had once explained to Jacob that they could remove all traces of gravitic interference, but the power requirements shot up exponentially—to the point where a ship like *Interceptor* would need another fusion reactor to cover the last one percent.

As a compromise, the original designers had decided to have controlled gravity expression. Of course, they had to figure out the right settings, and that took time and lives. When it was all over, though, they'd ended up with a design that made ship handling more intuitive.

Jacob didn't have to check when the guns and torpedoes fired—he could feel it. Acceleration and heading changes were the same. The only time it became dangerous, which a good coxswain could mitigate, was crossing a powerful gravwake behind a ship.

"Sir," Lieutenant Fawkes said through their private channel.

"Yes, Carter?"

"We have a problem. Sending it to your screen."

A second later, Jacob's MFD flashed, and a topographical map of the system appeared. Clearly, there was a lot more to a system map than a two-dimensional representation of orbital bodies. However, knowing the distance and relative location of every planet, moon, and large rock allowed for broad strategy.

Jacob leaned forward as much as his harness would allow, examining the map and trying to see the problem before Carter pointed it out.

The map showed Medial to their stern, several ships in orbit, and two ships breaking for the starlane—along with the heavy cruiser pursuing *Interceptor*. He spotted *Komodo's* transponder heading for the starlane. The other he didn't recognize. It had a higher power curve and accelerated faster than *Komodo*. He'd certainly raised enough Cain in orbit to warrant all the ships bugging out.

"I don't see it, Carter," he said.

"I ran this by Ensign Owusu just to make sure, sir, and he says it's spot on."

Jacob glanced up at his weapons officer. "Carter, I get it, but I'm not seeing it."

"Aye, sir, sorry, sir. Here, let me adjust the scan resolution," Carter said.

The bird's-eye of the map zoomed out. A green cone appeared in front of *Interceptor*. It was the degrees by which he could turn the ship and still maintain full velocity and acceleration. As they piled on velocity, the cone shrank.

Another green circle surrounded the space around *Interceptor*. There were five more reaching far back, each circle representing a location—or ship—the *Interceptor* could reach in a given time frame. Anything within the circle, they could catch if they went full stop and reversed course.

Jacob saw the problem. *Dammit. Just... Every time I think we're getting ahead here.*

The Caliphate heavy cruiser showed a yellow cone and circle. Due to its slower velocity and lower acceleration, the cone was thirty degrees wider than *Interceptor*'s. But her forward velocity and glacially slow turn radius weren't the problem. Her rear rings stretched out three times as far as *Interceptor*'s, not because she was faster, but because her base velocity was so much lower. It wouldn't take her long to full stop and do a one-eighty.

Those circles stretched out almost all the way to the starlane, which they'd designated as Point Echo. He either had to force them to speed up or get them to commit to a course directly opposite the starlane, because even the largest, slowest battleship could easily run down a civilian freighter. If the captain of Tango-One realized *Komodo* was actually Alliance, he could turn and engage the freighters long before they could flee the system.

In an effort to put distance between his ship and those damn guns, he'd ordered Suresh to flank speed, stretching their lead even farther, but also increasing the time it would take to turn around. Even as he watched, *Komodo* and the other ship passed through the final circle of *Interceptor*'s stern.

"I see it, Carter. Good man. Pass my compliments to Ensign Owusu if you will."

"Aye, Skipper, will do," Carter replied.

Jacob fiddled with the monitor controls, adding weapons range to the overlay. There was one more wrinkle in his plan. In order to entice Tango-One to chase him, he would have to let them stay in weapons range. Otherwise, it would all be for naught.

Which meant he needed to slow down. If he were too obvious about it, though, then they would suspect a trap and start looking for another reason.

He checked the mission clock. He needed to give *Komodo* one more hour. If Tango-One didn't turn around and head for the starlane within the next hour, then they would never catch *Komodo*.

One hour.

Jacob closed his eyes, spending a solid minute praying for guidance and inspiration. Begging for the lives of his crew.

"Chief Suresh, I want to reduce acceleration, but I want it to look like we've had a gravcoil failure," he said.

Her head snapped up, unable to hide her surprise. "Skipper?" she asked.

He double-checked and made sure his comms were open to the bridge. He didn't want to hide his plan from anyone. Not when he was about to ask them to risk their lives again after they thought they were in the clear.

"*Komodo* has to escape, Chief. If we don't let Tango-One gain on us, they could turn around and go after them, and we wouldn't be able to do anything about it. *Interceptor* must buy that ship one hour. One hour, and we can punch it for home."

"Aye, sir, I'll talk to Lieutenant Gonzales and figure out what we need to do," Suresh said.

"Make it snappy, Chief. They won't follow us for much longer."

On the bridge of *Divine Wind*, Captain Bitar watched the two ships running for the starlane on his plot. A moment later, more signatures broke free, running in multiple directions, but all away from the angry, heavy cruiser and the planet.

"Dammit," he muttered. The whole operation was blown. Alliance ships, ground forces, and the son of the Caliphate stuck on the planet. He was tempted to send his two remaining Dhibs after the first two ships that broke orbit, but... If he ended up boarding the destroyer, he would need them.

"Jamal," he said, "load up one Dhib with a platoon of Immortals and drop them. They can head back to the planet and secure our primary target."

"Aren't we chasing their only hope, sir?" his intelligence officer responded. "If we catch the destroyer, then any forces on the ground will have to surrender. The Alliance are cowards—they won't fight to the death or kill hostages."

Jamal wasn't wrong, but something about the situation bothered Bitar. Everything had caught him by surprise, happening so fast that he hadn't actually sat down and worked it out. If the troops on the ground came from the Alliance ship... how had they gotten there? Their ship was too small to carry a significant ground force. They must have arrived before *Divine Wind*.

"Comms, delay to planetary communications?" he asked.

"Ten seconds, sir. I think the jamming is lifted, but I can't reach anyone at their security offices."

Likely because their security offices floated in orbit and that damned destroyer had turned them to gas, along with all the satellites. Troops on the ground would still be organizing, trying to figure out who was in charge and what to do.

"Give me the priority channel," he ordered.

"Yes, sir. You're on," the young man said.

"Medial security, this is Captain Bitar of the *Divine Wind*. Come in. Over," he said.

He silently counted to twenty, praying each second that someone in authority would answer.

"Sir, this is Corporal al-Quresh, first responder brigade. I can't find anyone of higher rank on the net. Over."

Bitar ground his heel into the deck, clenching the arm of his command chair at the same time. There should be no less than a dozen officers and three times as many noncommissioned officers on the planet.

"Right. Okay, Corporal. This is important. I need you to get to the governor's residence and check on the status of the VIP there. I need you to do this in"—he looked at the clock—"fifteen minutes. This is of the highest priority. Understood? Over."

He waited for the response. Every second that ticked by drew him farther and farther away from the fleeing freighters. He couldn't just turn around, though, not with a flagged Alliance ship in his sights. Not for a guess. He needed to know.

"Yes, sir, I'm on it. Over."

"Bitar out," he said.

"Sir?" Jamal asked. "What's going on?"

"Just focus on that ship," he said.

It couldn't, though, could it? The Alliance wouldn't even know who the Caliph's son was. If he broke off pursuing the destroyer to take on the freighters, then he would look the fool for letting an easy kill get away. As long as they maintained contact with the Alliance ship, it couldn't leave the system. The moment they slowed to enter the starlane, Bitar would cripple their ship and—

"Sir!" Jamal shouted. "Alpha-one is slowing down. I registered a disruption in their gravwake, and then they lost half their acceleration."

Bitar laughed. "Allah be praised," he said. The bridge echoed with his sentiments. "We are victorious. Prepare to fire as soon as they are in range." He would crush the gnat, save the VIP, and stop the freighters.

Gonzales swore, wishing for the umpteenth time Redfern was aboard. The two-decades-older engineering chief knew the *Interceptor* backward and forward. When the captain had asked to simulate a gravcoil failure, Gonzales did the only thing he could think of. He caused the gravcoil to fail for real, but in a way he could easily repair on the go.

"Good man, Lieutenant Gonzales," Commander Grimm said over the helmet. "How long to bring the engines back up to full speed?"

Enzo Gonzales looked at the bank of flashing crimson warning lights with dread. The entire system had experienced backlash, and he'd gone from having every light green to the blinking red nightmare in front of him.

"Thirty minutes, sir," he said.

"Excellent. Keep me apprised. Grimm out."

Gonzales shook his head. What had possessed him to give such a ridiculous time frame? *Thirty minutes? More like thirty hours.* If he had learned one thing aboard *Interceptor*, though, it was "don't disappoint the skipper."

CHAPTER THIRTY-EIGHT

Jacob eyed the distance between the two ships warily. Once it hit one million kilometers, firing would commence. Tango-One had much more throw weight than *Interceptor*. Not to mention deeper magazines.

Interceptor didn't need to engage for very long, and they didn't need to win, just hold them for—he glanced at the mission clock—thirty-two more minutes.

"C'mon, girl," he said to his ship, "you can do it."

"One minute to weapons range. Sir, we could fire now, maybe get lucky," Lieutenant Carter Fawkes said.

"I know, but at this range, even with them down our wake, we would be wasting ordnance. They have sixteen point-defense turrets to our four. Six tubes to our two. Not to mention thicker armor. Besides, if we did get lucky, I don't want them spooking. We need them on us."

"Aye, sir." Fawkes went quiet.

Jacob studied the plot a moment longer. *Komodo* raced toward the starlane, still inside the yellow zone of the enemy cruiser. The second craft that left shortly after *Komodo* had passed her by, leading Jacob to suspect it was a smaller ship.

"We're going to lose sensor contact with *Komodo* soon," PO Tefiti said. "If you want to send a message, now is the time, sir."

Jacob shook his head. "Any signal could be intercepted, and if they think for a moment *Komodo* is with us, they will turn around and destroy her."

He would love to know what was going on with the ground team and *Komodo*, but that wasn't his mission. He trusted them to get the job done like they trusted him.

"Launch. Launch. Launch," Fawkes said over the bridge comms. To his credit, he kept his voice even.

"It's okay. We expected them to launch the moment they could. ETA to impact?" he asked.

Ensign Owusu answered, "Two-five-zero seconds, sir."

Jacob nodded. That put them right in the engagement envelope. In essence, the cruiser's torpedoes had to go twice as far to reach him. However, torpedoes were already fast, and launched from a speeding ship, even faster. They would hit *Interceptor* a few seconds before their gravcoils burned out if *Interceptor* did nothing.

"Carter, commence point-defense," he ordered.

"Aye, aye, sir. All turrets, commence point-defense."

A moment later, *Interceptor* shook as turrets three and four began firing twenty-millimeter nano-hardened tungsten rounds downrange. Unlike ships, torpedoes had only a limited ability to maneuver on the fly. They used calculations loaded into them at the time of launch to track their targets. Even if they were close enough to guide them via radio, it still wouldn't do much good with the small nature of the weapons—they could only carry so much fuel for maneuvering. Aimed in the general vicinity of their target, their limited AI took over and maneuvered them the rest of the way.

"Second launch. Six more in space, sir," Fawkes announced.

Forty seconds to fire six torpedoes. Which meant they could

launch eighteen at his little ship in the same two minutes it took him to answer with eight. "Range?" he asked.

Owusu threw the counter up on his screen. "Eight-five-three thousand klicks and gaining."

Jacob hated to risk his crew when he didn't have to, but he had to let that ship move closer. No captain from any navy would stop pursuit when victory was in their grasp. "Chief Suresh, slalom," he ordered. "Carter, have one and two start firing at the heavy cruiser."

"Aye, aye, sir, slalom," Chief Suresh replied.

"Turrets one and two fire on target. Aye, aye, sir." The ship shook again as the turrets continued firing on the torpedoes. Twenty-millimeter rounds flew through space at ten thousand KPS, some aiming for the torpedoes and some for the cruiser.

Interceptor banked to port as Chief Suresh took manual control, maneuvering the ship through shallow S-curves to allow all four turrets to fire on a near continuous basis. The range between the ships dropped faster as *Interceptor* gave up some of her acceleration to maneuver.

Bitar's unease grew with each passing second. Something wasn't right. The destroyer had lost speed, yes, but not so much. They were gaining slowly. *Divine Wind* crept up on her, kilometer by kilometer, firing a barrage of torpedoes and receiving light return fire.

"Sir, they're taking out our torpedoes without much effort. None have closed to more than three hundred thousand klicks."

Bitar knew torps were best against large, slow-moving targets. Destroyers were nimble and their guns agile; it would take much luck to hit them with one of his plasma torpedoes. Of course, it would only take one. Destroyers were a nuisance for his weapon systems.

"At six hundred thousand, go rapid fire on all tubes. Activate turrets one through eight and fire."

His turrets commenced firing, sending bolts of stable plasma shooting through space at thousands of kilometers per second. The bolts glowed green as they left, but turned yellow, orange, and finally red as they disappeared before reaching the enemy ship.

Bitar didn't expect any to hit, but if he could slow the ship down, then he was all for it. After all, firing eight quad-turrets cost him nothing.

"Sir, message from Medial," Jamal said. "They've arrived at the compound. No sign of the VIP and"—he held his hand over his ear to better hear the garbled communications—"he's saying it looks like a war zone, sir. Dead bodies everywhere, blown-up IFVs…"

Bitar bit back his curse. He was afraid of that, but the jamming had kept him from confirming it. Still, they had nowhere to go. Once he swatted the destroyer, he would go back and smash the ground forces on the planet.

———

Interceptor rolled through another S curve, Chief Suresh taking the ship further on her axis and against the gravwake than usual.

The momentary conflicting gravity pressed Jacob hard into his chair. He was about to ask why when the answer presented itself.

Green bolts of stable plasma slashed by the ship, missing by only a few hundred kilometers.

"They've commenced firing their turrets. Sorry, sir," Carter said. "I didn't catch it on the readout."

Jacob gave the young man a small hand gesture letting him know it was okay. "Let's not make a habit of it, Carter. One of their turrets is enough to seriously damage us," he said.

"Aye, sir. I'm on it."

Despite Jacob's calm exterior, he knew the truth; Suresh had saved every spacer aboard with her quick reaction.

"Chief, why don't we bump the acceleration up and at the same time widen our curve. I'd like to return a little more fire."

"Aye, sir, increasing acceleration to compensate, increasing slalom," she replied.

In the grand scheme of things, even though Tango-One was easily five times larger than *Interceptor*, she was still hard to hit. A tiny moving speck against a vast backdrop of space.

"Range, six hundred thousand, sir," Owusu said.

That should be enough, Jacob decided. No need to let them any closer unle—

"Sir, twelve torpedoes in space; they just doubled their volley!" Fawkes announced.

Twelve... that would mean she'd gone to rapid fire. Twelve every—

"Another volley. Six this time," Fawkes added.

Interceptor shook as Chief Suresh rolled her to one side and brought her back violently in the opposite direction.

Jacob checked the plot; Tango-One rapid fired her torpedoes and turrets. With no return fire, they could focus all their firepower on *Interceptor*, leaving nothing for point-defense.

"Weapons, commence firing tubes five and six," Jacob ordered.

"Aye, sir. Five and six firing."

The ship shuddered as twin massive torpedoes shot out the

back and ignited their own gravcoils to speed off toward the enemy.

He debated rapid-firing his weapons. It put a strain on crew and equipment, they had to work twice as hard, and there were more room for mistakes. His crew trained hard, though, and they wouldn't have to do it for very long. They could handle it. "Fawkes, rapid fire, all batteries," he ordered.

"Aye, sir. Rapid fire, all batteries," Fawkes replied.

"Launch! Torpedoes in space," Jamal said. "Just two, though."

Bitar laughed. If the situation on Medial weren't so critical, the match-up between his hundred-thousand-ton behemoth and the thirty-thousand-ton pipsqueak would be hilarious—though he was certain that was what *Jalut* had thought upon seeing *Dawud* with his slingshot.

The fact that this little ship was letting him close was a testament to how woefully unprepared the Alliance was to fight a war with the Caliphate of Hamid. They couldn't even maintain their own ships.

"All turrets, commence firing. Prioritize point-defense. Increase speed to flank."

PO Josh Mendez dropped through the hatch from the Long Nine, down onto the central deck in a way only the young could do. His knees flexed, and he took off running.

Torpedo room five lay all the way at the very stern of the ship, above the boat bay and past the aft ammo storage.

"DCS, PO Mendez. I'm on the way. What did you say the problem was, ma'am?"

"Mendez, DCS. The torpedo lifter is jammed up. With the new systems installed, I'm thinking one of the rails is bent. If you can locate it, I can have a team there in a minute with a replacement."

"Aye, aye, ma'am. I'm on it."

His ship was old, there was no doubt about it. They could only test so many systems, and the after-torpedo rooms and surrounding hull were all brand new, fabricated and rebuilt after the devastating hit they took in Wonderland.

Since he'd helped with the installation and fabrication, it only made sense for him to go locate the problem before it became a catastrophe. Torpedo rooms held enough ammo for six volleys. The loader would bring up more munitions; then the room team would slide them into place—not unlike how the Long Nine worked.

If the rails were bent or obstructed though, it wouldn't be long before they couldn't return fire and—

Interceptor heaved. Mendez's boots locked into place, preventing him from smashing into the hull but not stopping him from slamming forward onto the deck.

His suit flashed red, alerting him to a hull breach.

"Where?" Jacob asked after he'd regained his senses.

"Deck three, mess, port side is open to space, Skipper," Yuki told him from DCS. "No casualties."

Jacob sat back, relieved at the news. They were fifteen minutes into the engagement. Halfway through. If they could hang on for another fifteen, they could run for it—if they managed to avoid any serious damage that crippled their acceleration.

"Chief, what happened?" Jacob asked his coxswain as he looked at her face in the mirror.

"Sir, they're firing sixteen turrets with four barrels each. They've got the firepower to spare. That wasn't even a direct hit, just a graze as I came out of the turn."

"Sorry, Chief. Of course you're doing excellent. Hang in there."

She didn't respond. They both knew the odds they faced—her better than anyone aboard. The only advantage he had was that he didn't have to fight them. They didn't know it, but this was a battle for time. Time that was running out. He just needed it to run out on the clock before it ran out on his ship.

"Sir, torpedo room five is reporting empty magazine. DCS has a man looking into it, but we're down to six only," Carter said.

"We need that tube," Jacob said. "Make it a priority."

CHAPTER THIRTY-NINE

Bitar smiled like a predator. Even though the little ship was holding them at six hundred thousand klicks, they'd scored a hit. Just the one, but it showed. A field of debris blossomed on the radar like so much glittering sand on a shore.

The Alliance ship turned a little sharper, a little less precisely, as if whoever piloted her had decided speed in the maneuvers was more important than finesse.

"Good work, Jamal. Now do it again," he ordered.

Lights flashed on the bridge.

"We're hit, sir. Three impacts, no armor penetration," Jamal said.

Bitar's confidence returned, and he felt reassured that he'd made the right decision. *Divine Wind*'s armor was too strong for the Alliance turrets. Even if they scored more hits, it likely wouldn't hurt them.

"Sir, we must have damaged them worse than I thought. They're only firing one torpedo," Jamal said.

As Bitar watched, a single light blipped from the aft of the destroyer, speeding toward his ship.

Lighting in the aft armory flickered as Mendez climbed the ladder next to the loader. With one hand for balance, he pulled his harness and clipped it onto the ship's safety catch. At the very least, he wouldn't go flying across the compartment.

"LED," he said to activate the ELS suit's external lights. Two bright beams shot out from either side of the visor, illuminating the room as bright as a noonday sun.

In order to make the rail as easy as possible to replace, both in combat and for maintenance, they were marked every ten centimeters. Like a puzzle, each piece could be ejected and a new piece put in.

"XO, Mendez. No joy yet, ma'am. The rail looks good. Run the loader so I can see where it stops," he said.

"Roger that. Wait one," Yuki replied.

A moment later, the articulating arm descended from the overhead. Its padded, six-clawed hand reached for the next torpedo in line, then froze a meter from picking it up. While Josh watched, the arm lifted up again and then down, unable to make it past one rail.

He dropped down to the bottom, shining the light on the rail in question. "Got it!" he shouted for joy. He knelt down next to the arm and reached behind it to unlatch the rail.

In that same moment, one of dozens of stable plasma bolts whizzing by the ship struck home like an executioner's axe.

Light flashed, and an explosion like a small sun ripped through the boat bay, blasting the doors to smithereens and sending razor-sharp fragments through the after section of the ship.

The internal armor stopped the worst of it, but the energy deflected upward, and a hundred tiny pieces of death ripped through the aft magazine storage. Shards of hull ricocheted silently around the room and Josh felt the vibrations as they pinged off every surface.

Several embedded in the overhead, and three more hit the torpedo storage rack, causing several of the five-hundred-kilogram warheads to roll onto the floor, smashing into the rail. Two hit the articulating arm, severing one claw and the battery cable.

One more hit next to Josh's head, leaving a red-hot fragment quivering a few centimeters from his face. Josh squeezed his eyes shut and waited to die. When that didn't happen, he opened one eye, then the other. Fragments were everywhere. The floor had enough holes in it to be Swiss cheese, and space was clearly visible through the rear of the compartment. Everywhere except for where one PO Josh Mendez knelt, reaching for the rail, had shards of red hot fragmented armor sticking out like some kind of dart board of carnage.

Some grace, some miracle, had spared him. He let out a long breath, his hands shaking. "XO," he said, his voice uneven but far calmer than he thought it should be, "we need a new rail and a battery cable and we're good to go."

"Team on the way. Well done, Mendez," Yuki said.

"Aye, ma'am," he replied. His hands shook as he pulled himself up. He didn't have time to wait for the team. Reaching down, he shifted the nearest torpedo and got to work.

Jacob's stare didn't leave his MFD. Chief Suresh did her best, but they were too outgunned. Every second they spent in contact with the Caliphate monstrosity was a second too many.

"Bridge, Gonzales. I've got the gravcoil back, sir. Flank speed available when you're ready."

"Good job, Enzo," Jacob said.

His ship cried in agony as another hit mangled her, sending a shiver of pain through the hull. The boat bay turned red as DCS flagged the section as open to space. Luckily, it was empty.

"Aft magazine stores are repaired. We've got two tubes again," Fawkes said with triumphant joy. "Firing."

In order to match up their launches, torpedo room six had to wait an extra fifteen seconds to fire. While it was only marginally more effective to fire them simultaneously, it was worth the wait.

———

The end was inevitable. The destroyer heaved from another hit and lost a good ten percent of her speed. Bitar looked out at his bridge crew, and they all saw it as well. For whatever reason, the ship hadn't run when it could have. In a few minutes, it would be nothing more than an expanding globe of plasma.

"Sir, incoming message from Medial," Jamal said.

"Put it through," he ordered.

The image of a young corporal materialized. He was standing in front of the governor's compound. Bitar clenched his jaw at the damage. It was indeed a war zone.

"Captain Bitar, everyone at the compound is dead, sir. All the human stock is gone as well. We have over thirty security forces KIA, and twice that wounded all over the city."

A destroyer could carry a strong force, perhaps a platoon. With powered armor, they could cause a lot of damage. How had they inserted them on the planet, though? Destroyers were small, stealthy, and fast, but to insert on the planet without alerting its security forces seemed unlikely.

The corporal looked off-screen for a moment, then turned back, and the color drained from his face. "Sir, uh, the spaceport is reporting the Imperial liner we were storing there for the mighty Caliph was stolen, the arena ransacked, and all the human stock from there was taken as well."

"Wait," Bitar said as confusion swept over him. A liner? No one told him about a liner. Only that they had a princess from the Empire on the planet. "What is he saying?" Bitar asked Jamal.

Jamal looked stricken. "Sir, we spotted several civilian ships leaving the planet. I marked them as freighters, but..." He fiddled with his controls until the first two ships they'd spotted popped up.

Bitar pointed at the second ship. "That one?"

"Yes, sir. It came from the surface. I didn't see it at the time, but... it did," Jamal said in a whisper.

Bitar's hand went to his throat unconsciously. He couldn't swallow. He could barely breathe. The son of the Caliphate was on that ship.

He checked the range... it was only just inside their envelope.

"Full reverse," he screamed. "Change course for the star-lane... now, dammit, now!" he bellowed. "One-eight-zero, one-eight-zero!"

Interceptor's acceleration faltered as another hit severed the power runs to three gravcoil rings. Backup power flowed through the redundant sources, but they weren't as strong as the primary runs. The ship's acceleration dropped another fifteen percent. If they lost too much speed, they wouldn't be able to escape.

"DCS, get on that," Jacob said.

Yuki didn't look up from her control station, instead acknowledging him with a thumbs-up.

They'd managed to hold the ship off at five hundred thousand klicks, but just barely. *Divine Wind* had so many damned turrets, they barely had to aim to hit *Interceptor*.

They only needed thirty more seconds. Just thirty!

"Sir, massive gravwake spike. They're decelerating at full power and coming about one-eight-zero relative," PO Tefiti said. A second later, the ship bucked as the gravwake rolled over it.

"No," he said. They needed more time.

"Helm, full reverse, come one-eight-zero," he ordered.

"Aye, sir, full reverse, one-eight-zero," Chief Suresh said.

Jacob changed his MFD to the radar signature on Tango-One; sure enough, she was turning. Heavy cruisers weren't destroyers, though. While the gravcoil propelled ships, reaction drives maneuvered them. *Interceptor* spun on a dime, bringing her bow around a mere three seconds after the order was given, while Tango-One was still only a quarter of a way through her turn.

"Fawkes, fire the Long Nine!" Jacob yelled.

His weapons officer didn't hesitate, pressing the button the moment the ships lined up.

Josh Mendez was barely back in his seat when the ship bucked as the twenty-nine-meter-long coil of the Long Nine propelled its nine-kilogram warhead into space at ninety thousand KPS. In its five-point-two-second journey, the shell of the sabot discarded, leaving only the nano-hardened tungsten arrow. It impacted with the force of a nuclear bomb and didn't care how much armor stood in its way.

Divine Wind lurched as the round penetrated the forward starboard hull plating, through the mess deck, the barracks, torpedo rooms three and four, the bow ammo storage, and out the other side.

Unlike Alliance ships, Caliphate ships didn't drain their atmosphere. Explosive decompression reverberated throughout the ship. Armor turned to deadly fragments, vaporizing everything in their way, leaving bloody, stained messes behind where crew had served.

It was no mortal blow, but it was enough.

"Chief," Jacob said as soon as the results from the shot were in, "Get us the hell out of here."

"Aye, sir, setting course for hell," she said with a grin. *Interceptor* spun on her axis one more time. Her gravcoil powered up, and she shot off at four hundred and eighty-six gravities of acceleration.

Jamal shook his head, trying to clear his blurry vision. The ship had taken a massive hit, though apparently not a fatal one, thank Allah. He tried to bring up his systems; red emergency lighting flickered to life as the circuit breakers kicked in, preventing electronics from exploding.

"Sir, they must have hit us with their main gun. Damage is coming in now. Power to the forward rings is out; we're going to need—" Jamal looked up and his mouth froze at the sight of what used to be his captain. Three shards of hull had penetrated the bridge, tearing right through comms and the poor kid who sat there, along with ripping his captain in half. Only his legs remained in the chair, the rest of him was smeared against the rear hull. Jamal put his hands over his mouth, desperate not to puke.

CHAPTER FORTY

Jacob cracked his neck, relieving the pressure that had built up all morning. His nondescript cell aboard the heavy cruiser *Hurricane* held only a plain bed with a single flat pillow, a blue blanket, and white sheets. He wore a stripped-down uniform with only his name and rank. Until such time as he was sentenced, he would retain his rank and privilege.

While there was never a real chance of destroying the heavy cruiser, they had removed it from play and allowed *Komodo* to escape. All the way back to the wormhole, he had worried about the fate of his ground crew and those aboard the freighter. How many had they saved? How many had they lost? Did Nadia make it? He practically melted in relief when they appeared in Zuckabar and were directed to park next to *Komodo* and the previously unknown Iron Empire liner.

Moments after they connected the umbilical to Kremlin Station, Rod Becket's security people had placed him under arrest. He spent fifteen days in solitary aboard USS *Hurricane* while he was returned to Alexandria for imprisonment and court-martial.

He knew going in this was always the way it would end up. No medals, no reprieves, no fame. Only incarceration. He had done his duty, though, and he felt deep satisfaction. Duty, honor, courage. They had delivered a devastating moral blow to the Caliphate, and their mission was victorious.

As long as his crew wasn't punished, he would call it a win. He knew his mother would be proud.

The hatch buzzed, and a marine sergeant entered, followed by a PFC.

"Prisoner, stand up," Sergeant Māhoe said. He was a big, dark-skinned man, probably from Ohana, if Jacob had to guess.

They gestured for him to hold his hands out, and they cuffed him before escorting him out to the boat bay, where they boarded a Corsair. No one spoke to him, and he didn't ask any questions. As far as they were concerned, he was scum. No better than a pirate. A mutineer who had stolen his own ship. He was okay with that, too. The people who mattered knew the truth.

The court-martial was a formality. After that, they could sentence him however they wanted. It would likely be a penal colony on the back side of Loki.

A shiver ran through the Corsair as it mated with another ship. He looked up, but again couldn't see anything outside, and no one talked to him. The PFC came over and undid his harness.

"Prisoner, stand," Sergeant Māhoe ordered. Jacob complied.

The side doors hummed open, and Jacob instantly recognized the *Alexander*'s boat bay. The flagship of the fleet was the newest, most advanced ship they had in the Alliance. Each of the two boat bays had four Corsairs docked inside.

"I'll take it from here, Sergeant," Jennings said from below.

Jacob's face split into a grin. His heart leapt, seeing her.

"Aye, aye, Gunny," Māhoe said.

Jacob hopped down and stood to his full height, towering

over the marine. "Gunny?" he asked with a raised eyebrow.

"Some damn fool of an officer put me in for a promotion... *Again*." Her icy voice was music to his ears. She hated awards and promotions. Twice he had bumped her up farther than her age would account for—and clearly the marine adjuncts who reviewed field promotions agreed.

"What are friends for?" he said.

She grabbed his arm, squeezed reassuringly, and led him to the lift. "Friends indeed, Skipper," she muttered.

Jennings guided him to the lift. The tube hummed as it carried him to his final destination.

"How many did we lose?" he asked. No one had told him anything after they returned. He'd hoped she would be different.

"I've been ordered not to speak, sir," Jennings said.

Not pressing her further, he swallowed again, trying to keep his mouth and throat working. When he first saw Jennings, his heart had skipped a beat, but then reality crashed back down on him.

The lift doors opened, and she guided him to where two plain-clothed guards stood. A man with tan skin and the heavyset shoulders and neck of MacGregor's World, and a blue-skinned woman who looked easily as dangerous, if not as thick, as the man.

Jennings grunted as she put Jacob in front of the man for examination. "Commander Grimm and escort here to see the president," Jennings said.

The man gave her a curt nod, and the hatch slid open.

Jacob's mind reeled at the revelation. Jennings prodded him in, forcing his feet forward; it was only by the grace of God he didn't fall flat on his face.

The room she ushered him into didn't belong on a starship. Instead of the metal bulkheads he expected, faux wood paneling lined the walls. Six old-fashioned oil paintings hung in perfect spacing around the room. All were previous holders of the office, but the largest one, situated behind the president, caught his attention.

The painting was of an older woman in her fifties, back when people still aged like that. She had keen blue eyes and blonde hair like Jennings'. It was pulled into a tight bun, also just like his gunny sergeant.

Jacob blinked. He looked at Jennings, then back at the painting, then back at Jennings. The only thing that differed between the two was Jennings' powerful shoulders and neck muscles.

He wanted to say something, ask her what the connection was, but the man behind the table required his immediate attention.

Jacob snapped to attention. He tried to salute, but the cuffs stopped him. Jennings moved forward and triggered the release.

He might be under arrest, but until such time as he was discharged, he was still an officer in the United Systems Alliance and would behave accordingly. Once his hands were free, he finished the salute.

"Lieutenant Commander Jacob T. Grimm reporting as ordered, sir."

"At ease, son," President Axwell said.

Jacob dropped his salute into attention, then snapped his legs into parade rest, and finally relaxed into at ease. President Axwell not only commanded the military, he commanded respect.

"So, Mr. Grimm, did you put everything in your report?" President Axwell asked.

Jacob tried to straighten his scrambled thoughts. He had spent half the trip home writing his report. He took three deep breaths, and things started to clear up. He hated lying, but he wasn't about to ruin the OP at the end. "Yes, sir," he said. "If I may ask, how is the rest of my crew? And Commander Dagher?"

"I told you," Admiral Villanueva said to the president. Jacob glanced over and saw Admiral DeBeck and a blue-skinned woman he didn't recognize. Opposite them was Senator Talmage, holding a white cup of tea and playing with his eye patch.

"I'll pay you later," Axwell replied to the fleet admiral.

Jacob tried to suppress a grin at the revelation and the irony. When Admiral DeBeck had approached him to go on the mission in the first place, it was because he knew the answer before he asked. They seemed to know him very well.

"They said that would be the first thing you asked."

"I'd like to think it's the first thing any captain would ask, sir," Jacob said.

President Axwell betrayed no emotion other than a small smile that didn't touch his eyes. "I'd like to think so too. I'm a supporter of the navy, Jacob. Always have been. But fear is a powerful thing. Fear has controlled our society for too long.

"And then here you come, raising all kinds of trouble for me while I'm struggling to put the navy back together."

"Sorry, sir. It wasn't my intent," Jacob said.

Axwell spread his hands out wide. "Yet here we are."

"My mother taught me to always do my duty, sir. I can't turn that off. Not for anything. It's... it's all I have left of her," Jacob said, his voice lowering as he spoke.

"I read her record too. She was quite the woman," the president said.

Jacob nodded, not trusting himself to speak. The president still hadn't answered his question, and the knot of fear he had felt all the way back from Zuckabar grew with each second. He forced himself to swallow and stay calm. Were they not telling him because of how badly it had ended? Jennings was here, and if she was here, then some must have survived.

"So, Commander," Axwell continued, "I'm sorry to inform you one of your marines, Private Cole, was KIA."

Jacob swallowed hard, glancing back at Gunny, who simply stood rock solid next to the hatch. Cole was just a kid... they were all just kids.

"Who else, sir?" he asked.

Axwell shook his head. "No one else, son. Your marines kicked ass and took names. When it was all said and done, not only did they rescue over five thousand former slaves, but they secured two VIPs who will likely keep us from having to fight this war until we decide to. There's more beyond that, I'm told, but it is classified at the moment. Perhaps Nadia Dagher could fill you in at some later date."

Nadia survived. Relief flooded through him, followed by a stab of guilt. He'd lost six crew in the brief battle, plus one marine, yet he celebrated Nadia's survival.

"I'm glad it worked out, sir. I know I have no right to ask, but for my own ease of conscience, I want to know—my crew won't be punished for my actions, will they?"

"Punished for what?" Admiral DeBeck asked.

Jacob glanced sideways at him where he sat stern faced and unreadable. Next to him, Fleet Admiral Villanueva cracked a smile. "*Mon ami,* punishment is the opposite of what we intend," she said.

President Johan Sebastian Axwell stood up from behind his desk and walked around to stand directly in front of Jacob. "I wish we could do this more publicly, Commander," the president said, "but there are still limitations. Rest assured, though, it will all come out. Eventually."

Senator Talmage and Admiral Villanueva stood next to the president. Jacob snapped to attention.

DeBeck remained seated. "Wait," the ONI spymaster said. "Gunny, if you will?"

"Aye, aye, sir," Jennings said.

Jacob couldn't see her, but he heard her sharp heel turn. The hatch opened, and someone else walked in. Out of the corner of his eye, he saw his father stand next to DeBeck. He gave his son a nod. That one motion made everything Jacob had ever suffered worth it. If no one ever knew what his crew had gone through, at least the people who mattered would.

"Lieutenant Commander Jacob T. Grimm," Admiral Villanueva said, "with the authority of my office and in conjunction with NavPer, I hereby award you the promotion to *full* commander, and all the privileges and responsibility commensurate with your rank."

She reached to his lapel, removed his golden oak leaf, then pulled out a small box. "These were mine. I would be honored if you wore them." A pair of silver oak leaves, slightly tarnished from use, sat in the box.

"Aye, ma'am," he said, not trusting himself to speak further.

After she placed the ranks on his lapel, she stepped back and saluted, which he returned.

"My turn," Senator Talmage said. "This is getting to be a ritual I enjoy. Commander Jacob T. Grimm, for your actions in saving the lives of thousands of civilians while facing an undefeatable enemy force, and for going above and beyond the call of duty, it is my honor and duty to present you with this Silver Star. I know it will look illustrious next to your other awards." He pinned the medal to Jacob's chest.

Jacob desperately wanted to look over at his father, but he held fast at attention. The senator shook his hand.

"And last but not least," President Axwell said.

Jacob's mind reeled. What more could they do? He was still coming to grips with the fact that they weren't kicking him out.

"This one isn't for you per se," he said. "However, we're breaking ground on the new naval HQ this month. Because of the attack, SecNav and Congress have decided to place the base far away from any other potential targets in case, God forbid, we're ever attacked like that from orbit again."

It made sense. With modern orbital defense and detection, everyone assumed they could not be hit without warning. The Guild and Caliphate had shown them how wrong they were.

"Therefore," Axwell continued, "I am happy to announce that the Melinda Grimm Naval Base will be constructed on Alexandria and will be the center of the navy going forth."

Jacob had no words. He broke attention and looked at his father. Red-rimmed eyes gleamed back at him.

"She would be proud, son," Jacob's father said. "Just like me."

A wake-up alarm as old as mankind itself echoed through the small farmhouse as the roosters began their serenade to the sun.

Jacob stretched languidly in the sunlight peeking through his windows. Confusion washed over him for a moment. Through the haze of sleep, his mind tried to come to grips with what felt wrong.

He could see the sun... which shouldn't be possible. And there was a warm mass of flesh pressed up against him. After a long moment, his mind caught up, reminding him that he wasn't on a ship but in his old bedroom on his family ranch, and that the warm mass of flesh was indeed Nadia, who currently snored lightly, her face pressed up against his chest.

Carefully, so as not to disturb her sleep, he extracted himself from her warmth and made his way to the small bathroom down the hall. His father had never expanded the house, even though he could afford it. It remained a modest, one-level, three-bedroom home.

When he finished, he threw on a shirt and went to make Nadia breakfast. The kitchen was empty, but there were signs his father had already risen. The only people who worked harder than the military had to be farmers and ranchers.

He poured a cup of coffee for Nadia and a glass of orange juice for himself. Warm hands slid around his waist, and hot breath flushed against his back as Nadia encircled him in a hug.

"Good morning," she purred.

"I made coffee," he said.

"You're a saint." She took the offered cup, sipping it while leaning against the counter.

Jacob let out a sigh as she leaned against the counter. She was wearing one of his button-up flannel shirts, her long legs bare to the floor.

"You look magnificent," he said.

She winked at him from behind her coffee cup. "I know."

They stared at each other; for how long, they didn't care. All they cared about was the other person. No mission, no enemy, no conflict to come between them.

As if by magic, the spell broke, and they moved at the same time. Jacob engulfed her in a kiss that channeled all his heart, passion, and desire into her.

When they finally broke, they were left breathless.

"Wow," she said. "That was some kind of kiss."

"You're some kind of woman," he whispered back.

Commander Jacob T. Grimm will return as captain of the USS *Interceptor*.

BLOODED: A GRIMM'S WAR STORY

@2022 JOSH HAYES

BY JOSH HAYES

CHAPTER ONE

The Corsair's engines whined as the dropship banked to port, lining up on its approach to Mining Outpost H267. Private Allison Jennings managed to catch a glimpse of the small settlement through the pilot's viewport, then sat back, returning her focus to not throwing up. She tightened her grip on her seat's harness and forced herself to repeat the mental inventory she'd put herself through a dozen times already.

"There's the merc's ship," Staff Sergeant Nealon said, pointing at something Jennings couldn't see. "Looks like it's blasted all to junk. I guess that's why they haven't left yet."

He turned from the pilot's cabin to the face the rest of the team, sitting on either side of the Corsair's large cargo compartment. His USMC grey and white combat fatigues fit his athletic frame perfectly, almost like they'd been tailored. He stood with his helmet under one arm, the other hand resting on one of six extra magazines in pouches on the front of his tactical armor. The nanite-infused fibers of his uniform provided excellent protection from kinetics and fragmentation, but any high-powered plasma rifle would burn through them like they were paper, hence the extra armor in the vest. His MP-17, the newest firearm in the USMC's arsenal, was holstered on his right thigh.

"Jennings, you good?" Staff Sergeant Nealon asked, stopping in front of her seat, hand on the overhead rail, body swaying with the dropship's motion.

She swallowed, steeling herself before looking into her team leader's dark eyes. "Oorah, Staff Sergeant."

Across the compartment, Corporal Nix, the team's designated marksmen, pointed to her gear. "Don't worry, Jennings. If you lose any of that, the Corps will just take it out of your rear. Good thing you brought your K2 though, you'll definitely need that." The way he'd said it suggested he was being sarcastic, but it was hard to tell through his Old Earth southern drawl.

Unconsciously, Jennings put a hand on the hilt of her standard issue Marine combat knife. The primitive weapon was the only piece of gear she'd questioned when she'd left the supply, wondering why with all their advanced armor and weaponry, the Marines still insisted on issuing combat knives. Then again, who was she to question anything? She'd only technically been a Marine for two months, and before that she'd been a recruit in training. In the eyes of the Corps, her opinions meant absolutely nothing, less even.

Nix laughed. Sergeant Nealon grinned. Jennings took a second to glance over Nix's gear. He wasn't wearing one, and while technically a required piece of equipment, she'd noticed that some regulations were more flexible than others, especially to those with some rank. As a designated marksman, Nix had even more leeway when it came to gear, because of his role in providing overwatch for the rest of the squad. Everyone wanted the people responsible for potentially saving them from unseen or nearby threats to be as comfortable as possible.

"Once you've been blooded, it's on you to bring what you

need," Sergeant Nealon explained. "Until then, you bring what I tell you to bring."

"Roger that, Staff Sergeant."

The tone of the engines shifted again, and the pilot's voice came over the Corsair's intercom. "One minute out!"

"Roger, one minute!" Sergeant Nealon called over his shoulder. To his team, he said, "All right, helmets on! Remember, keep your safeties on and your damn fingers off the triggers, understood?"

The chorus of affirmatives echoed through the compartment. Jennings glanced around at the rest of the team as Sergeant Nealon made his way to the rear cargo ramp. They looked calm and collected, every bit the professionals Marine Corps was known for. As if on cue, the team's nonchalant, jocular attitude vanished, replaced by a stoicism reserved for those preparing themselves for combat. In her mind, Jennings ran through the multiple training scenarios she'd gone through and tried to call everything her instructors had told her about combat.

Every member of the squad, except for Jennings, had seen action in one form or another. With the possible exception of Sergeant Nealon, Nix was the most experienced Marine of the group, having served two tours in Malia during the revolution. He'd didn't talk about his missions often, but the rest of the team had built up a kind of lore around him, and he made no effort to correct them. Though technically not a part of their squad, Sergeant Nealon had talked their platoon leader into giving him an extra set of eyes.

He looked bored, and from everything that Jennings knew about their mission, he had every right to be. Not even Lieutenant Jorge had considered this mission critical enough to accompany his men down to the planet's surface, and Jennings couldn't help but feel disappointed that her first mission would be so... mundane.

The ramp opened with a mechanical hum and warm desert air flooded the cabin. Even through her full-faced, Advanced Protective Systems assault helmet, Jennings could taste the sand on the dry wind. She snapped the chin strap and tapped button on the backside, activating the augmented visor. The APS7's visor allowed its wearer to see in multiple spectrums when necessary and was tied into the squad's tacnet. When Sergeant Nealon spoke his rank and name appeared on the bottom left corner of the screen and a small directional arrow pointed toward his position relative to Jennings.

"Stay close to me Jennings."

She nodded, but said nothing, not wanting her voice to betray her nervousness.

The Corsairs wings rotated and the plasma engines flared, kicking up a cloud of dust that swirled in around them as it touched down onto the hardpack. It'd barely settled onto its landing struts when Nealon shouted for them all to, "Go, go, go!"

At the back of the line, Jennings followed Nix down into the hot air. Her visor automatically darkened, protecting her vision from the bright afternoon sunlight, and for the first time in her life, Allison Jennings stepped foot on an unknown world as a United Systems Marine.

CHAPTER TWO

The outpost was little more than a cluster of prefabricated buildings erected in a square next to the giant ore processor. The machines inside the hundred-meter-long rectangular complex thumped and clanked incessantly and several exhaust vents along the roof pumped grey steam and smoke into the air. The complex was actually several buildings attached to each other, each segment containing different equipment performing different functions.

Sergeant Nealon led the squad away from the Corsair, which lifted off behind them, moving to take up an orbiting patrol above the plant. One of the first things Jennings had learned about Marine pilots was that they absolutely hated sitting on the ground. Flying in circles for a few hours was definitely more preferable to being a stationary target of opportunity for any amount of time.

A group of locals approached from the far side of the landing area, several of them armed with rifles, the rest with pistols holstered on hips. Their leader, dressed in a tan vest, light blue work pants and matching shirt, sleeves rolled up just below his elbows. The badge on his vest marked him as the outpost's marshal, but the expression on his face told Jennings he was most definitely out of his element.

"Thank you for coming, Captain," the man said, putting out his hand. "I'm Marshal Gillam, these are my men, such as they are."

"It's sergeant actually. And no thanks are needed. Do you have an update on the situation?"

"They're still hold up in the central control station," the marshal said. "Five of them. Joey here shot one of them when it all went sideways." He motioned to a man behind him whose arm was tied up in a sling. "And we managed to disable their shuttle, but ain't got the firepower to do much else."

"Then it's a good thing we do," Nealon said. "You have a command post?"

The marshal frowned. "Uh..."

"Where are you coordinating your response?"

"We're operating out of Tim's place right now, it's the closest building to the processor."

"Tim's place?"

"That's right. I'll take you there. Follow me." The marshal turned and started off toward the outpost proper.

Before following, Nealon turned to the squad. "Nix, find a perch and stay there. Masterson, take the One-Two Corner, Walters you have Three-Four. Remember they have hostages, identify your targets before doing anything. I'll get you IDs of the townsfolk as soon as I can. The rest of you, with me."

The three men acknowledged their orders and headed off to carry them out. Jennings followed silently as the marshal led them through the small outpost. Tim's, as it turned out, was the local bar complete with old-style batwing doors and worn oak bar. A handful of square tables had been pushed together in the center of the room, where a holographic, wireframe representation of the processor flickered above the palm-sized projector.

The marshal walked around to the far side of the table and pointed. "As far as we can tell, they're all on the second level, here, in the control center."

"And the hostages?"

"There's five of them. Fred, Stacy, Reynolds and his wife, Fran, and their daughter Macy."

"Daughter?"

The marshal shrugged. "Not much else folks can do when they have to pull shifts and childcare ain't available."

"Fantastic. Where are your men stationed?"

"Got a couple here to the north and my deputies Jackson and Ham are here on the southside."

"I assume they're armed."

"Got a pair of K97s between them. High-powered weapons aren't high up on the company's priority list is you catch what I'm throwin'."

Nealon chuckled. "Yeah, I hear you. So, any word on demands? I'm guessing the score was the refined ore?"

"That's right," Gilliam said. "Most of it was already loaded into containers, ready to ship out at the end of the week. Course, when we drove a rover into their shuttle, it put a little dent into their operation. That's when they took the hostages."

"I don't understand," a bearded man, wearing dark blue overalls with the company logo on the breast pocket asked. "Where's the rest?"

"The rest, sir?"

"Yeah, the rest of your guys." The man motioned between Nealon and the rest of the squad.

Nealon met the eyes of everyone on the team, then turned back to the man. "We're what the Man sent, sir. This is what you get."

"And I'm sure it'll be enough, Watson," Gilliam said, giving the man a sidelong glance.

Jennings watched, and listened, as Nealon talked with the locals about the specifics of the complex, entrances and exits, what was stored where, potential danger zones, anything and everything that could slow them down or hurt them. The sergeant had never come off as an overly talkative type, but he sure did play it off with these men. He communicated with them on their level, presenting himself as just another backwater worker, making them feel comfortable and within minutes they'd apparently forgotten he was an outsider here.

"You're all right, you know it," Gilliam said with a grin and a hand on Nealon's shoulder. "And here I thought all you Alliance navy types were all stuck up paper pushers."

"Oh, they definitely are, sir," Nealon said. "I guess it's a good thing we're Marines."

The man Gilliam had called Watson leaned forward, both palms flat on the table. "You going to get our people back?"

Nealon considered the man for a moment, then said, "We're going to do our best."

"Your best?" The man straightened and crossed his arms.

"Watson..." Gilliam gave the man a sidelong, warning glare.

The man ignored the marshal. "The hell you mean 'your best'? I thought you were some badass military types? You don't impress me none, with your gear and guns. Ya'll as like to get our friends shot up as we are."

"Would you prefer I lie to you? Prefer I say, we'll get your people out of harm's way, no problem at all? Then we fail? Then what? I'm not in the business of false comfort, sir. I call it like it is because that's how it is. It might not be pretty, it might not be what you want to hear, but it's the truth. You don't have to like it." Nealon took a breath, almost challenging the man to counter him, then continued, "My team and I are going to do our best to get resolve this situation and save as many lives as we can. We're professionals, sir, and I can assure you we take our work as serious as anyone can. If that's not good enough for you, well..."

The marshal raised his hands in surrender and stepped between the man and Nealon. "All right now, Watson ain't mean nothing wrong by that. He's just a bit amped up, ya know. Hell, an honest word is how we all prefer it out here in Beyond."

"What's this here?" Corporal Grant asked, stepping up to the table and pointing at the rows of tanks along the northside of the complex. "High pressure compression tanks, yeah?"

Watson nodded. "That's right. Don't be shootin' around them, you'll have a bad bay."

"There's going to be a lot of pressure values and conduits along this end," Grant said, tracing the lines on the map with his finger. "If they're in the control room they're going to have access to master flow control. If they figure that out we could be in for a bad time."

"Oh?" Nealon asked.

Gilliam looked at the gathered worked, all still dressed in their dark brown work coveralls, then turned back to Nealon. "Well, uh, because they can blow it all to hell, if they wanted to. And the town with it."

CHAPTER THREE

Nealon considered the marshal for a minute, as if trying to work out whether the man was being hyperbolic or being serious. Jennings knew a lot of combat missions ran on a clock but running against one that ended with a town-flattening explosion put this mission in a completely different light. Even without the breadth of experience of the rest of her teammates in this room, Jennings knew they didn't have time to stand around and debate. They needed to act.

"He ain't lying," one of the other men said, his hands resting on his hips, chewing something tucked into his cheek. "The powerplant is an old TX86, not state of the art by any means, but the top end of the company's budget if ya' know what I mean."

"I get it," Nealon said. He pointed to the east end of the complex. "With the way their shuttle's smoking, it should give us at least some concealment on the way in. Five of your people are in there?"

"That's right." Gillam held out a pad with personal information and pictures of the hostages.

Nealon flipped through it then handed it to Grant. "Get those to the rest of the team."

"Roger that," Grant said, and pulled his handheld out to relay the intel.

Jennings's own pad vibrated a second later. She flipped open the ruggedized case at the top of her tactical vest and tapped the screen with a finger. The images of the five hostages arrayed themselves side-by-side, their names appeared at the bottom edge of the pictures. She stared at the faces for several long moments, burning their images into her mind. She couldn't begin to imagine what must be going through their heads right now. She shook herself and closed the case. She needed to focus on what she could control.

She looked over the holographic wire-framed image. She was no stranger to the large industrial processors; McGregor's World was home to dozens and dozens of corporations looking to take advantage of the planet's high metal and mineral content. Her parents had owned a small shipping and transport company, and Jennings had spent the majority of her childhood riding in the back of their mountain crawler as her father moved loads of ore from what place to another.

"And you've talked to them right? Since they've hold up?" Nealon asked. "Have they said anything more?"

Gilliam nodded. "Just that they wanted a shuttle to transport them and their load out. Said if we tried to make entry they'd kill the hostages."

"I doubt their plan is to let them go at all now," Grant said. "With us down here and *Brewton* in orbit, they're going to need the insurance."

Watson looked like he was about to protest Nealon's terminology but kept silent at a look from the marshal. "If they board that shuttle, we'll never see our people again, Sergeant."

Nealon seemed to consider that for a moment, then asked,

"It's possible they didn't see us come in. Can you raise him? Don't say anything about us, but I want to keep them talking."

Marshall Gilliam nodded and held his hand out to one of his companions who gave him a small handheld comm. He took a deep breath, then keyed the unit. "H-hello? Are you still there?"

It took a few moments for the person on the other end to answer. *"You got that shuttle for us yet?"*

Nealon shook his head. He mouthed, "Working on it."

"W-we, we're working on it."

"Don't want to hear 'working on it'," the merc said. *"I want to see that damn bird landing outside this here building, and I want to see it in the next five minutes or I'm going to start blasting. Maybe I'll start with this little tasty morsel right here."*

In the background a woman's voice cried out.

"Get back!" the merc shouted. The wet sound of a smack echoed through the comm and Jennings winced. *"Damn whore! Now, marshal, are you listening to me? Because I want to make damn sure you understand what I'm about to tell you."*

Gilliam swallowed hard. "I'm... I'm listening."

"I want that shuttle on the ground and ready to fly in five minutes. No more excuses, no more delays. If you don't have the shuttle on the ground in five minutes I will kill a hostage, and I will continue killing until we have the shuttle or until all these pitiful bastards are lying dead on the floor. You understand, is that clear enough for you?"

"I understand."

"Good. There will be no more communications."

The comm went dead. Gilliam's already anxious expression had shifted to one of pure horror. He looked from the little unit in his hand to Nealon, his mouth opened and closed, no words came.

"We can't wait any more," Watson said. "We need to get

them that shuttle. I know there's one on Pad 3, we had a scheduled supply pick up this afternoon."

"If we give them a transport those people are dead," Nealon said. "I know how these mercs think. They've already killed at least once, they're not going to have any qualms about leaving anymore bodies in the wake."

"We don't know that," Watson said.

"The Alliance doesn't negotiate with terrorists, period. The only way those bastards are leaving this planet are in cuffs or in a box."

Marshal Gilliam exchanged looks with the rest of his men, then turned back to Nealon, expression resolute. "What is your plan?"

"We'll make entry here," Nealon said, pointing at the south side of the building. "Grant, you and Lincoln will flank on this ladder, here, Jennings and I will take the central stairs, here. Ginelli and Walters will take the roof access, here. We take them simultaneously from multiple directions. They'll never know what hit them." He nodded to Grant. "You got your bangers?"

Grant patted a pouch on his tactical vest. "Always, Sarge."

"All right. Marshal Gilliam, you and your men hold the perimeter and make sure none of those bastards make it past us."

"The perimeter?" Watson asked, incredulous. "The hell you mean, the perimeter? We should get them what they want. Get them the shuttle and they said they'd give our people back. Come on, Cory, you can't seriously believe this is the best course?"

"It's the only course," the marshal said. "The sergeant is right. If they get off the surface we'll never see them again."

"I don't believe you."

"You don't need to believe," Nealon said, not bothering to hide his obvious growing frustration.

"At least let us help you," Gilliam said. "Increase the odds."

Nealon shook his head. "This is a Marine operation now. We don't need to give these guys anyone else to shoot at."

"All right, then, we'll handle the perimeter," Marshal Gilliam said, raising a hand as the others started to protest. "Just, please, get our friends back safety."

Nealon nodded, instructed the men on where to go, then eyed the rest of squad and jerked his head toward the door. "Let's roll."

Jennings gave the men a final look, then followed the squad outside. On McGregor's World there'd aways been a general distain for the Alliance, so it made sense it would be shared by others, but she'd never experienced that distain as a *Marine*. Granted, she'd only been a part of the organization for a few months, but she felt more at home with the men and women of her unit that she'd ever felt back home, more than she'd ever felt anywhere. For all intents and purposes, the Alliance was her home now, and she didn't appreciate anyone disparaging it.

CHAPTER FOUR

Outside, Sergeant Nealon adjusted the position of his MP-17 on his tactical sling, and turned to face his people. "All right, these bastards have had enough time to settle in and find good positions. We're going to have to go in fast but soft; there are too many unknown variables in that place, including the child. I don't know about any of you, but I don't need that on my conscience.

The rest of the team nodded.

"Tap and go, sarge?" Grant asked.

Almost immediately the term registered in Jennings's mind, a slang not exactly taught during close-quarters combat training, but one that all Marines knew regardless. In a majority of situations, the general rule of any engagement was to wait until taking fire to engage, however in some rare circumstances, that rule was set aside in favor or a more direct approach. Shooting —tapping—without warning, then proceeding on mission put the enemy immediately on the defensive and put the Marines where they always preferred to be, on offense.

Nealon nodded in response and keyed his radio. "Nix, you have eyes on?"

"I'm in position. I've got them on IR, but without positive IDs I'm looking at a whole bunch of unknowns."

"I copy. Stand by."

Marshal Gilliam and the rest of his rag-tag posse filed out of Tim's Bar and headed off to man their positions around the complex. Jennings knew the chances of the mercs getting past her squad was slim to none, and the posse Gilliam had put together had even less of a chance to stop them if they did. She just hoped they wouldn't accidently shoot her or any of her fellow Marines in the process.

"Walters, Masterson, you've got civies coming to relieve you. Rally with us on the south side, how copy?"

"Good copy, Sarge," Masterson replied.

"Roger that," Walters said.

The merc's shuttle was a mess of burning, twisted steel. Grant whistled as they approached. Jennings twisted her nose up at the scent of ozone and burning rubber. The wind had died down a bit, but the thick black smoke still blanketed the ground between the shuttle and the complex's south entrance. Along with the scattered counter-grav carts, haulers and loaders, their approach was almost textbook.

When the other two Marines joined them, Nealon ran down the plan once more, then Ginelli, Walters, Grant, and Lincoln headed off through the smoke, their weapons up and scanning. Nix advised over the radio that he had them covered, and they started up the ladder. Jennings looked over her shoulder, trying to see where Nix had posted up at, but saw nothing. Ginelli and Walters broke off at the ladder and quickly began to climb up as the other two continued on down to the west side of the building.

"All right," Nealon said to Jennings and Masterson. "We're going to move straight through those doors, standard area move-and-clear to the central stairs, got it?"

"Roger that," Masterson said.

Jennings nodded but said nothing, worried the small amount of breakfast she'd had earlier would come up. Despite repeatedly telling herself she was ready for her first mission; her nerves were threatening to get the best of her. She took a deep breath and adjusted her grip on her MP-17, now extended to rifle length, the nano-configurable ammunition set to anti-personnel.

Nealon pointed a finger at Jennings. "Stay on my six, got it."

"Affirmative."

"Let's move out."

CHAPTER FIVE

Jennings followed Nealon across the hardpack ground, staying low and weaving through the collection of loaders and haulers. She'd driven many similar vehicles in her youth and could tell these vehicles were in much need of repair. The sound of the machinery inside the processor drowned out any noise they might have made, leaving their only concern the sight lines from the many open windows looking down across the open area between the town and the complex. Fortunately, with Nix as overwatch, anyone stupid enough to pop up and take a look wouldn't have long to see anything.

They reached the south entrance, a short security tunnel where a guard should've been keeping watch but now stood empty. Masterson took point, sliding through the entryway then rolling left, his weapon up and scanning. Nealon followed, rolling right. Jennings came through on his heels, her weapon pulled tight into her shoulder, eyes sweeping up and around the center of the wide chamber that stretched away from the entrance.

Like the processors of her homeworld, this too was filled

with catwalks, conduits, cables, piping and large machines. The noise was deafening. Were it not for their helmets' sound dampening headphones, they wouldn't've been able to hear each other scream, much less communicate effectively. Even without an active work crew, the machinery still thumped incessantly away, power generators still hummed with power.

She stopped at steel support pylon that stretched to the building's ceiling and surveyed the area. The processor's main transfer line sat directly in front of her, a rectangular metal tunnel that ran half the length of the building. She slipped past the pylon and crouched low against the tunnel's exterior wall, keeping her MP-17 pointed up and ahead. Through small circular windows, she could see the belt inside moving, carrying pieces of rock and ore to be sorted at various stations deeper inside the plant.

On the smooth concrete floor, ten meters away, a body lay face down, a pool of blood darkened the floor around it. The man's hardhat lay upside-down several meters away, the large wrench he'd apparently been carrying discarded on the ground next to him. Even if he'd seen them coming, he would've never had a chance.

Jennings glanced to her left, saw Sergeant Nealon advancing behind a row of storage lockers and tool racks. She took a breath, checked the catwalk above her, saw it was clear, then started moving along the side of the thin metal wall, knowing it provided only concealment and wouldn't stop a poorly aimed rock.

The plant's main control station was in an elevated office in the middle of the large building. Multiple catwalks led to various workstations and several secondary offices around the plant. The control station itself was twenty meters square, with sheet metal walls and frosted glass windows. A large second floor area extended for another twenty meters around the office, filled with storage containers and equipment racks. Clusters of hard plastic containers, cylindrical tanks and other piles of equipment had been stacked up to form several impromptu fighting positions, but none of the mercenaries were in sight.

"All right, Sarge, we're making entry now," Grant advised over the comm.

"Roger. I'm going to work my way up. Masterson, meet me at the stairs, Jennings keep us covered."

She was about to argue but held her peace. The sergeant knew what he was doing. Who was she to question? She adjusted her MP-17 in her shoulder pocket and shifted her cheek-weld slightly on the weapon's extended stock. In her peripheral she watched Sergeant Nealon work his way to the base of the stairwell, all the while keeping his weapon up and ready. Masterson made it there just after Nealon, and one by one they began making their way up. They took careful steps, but Jennings doubted anyone would hear them coming, not over the incessant cacophony of the machinery around them.

Movement caught her attention, and she froze, crouching lower and centering her sights on the lone figure standing on the catwalk twenty meters above. The man wore mismatched combat fatigues, his pants olive drab, his shirt charcoal grey. The tactical vest looked at least twenty years old. His rifle, held at low-ready, looked about the same age. Jennings was no "gun-nut" but like every Marine recruit she'd studied weapons and ammunition in training. It looked like an old Alliance X34, an automatic rifle, capable of firing a caseless 6mm round at 1,066 meters per second. Not state-of-the-art by any means but it would kill just the same.

She keyed her comm. "Tango sighted. Twelve o'clock, high. On the catwalk. He hasn't seen me."

"Roger," Nealon replied, slowing his ascent, peering out

from underneath the first landing, trying to get a bead on the enemy mercenary.

Almost casually, the man surveyed the plant ahead of him, then turned and started back the other direction, away from Jennings. He stopped every few meters to peer down into the intricate maze of machinery and equipment. He seemed almost nonchalant about his patrol, like he was sure the locals wouldn't dare to engage them.

"I have a shot," Jennings whispered, blood pounding in her ears. She forced herself to keep her finger on the trigger guard, not trusting herself to keep the pressure off.

"Stand by," Nealon ordered. *"Looks like he's by himself. Nix, how many targets are you seeing up there?"*

"I've got eight inside," the marksmen said. *"I'm pretty sure I've ID'd little girl, but it's hard to tell with all the interference."*

Jennings ground her teeth, her finger tensing on the frame of her weapon, her holographic reticle hovering over the mercenary's chest. The thought of that little girl huddled in that room, terrified, confused, helpless, turned her stomach.

"That means there's one still unaccounted for. Still no shot?"

"Negative. Nothing clean anyway."

"All right, we don't want to push until we know where they all are. Ginelli, Walters, you two in position?"

There was a brief moment of silence, then Ginelli came over the comm, his voice sounding slightly winded. "Almost. There's a skylight ahead that should give us a good entry point or at the very least an excellent shooting position."

"Roger. Grant, any sign of the last merc?"

"Negative. We came in through a service hatch on the lower level, coming up into the main area now. No sign."

"Keep your eyes open people, he's in here somewhere."

CHAPTER SIX

Jennings turned her attention away from the lone merc to scan the rest of the space that she could see. The last merc could be anywhere, hiding among the large industrial components and machinery, but he had to be close. The mercs expected the shuttle to be outside in a matter of minutes and that meant the fifth man wouldn't be too far away; within running distance at the very least.

"We're running short on time," Nix said over the comms, mirroring her own thoughts.

She keyed her comm. *"I can sweep west if Grant comes east. We might be able to flush him out."*

Nealon was silent for a second to think about it, looking down at her from his position on the stairs, then nodded. *"Do it."*

Jennings gave the merc one final look, then moved left, weaving through a maze of machinery, conduits and walkways. She paused halfway across the space, pressed her back up to the metal casing on one of the machines, then checked over her shoulder. After ensuring the merc hadn't seen her, she continued through the plant, forcing herself to move carefully, resisting the urge to run.

She kept low, scanning down walkways, in work alcoves and around tanks and transfer lines. Even if they'd had a full platoon, it would've taken hours to effectively clear the entire building; there were just too many small spaces throughout the building to check every single one in turn. Jennings forced herself to ignore the fact that she might've passed him already, but none-the-less checked behind her periodically as she proceeded deeper into the plant.

"All elements, report status," Nealon said over the comm.

The squad members sounded off in turn; no changes. Jennings was about to key her comm and advise the same when movement caught her eye. She froze, MP-17 coming up to her eye, the holographic optic outlining the edge of what had to be a human figure ten meters ahead. She held her breath. She was too close to verbally answer, so she clicked her mic and waited.

"Jennings?" Nealon's voice was a whisper now, despite his voice only coming through her earpiece.

She clicked the mic again and took a step forward. Outlined in high-contrast yellow, the human shape shifted, apparently adjusting its stance. The merc hadn't seen her, and as she stepped closer, realized he was looking down.

Jennings made her decision, quickly crossed the distance, and jabbed her MP-17's barrel into the side of the man's head. "Move and you die."

The man's head came up, eyes filled with fear and confusion. Jennings looked down and couldn't believe what she saw. The man had been in the middle of relieving himself, his manhood still in his hand. He opened his mouth to say something and she cut him off with an abrupt shake of her head.

Then, as the adrenaline started to wear off, she recognized him. "Marshal?"

Still obviously terrified, the man nodded open-mouthed.

"What the hell are you doing in here?" Jennings asked under her breath, keeping her rifle against his skull.

"Jennings, report," Nealon demanded through the comm.

Gilliam swallowed. "I... I was trying to help."

"You've got to be kidding me," Jennings muttered, taking a hand off her weapon to key her comm. "I'm good. One of the workers came in to—"

Sparks exploded off the metal housing next to the marshal's head. Instinctively, she ducked, pulling Gilliam down with her even as he screamed in terror. A second burst of fire raked the machinery above them as Jennings pushed him back, forcing him to move and get off the "X".

"Go!" Jennings growled, glancing over her shoulder, trying to locate the shooter.

She pushed Gilliam around a corner, then pulled him to a stop and keyed her comm again. "Contact!"

CHAPTER SEVEN

Jennings got her MP-17 back into her shoulder, blew out a breath, then ducked across the narrow walkway, putting distance between her and the terrified civilian. When no gunfire erupted, she paused, turned back to the marshal, and pointed. "Stay here."

The man only managed to nod, the look of terror and confusion still plastered on his face. A person can talk about charging into battle all day long, but once the bullets start flying, words can only get you so far. Jennings had never been in combat, but she'd been through enough real-world training scenarios that even though the gunfire scared the ever-living daylights out of her, it didn't shut her down.

She was a United Systems Marine, her job was to run into the fire.

Jennings took another breath the slipped through a narrow space between two three-meter-high transfer cases, her rifle pulled tight into her shoulder, eyes scanning the space ahead through her sights. The shooter had likely already changed positions, but at least he'd be on the move now and not stationary. In theory, that would make him easier to spot.

"Target One moving," Masterson advised over the comm.

"I see him," Nealon replied. *"Jennings, what's your status?"*

"I'm good. Tracking the shooter. Shots came from the north side." Jennings shot a glance over the rows of machinery to where Nealon stood at the third landing, ten meters up. He had his MP-17 up and was scanning the plant in her direction.

"No contact," he reported.

The mercenary on the walkway above Nealon came into view on the top landing, his old-style rifle sweeping over the side of the railing. Jennings shifted aim and fired. Sparks danced off the railing and the mercenary ducked back around a steel support pylon. Another barrage of shots echoed around the plant, making it impossible to identify the origin. Jennings ducked anyway, waiting until the shooting subsided, before moving.

"Moving to contact," Nealon said.

In her mind, Jennings knew the sergeant was now pressing his attack up the stairs and she fought the urge to watch. There was still another shooter down here, and it was her job to find him. The thought of the hostages and what their captors were doing now flashed through her mind, but she pushed it away almost immediately. She was doing everything she could for them right now, and she couldn't afford to waste time and energy thinking about something she couldn't control. She had her own problems to face right in front of her, she just had to trust that the other members of her team would be able to handle the rest.

More shots rang out, echoing through the expansive building. Her squad mates shouted over the comms as they converged on the known threats. Ginelli advised another merc appearing from the central control station, then more gunfire. Again, Jennings fought the urge to look and forced herself to push forward, keeping her attention solely focused on her task.

She slipped into another narrow walkway, moved forward several meters, then slid sideways between to large pipes that curved up from the floor and snaked around the larger equipment in the area. Jennings ignored the heat radiating off the metallic surfaces and continued through into a small work area where she paused and scanned her surroundings.

She flinched as more shots rang out.

"Masterson's hit!" Nealon shouted over the comm.

"Moving!" Ginelli answered.

This time Jennings did look. Masterson was pushing himself off the railing on the second landing, one hand pressed against his shoulder.

"I'm good," Masterson said. *"No penetrat—"*

Another burst of gunfire cut him off as additional rounds smacked into his chest, knocking him over the railing and sending him plummeting through the air. His feet slammed into a metal housing, flipping him end over end, before the back of his head hit a pipe and his body went limp before landing on a rack of electronics.

A curse caught in Jennings's throat as she froze, stunned by the attack. She watched, helpless, as Nealon charged up the stairs, his weapon up and searching for a target. The mercenary was already moving, running back along the walkway toward the protection of the piles of tanks and equipment stacked in front of the control center. Jennings leveled her rifle and fired, sending three bursts down range in quick succession.

Sparks danced of the walkway and railing behind the mercenary, then off a stack of storage crates he jumped behind. Jennings cursed and ducked under pipe, moving laterally right to try and get a better shot.

Something flashed in her peripheral a split second before her head erupted in pain. Her helmet protected her from any real damage from the blow, but the impact sent her stumbling back none-the-less. Partially stunned, Jennings struggled to regain her footing as the buttstock of a rifle knocked her weapon aside and the mercenary appeared from behind a wall. A foot came up and connected with her pelvis, knocking her off balance and into a rack of pressure controls.

A valve wheel stabbed into her back. She ignored the pain, already pushing herself upright as her attacker came on. She grabbed her MP-17 by the stock and barrel and rammed it forward, slamming the side of the weapon into the man's chest. He growled, dropped his rifle and grabbed hers, his face a mask of contempt and rage. He jerked hard, attempting to yank it free, but Jennings held tight, knowing if she lost her weapon she would die.

She tried to kick him, but he pulled himself in closer as she'd shifted her weight, closing the distance and rendering her attack useless. She could smell his breath, practically feel the hatred radiating off his body. His menacing glare turned into a sneer as he pushed her back into the control panel and jerked the weapon again. Jennings held firm, using her McGregor's World strength to her advantage.

Even in bootcamp, her instructors had underestimated her, judging her abilities based solely on her short physical stature, but never considering the underlying reasons for her height. Born to a world where the gravity was 1.4 Earth standard and an atmosphere twice as dense, her bones and muscles had developed accordingly, giving her uncommon strength for her size.

He mercenary's sneer shifted to confusion as he jerked again, and again Jennings held firm. Then she jerked back and twisted, wrenching the MP-17 from his grip and sending him stumbling sideways. He recovered quickly however and was on her before she could get the weapon up to fire. He lunged forward and planted the sole of his boot squarely into her chest, again knocking her back a third time.

Her helmet smacked against the panel and despite the padding inside, stars danced in her vision. Somewhere in the distance, almost seemingly in another world, a chest-rattling boom reverberated through space. The merc fell on her again, pinning her against the control panel. He shouted something Jennings didn't understand then grabbed her weapon and slammed the barrel back into her helmet's visor. Cracks spider-webbed across her vision as he repeatedly hit her visor. Her mind raced for a solution as she desperately grabbed for the weapon, knowing the nano-reinforced polycarbonate visor would likely only hold for a couple more strikes. Then, almost as an afterthought, she dropped to her knees. The man fell forward, off balance, and before he was able to right himself, she rammed the blade of her K2 up onto the man's groin.

He screamed, dropping the rifle and grabbing Jennings's gloved hands as she twisted the knife. He pounded a fist into the top of her helmet, his voice cracking in pain. She tensed, holding her breath, then exploded upward, ramming the knife deeper into his flesh and lifting him off his feet. He slammed against the rail behind him and lost his grip on her hand. Jennings gave a war cry of her own, ripped the knife free then slammed it back in again, and again, and again.

The man pleaded for help, his voice tinged with horror and agony. His hands slapped ineffectually against her helmet and shoulders, he kicked out, his boots glancing off her as his life's blood spilled out over her hands. Pinned against Jennings and the rail, his body went limp then finally she retreated, allowing his corpse to collapse to the grated metal floor.

CHAPTER EIGHT

Her breaths came in ragged gasps as she stared down at the man's body, blood spurting from several severed arteries. Her hands shook, fingers throbbed from holding the K2's handle so tightly, every muscle tensed and aching. She swallowed hard, then looked up as the sounds of battle intensified around her, returning from merely muffled pops in the distance. Voices returned to her ears through the comm.

"...anyone copy? I say again, is everyone all right in there?" Nix demanded.

As the plant came back into focus, the odor of smoke and fire reached Jennings and she looked up to see a fire raging along the walkways outside of central control. The valve of a metal cylinder exploded and sent the tank careening through the air, trailing think white smoke behind it. Another explosion rocked the platform, throwing half a dozen hard plastic containers into the air along with several loose pieces of equipment and other debris.

Jennings keyed her comm. "Jennings up!"

"Jennings, what the hell happened in there?" Nix asked, sounding out of breath.

"I... I don't know. Something exploded."

Jennings unfastened her helmet and pulled it off; with the visor cracked as it was it was useless and inhibited her vision. With it off she could see the destruction upstairs had been significant. She searched back and forth along the catwalk but saw no sign of her teammates.

She pulled the comm set out of the helmet, wrapped it over one ear, adjusted the mic, then said, "I don't see Nealon or Ginelli."

Two figures appeared through the smoke outside the back of control center, then a third and fourth. The first held weapons, the same old X-34 model their companion had shot at her with, the next two appeared unarmed and a fifth was obviously a child. A sixth mercenary materialized through the smoke, coughing and waving the others forward. The group turned and made their way across the elevated walkway, heading east away from Jennings.

She lifted her MP-17, aimed, but had no shot. She keyed her comm. "Sergeant Nealon? Ginelli? Grant?"

"Almost there," Grant advised, sounding out of breath. *"I've got six heading east through plant!"*

"Ginelli is up. Walters is hurt bad. That explosion messed him up pretty good."

"They've got hostages with them," Jennings warned. "Sergeant Nealon are you there?"

No response.

Movement to her left drew her attention to see Grant and Walters running across the elevated walkway, only to slow and stop at a large gaping hole caused by the explosion.

"We're going to have to find another way around," Grant said.

"All units, be advised, a shuttle is inbound, looks like its heading for the eastside of the building. I'm shifting pos." Nix said.

"Shuttle? Where the hell did it come from?" Grant demanded.

"The locals must have folded," Jennings said, looking around but seeing no sign of Watson anywhere.

Jennings turned back to the mercenaries, now halfway across the plant, whispered a curse, then took off after them. She weaved through the maze of machinery and equipment, remembering the years of doing the exact same thing as a little girl waiting on her father to load his cargo for distribution. She couldn't see the exit, but instinctively she knew she was heading directly for it. Surrounded by a forest of steel, she was as much at home here as she was anywhere.

Occasionally, Jennings raised her weapon, ensuring she didn't have a shoot, then continued after them. She reached recessed ladder in the plant's wall, nestled in-between two large support pylons, and pulled herself up two rungs at a time. What amounted to normal gravity for everyone else, felt like she was practically flying, her McGregor's World strength propelling her up the ladder with uncommon speed. In training, she'd actually held herself back quite a bit, not wanting to stand out too much, knowing she'd likely make a name for herself, and in USMC bootcamp, standing out for any reason wasn't exactly ideal.

She skipped the second level and continued all the way to the top, wanting a better angle on the mercenaries and hoping they wouldn't look up as she closed on them. Bringing the MP-17 into her shoulder she started off down the side access, but with the sheer mountain of equipment rising up through the plant she had no line of sight to the mercenaries. She needed to beat them to the far end or risk losing them forever.

"I'm going to try and cut them off," Jennings said, increasing her pace. With all the ducts and cabling and low-hanging machinery, she couldn't quite push herself to an all-out sprint, but she raced on as fast as she could manage.

"Wait for us," Grant called through the comm, his voice strained, obviously out of breath. *"We're coming to you."*

"There's no time," Jennings argued, slowing to duck under a transfer belt. She scanned ahead and realized unlike the multiple processing stations she visited as a child, there was no direct access to the middle work area of the plant from this level. This walkway was solely here to provide access to the machinery for maintenance.

Her mind raced, searching for options, then, without pausing to think about what she was going to do, she pulled herself up onto the next transfer belt, knocking several loose rocks off in the process, and moved inward struggling to keep her balance on the uneven rollers. She glanced down at the central walkway and saw one of the hostages trip, knocking over several hard-plastic containers as he did so.

"That's it," Jennings whispered to herself. "Slow them down, give me some time."

The merc in the rear jerked the man back to his feet, then pushed him along after the others. The man stumbled but managed to keep his footing. Another merc had ahold of the little girl and was pulling her along, barely allowing her feet to touch the walkway. The lead merc pushed the final hostage, a woman, ahead of him, checked behind him for the other two, then proceeded forward, holding his X-34 in one hand, the muzzle pointing down.

Jennings slowed, lined up a shot, but with all six of them moving, any shot would put the hostages at risk. She held her sights on the group for another few seconds as she continued to advance after them, then finally muttered a silent curse, lowered her rifle, and started running.

A low rumble reverberated through the building as a

shadow passed by overhead, the shuttle's engines ratting the frosted glass windows ten meters above Jennings. It flew slow, obviously on its final approach and Jennings knew in the very depths of her soul she could not allow those men to take the hostages on board.

She ignored repeated calls from her teammates to slow down and wait for them. There was no time for that; if she waited, she'd lose them. She jumped over a low pipe, rocking the walkway when she landed with a resounding bang. The commotion drew the attention of rear-most merc who turned, face skewed up in confusion as he looked for the cause of the racket. Jennings leveled her MP-17 just as he found her and started bringing up his own weapon.

Her rifle whined, sending two bursts of nano-reinforced anti-personnel rounds raining down on her target. The man returned fire before duking out of the way as her rounds chewed through the metal walkway. The mercenary rolled behind a cluster of pipes, gaining cover against Jennings's attack as the second mercenary turned and engaged.

Jennings jumped off the walkway onto a flat metal housing, causing the metal to bend and groan under her weight. She pulled herself over the far edge, coming to crouch behind a scanning station and took a minute to catch her breath. More gunshots rang out, the twangs of nearby hits reverberating through the metal around her.

"Engaging!" Grant shouted, his voice coming through Jennings's earpiece a split second before his shots echoed through the space beneath her.

She peered over the edge of the housing and caught sight of the Marine advancing toward the mercenaries on the central walkway below her. Their return fire forced the merc to take cover behind an equipment rack, where he waited for their shots to subside, then poked around the edge and continued to engage. She worked her way to the other edge of the metal housing she was on and craned her head to look down at the fleeing mercs and their prisoners. The lead man was almost at the stairway leading down to ground level.

"Nix! They're going to be exiting in about thirty seconds!" Jennings shouted before pulling herself forward, onto a pipe that spanned a four-meter gap between the housing and another horizontal support girdle.

"Roger!"

Jennings tested the pipe, slowly putting more and more weight on it until she was sure it would hold her, then quickly crossed it without looking at the floor dozens of meters below. She reached the support girdle, let her MP-17 hang on its sling and pulled herself up and over. Another beam ran parallel to the center of the building, just below the walkway she'd just been on, and she carefully stepped around to move along that beam, picking up speed as she went.

Below, the rest of the mercenaries had reached the ground level and were busy ushering their hostages down the stairs to the exit below. As Jennings made her way across the beam, the sound of the shuttle's engines mixed with the humming and thumping of the plant's machinery and knew she was running out time.

CHAPTER NINE

"I don't have a shot," Nix said. "*Damn it, shifting pos.*"

Ahead, the upper walkway ended at a frosted glass window three meters across. Jennings gritted her teeth, reached up and pulled herself over the edge of the walkway, hesitated for a just a moment, then slipped her MP-17 off and swung it like a bat, shattering the window. Outside, the building's metal roof sloped away at a slight angle, and mentally estimated how high she was she cleared the remaining shards of glass from the bottom of the frame.

"*Jennings what the hell are you doing?*" Nix demanded through the comm.

She ignored him, hearing shuttle's engines spinning up. She hopped through the window and slipped her arm back through her combat sling before bringing her rifle back up to her shoulder. Keeping it at low-ready, she started across the roof, her boots clanging against the metal. She ignored Nix's continued protests, and her own doubts, as she fully committed, mentally marking out the line of no return and sprinting past it.

The shuttle's hull came into view just before she reached the edge of the roof. She screamed as she kicked off the edge and launched herself into the air. The shuttle's tail section came up to meet her. She landed and rolled across the hull, losing her grip on her MP-17 as she did so. The weapon bounced along behind her, pulled by its sling until she managed to stop herself and catch her bearings.

"*Holy shit, that's the craziest thing I've ever seen,*" Nix said.

Jennings pushed herself to her feet. "The ramp, is it still open?"

"Yeah, but..."

Jennings took off before he could finish, crossing the six meters to the shuttle's tail. She tapped the selector switch for her MP17 and it folded in on itself, reverting to the smaller, more manageable pistol size used for storage and close quarters engagements. Before she could talk herself out of it, she dropped to the hull, slid over the edge and down to the ramp below.

Still holding the bulkhead above, she brought her MP-17 up, one-handed, and put two shots in the back of the nearest mercenary. He'd never even known she was there. The shuttle banked right and pulled up slightly, sending the body sliding down the ramp and over the edge.

Jennings started up the ramp as it closed.

"What the—" the second mercenary blurted out before Jennings put three rounds center mass. He jerked back under the impact and bounced off the bulkhead and collapsed to the deck.

The two hostages directly ahead of her screamed as she approached, ducking away from her pistol as she searched for her final target. The girl dropped to the deck, wailing, hands over her head as she curled into the fetal position.

The final mercenary stood with his rifle half raised, frozen as Jennings leveled her pistol.

"Alliance Marines, you move you die!" Jennings shouted

over the wind and roar of the shuttle's engines, her MP-17's reticle aimed directly at his face.

He glared at Jennings, eyes burning with hatred and rage. Blood pounded in her ears as she glared right back. The shuttle's interior faded away, a distant memory in the back of her mind, every fiber of her being focused on the man's rifle and where the muzzle was pointing. Her finger tensed on the trigger but there was no confusion in her mind about what would happen next.

"If you—"

The man's expression changed. It was a subtle movement, but Jennings saw it, nonetheless. His body position shifted, his hands moved, and the muzzle of the X-34 started to come up.

Jennings shouted, but the report of her weapon drowned out her words. Three rounds slammed home. The first punctured his left sinus, tearing through soft cartilage and muscle before punching a hole through his pituitary. The second tore through his left eye, severing the optic nerve before entering his frontal lobe. The third bullet fractured his skull, then took a course through his parietal lobe before exploding out of the back of his head, spraying the bulkhead with blood and gore. His body jerked with each impact. Hands opened and his rifle clattered to the deck as his body toppled backward, crashing to the deck with a sickening wet smack.

Her breathing echoed in her ears, fingers tingling as she watched the man's blood pool around his lifeless body. She shuttle's deck shifted underneath her, and she had to shake herself as the world around her came back into focus. A chorus of screams filled the cabin, jolting her back to reality.

A meter away, the girl briefly glanced up at Jennings, then recoiled in terror, burying her head in her arms, her body quivering. The two other hostages were getting to their knees, distant expressions seemed to not comprehend that had just transpired. A voice in her head told Jennings to comfort them, and even though she'd never quite thought of herself as caregiver, she knelt beside the girl and put a hand on her shoulder.

"It's going to be okay," Jennings told her. "You're safe now."

The girl pulled away from her, slapping at Jennings's hand. She pushed herself across the deck in a desperate attempt to put more space between them, stopped only by the bulkhead behind her. Pressed against the shuttle's steel interior, the girl locked bloodshot, tear-filled eyes on Jennings, fear, confusion, and hatred burning within her.

Jennings stood, not wanting to press the issue and make the girls condition any worse. Traumatic stress did strange things to people and while she was an accomplished at many things, helping people through their trauma was not one of them. Instead, she turned to the other two hostages, the male now on his feet, taking long, measured breaths.

"Thank you," he said, his eyes locked on the final dead mercenary. "I didn't think... I mean after the... thank you."

"You're welcome," Jennings replied, slipping her retracted MP-17 back into its holster. She turned and stepped over the body, reaching the cockpit a moment later where she told the pilot to land.

She realized her earpiece had fallen out at some point during her jump and fished the wire out of her shirt.

"...report! Are you okay?" Nix's voice tinged with more than a little anxiousness.

Jennings keyed her comm. "I'm okay. All tangos down."

"Jennings, that was some ballsy move you just did. What the hell were you thinking?"

She looked down at the dead mercenary and shoot her head. "I wasn't. I just did what I needed to do."

CHAPTER TEN

The shuttle flared briefly before settling back down to the ground where Jennings was met by what was left of her team. Nix held his MP-17 still in its sniper rifle configuration, the weapon draped across his chest, held in the crook of his arm. Grant and Lincoln and Ginelli stood with him, their helmets off, their expressions all equally intrigued at what their short, stocky recruit had managed to pull off. Walters lay in the back seat of an open-top rover they'd apparently commandeered from somewhere.

"Where's Sergeant Nealon?" Jennings asked.

Nix shook his head. "Whatever caused that explosion back there got him. Him and several of the hostages. Masterson—"

"I saw," Jennings said, not wanting to see his body hit again.

"Come on," Grant said, moving around Jennings, up into the shuttle's bay to help the closest hostage. He took the woman gently by the arm and lead her down the ramp. She was seemingly oblivious to his words, stared blankly at the ground. Lincoln moved in to help the man to his feet. The man waved him off, moving instead to help the girl.

Jennings and the rest of the squad turned as the sound of rovers approaching reached them, all three kicking up dust clouds in their wakes. Marshal Gilliam hopped out of the first one, followed by Watson and the others.

Gilliam his arms held out to his sides. "What the hell happened in there? Ya'll were supposed to save those people, not blow up half the blasted plant!"

Jennings opened her mouth to answer, but no words came out. Instead, she looked to Nix, the next highest rank after Sergeant Nealon, and by default, the squad's new leader.

"Sir, I—"

"They killed them!" a tiny voice screamed, her voice cracking with the effort.

Jennings and the rest of the squad turned and saw the girl holding onto the man, tears streaming down her face, cheeks flushed with hatred and pain. She pointed at Jennings with a quivering finger, teeth bared.

"She killed them!"

"I..." Jennings didn't know what to say.

Two of Gilliam's men rushed up the ramp to help the man and the girl, picking her up and attempting to hide her face from the Marines. She fought against him, however, and turned to face them as he carried her past.

"Why? Why did you kill them?" she screamed, again pointing a tiny, quivering finger at them as she was taken to one of the trucks. "Why?"

Jennings exchanged a confused looked with Nix, opened her mouth to explain, but the corporal waved her off. "We know. It's okay."

"Okay?" Gilliam demanded. "Okay? What the hell makes you think any of this is, okay?"

Watson stepped up next to him. "Do you have any idea how

many credits' worth of machinery were destroyed in there? Not to mention the lives of our people."

"Hey asshole, in case you didn't notice, we lost some good people too. How about a little respect, huh? Some good men lost their lives today trying to save your people."

"It's just like you Alliance types to come in here, blow our town all to hell, get our people killed, and think, 'Hey, we saved the day'."

"If we hadn't come, *all* of those people would be gone right now."

"Yeah, but maybe they'd still be alive," Watson argued. "You should've let the shuttle go!"

Nix scoffed, obviously not believing what he was hearing. He stepped forward, hand on his rifle, and pointing.

"I'm sorry," Jennings said, before Nix could get his next words out, stopping the corporal mid-step. She held the Gilliam's gaze for several long moments, then said, "Can you tell her I'm sorry."

It seemed to take him a second to realize who Jennings meant, then he nodded without saying a word. He gave Nix a final look, then turned and motioned for the rest of his men to follow. "Come on, boys, we still got work to do."

When they were out of earshot, Nix muttered, "Ungrateful bastards. Do they have any idea?"

Grant put a hand on his shoulder. "Let it go, brother. Let's go get Sarge and the others. These backwater bumkins only care about themselves and their credits. They don't give a crap about us or anyone else."

It took them twenty minutes to find their fallen teammates and get them into the dropship. They didn't have flags to drape over their bodies, so they pulled out their emergency blankets from their survival gear and laid the silver material over their friends.

None of the townsfolk saw them off, or even contacted them again before the Corsair lifted off, and if Jennings was being honest, she didn't know how she felt about that. She wasn't looking for a parade, but to be blamed for the deaths of the hostages...

"Does anyone know what caused it?" Jennings asked as the ramp closed. "The explosion I mean."

Nix shook his head. "I didn't see a thing."

"There were a lot of tanks around the main control center," Grant said. "Might've been a missed shot. One of those dudes you shot on the shuttle had a fragger on his vest, might have been one of those."

Jennings nodded but didn't respond. Not knowing was almost worse. What if they were responsible? What if it had been one of their rounds? What if it had been her?

"Don't think about it too hard, Private," Nix said. "We'll work through the AAR when we get back to the *Brewton*. But you can be damn sure, the blame for all of this lies at the feet of those guys you killed back there. No one else's, okay?"

Jennings nodded again, not sure she completely believed him. She kept seeing that screaming, terrified little girl, her accusatory finger. Finally, she said, "I just..."

"Just what?"

"I just hope we did more good than bad."

"Hell, Jennings, that's all any of us can hope for," Nix said. "And believe you me, you've got a whole career of asking yourself that exact same question."

"How do you decide?"

Nix shrugged. "Ultimately, that determination falls on you, but for me, I look at the man or woman next to me and ask if I'd done everything I could to make sure they made it back with me. And if I have, then the answer is yes."

Jennings looked down at their fallen comrades. "And if they didn't?"

"Then I make their sacrifice worth it."

THE END

THANK YOU FOR READING ONE DECISIVE VICTORY

We hope you enjoyed it as much as we enjoyed bringing it to you. We just wanted to take a moment to encourage you to review the book. Follow this link: One Decisive Victory to be directed to the book's Amazon product page to leave your review.

Every review helps further the author's reach and, ultimately, helps them continue writing fantastic books for us all to enjoy.

———

ALSO IN SERIES
AGAINST ALL ODDS
WITH GRIMM RESOLVE
ONE DECISIVE VICTORY

———

You can also join our non-spam mailing list by visiting www.subscribepage.com/AethonReadersGroup and never miss out on future releases. You'll also receive three full books completely Free as our thanks to you.

Facebook | Instagram | Twitter | Website

Want to discuss our books with other readers and even the authors? Join our Discord server today and be a part of the Aethon community.

LOOKING FOR MORE GREAT SCIENCE FICTION AND FANTASY?

In the West, there are worse things to fear than bandits and outlaws. *Demons. Monsters. Witches. James Crowley's sacred duty as a Black Badge is to hunt them down and send them packing, banish them from the mortal realm for good. He didn't choose this life. No. He didn't choose life at all. Shot dead in a gunfight many years ago, now he's stuck in purgatory, serving the whims of the White Throne to avoid falling to hell. Not quite undead, though not alive either, the best he can hope for is to work off his penance and fade away. This time, the White Throne has sent him investigate a strange bank robbery in Lonely Hill. An outlaw with the ability to conjure ice has frozen and shattered open the bank vault and is now on a spree, robbing the region for all it's worth. In his quest to track down the ice-wielder and suss out which demon is behind granting a mortal such power, Crowley finds himself face-to-face with hellish beasts, shapeshifters, and, worse ... temptation. But the truth behind the attacks is worse than he ever imagined ...* **The Witcher *meets* The Dresden Files *in this weird Western series by the Audible number-one bestselling duo behind* Dead Acre.**

GET COLD AS HELL NOW AND EXPERIENCE WHAT PUBLISHER'S WEEKLY CALLED PERFECT FOR FANS OF JIM BUTCHER AND MIKE CAREY.

Also available on audio, voiced by Red Dead Redemption 2's Roger Clark (Arthur Morgan)

They've plundered their way across the galaxy and just found the score of a lifetime. All they have to do is steal from the most ruthless crime lord in the galaxy. What could possibly go wrong? Yan and his band of rogues are intent on plundering their way to fame and fortune. When they stumble across the score of a lifetime, they quickly go all in for one last job. With everything on the line, there's no way they can fail. At least that's what they're hoping. In the end, they just might have gotten into something bigger than they ever imagined possible.

GET MOST WANTED NOW!

Earth is a frozen wasteland... The victim of a war we hadn't realized we were fighting. Opportunities there are few and far between... that is unless you're willing to put on a uniform. For ace-pilot Deborah Allen Riker (a.k.a "Admiral Dare"), life had never been easy. She's defended Earth against countless enemies, both alien and human alike. Now a civilian and academic living on the fringes of civilized space, she has committed herself to a life of solitude and studying a race of long-dead aliens. Everything was great... until she finds herself dragged into a new conflict. A conflict she never saw coming. One of the great Arks built to carry the last vestiges of humanity into the deepest reaches of space goes missing. And she's just the gal to find it.

GET THE EXODUS EARTH NOW!

For all our Sci-Fi books, visit our website.

ABOUT THE AUTHOR

Join Jeffery on his mailing list to receive the latest information about his writing. Find his other books on Amazon.com under Jeffery H. Haskell.

https://goo.gl/LJdYDn

Or via his website @ Jefferyhhaskell.com

A quick note on technology.

I expect that in one thousand years things will be very different than how I imagine. In fact, I would bet they will be unrecognizable. If you go back a thousand years from today, to 1022, it would be almost impossible for those people to understand the technology of today. Swords and lances were the hi-tech weapons of war.

I don't pretend I'm doing anything new with my writing. I love military sci-fi for the stories of survival and brotherhood they tell. Seeing a crew pull together to overcome adversity and succeed against overwhelming odds. For those stories to work, for the technology and the ships to play an important part in those stories, the author and the reader must understand them fully.

Thus I chose to limit the advance of technology even though it's a thousand years in the future. I didn't want to spend all my time reading about quantum physics and nano-carbon tubes in order to write. I spend enough time doing that for fun as it is!

Instead I kept things at a level that I could understand well enough to describe in a way that average readers will understand. When they launch torpedoes, you can see it. When the ship shakes from the turrets firing, you can feel it.

There are spots for high-technology, but I try to keep it grounded in what we know today. You may be surprised to learn (or not, you all are pretty intelligent) that the gravity coil FTL is based on a theory about gravity manifolds that actually exist as a natural phenomenon.

Pretty cool if you ask me.

I strive to improve with each book. I'm not satisfied to stand still and just do what I did before. If you do see a cool piece of tech out there you think would be a good fit for the Grimmverse, let me know at Jeffery.haskell@gmail.com I'd love to hear from you.

Printed in Great Britain
by Amazon